'A spellbinding tale of an unholy lust for power that
reaches from beyond the grave . . . A cataclysmic finale
will put readers in mind of some of the best recent works of
supernatural horror, among which this book ranks.'
Publishers Weekly starred review

'Fantastically well-written . . . excellent characterisation and
great pace. Just the thing to induce a chill on the back of the
neck during the long, hot summer.'
Shotsmag.co.uk

'This novel builds slowly yet relentlessly, cranking up
the suspense until it's taut as a bowstring . . . Believable
characters, an eye for detail and an ear for dialogue . . .
Michael Koryta is a master storyteller.'
WarpcoreSF.co.uk

'A story so chilling it would keep Stephen King up all night'
Peterborough Evening Telegraph

SO COLD
THE RIVER

MICHAEL
KORYTA

HODDER

First published in Great Britain in 2010 by Hodder & Stoughton
An Hachette UK company

This paperback edition first published in 2011 by Hodder & Stoughton

2

A CIP catalogue record for this title is available from the British Library.

Paperback B format ISBN 978 0 340 99824 3
Paperback A format ISBN 978 1 444 72193 5

Printed and bound in the UK by CPI Mackays, Chatham ME5 8TD

Hodder & Stoughton policy is to use papers that are natural, renewable
and recyclable products and made from wood grown in sustainable forests.
The logging and manufacturing processes are expected to conform to the
environmental regulations of the country of origin.

Hodder & Stoughton Ltd
338 Euston Road
London NW1 3BH

www.hodder.co.uk

For Christine, who wouldn't let me talk myself out of this one

Part One

CURER OF ILLS

I

You looked for the artifacts of their ambition. That was what a sociology professor had said one day in a freshman seminar, and Eric Shaw had liked something about the phrase, wrote it and only it in a notebook that would soon be forgotten and then discarded. *Artifacts of their ambition.* Only through study of those things could you truly understand people long departed. General artifacts could be overanalyzed, layered with undue importance. It was critical to find things that indicated ambitions and aspirations, that tired bit about hopes and dreams. The reality of someone's heart lay in the objects of their desires. Whether those things were achieved did not matter nearly so much as what they had been.

The phrase returned to Eric almost two decades later as he prepared a video montage for a dead woman's memorial service. *Video life portraits,* that's what he called them, an attempt to lend some credibility to what was essentially a glorified slide show.

There'd been a time when neither Eric nor anyone who knew him would have been able to believe this sort of career lay ahead for him. He still had trouble believing it, in fact. You could live a life and never comprehend exactly how you found yourself in it. Hell of a thing.

If he were fresh out of film school, he might have been able to convince himself that this was merely part of the artist's struggle, a way to pay the bills before that first big break. Truth was, it had been twelve years since Eric claimed his film school's highest honor, *twelve years*. Two years since he'd moved to Chicago to escape the train wreck of his time in L.A.

During his peak, thirty years old and landing bigger jobs with regularity, his cinematography had been publicly praised by one of the most successful movie directors in the world. Now Eric made videos for graduations and weddings, birthdays and anniversaries. And funerals. Lots of funerals. That had somehow become his niche. Word of mouth sustained a business like his, and the word of mouth about Eric seemed to focus on funerals. His clients were generally pleased by his videos, but the funeral parties were elated. Maybe on some subconscious level he was more motivated when his work concerned the dead. There was a greater burden of responsibility there. Truth be told, he operated more instinctively when he prepared a memorial video than when he did anything else. There seemed to be a muse working then, some innate guiding sense that was almost always right.

Today, standing outside a suburban funeral parlor with a service about to commence, he felt an unusual sense of anticipation. He'd spent all of the previous day—fifteen hours straight—preparing this piece, a rush job for the family of a forty-four-year-old woman who'd been killed in a car accident on the Dan Ryan Expressway. They'd turned over photo albums and scrapbooks and select keepsakes, and he'd gotten to work arranging images and creating a sound track. He took pictures of pictures and blended those with home video clips and then rolled it all together and put it to music and tried to give some sense of a life. Generally the crowd would weep and occasionally they would laugh and always they would murmur and shake their heads at forgotten moments and treasured memories. Then they'd take Eric's hand and thank him and marvel at how he'd gotten it just right.

Eric didn't always attend the services, but Eve Harrelson's family had asked him to do so today and he was glad to say yes. He wanted to see the audience reaction to this one.

It had started the previous day in his apartment on Dearborn as he was sitting on the floor, his back against the couch and the collection of Eve Harrelson's personal effects surrounding him, sorting and studying and selecting. At some point in that process, the old phrase came back to him, the *artifacts of their ambition,* and he'd thought again that it had a nice sound. Then, with the phrase as a tepid motivator, he'd gone back through an already reviewed stack of photographs, thinking that he had to find some hint of Eve Harrelson's dreams.

The photographs were the monotonous sort, really — everybody posed and smiling too big or trying too hard to look carefree and indifferent. In fact, the entire Harrelson collection was bland. They'd been a photo family, not a video family, and that was a bad start. Video cameras gave you motion and voice and spirit. You could create the same sense with still photographs, but it was harder, certainly, and the Harrelson albums weren't promising.

He'd been planning to focus the presentation around Eve's children — a counterintuitive move but one he thought would work well. The children were her legacy, after all, guaranteed to strike a chord with family and friends. But as he sorted through the stack of loose photographs, he stopped abruptly on a picture of a red cottage. There was no person in the shot, just an A-frame cottage painted a deep burgundy. The windows were bathed in shadow, nothing of the interior visible. Pine trees bordered it on both sides, but the framing was so tight there was no clear indication of what else was nearby. As he stared at the picture, Eric became convinced that the cottage faced a lake. There was nothing to suggest that, but he was sure of it. It was on a lake, and if you could expand the frame, you'd see there were autumn leaves bursting into color beyond the pines, their shades reflecting on the surface of choppy, wind-blown water.

This place had mattered to Eve Harrelson. Mattered deeply. The longer he held the photograph, the stronger that conviction grew. He felt a prickle along his arms and at the base of his neck and thought, *She made love here. And not to her husband.*

It was a crazy idea. He pushed the picture back into the stack and moved on and later, after going through several hundred photographs, confirmed that there was only one of the cottage. Clearly, the place hadn't been that special; you didn't take just one picture of a place that you loved.

Nine hours of frustration later, nothing about the project coming together the way he wanted, Eric found the photo back in his hand, the same deep certainty in his brain. The cottage was special. The cottage was sacred. And so he included it, this lone shot of an empty building, worked it into the mix and felt the whole presentation come together as if the photograph were the keystone.

Now it was time to play the video, the first time anyone from the family would see it, and while Eric told himself his curiosity was general — you always wanted to know what your clients thought of your work — in the back of his mind it came down to just one photograph.

He entered the room ten minutes before the service was to begin, took his place in the back beside the DVD player and projector. Thanks to a Xanax and an Inderal, he felt mellow and detached. He'd assured his new doctor that he needed the prescriptions only because of a general sense of stress since Claire left, but the truth was he took the pills anytime he had to show his work. Professional nerves, he liked to think. Too bad he hadn't had such nerves back when he'd made real films. It was the ever-present sense of failure that made the pills necessary, the cold touch of shame.

Eve Harrelson's husband, Blake, a stern-faced man with thick dark hair and bifocals, took the podium first. The couple's children sat in the front row. Eric tried not to focus on them. He was never comfortable putting together a piece like this when there were children to watch it.

Blake Harrelson said a few words of thanks to those in attendance, and then announced that they would begin with a short tribute film. He did not name Eric or even indicate him, just nodded at a man by the light switch when he stepped aside.

Showtime, Eric thought as the lights went off, and he pressed play. The projector had already been focused and adjusted, and the screen filled with a close-up of Eve and her children. He'd opened with some lighthearted shots — that was always the way to go at a heavy event like this — and the accompanying music immediately got a few titters of appreciative laughter. Amidst the handful of favorite CDs her family had provided, Eric had found a recording of Eve playing the piano while her daughter sang for some music recital, the timing off from the beginning and getting worse, and in the middle you could hear them both fighting laughter.

It went on like that for a few minutes, scattered laughter and some tears and a few shoulder squeezes with whispered words of comfort. Eric stood and watched and silently thanked whatever chemist had come up with the calming drugs in his bloodstream. If there was a more intense sort of pressure than watching a grieving group like this take in your film, he couldn't imagine what it was. Oh, wait, yes he could — making a real film. That had been pressure, too. And he'd folded under it.

The cottage shot was six minutes and ten seconds into the nine-minute piece. He'd kept most pictures in the frame for no more than five seconds, but he'd given the cottage twice that. That's how curious he was for the reaction.

The song changed a few seconds before the cottage appeared, cut from an upbeat Queen number — Eve Harrelson's favorite band — to Ryan Adams covering the Oasis song "Wonderwall." The family had given Eric the Oasis album, another of Eve's favorites, but he'd replaced their version with the Adams cover during his final edit. It was slower, sadder, more haunting. It was right.

For the first few seconds he could detect no reaction. He stood scanning the crowd and saw no real interest in their faces, only patience or, in a few cases, confusion. Then, just before the picture changed, his eyes fell on a blond woman in a black dress at the end of the third row. She'd turned completely around and was staring back into the harsh light of the projector, searching for him. Something in her gaze made him shift to the side, behind the light. The frame changed and the music went with it and still she stared. Then the man beside her said something and touched her arm and she turned back to the screen, turned reluctantly. Eric let out his breath, felt that tightness in his neck again. He wasn't crazy. There was something about that picture.

He was hardly aware of the rest of the film. When it ended, he disconnected the equipment and packed up to leave. He'd never done that before — he always waited respectfully for the conclusion of the service and then spoke to the family — but today he just

8

wanted out, wanted back into the sunlight and fresh air and away from that woman with the black dress and the intense stare.

He'd slipped out of the double doors with the projector in his arms and was headed through the foyer and toward the exit when a voice from behind him said, "Why did you use that picture?"

It was her. The blond woman in black. He turned to face her, caught a blast of that stare again, able now to see that it came from intense blue eyes.

"The cottage?"

"Yes. Why did you use it?"

He wet his lips, shifted the weight of the projector. "I'm not really sure."

"Please don't lie to me. Who told you to use it?"

"No one."

"I want to know who told you to use it!" Her voice a hiss.

"Nobody said a word to me about that picture. I assumed people would think I was crazy for putting it up there. It's just a house."

"If it's just a house," she said, "then why did you want to include it?"

This was Eve Harrelson's younger sister, he realized. Her name was Alyssa Bradford now, and she was in several of the photographs he'd used. Back in the main room someone was speaking, offering tribute to Eve, but this woman did not seem to care in the least. All of her attention was on him.

"It felt special," he said. "I can't explain it any better than that. Sometimes I just get a sense. It was the only picture of the place, and there were no people in it. I thought that was unusual. The longer I looked at it...I don't know, I just thought it belonged. I'm sorry if it offended you."

"No. It's not that."

It was quiet for a moment, both of them standing outside while the service continued inside.

"What was that place?" he said. "And why are you the only one who reacted?"

She looked over her shoulder then, as if making sure the doors were closed.

"My sister had an affair," she said softly, and Eric felt something cold and spidery work through his chest. "I'm the only person who knows. At least that's what she told me. It was with a man she dated in college and during a rough time she had with Blake. . . . He's a bastard, I'll never forgive him for some of the things he did, and I think she should have left him. Our parents were divorced, though, and it was an ugly divorce, and she didn't want to do that to her kids."

This sort of disclosure wasn't all that uncommon. Eric had grown used to family members sharing more than seemed prudent. Grief sent secrets spilling past the old restraints, and it was easier to do with a stranger sometimes. Maybe every time.

"That cottage is in Michigan," she said. "Some little lake in the Upper Peninsula. She spent a week there with this man, and then she came back, and she never saw him again. It was the children, you know, they were all that kept her. She was in love with him, though. I know that."

What could he say to that? Eric shifted the projector again, didn't speak.

"She didn't keep any pictures of him," Alyssa Bradford said, and there were tears in her eyes now. "Tore apart the photo albums she had from college, too, and burned every picture he was in. Not out of anger, but because she had to if she was going to stay. I was with her when she burned them, and she kept that one, that single shot, because there was nobody in it. That's all she kept to remember him."

"It just seemed to belong," Eric said again.

"And that song," she said, her eyes piercing again after she'd blinked the tears back. "How on earth did you select that song?"

They made love to it, he thought, *probably for the first time, or if not that, then certainly for the best time, the one that she remembered longest, the one that she remembered not long before she died. They made love to that song and he pulled her hair and she leaned her head back and moaned in his ear and afterward they lay together and listened to the wind howl around that cottage with the deep red paint. It was warm and windy and they thought that it would rain soon. They were sure of it.*

The woman was staring at him, this woman who was the only person alive who knew of her dead sister's affair, of the week she'd spent in that cottage. The only person alive other than the lover, at least. And now Eric. He looked back into her eyes, and he shrugged.

"It just felt right, that's all. I try to match the music to the mood."

And he did, on every project. That much was true. Everything else, that strange but absolute sense of the importance of the song, couldn't possibly be more than trickery of the mind. Any other notion was absurd. So very absurd.

Eve Harrelson's sister gave him a hundred-dollar bill before she left to return to the service, a fresh wave of tears cresting in her eyes. Eric wasn't sure if it was a tip or a bribe for silence, and he didn't ask. Once his equipment was packed up and he was sitting in the driver's seat of the Acura MDX that Claire had paid for, he transferred the bill from his pocket to his wallet. He tried not to notice that his hands were shaking.

2

IT WASN'T THE FIRST time. Over the years, Eric had grown used to sensing some unexplained tug over a specific sight. It was one of the reasons his finest work came on historical projects. The last film of note that he'd worked on was an HBO historical drama about the flight of the Nez Perce in 1877, an amazing and tragic story, and one Eric connected with from the start. They'd been shooting in the Bear Paw Mountains in northern Montana, at the spot where the fifteen-hundred-mile retreat had ended about forty miles from the Canadian border, which the Indians were trying desperately to reach. There was a team of historians along, people who'd devoted countless hours to the story and believed they had an accurate sense of the key locations. The crew spent about six hours getting things set up and was nearly ready to shoot when Eric rode to a rise that looked down on another valley. This one was smaller and on the surface less visually appealing. A little bit of snow was blowing and the sun was losing a struggle with the clouds. It was as that last shaft of sunlight receded that he looked down at the smaller valley and knew that this was where they'd been. The Nez Perce. Chief Joseph and about seven hundred exhausted and starving followers, fewer than two hundred of them warriors. General William Tecumseh Sherman and two *thousand* well-equipped U.S. soldiers on their heels.

Eric spent a few more minutes up on the ridge, then rode back down and embarked on a furious argument to pack everything up and move the upcoming scene into the smaller valley. The director was Douglass Wainberg, a short Jewish guy who insisted on wearing cowboy hats throughout the whole project, and while he had plenty of faults, he also had a trust in talent. He relented after Eric went on a tirade about light and horizon lines that was total bullshit — the only reason he wanted to move was that he knew they were in the wrong valley — and they wasted most of a day relocating. One of the historians took issue with the decision, said it was sad to see accuracy sacrificed for lighting concerns, and Eric had ignored him, confident that the guy was wrong. The Nez Perce had never been in his damn valley.

That was the strongest sense he'd ever had about the significance of a single shot until the picture of the red cottage. And his previous senses had always seemed to be closer to illusions, something that vanished as soon as you tried to close your fist over it.

Eve Harrelson's sister called a week after the service, around the time he'd begun to smile ruefully at the way his imagination had gotten away from him.

"I hope that you won't let the . . . odd moment from Eve's service discourage you from working with me" were Alyssa Bradford's first words when they met the day after her call. They were sitting on the patio outside a coffee shop on Michigan Avenue, and she had two shopping bags on either side of her chair and wore probably two thousand dollars' worth of clothes, carefully styled to seem casual. The woman reeked of money. Eric had no idea where it came from. He'd gotten to know the Harrelson side of the family, and they were middle class at best. Evidently, Alyssa had married up.

"Of course not," he said. "I understand your reaction."

"I called you only because of the quality of your film," she said. "The way you worked it all together, and the music . . . just wonderful. Everyone who was there was touched by it. *Everyone*."

"I'm glad."

"It triggered something in my mind. Something I could do for my husband. My father-in-law — his name is Campbell Bradford — is in extremely poor health, close to the end, I'm afraid. But he's a remarkable man, and has a remarkable story, and after seeing your film I thought, *This would be perfect.* An absolutely perfect tribute, something lovely for his family to have."

"Well, I'm glad it made a favorable impression. After seeing that one, you have a pretty good idea of what I'll need, and —"

He stopped talking when she held up a hand.

"We won't be doing quite the same thing. See, I want to contract your services for a longer period of time. I'd like to send you somewhere."

"Send me somewhere?"

"If you're willing. You have experience with bigger projects is my understanding."

Experience with bigger projects. He looked at her with a small smile and managed a nod, the shame landing on him again, almost enough to drive him from the chair.

"I've done a lot of work in film," he said. It was as difficult a sentence as he'd ever uttered.

"That's what I thought. I read about you online, and I was so surprised to see that you'd come back to Chicago."

The sidewalk was calling to him now, screaming at him. *Get up, get your ass out of that chair and walk away from this disrespect. You were big once. Big, and ready to be* huge. *Remember that?*

"I thought that it was probably a family decision," Alyssa Bradford said.

"Yes," he said. A family decision that when your career imploded, it was time to come home.

"Well, this is a family matter, too. My father-in-law has an extraordinary story. He ran away from home in his early teens, came to Chicago in the midst of the Depression, and made a success of himself. A *massive* success. He's worth well over two hundred million today. It was a quiet fortune, too. Until very recently, no one in the family knew exactly what he was worth. We knew he was rich, but not *that* rich. Then he got sick and the legal discussions started and it came out. Now can you see why I'd like to tell his story?"

"What did he do to make the money?"

"Investments. Stocks, commodities, bonds, real estate, you name it. He's just had a golden touch."

"I guess so." Eric was having trouble looking her in the eye for some reason. Her stare, that intense blue-eyed stare, reminded him of the way she'd cornered him during the memorial service.

"The town where he was born, and where I want to send you, is in southern Indiana, a truly odd place, and beautiful. Have you ever heard of French Lick?"

"Larry Bird," he said, and she laughed and nodded.

"That's the general response, but at one point it was one of the great resorts in the world. There are two towns there, actually, West Baden and French Lick, side by side, and they each have a hotel that will take your breath away. Particularly the one in West Baden. It's unlike anything I've ever seen, and yet it's built out in the middle of nowhere, this tiny town in farm country."

"You want me to go there?"

"That's what I'm hoping, yes. It's where my father-in-law is from, and he grew up in the era when it was really alive, when people like Franklin D. Roosevelt and Al Capone were visitors. That's what he saw in his childhood. I visited the place for the first time last year after reading that they had restored the hotels. I was there only for a day, but long enough to see that the place is just surreal."

"Are you looking for a video history of the place, or of his life, or —"

"A combination. I'm prepared to pay for you to be down there for two weeks, and then take whatever time you need to finalize it once you're back."

"Two weeks sounds like an inordinate amount of time. Not to mention cost."

"I don't think so. My father-in-law didn't speak much of his childhood, or his family. He'd talk about the area, all these stories about the town and times, but hardly anything about his own life. All we know is that he ran away from home when he was in his teens. His relationship with his family ended then."

"If that's the case," Eric said, "he might not enjoy seeing me present the family history on video."

"You could be right. This isn't just for him, though — it's for my husband and the rest of the family."

"I'm certainly interested," he said, "but I do think two weeks sounds a bit —"

"Oh, I forgot to tell you the price. I'd pay twenty thousand dollars for the completed product. I'll give you five of that in advance."

It was amazing that his first instinct was to think that dollar figure unimpressive. His mind still went to real film budget numbers initially. Then he considered it again and realized that twenty thousand dollars was half of what he'd made all last year. And twenty thousand *more* than he'd made the year before that. He closed his mouth on the hedging *I don't know if I can invest all that time* argument that had been forthcoming, leaned back in his chair, and raised his eyebrows at Alyssa Bradford.

"I don't see how I can turn it down."

"Excellent. Once you see the town and the hotels and learn about the history, I think you'll find the whole project very suited to you. Suited to someone of your gifts."

"My gifts."

She hesitated, the first time she'd shown anything but total self-assurance, and then said, "You know, taking things that are gone and bringing them back to life."

Eric said, "I'd like to interview him. Something of this length, interviews will be important."

She nodded, but the smile was fading. "I understand that, but I don't know how much you'll get. He's ninety-five and in very poor health. Conversations are difficult."

"Sometimes one sentence is enough to make a hell of a difference. If it's the right words, the right sound...it can have an impact."

"Then I'll arrange a time for you to visit. I also know that you like to have photos and family artifacts. I already brought something for you."

She reached into her purse and withdrew a glass bottle, maybe eleven inches tall. Her purse had been resting in the sunlight, but the bottle was surprisingly cold when she passed it into his hand. Light green glass, with etching across it that said *Pluto Water, America's Physic*.

"Look at the bottom," Alyssa Bradford said.

He turned the bottle over and found another etching, this one the image of a jaunty devil with horns, forked tail, and a sword in his belt. One hand was raised, as if in a wave. The word *Pluto* was etched beneath the figure.

"What is it?"

"Mineral water. That's what made the town famous, and what built the hotels and brought people in from all over the world."

There was a stopper held in place with a wire press-down, and below it the bottle was filled with a cloudy liquid the color of sandstone.

"They drank this stuff?" Eric said.

"Drank it out of the bottles, yes, but they also had spas, springs you'd sit in that would supposedly cure physical ailments. That was the big deal at the resorts. People would come from all over the world to visit those springs for the healing effects."

Eric was running his thumb over that etched figure on the base, watching sediment rise and settle inside the glass with his motions.

"Isn't it just a gorgeous bottle?" Alyssa Bradford said. "It's the one thing I found that had something to do with his hometown. I think it's fantastic that he kept it all these years. That bottle is about eighty years old. Maybe more."

"What's with the devil?"

"He's Pluto. It's the Roman version of Hades. God of the underworld."

"Seems like a strange mascot for a company to choose."

"Well, the mineral water came from underground springs. I suppose that inspired them. Anyhow, he's a happy-looking devil, isn't he?"

He was that. Cheerful, welcoming. That water inside the bottle, though, was a different story. Something about its odd color and those fine, grainy flakes of sediment turned Eric's stomach, and he set the bottle on the table and slid it back to her.

"No, you can keep it for now," she said. "I'd like you to take it with you. See if you can find someone who can give an accurate date for it."

He didn't want the bottle at all, but he accepted it when she pushed it across the table, wrapped his hand around it and felt that unnatural penetrating cold from within.

"What do you have in that purse, dry ice?"

"It always feels that way, actually," she said. "I don't understand why. Something about the mineral content? Or maybe that old glass."

He put the bottle in his briefcase and refilled his coffee while she wrote him a five-thousand-dollar check, keeping his palm pressed against the warm side of the mug until she'd signed it and torn it free and handed it to him.

3

It was the sort of story that begged for telling, and with the addition of those wild, extravagant hotels in so rural a place, it was a story with a strong visual component. Perfect for film. Maybe this could go somewhere beyond the Bradfords. Maybe, if he did it right, this could open some doors that had swung shut in his face out in L.A.

Before even setting foot in the town, Eric had swiftly developed a sort of possessive fear about the place, a worry that somebody else was going to get there first. The stories he'd found in his first pass of research were countless. Rich and poor, gangsters and politicians, the explosion and then death of the passenger trains, Prohibition and the effects of the stock-market collapse—all of it had swirled through these bizarre little towns. They were a microcosm, really, a story of America. It was a chance to do something real again.

Alyssa Bradford called him three days after their meeting to say he could check into the West Baden Springs Hotel on the first Friday of May. That was just one week away, and she'd arranged for him to have his first—maybe his only, depending on the man's health—chance to talk with Campbell Bradford on the Thursday prior. Alyssa warned that the old man was not well, might not be able to communicate. Eric said he still wanted to give it a shot.

Claire called that night, and when he saw her number on the caller ID, he felt flushed with relief and gratitude—it had been a week since they'd spoken, and each day was drawing longer and harder on him. Then she said, "I was just calling to check on you," and that was all it took to erase the positive feelings. Calling to check on him? Like he was suicidal or something now that they weren't together, incapable of maintaining a life without her in it?

He made a few cutting remarks, threw in one jab about her father, and guided her toward an early hang-up like a dog herding cattle toward an open gate. When she invited him to give her a call in a few days, he said not to count on it.

"I'm headed out of town for a while," he said. "Few weeks, maybe a month."

"Spontaneous vacation?" she said after a beat of silence.

"Work."

"And where are you going?"

"Indiana," he said, biting off the word with pain.

"How exotic."

"It's a hell of a story. Believe it or not, those don't always come from Maui or Manhattan."

"I'm just kidding. Tell me about the story."

"Maybe later. I've got a lot to do, Claire."

"Okay." Her voice had some sorrow in it, and that pleased him. "Well, I hope it goes great for you, whatever it is."

He swung a closed fist toward the wall, pulled the punch at the last minute, and landed it with a soft thump, no real pain. Damn her *hopes* for him, her well wishes, and her blessings.

"I'm sure that it will," he said. "I've got a good feeling about it. Things just seem to be looking up for me lately."

That was a cruel parting line, and he knew from her frigid *Good-bye, Eric,* and the click of the breaking connection that it had scored a direct hit. He turned off his phone and went to the kitchen and poured himself two fingers of Scotch. *No, hell with it, pour four.* He dropped an ice cube into that — *Water the drink down a touch, and the quantity becomes no problem at all, right?* — and then went into the living room and began scanning through the DVD collection, looking for something to take his thoughts away. Something by one of his old favorites, Huston or Peckinpah, maybe. Yes, Peckinpah. Make it bloody and loud. That seemed right tonight.

He'd watched *Straw Dogs* and had another Scotch and tried without success to sleep before he found himself back at the computer, researching again. He'd found there were matches for the correct Campbell Bradford — though it appeared in most formal circumstances he referred to himself as C. L. Bradford — but all of them had to do with his philanthropy. For a man of such great wealth, he'd lived a remarkably quiet existence. Eric couldn't find so much as a short bio paragraph on the Web, just the name on list after list of contributors for various causes. His donations spanned a wide spectrum, too wide to tell Eric much about the man, but it was obvious he was partial to liberal politics and a supporter of the arts, particularly music. He'd made sizable donations to various community orchestras, but Eric noted that they seemed to be small or rural groups, with names like Hendricks

County Philharmonic, rather than the prestigious symphonies. Perhaps he assumed—correctly, no doubt—that the large ones were better funded.

After cycling through pages of results without finding anything of interest, Eric went back and ran a search for Campbell along with the words "West Baden" and got nothing. He tried again with "French Lick" and was surprised to find three results. A closer look revealed all three were basically the same thing—a request for information on Campbell and a handful of others posted by an Indiana University graduate student named Kellen Cage. The student explained that he was researching the area's history for a thesis and was hoping for any information about a handful of people—particularly, he'd written, Campbell Bradford and Shadrach Hunter. The latter name meant nothing to Eric. There was an e-mail address listed, though, so Eric went ahead and dropped him a note. If the kid was intrigued by Campbell, that meant he'd heard some stories already, which put him well ahead of Eric. And, for that matter, Campbell's family.

After exhausting the minimal possibilities for Campbell, he turned to searching for Pluto Water and soon found some old ads that he'd have to include in the film. They were priceless. Pluto Water cured damn near everything, it seemed. Alcoholism, asthma, obesity, paralysis, pimples, hives, influenza, insomnia, malaria, and venereal disease all made the list. It turned out the product was nothing more than a laxative, but even after that was known, the company still made millions bottling and selling it with the charming slogan *When nature won't, Pluto will.*

The ads themselves were amazing things, too, perfect images of a time and place and people. Women in flowing gowns, men in suits, and that silly smiling devil always present. Eric was particularly taken with one of a man standing in front of a basin sink and mirror. In the illustration he looked back at himself in what appeared to be true and total horror, and the text beside his head read, *What's wrong with me?*

He got to his feet, planning on another Scotch but then thought better of it. Maybe because the room reeled a little around him, maybe because he'd just seen the word *alcoholism* on those lists. Didn't want to dance too close to that partner, no.

But he was on his feet, and he felt like he was in search of something.

The Pluto Water. He went into the living room and found his briefcase and opened it, wrapped his hand around the bottle. Still cold. Still *oddly* cold, in fact. How could water sit in a room for so long and never absorb its temperature? He hadn't read anything about that quality in his research.

"Curer of ills," he said, running his thumb over the etchings. The water looked hideous, but millions of bottles had been consumed over the years. Had to be safe. Mineral water didn't go bad, did it? Then again, wouldn't *anything* go bad after so long?

Only one way to find out, but of course he couldn't do that.

Why not?

For one thing, the water could be tainted, could poison his ass, leave him dead on the living room floor from one tiny taste.

You know that won't happen. That water is natural, came out of a spring, not a chemistry set.

But there were other reasons, those of the courteous, professional sort, not to crack into an artifact the old man had for some reason left untouched all these years.

It has a cap. You open it, take a sip, put the damn cap back on. Who's to know?

He felt like a young boy standing in front of the liquor cabinet, pondering his first taste of the sauce. Drink some of it down, then fill it up with water—maybe apple juice for color—and they'll never know. What the hell was his problem? It was a bottle of old mineral water. Why did he want to know what it tasted like? It tasted, no doubt, like shit.

Scared of it. For some reason, you're scared *of it, you pussy.*

It was true, he realized as he stood there staring at the bottle, it was true and it was pathetic, and there was only one way to slap that fear down. He forced the old wires up and loosened the stopper. It was a terrible thing to do — he'd probably just cut the bottle's value in half by opening it, and it wasn't even his bottle — but after the whiskeys and the bad conversation with Claire and the realization that for some inexplicable reason he was frightened of this bottle, he no longer cared about that. He just wanted a taste.

There was a sulfuric smell to the water, and he felt mildly repulsed as he lifted the bottle to take a drink. He was almost unable to bear the smell of the stuff; how had so many people actually ingested it?

The bottle hit his lips and tilted and a splash of the contents sloshed over the rim and into his mouth and found his throat.

And Eric gagged.

Dropped to his knees and spat the foulness onto the carpet, the taste more corrupt than anything he'd ever experienced, a taste of rot, of death.

He set the bottle on the floor, spat onto the carpet again as he took a shuddering breath through his nose, and then felt another gag coming on and knew this time it wasn't going to be so clean, made it halfway into the bathroom before vomiting violently onto the floor. The whiskey scorched through his throat and burned his nostrils and he fought his way to the toilet and hung on to the bowl and emptied again, felt his temples throb and saw his vision go cloudy with tears from the force of it, the terrible exertion.

The next bout was worse, an awful wrenching from deep in

his stomach, like somebody twisting a wet towel until the fibers screamed with strain. When he finished, he was facedown on the floor, the tile cold on his cheek.

It was an hour before he left the bathroom. An hour before he felt strong enough to stand. He got out the mop and a bucket and some disinfectant spray and went to work. When the bathroom was clean, he returned to the living room, avoiding the clock that announced it was four in the morning, long past the hour that decent people had found their beds, and picked up the Pluto bottle. The smell rose again, and he clenched his teeth as he fastened the cap, holding his breath until the bottle was in his briefcase.

Curer of ills, indeed.

4

THE NEXT DAY HE took some Excedrin and drank about a gallon of iced tea and waited until evening to eat, and that night he did not allow himself so much as a beer or a glass of wine.

There were no other jobs in play, just the Bradford project, so he spent the rest of the week on research and equipment shopping, considering spending Alyssa Bradford's advance check on a new camera. He wanted to upgrade partially for the quality improvement and partially to stop using the camera Claire's father had given him as a present after things bottomed out in L.A. and Eric followed Claire to Chicago. That pretentious bastard. His latest novel had just come out this week. Eric wouldn't read the book, that was for damn sure, but if he heard of a bad review, he'd absolutely read *that*.

He didn't talk to Claire again before his meeting with Campbell Bradford. By the morning after their last phone call, which he awoke to with a headache that clearly intended to linger for a few hours, he wished that he'd told her more. It would've interested her, and she would've listened. One thing about Claire, she always listened.

But he didn't call, and she didn't either. He checked the caller ID every day, and that ritual became maddening—she was his *wife,* and here he was, checking to see if she might have called.

His wife.

He stopped by the apartment to pick up his equipment the night of his interview with Campbell Bradford and saw the message light blinking on the answering machine, thought perhaps Claire had called, then hated himself for such hopefulness. He didn't allow himself to even check the message, ignoring the machine while he picked up his camera and tripod and briefcase. When he opened the case to put his recorder inside—always good to have an audio backup—he saw the pale green bottle and felt a wave of nausea. He started to remove the bottle, then changed his mind. Maybe he'd show it to old Campbell and see what sort of response it triggered.

Alyssa Bradford had told him to go by the hospital around seven. He went through the building as quickly as he could, long, fast strides, the camera bag banging against his leg. He hated hospitals, always had. When he found the right room number—712—he discovered the door was closed. Rapped lightly on it with his knuckles.

"Hello?" he said, pushing it open, poking his head inside. "Mr. Bradford?"

There were two beds in the room, but only one was occupied. The man in it turned to look at Eric, one half of his face lit by a small fluorescent lamp above the bed. Otherwise the room was dark. The sheets were pulled up to the man's neck, and the face above them was weathered and gaunt, with sunken blue eyes that announced his sickness even more than the hospital room itself. Loose skin hung off a jaw that once would have been hard and square, and though the hands resting on top of the sheets were thin and brittle, they were large. Would have been powerful, once.

"Mr. Bradford?" Eric said again, and the old man seemed to nod.

"Your daughter-in-law said she told you I'd be coming," Eric said, crossing to the foot of the bed and pulling up a plastic chair. "I hope I'm not here at a bad time."

No answer. Not a word, or a blink. But the eyes followed Eric.

"I think Alyssa told you what I was going to be doing?" Eric said. He was reaching into his camera bag now, rushing things along because the old man's unresponsive stare was unsettling.

"I was hoping I could hear some of the stories you've got to tell," he continued as he removed the camera. "Alyssa promised me you've got some good ones."

Campbell Bradford's breath came and went in soft, barely audible hisses, and when Eric became aware of the sound, he wanted out of the room, cursed himself for forcing this suggestion on Alyssa in the first place. This man was dying. He was not months away, or even weeks away. Death was close. He could hear it in those little puffing hisses from Campbell's nose.

It hadn't been so many years ago that Eric could be in the presence of an old, sick person like this and feel sorrow. Now he felt fear. The buffer zone of years was thinning too fast. He'd be here soon.

"I'll just let you talk as much as you want, and whenever you're ready for me to go, I'll get lost," he said, unfolding the tripod and fastening the camera to it. When he stole a glance at Campbell, he saw the same blank face and thought, *Well, this isn't going to take long*. The man was not going to be able to talk to him. Then Eric took the lens cap off and dropped his eye to the viewfinder to check the focus and felt his next words die in his chest, pulled down by a cold fist of fear. In the viewfinder Campbell Bradford was watching him with an entirely different expression, the blue eyes hard and penetrating and astonishingly alert. They were the eyes of a young man, a strong man.

Eric lifted his head slowly, turned from the camera to the man in the bed and felt that cold fist in his chest open and flutter its fingers.

Campbell Bradford's face had not changed. The eyes looked just as dim, just as unaware. Eric looked at the door, wishing now that he'd left it open.

"You going to talk to me?" Eric asked.

A slow blink, another hissed breath. Nothing else.

Eric looked at him, then thought, *Okay, let's try it again,* and lowered his eye to the viewfinder. There was Campbell, still in the bed, still watching him, still with alert blue eyes that looked nothing like the ones Eric had just been staring into.

He wanted to look up again but didn't, kept his eye to the camera instead. Give Paul Porter credit — he might be an asshole, but the man bought one hell of a camera. It was amazing, the way the thing picked up the life in Campbell Bradford's eyes.

"Are you going to talk to me tonight?" Eric asked again, this time with his eye to the camera.

"Yes," Campbell Bradford said, voice clear and strong.

Eric jerked his head up, bumped the tripod with his knee, and nearly knocked the camera over. Campbell looked back at him, face empty.

"Great," Eric said, steadying the camera and facing Campbell. "Where would you like to start? What would you like to tell me?"

Nothing.

What in the hell was this about? The old bastard spoke only when Eric was looking at him through the camera. He waited, and still Campbell was silent. Eric pursed his lips, exhaled, shook his head. *Okay, Gramps, I'll look away again.* He put his eye to the viewfinder and said, "I'd like to ask you about your childhood. Is that okay?"

"I don't really have much to say about that," Campbell Bradford said. His face was unchanged in the camera, the skin still loose and sallow, the sickness still clear. In fact, nothing had changed except the look in his eyes. For the first time, Eric considered that the old man could be screwing with him. That blank-faced look could be forced.

"Can I ask you something off topic?" Eric said.

"Yes." The voice was clear enough, but not youthful. It was an elderly man's voice. A sick man's voice.

"Are you going to talk to me only when I'm looking through the camera?"

Campbell Bradford smiled.

"That," Eric said, "is one wicked sense of humor."

He lifted his head again, and Campbell went back to the vacant expression, and Eric laughed.

"Okay, I'll play the game." He moved the camera over and flicked the viewing display open so he could look through the camera without having to keep his eye to the tiny viewfinder. "Why don't you want to talk to me about your childhood?"

"Not much to say."

The old man was good. He could time it right, speak just as Eric dropped his eyes to the display, stop just as he flicked his eyes up. What a case.

"Tell me about the town, maybe. West Baden, isn't that it?"

"Nice town," Campbell said, and his voice seemed tired now.

"Did you live by the hotel?" Eric said and waited a long time on this one, staring right at Campbell, waiting for him to crack. He didn't, and Eric dropped his eyes to the camera, and Campbell said, "Sure."

Shit, he wasn't going to give it up.

"How long did you live there?" Eric said, eyes still on the camera.

"A while." The fatigue appeared to be taking Campbell quickly, and Eric wondered if the game he'd played had sapped his strength.

Show him the bottle, maybe. Tell him the way that shit had tasted, see if he could get a laugh or a response of any depth. Eric took the bottle out. *Damn* but that thing was cold.

"Alyssa gave me this," he said, pushing it into the old man's hand, and for the first time Campbell's face changed while Eric had his eyes away from the camera, went drawn and lined with concern.

"You shouldn't have this," he said.

"I'm sorry. She brought it to me."

Campbell's long, ancient fingers opened and he lifted his hand from the bottle, found Eric's forearm and squeezed with surprising strength.

"It was *so cold*," he said.

"The bottle? Yeah, I know. Weird stuff."

"No!" Campbell's eyes were wide now, full of emotion, the game forgotten.

"What?"

"Not the bottle."

"Well, I thought it was plenty cold. When I touched—"

"Not the bottle."

Eric said, "What, then? What are you talking about?"

"So cold."

"What was?"

"The river."

"What river are you talking about?"

"It was *so cold.*"

Eric wanted to say something about Bradford's sense of humor again, wanted to give him some credit for this unnerving and inventive-as-hell prank, but he couldn't get the words out, couldn't even get them formed, because he was staring into the man's face and unable to believe that any drama school on earth had ever produced a talent like this. He wasn't acting. He was lost in some frozen memory. One that terrified him.

"So cold the river," Campbell Bradford repeated, his voice now dropping to a whisper as he lowered his head back to the pillow. "So cold the river."

"What river? I don't understand what you're talking about, sir."

Nothing.

Eric said, "Mr. Bradford? I'm sorry I brought the bottle."

Silence. The amazing job of blank-faced posing he'd done before paled in comparison to this.

"Mr. Bradford, I was hoping to talk to you about your life. If you don't want to talk about West Baden or your childhood, that's fine with me. Let's talk about your career, then. Your kids."

But it wasn't going to work. Not anymore. The old man was stone silent. Game or not, Eric wasn't going to wait all night. He let five minutes pass, asked a few more questions, got no response.

"All right," he said, removing the camera from the tripod. "I think you were messing with me earlier, and I hope you are now. I'm sorry if I upset you."

That got a languid blink. When Eric picked up the bottle from the bed and put it back in his briefcase, Campbell followed it with his eyes but said nothing.

"Okay," Eric said. "Take care, Mr. Bradford."

He left the hospital and drove back to the apartment, opened a beer and leaned against the refrigerator while he drank it, holding the bottle to his forehead between sips. What a weird guy. What a weird night.

It was the sort of story he'd have shared with Claire once, and that thought reminded him of the message he still hadn't checked. Maybe it was her. *Hopefully,* it was her. If she'd called, he was justified in calling her back. It would give him the excuse.

When he played the message, though, it wasn't Claire's voice.

"Eric, hey, I hope this catches you! This is Alyssa Bradford, and I'm calling to tell you not to waste your time driving to the hospital tonight. My father-in-law took a turn for the worse this week. I went down there yesterday and he couldn't say a word, would just look at me and stare. The doctors said he hasn't spoken since Monday. I'm so sorry it won't work out. I wish you could have talked with him. He had such a sense of humor. I guess the last time he spoke, it was to tell the nurse she needed to get a new outfit. That was just like him. If those were his last words, at least they were a joke."

She wished him luck in West Baden and hung up. Eric finished the rest of his beer in a long swallow and deleted the message.

"Hate to tell you, Alyssa," he said aloud, "but those weren't his last words."

5

It hit ninety on the first Friday of May, and everyone Anne McKinney spoke with commented on the heat, shook their heads, and expressed disbelief. Anne, of course, had seen this coming about six weeks earlier, when spring arrived early and emphatically. It had been in the high sixties throughout the third week of March, and while the TV people were busy talking about when it would break, Anne knew by the fourth day that it would not. Not really, not in the way of a normal Indiana spring, with those wild swings, seventy one day and thirty the next.

No, this year spring settled in and put up its feet, and winter didn't have much to say about it, just a few overnight grumblings of cold rain and wind. There had been five days in the eighties during April, and the rain that came was gentle. Nurturing. The entire town was in bloom now, everything lush and green and unpunished. The grounds around the hotel were particularly stunning. Always were, of course — full-time landscapers could do that for you—but Anne had seen eighty-six springs in West Baden, remembered about eighty of those pretty well, and this was as beautiful as any of them.

And as hot.

She couldn't avoid the weather conversations even if she'd wanted to; it was her identity in town, the only thing most people could think to mention when they saw her. Sometimes the topic came up casually, other times with genuine interest and inquiry, and, often enough, with winks and smiles. It amused some people, her fascination with weather, her house on the hill filled with barometers and thermometers and surrounded by weather vanes and wind chimes. That was fine by Anne. To each his own, as they said. She knew what she was waiting for.

Truth be told, there were times when she thought she might never see it either. See the real storm, the one she'd been counting on since she was a girl. The last few years, maybe she'd let her eye wander a bit, let her interest dim. She still kept the daily records, of course, still knew every shift and eddy of the winds, but it was more observation and less expectation.

But now it was ninety on the first Friday of May, the air so still it was as if the wind had lost its job here, headed elsewhere in search of work. The barometer sat at 30.08 and steady, indicating no change soon. Just heat and blue skies and stillness, the summer humidity yet to arrive, that ninety more tolerable than it would be in July.

All peaceful signs really. Anne didn't believe any of them.

She went into the West Baden hotel at three and sat in one of the luxurious velvet-covered chairs near the bar and had her afternoon cocktail. Brian, the bartender, gave a wink to one of his coworkers when he fixed Anne's drink, as if she didn't know he put only the barest splash of Tanqueray in the tonic before squeezing the lime. A splash was all she needed these days. Hell, she was eighty-six years old. What did the boy think she was coming down here for, to end up three sheets to the wind?

No, it was the routine. A ritual of thanks more than anything else, an appreciation for continued health, health that she couldn't ask for at this age. She still made it up all those front steps, didn't use a cane or a walker or a stranger's arm. Walked in under the dome and had herself a seat and a sip. The day she couldn't do that, well, go ahead and pop the lid on the pine box.

There wasn't a soul in the world who would understand how it made Anne feel to come in here and see the place alive. The day it had finally reopened, she walked into the rotunda beneath that towering dome of glass and burst into tears. Had to sit down on a chair and cry, and people just smiled sympathetic-like at her, seeing an old woman having an old woman's moment. They couldn't understand what it meant, couldn't understand the way this place had looked when she was a girl, the most amazing place she could ever have imagined in the world.

It had been mostly a ruin for years. Decades. She'd come and gone through the town daily, looking up to see the crumbling stone and cracked marble, and with every day and every look, a little piece of her died a wailing, anguished death.

But she'd never lost hope either. The place was special, and she just couldn't imagine that it would go on like that forever. The hotel's return, much like the big storm, was something she'd believed in without fail. You called that sort of thing faith.

Her faith had been rewarded. Bill Cook, the man's name. Awful plain name, she thought, but he'd made a few billion dollars on it with a medical company up in Bloomington, and then he'd found his way down here and not only seen what had to be done but could afford to *have* it done.

So now they were back, both of them, the West Baden Springs Hotel and the French Lick Springs Resort, buildings that seemed as out of place in this valley as a pair of giraffes at a dog show, and though she had no use for the ugly fake riverboat casino that was built to draw people down, she understood its purpose. Most irksome part of that was that the thing wasn't really a riverboat, was nothing but a building with a moat around it, but evidently that was enough to please the legislators, who wouldn't allow anything but riverboat casinos in the state. You had to wonder what that said about the quality of brains in the statehouse, that they could fool themselves into thinking a building was a boat just because you filled a ditch around it with water, but Anne had been around for too many years to hold much hope for government anyhow. They could have declared the thing a spaceship for all she cared as long as it allowed the hotels to come back.

She'd lived to see it. That was a special thing, and one that returned her faith in the storm. It was coming, someday, a dark, furious cloud, and though she didn't know what role she would play in that, she knew it was important that she be ready. Part of her wanted the storm; part of her dreaded it. As much as she loved them — those brilliant flashes of lightning, the terrible screaming winds — she feared them, too. They took all the powers of man and sneered at them.

A convention of some sort was in the hotel today, and the place was particularly active, echoing with voices and laughter and footfalls on the parquet. It soothed her like a hand on the shoulder. She asked Brian for one more, smiled to herself as she saw him fill the short glass with nothing but tonic and ice before adding the lime. He knew the rules. Anne was here for the sounds and the sights, not the sauce.

She took the tonic in slow, and by the time it was gone, that comforting noise and bustle and the soft velvet armchair were pulling her down to sleep, and she knew it was time to go. Start falling asleep down here and she'd begin to seem less charming to the staff. Right now, with her daily gin and her smiles and occasional barbed jokes, she was something of a local treasure. Valued, appreciated, even by the younger ones. She liked that role, and understood all too well that it could quickly be erased by one drooling nap.

She got to her feet, taking care to relish that tug of pain in her lower back, a tug that she wouldn't have if she couldn't still get to her feet. Left a few dollars for Brian — *Thank you, Mrs. McKinney, have a good day and we'll see you tomorrow* — and walked away from the bar and back into the rotunda. Stood in the middle and looked up at the dome, with the sun shining down and the place glittering, took a deep breath, and thanked the good Lord for one more afternoon like this. Precious things. Precious.

Out the main doors and back onto the steps and what do you know — there was some wind to greet her. First she'd felt all day. Nothing of real notice, just a gentle, experimental puff, like the breeze wasn't sure about it yet, but it was there all the same. She stood at the top of the steps and watched the bushes rustle and the leaves turn and flutter, saw that the wind was coming up out of the southwest now. Interesting. She hadn't expected the shift today. The air was still hot, might've even pushed a few degrees past ninety by now, but she thought she could detect a chill to the wind, almost as if there was some cold trapped in it, surrounded by warmth but still there nevertheless.

She'd go home and take a few readings, see what sense she could make of it. All she knew now was that there was something in the air. Something on the way.

6

IT WAS A SIX-HOUR drive, the final third a hell of a lot more pleasant than the first two. Getting out of the city and into Indiana was a nightmare in itself, and then Eric was rewarded by only as bleak a drive as he could think of, Chicago to Indianapolis. South of Indy, though, things began to turn. The flatlands turned into hills, the endless fields filled with trees, the straight road began to curve. He stopped for lunch in Bloomington, left the highway and drove into town to see the campus, one he'd always heard was beautiful. It didn't disappoint. He had a burger and a beer at a place called Nick's, the beer something local, Upland Wheat. When in Rome, right? Turned out to be as good a warm-weather beer as he'd ever tasted, sort of thing made you want to stretch out in the sun and relax for a while. There was driving to be done, though, so he left it at just the one beer and got back into the Acura and pushed south.

Past Bloomington to Bedford, and then the highway hooked

and lost a lane in a town called Mitchell and began to dip and rise as it carved through the hills. Everything was green, lush, and alive, and now and then flatbed trucks loaded with fresh-quarried limestone lumbered by. There weren't many houses along this stretch of the highway, but if Eric had had a dollar for every one with a basketball hoop outside, he'd have been a rich man by the time he hit Paoli.

He knew from the map that Paoli meant he was close, and once he figured out what road to take away from the square — a mural covering the entire side of a building pointed the way to French Lick — he laid a little heavier on the gas, ready to have this drive done.

A dull, constant headache that had lodged in the back of his skull somewhere north of Indianapolis, then faded while he had his beer, now returned with a little stronger pulse to it, one that made him wince every now and then as it hit a particularly inspired chord. He had Excedrin in the suitcase, would have to take some as soon as he got to the hotel. He'd hoped things might turn a little more exotic as he neared West Baden and French Lick, but there was just more farm country. He ran past one white rail fence that seemed to stretch for a mile — would hate to paint that thing — and not much else that was worth notice. Then a few buildings began to show themselves, and a sign told him he'd reached West Baden, and he thought, *You've got to be kidding me.*

Because there was nothing here. A cluster of old buildings and a barbecue stand, and that was it. Then he felt his eyes drawn away from the road, up the hill to the right, and he let off the gas and felt his breath catch in his chest as the speed fell off.

There was the hotel. And Alyssa Bradford had used the correct word in describing it, because only one word came close — *surreal.* The place was that, and then some. Pale yellow towers flanked a mammoth crimson dome, and the rest of the structure fell away beneath, hundreds of windows visible in the stone. It looked more like a castle than a hotel, something that belonged in Europe, not on this stretch of farmland.

A horn blew behind him, and Eric realized he'd coasted almost to a stop in the middle of the road. He pushed on the gas again, found a set of twin stone arches that guarded a long, winding brick drive that led up to the hotel. *West Baden Springs — Carlsbad of America,* the arches said. He knew from his research that referred to a famed European mineral spa.

The place gave him an immediate desire to reach for the camera, get this recorded now, as if it might soon disappear.

He wasn't certain the brick road was a legitimate entrance, so he drove past the stone arches in search of the parking lot and, within the space of a blink and a yawn, found himself in French Lick. Out of one town and into the other, all in what felt like six city blocks. They were separate towns, but the reality was, they felt like one place, and the only reason they hadn't merged into one town over the years was those hotels. They'd been rivals at one time, French Lick and West Baden, and many locals just referred to the area as Springs Valley.

He passed the French Lick Springs Resort, which held the grandeur of its West Baden partner but not the magic. The architecture was more traditional, that was all. A good-looking building, but a building nonetheless. The West Baden hotel, with its dome and towers, quickened the pulse more. The owner of the French Lick hotel, Thomas Taggart, had been a fierce rival of the West Baden Springs Hotel owner, Lee Sinclair — in business and politics, with Taggart a key Democrat in the state and Sinclair an equally powerful Republican. For decades those two had dueled for superiority in the valley, and while Sinclair's hotel may have won out, Taggart created a million-dollar business with his Pluto Water, while Sinclair's Sprudel Water — virtually the same product — had somehow failed, eventually forcing him to sell his interest in the water to Taggart.

Eric turned at the casino and drove up the road in search of the entrance for the West Baden hotel. The parking lot was set to the side and above the hotel, and he parked and took his bags out and walked toward the entrance, looking out at the grounds as he went. A creek cut through the middle, surrounded by flowering trees and flowerbeds and emerald-colored grass. The smell of the grass was in the air, freshly cut, and something about that drew him away from the parking lot entrance and around to the front of the building. He set his bags down on the steps and inhaled and looked off down the long brick drive.

"What a place." He said it aloud, but softly, and was surprised when someone said, "Wait'll you see the inside."

He turned and saw an elderly woman heading down the steps toward him. She looked at least eighty but walked with a firm, steady stride and wore makeup and jewelry, a pocketbook held between her upper arm and her side.

"I'm looking forward to it," he said, stepping aside so she could come down. "Have been for a while."

"I know the feeling," she said. "And don't worry, it won't disappoint."

He picked up his bags and went up the steps and through the doors and into the atrium. Made it about twenty feet inside before he had to drop the bags again — not because they were heavy but because taking the place in called for energy.

The dome was three times as wide as he'd expected and twice as tall, a tremendous globe of glass resting on white steel ribs. The design had been truly ingenious in its time — hell, it still was. Harrison Albright, the architect who had conceived of the whole amazing design, came up with the umbrella-like supports to hold the dome up, but he had concerns that temperature changes would cause it to expand and contract at a different rate than the building below — a sure recipe for disaster, a collapse of the dome that would shower those beneath with glass and humiliate its creator. As a solution, Albright rested the steel support ribs on ball bearings, allowing the dome to expand and contract at a different rate than the building below. This idea in 1901.

There were ten thousand square feet of glass in the dome alone. More glass than in any other building in the world at the time of its construction, more even than London's Crystal Palace. It was one thing to read details like that on the Internet, another to see it. One of the stories Eric had found said that when they removed the supports beneath the dome, many spectators, including Sinclair, weren't certain the thing would avoid collapse. In response, Albright insisted on climbing to the roof and standing dead center on top of the dome when they removed the last of the scaffolding. He'd been sure of his math, even if nobody else was.

The atrium stretched out beneath the dome, shining floor and ornate rugs and potted ferns, lots of gold trim on the perimeter. They'd redone the tile — twelve *million* marble mosaics were hand-laid in the original floor — and matched the paint to the original color, matched the rugs, matched damn near everything that could be matched. Eric had seen impressive renovations but nothing with such attention to detail.

Some of the rooms had balconies that looked out over the atrium, and he hoped Alyssa Bradford had come through with one of those for him. He wanted to sit out there at night and have a drink and watch the place quiet down. *Probably see ghosts,* he thought, and smiled.

The hotel had that kind of feel, though. It started with that misplaced quality, floating out here in the middle of nowhere, and then built on the astonishing design and a restoration job so carefully and perfectly completed that entering the building was like walking out of one century and into another.

He took a few steps away from his luggage, more into the center of the room, and then tilted his head back to look directly up at the dome. When he did that, the headache that had been momentarily forgotten bloomed bright behind his eyes, a swift, jagged pain. He winced and dropped his eyes, shaded them with his hand. Bad idea, looking up into the light like that. Light always exacerbated a headache.

He returned to his bags and brought them to the reception desk and checked in. Took the keycard for his room — 418 — and then went up and got the luggage stowed. The room was a reflection of everything else — ornate, luxurious, reminiscent of times gone by. And it had the balcony. Alyssa Bradford had done well.

He was distracted from enjoying the room, though, because the headache was getting to him now. He opened the suitcase and took out the Excedrin, shook three tablets into his palm, and went into the bathroom and poured a glass of water and washed them down.

That should help. A drink didn't sound like a bad idea either. He wanted to sit down at the bar under the dome and sip one slow. Give the Excedrin a little while to work, and then he'd come back up and get the camera and start the job.

Josiah Bradford had hardly gotten his cigarette lit before Amos came boiling around the corner, telling him to put it out. Had one tantalizing puff and then he was smashing it under his foot and Amos was bitching at him.

"How many times I got to tell you, we don't smoke on the job, Josiah. You think I want the guests to come outside to enjoy the day and have to breathe in the cigarette smoke from my land-scaping crew? I swear, son, you get told and told again and it don't mean a thing to you."

Josiah bit down his response, shoved past Amos's wide paunch and threw the cigarette into the trash, and took his weed eater and fired it up with a theatrical flourish, pumping the throttle trigger with his index finger to turn the thing's whine into a scream and drown out Amos's voice. Shit, it was a cigarette, not an atom bomb. Amos needed to get his ass some perspective.

Josiah went off down the brick road, trimming edges that didn't need trimmed, keeping his back to Amos until he heard the Gator come to life and drive away. Then he let off the trigger, turned to Amos departing in the stupid little cart, and sent a thick wad of spit in his direction. Didn't come close, but it was the gesture that counted.

It was too damn hot for May. The skin on Josiah's arms and the back of his neck had gone dark brown by mid-April, and now he could feel the sweat soaking through his shirt and holding his hair to his neck in damp tangles. Had been a time, not all that long ago, that he'd been griping about the cold. Now he wished fall would hustle along.

He worked all the way down the brick drive to the stone arches and the old building beside them that had once been a bank. Then he crossed to the other side and paused before start-ing his return trip, looking up at the length of the drive at the work yet to be done. Looking up at that damned hotel.

Oh, he'd liked it at one time. Had been excited, same as every-body, when word came down that the place was going to be restored, that the casino was on its way. Jobs aplenty, that was the word. Well, he had his job now. Had his callused hands and sunburn. Some fortune.

The resorts were supposed to be a big deal for the locals.

Provide a — what was the word that politician had said? — a *boon*, that was it. A boon. Shit.

Thing these damn hotels provided, so far as Josiah was concerned, was torment. Rich folks coming in again, the way they had so long ago, and all of a sudden you were more aware of your place in the world. More aware of your fifteen-year-old Ford pickup when it was idling next to a Mercedes with Massachusetts plates, waiting for a green light. More aware of the Keystone Ice you bought in thirty-packs when you saw somebody in an Armani suit throw down a twenty for a Grey Goose martini and then wave off the change.

They said all this was going to boost the local economy, and they'd been right. Josiah made eight thousand dollars more per year now than he had before the restorations began. But he did it trimming weeds in front of people who made eighty grand more than that. Eight hundred grand more than that. Worse than the money was the anonymity — people coming and going right past you all day and never giving you so much as a blink. Wasn't that they disrespected you outright; they didn't even realize you were there.

It vexed him. Had almost from the day the hotel doors opened and he saw all that gold and glitter, from the first time he'd walked through the casino with his hand wrapped tight around the ten-dollar bill that was all he could afford to gamble with. Because Josiah Bradford's family had been in this valley for generations, and there was a time, back when the resorts were flourishing in the Prohibition days, when they were powerful. Noticed and known. Somehow, seeing the place come back to life while he held a weed eater in his hands felt beyond wrong — felt intolerable.

Why, wasn't but a month ago that some black kid from IU came to Josiah's home in a damned Porsche Cayenne, just dripping money, and said he wanted to talk about Josiah's great-grandfather, Campbell, the man who'd controlled this valley once. Granted, he'd run off and left his family, taking with him every dime they had — and according to the stories, plenty of dimes they didn't have, too — but in his time he'd been as powerful as anyone who ever walked through that damn rotunda. A behind-the-scenes sort of influence, the kind you built with brass knuckles and brass balls, the only kind Josiah'd ever respected. Campbell's legacy was an infamous one, but Josiah had always felt a strange kind of pride in him anyhow. Then the black kid showed up, some rich student, wanting to talk about the tales, put his own version of the Bradford family history down on paper. Josiah threw him the hell out of his house and hadn't heard from him since, but the car was around often enough, a 450-horse motor in a frigging SUV, dumbest thing Josiah had ever seen, seventy thousand-some dollars' worth of stupid.

Every insult was fuel for the fire, though. That's what he told himself day in and day out, what kept him here, putting cigarettes out before he'd even had a chance to smoke them, saying yessir and nosir to that fat bastard Amos. It wouldn't last forever. You could bet your sweet ass on that. There'd come a day when he'd walk back into this shit-hole town and make 'em stir, swagger into that casino and toss a few thousand on the table, look bored when he won and amused when he lost, have the crowd hanging on it.

You had to be ambitious. Josiah figured that out early, knew even when he dropped out of high school that he would rise above all this crap. He didn't *need* high school, that was all. Had all As and Bs except for a C in chemistry when he quit. But what was he going to do, earn a scholarship, go up to IU or Purdue and get some bullshit degree that landed him a four-bedroom house with a thirty-year mortgage and a leased Volvo? Please.

What he had his sights on was a good deal bigger than that, and you didn't need the schooling to get it. What you needed was the hunger. And Josiah Bradford had that in spades. *Fire in the belly,* his old man had called it just before tying one on up in Bedford and wrapping his Trans Am around a tree on US 50, killing himself before Josiah had the pleasure.

Better believe it was a fire. Burned hotter every day, but Josiah was no idiot, knew that it required a touch of patience, required waiting for the right opportunity.

The puttering sound of the Gator's little motor broke him out of his reverie, and he bowed his head and extended the weed eater again, let the sun scorch on his back as he began to make the slow trip back up the brick drive to the hotel.

The Bradford name had meant something in this town once.

It would again.

7

THERE WAS A COCKTAIL waitress at the bar who reminded
Eric of Claire, the same willowy build and glossy dark hair
and easy laugh, so he decided not to linger over that drink so
long after all. He settled for one beer again and then went up
to the room and took his shoes off and lay on the bed, thinking he'd rest for a few minutes. Evidently the drive and the beer
were enough to coax sleep along, because when he opened his
eyes again the bedside clock showed that he'd slept for nearly
two hours. It was past five now. Time to get into action.

He sat up with a grunt, still feeling foggy with sleep, and
swung his feet to the floor and went to get his briefcase. There
was a legal pad in it on which he'd sketched a rough outline
of what he wanted to get done first. All he had scheduled for
today was an evening meeting with that graduate student who'd
posted about Campbell on the Internet, but he'd like to get some
film done, too, get things rolling as much as possible.

Inside the briefcase he found the legal pad and the bottle of Pluto Water, which reminded him that he needed to check on that, get an accurate date if possible.

When he took the bottle out of the briefcase, he could've sworn it was even colder than when he'd last touched it in Chicago. It had always been unnaturally cool, but now it felt as if it had just come out of a refrigerator. It was hard to believe, considering his last experience with it, but somehow the bottle looked almost tempting today. Almost refreshing.

"No way," he said, thinking about another taste. He couldn't ever stomach that again. Who knew what was wrong with it. Stuff would probably kill you.

All the same, he loosened the cap again. Lowered his nose to it and took a quick sniff, bracing for that noxious, stomach-turning scent.

He didn't get it. A trace, maybe, but nothing so foul as last time. In fact, it smelled mild now, almost sweet. That was odd. Must have released the worst of the smell as soon as it was opened. Maybe that's how they did it in the old days, let the stuff sit open for a while before consumption.

Oh, hell, he thought, *go on and get a little on your tongue.*

He poured a few drops into a cupped palm, then held it to his face and dipped the tip of his tongue into it, expecting the worst.

It wasn't so bad at all. Just a barely perceptible sweetness. It must have needed to breathe a little. No way he was going to brave an actual swallow of it again, though. No way.

He put the cap back on and left the room.

That first afternoon it felt right to just wander. He opened with a few shots of the dome and the atrium and the rest of the interior splendor, then moved on outside and explored the grounds.

There were a handful of beautiful but small stone buildings that had once housed some of the mineral spas. A fountain highlighted the center of the garden, and Eric discovered there was a small cemetery on the hill above, looking down at the dome. He took a few experimental shots from the ground, shooting at the hotel past the tilted gravestones, and was pleased with the results. This spot needed to be incorporated into whatever he did—anytime you could shoot down on something so grand with gravestones in the forefront, you should.

He went back down the hill, amazed at the heat on this first weekend of May, his shirt already clinging to his back, his forehead wet with perspiration, and then walked to the end of the brick drive—past an even more sweat-soaked man with a weed eater, who returned Eric's nod with a surly look—and then stood beneath the stone arches and shot back up at the hotel. The sun was still high, glaring off the dome, and he thought that it would probably be pretty powerful if he could catch it at just the right stage of twilight some night, as the sun fell and those old-fashioned lamps came on.

There was no shortage of options and angles here; the place offered a sort of visual potential he hadn't seen anywhere else. He took some shots up from outside the arches, using a slow zoom up the brick drive, trying to create the effect of walking up on the place, then went back to the car and headed toward French Lick. It was within walking distance, but not when lugging his equipment under the scorching sun.

Once inside, he had to give the French Lick hotel a bit more credit—it was pretty amazing in its own right. It would have seemed extraordinary in this little town were it not for the big brother up the road. As he walked through, Eric felt a mild sense of sympathy for Thomas Taggart. He'd built a hell of a place here, only to have it outshined by something a mile away. That's how it could go, though — there was always somebody a little bit better.

He shot video in the hotel and the casino, wandering, and found himself drinking another beer in a basement bar, where the walls were adorned with antique electrical switchgear. The Power Plant, they called it. Whatever — the beer was cold, and the lights were dim, and that helped his headache. He wasn't sure what that was all about. Eric had never been prone to headaches, but this persistent little bastard had been with him all day. Could be he was coming down with something.

He ate dinner at the casino's buffet, taking his time, nothing left to do until nine, when he was supposed to meet the graduate student. The kid had told Eric he'd be driving down from Bloomington that night, so they'd agreed to meet late and grab a drink at the hotel bar. Not much else had been said in the e-mail exchange, so Eric had no idea how helpful the kid might be.

When he got back outside, the grounds were bathed in long shadows, the sun fading behind the tree-covered hills above. There was a back road connecting the two hotels and the casino, used by shuttles to ferry gamblers back and forth, and he took that on the return trip. Ahead of him was an old Chevy Blazer with a worn-out muffler, steep tree-lined hills on the left, a low valley with train tracks on the right. Four deer stood grazing in the valley, regarding the cars curiously but not fearfully. He had the windows down and his arm resting across the door and his mind was on Claire, disconnected from his surroundings, until he saw the leaves.

They were down on the right, in a short field that ran between the railroad tracks and a creek. A cluster of dead leaves soaked by winter snows and spring rains and then baked to parchment under this unseasonable sun. He looked away from the road as the Blazer in front of him crackled and roared and pulled away, put his foot on the brake and turned the wheel, and brought the Acura to a stop on the side of the road, watching.

The leaves were spinning in a circle, rising several feet off the ground but remaining tightly packed, swirling in a perfect vortex. It was the sort of thing you'd see during the fall in Chicago, where the winds eddied between buildings, trapped by tons of concrete and steel and forced into unusual patterns. But out here, in an open field, when the wind seemed to blow only out of the west and had nothing to redirect it, that circle was unusual. Even the wind itself seemed tremulous, lending an uneasy quality to the way those leaves danced and spun. Yes, that was the word. *Uneasy.*

He put the car in park and opened his door and stepped out into the wind, felt it wrap his shirt around his body and lift warm road dust to his nostrils, a smell that reminded him of summer labor during college, when he'd hauled wheelbarrows around construction sites for a Missouri masonry company. He left the road with the car running and the door only half closed, an electronic chime pinging after him, and walked down the short hill and into the tall grass on the other side. Up the little ridge and onto the tracks, and then he stopped, looking down at those leaves.

The vortex had thickened now, attracting more leaves. It was at least eight feet tall and maybe four feet in diameter at the top and one foot at the bottom. Swirling clockwise, a little rise and fall in the motion, but generally a perfect circle.

For a moment he was completely captivated, holding his breath and staring, but then his mind kicked into gear and he thought, *Get the camera, dumbass.*

He hurried back to the Acura and dug the camera and tripod out, sure that when he turned his back, the leaves would have settled, this rapturous moment gone. They were still turning, though, and he walked up to the gravel ridge where the train tracks ran and got the camera set up and turned on.

For this he wanted the zoom reduced as much as possible, a wide-angle shot that captured the bizarre look. The light was poor, the gray gloom of twilight, but it was enough to work with. Behind the swirling leaves the deer stood at the edge of the tree line and stared at him. He'd been standing with his eye to the viewfinder for a few seconds before their ears rose and, one after another in a silent sequence, they took quick leaps into the trees and vanished. It wasn't until the last one disappeared that he became aware of a sound, faint at first but building rapidly. Wind was part of the sound — more wind in his ears than there was in the air, heavy and roaring. There was something else over the top of it, though, light and lilting. A violin.

Now a third sound joined in, lower than both the violin and the wind, and at first he thought it was the steady plucking of a cello or bass. Then it grew louder and he realized it wasn't an instrument at all, but an engine, the sound of heavy gears straining, pounding along in constant rhythm. The violin rose to a frantic shrieking and then vanished abruptly, and the wind died down and the leaves fell out of the vortex and scattered over the ground, one blowing across the grass and trapping itself against Eric's leg.

The engine sound was louder than ever, approaching fast, and Eric turned from the camera and looked up the railroad tracks and saw the cloud. It was a roiling, midnight-colored mass sitting low on the horizon and blowing in fast. He stood in the middle of the tracks and stared up at it, feeling the fading sun on the back of his neck but seeing nothing but darkness ahead, and then the clouds parted and fell back and a train emerged from the center.

It was a locomotive, and that malevolent dark cloud was boiling out of its stack, thick snakes of black steam. A whistle screamed, and Eric could feel the vibrations under his feet now, the rails trembling with the approaching weight, loose gravel rattling.

The train was moving faster than any he'd ever seen, and he was standing right in its path. He stepped to the side and caught the tip of one shoe on the rail, stumbled and almost fell as he lifted the tripod and scrambled down off the tracks and into the grass where the fallen leaves lay. When the locomotive thundered by him, he had to turn from the tracks and lift one arm to shield his face. Then the whistle split the air again and he looked up at the boxcars whirling by and saw that the train was colorless, all shades of black and gray except for one white car with a splash of red in the Pluto Water logo. The door of this car was open and a man hung from it, his feet inside the car and his torso extended, weight resting on the hand clasped to the edge of the door. He wore an old-fashioned suit with a vest and a bowler hat. As the car approached he looked at Eric and smiled and tipped his hat. It seemed like a gesture of gratitude. His dark brown eyes held a liquid quality, shimmering, and Eric could see that he was standing in water, some of it splashing over the side, glistening in the darkness that surrounded the train.

Then the train was by, an all-black caboose at the end, and the accompanying cloud lifted and Eric stood staring into the sky, looking at nothing. A car came down the road, swerving into the oncoming lane briefly as it passed the Acura, and the woman behind the wheel gave Eric a curious look but didn't slow, went on toward West Baden Springs on the heels of a train she clearly hadn't seen.

8

THE SENSE THAT CREPT over him then was unlike anything he'd ever experienced before, reality and the world he knew separating and speeding away from each other. He'd seen the train so clearly, had smelled the heat and felt the earth shudder. It had been *real*, damn it.

But now it was gone. Faded into the evening air like an apparition, and he was sure that the woman who'd just passed by had not seen a thing. There was not so much as a trace of smoke in the sky.

Even the wind was gone. That thought brought the spinning leaves back into his mind, and he turned to the camera and flicked open the display window. The leaves had been real. He had *that* crazy shit on tape.

He punched the rewind button and then play, jumped through some film from the casino until he reached the gloomy field and train tracks and the . . .

empty sky.

There were no leaves in the air on this tape. Nothing except the tracks and the trees and the tall grass waving in the wind.

He went back to the casino shots again, played the video all the way through, squinting at the screen, and again saw no trace of the spinning leaves.

"Bullshit," he said aloud, staring at display. "Bullshit, you are so full of shit..."

"I thought a camera could never lie," someone said from above him, and Eric lifted his head and looked up to see a young black guy watching him. He'd pulled up behind the Acura and gotten out of his car and Eric hadn't noticed any of it as he stood there staring obsessively at a camera that was calling him a liar.

"I'm not certain," the guy said, "but I think I was on my way to meet you."

Eric cocked his head and gave a closer look. The guy was tall, probably six four at least, and very dark, with short hair and wide shoulders. Dressed in jeans and a white button-down shirt that hung loose and untucked.

"Kellen Cage?" Eric said. This was not who he'd expected to be doing a thesis on the history of a rural Indiana town.

"Ah, so you are Eric."

"How did you figure that out?"

"In your e-mail you said you were working on some sort of film project. And I'm no detective but I can't imagine there are many people walking around here with a camera like that."

"Right."

"What are you shooting?" Cage said, surveying the area.

"Ah, nothing. Landscape, you know."

"Yeah? Well, you ought to park somewhere else, man, or at least close the door. Somebody's gonna take it off, you leave it like that."

Kellen Cage had walked closer, all the way down the hill, and he looked even younger now. Maybe twenty-five, twenty-six at best. His size was more evident down here, too. Eric wasn't a small guy — six feet and one hundred and eighty pounds that had been pretty hard pounds before he'd left L.A. — but this Kellen Cage, taller and broader and knotted with muscle, made Eric feel tiny.

"So what's the problem with your camera?" Cage said when Eric didn't respond.

"Nothing, man. Nothing."

"You were giving it one hell of a lecture over nothing." He had his head leaned to the side, was studying Eric with a skeptical look. Eric didn't answer, just set to work removing the camera from the tripod and replacing it in its case.

"So what kind of film are you doing?" Kellen Cage asked.

"Oh, just a minor thing, nothing worth talking about but something that pays, and considering doing more. What about you?"

He was struggling with the camera because his hands were shaking, and he hoped Cage hadn't noticed.

"Been coming down here for months," Cage said. "Working on a thesis for my doctorate up at Indiana. I'd like to get a book out of it, though. Came down and thought, man, there's a lot here. Hate to waste it."

"Focusing on the hotel?"

"Nope. All the historical attention paid to this place has revolved around the hotels and Taggart and Sinclair, but there's a strong black history, too. Joe Louis came down here all the time, used to train here before big fights, thought there was some sort of magic to the springs. Swore he never lost a fight after leaving the place. He didn't stay in this hotel, though — stayed at a place called the Waddy that was for blacks. And they had a baseball team made up of porters and cooks and groundskeepers from the hotels who played with the major-league clubs that came down here for spring training. Played *well* with them, is the way it's told, beat the Pirates once. The black teams they had down here could've played with anybody."

Eric finally had the camera in the bag. It took him a few seconds to realize that Kellen Cage had stopped talking and was waiting on a response.

"I read some about Louis," Eric said. "Didn't know the baseball stuff."

"Oh, there's plenty of more important elements to it, but I always catch myself telling the sports side first. Most of what I'm doing is focused around that Waddy Hotel. It's important to bring these two hotels back to life. I just want to make sure the Waddy doesn't get forgotten."

Eric slid the camera bag over his shoulder, then went to pick up the tripod, dropped it, and nearly lost the camera bag when he bent over to pick it up. Kellen Cage reached down and took the tripod.

"You want to go on to the hotel and grab that drink as planned?" he said. "No offense, my man, but you look like you *need* one."

"Yeah," Eric said. "Yeah, I could definitely use a drink."

9

H e didn't go up to the room, choosing instead to bring the camera along with him as they walked across the atrium, Kellen explaining something about the bar's hours and Eric hardly hearing him.

Don't overthink it, Eric, the way you did with the Harrelson tape. The way you did in that valley in the Bear Paws. In fact, those aren't fair comparisons. There might have been some sort of a tug, those times. Some sort of intuition. But this thing? That train was in your imagination, brother. Nothing else.

Eric was actually pleased to have Kellen Cage walking along-side him now. Cage promised something valuable — a distraction. Talk to him, have a few drinks, forget this moment. Forget this trembling in the gut, this foolish, ominous sense.

"What're you having?" Cage said when they reached the bar.

"Grey Goose on the rocks with a lemon."

Cage turned and spoke to the bartender and Eric eased onto

the stool, turned and looked back at the sprawling atrium and took a deep breath. He just needed to relax. This thing, well, it wasn't anything, really. Not even worth analyzing. Just forget it.

"So, I'm truly happy to hear you're interested in Campbell Bradford," Kellen said, "because he's one of the biggest question marks I've got left. The old boy just disappeared when he left town."

"Made a pile of money after he went," Eric said. "His daughter-in-law's the one who hired me. Said he's worth two hundred million or somewhere in that neighborhood."

"You mean he *was* worth that much," Kellen said. "Not is. Was. Has to be dead."

"No, but he's close."

Kellen tilted his head back and arched an eyebrow. "The man is alive?"

"He was when I left Chicago, at least."

Kellen shook his head. "No way. Not the same Campbell."

Eric frowned. "His daughter-in-law told me he'd grown up here and then ran away as a kid."

"The Campbell Bradford I know of ran away from town, too. But he was a grown man, left a wife and kid behind. And he was born in eighteen ninety-two, which would put him at, what, one hundred and sixteen now? Your man can't be *that* old, right?"

"He's ninety-five."

"Then he ain't the same guy."

"Well, must be two people with that name. Maybe my guy is your guy's son?"

"He had a son named William who stayed in town." Kellen's face was tinged with disappointment. "Hell, you're not going to be able to help me. We got two different people."

"They have to be connected," Eric said. "Name like that, town like this? Have to be related somehow."

Kellen took a drink, then said, "The Campbell I know of, he was a dark man."

"How so?"

"There was a time this area was a gambler's paradise, back in the twenties. Bunch of money poured in, bunch of debts piled up, and Campbell Bradford was the man who saw to balancing the scales."

"Some sort of enforcer?" Eric said.

"You got it. He was the muscle, the debt collector. People were *terrified* of the man. Thought he was evil. The story I'm interested in, the way this guy intersects with my own project, is that there's a legend he murdered Shadrach Hunter after the stock market collapsed in 1929, just as this town dried up. It's unreal how fast this place emptied out after Black Tuesday. One day this was among the world's elite resorts, a year later it's empty and on its way to being a ruin. Pretty damn fast change, you know?"

"Who was Shadrach Hunter?"

"Ran the black casino," Kellen said. "And, yes, there was such a thing. Started out as a small poker game in a shitty back room, and grew. There were so many blacks down here working at the hotels, but they couldn't socialize there, so they threw dice and played cards down at Shadrach's. Before long, though, the thing grew some legs. Campbell Bradford was helping control all the gaming in the valley for white people — working with Ed Ballard, who owned this hotel, only Campbell was a lot dirtier than Ballard, who was far from clean himself — but he didn't have anything to do with Shad's game. According to the legend, Shad was a miser, skimmed money from every game and saved it, just stockpiled. Always wore a gun in his belt and had a couple big guys running with him at all times, bodyguards.

"Well, after the market crashed, this whole town shut down and the cash flow vanished. 'Round that time, Shadrach Hunter was murdered, and Campbell Bradford disappeared, leaving his family penniless." Kellen spread his hands. "So, you can see where the myth developed. I've got some great stories about it but damn few facts. Was hoping you could offer some."

"All I've got is a dying old millionaire in Chicago who goes by the same name."

"No way it can be the same guy?"

"He's old, but he's not a hundred and sixteen."

"Well, I'll put you in touch with a man named Edgar Hastings tomorrow," Kellen said. "I'll be interested to see what he thinks. He knew the family, is one of the last people alive in this town who has clear memories of Campbell Bradford. Campbell's got a great-grandson left in the area, too, but I won't put you in touch with him."

There was a dry smile on his lips. Eric said, "What's his deal?"

"Oh, a bit on the surly side. Edgar warned me, said it would be best not to talk to him, but I ignored that advice and went to his house. Took about two minutes for him to run me off the place. Threw a beer bottle at my car as I was leaving."

"Charming."

"Hospitable, no question. But assuming he isn't going to be more helpful with you than he was with me, Edgar's all I have to offer."

"Okay."

"So, how'd you get into this business?" Kellen said. "Want to be a filmmaker all along, or was it a hobby that turned professional, or...?"

He let his voice trail off, waiting, the question asked in absolute innocence, but Eric was feeling anger bleed through him. *I was a filmmaker,* he wanted to shout, *and if a few breaks had gone my way and a few assholes had stayed out of it, you'd be asking me for an autograph right now.*

"I went to film school," he said, trying to keep his voice loose. "And then I worked out in California for a while. I was a director of photography on some stuff."

"Things I'd know?"

Yes, things he would know. But if he named those, he saw the inevitable follow-up question—*What films have you worked on recently?* And what would Eric say to that? *Why, you mean you haven't seen the Anderson wedding video? Or the Harrelson funeral piece? What, you live in a cave, man?*

"Probably not," he said. "I couldn't stick it out there, so I came back to Chicago and started doing my own thing."

Kellen nodded. "'Director of photography'—what's that mean, exactly?"

"You run the cameras and the lighting crew. The director's in charge of the film as a whole, obviously, but the DP is in charge of the images."

"Getting the ones the director wants?"

Eric gave a small smile. "Getting the ones he needs. Sometimes those are the same. Sometimes they aren't."

Kellen's face was showing genuine interest, but Eric didn't want to step any deeper into this conversation. He said, "You know, I'd actually like to get a few shots in here," basically just to buy some silence.

"You got plenty to work with," Kellen said. "Check out the fireplace."

Eric turned to look at the fireplace near the bar. It, like the hotel, was both beautiful and massive. The facade was built out of river stones, with a mural painted across their surfaces. The mural depicted swirling blue waters and lush green fields, a small image of the hotel set back and to the left, behind a buckeye tree. In the upper-right corner, perched above the tumbling water, was Sprudel—the West Baden companion to French Lick's Pluto;

god of the underworld. He looked more like a gnome than a devil, but it was enough to remind Eric of the black train, and that sent a dark flourish through him. He *had* seen the train. No doubt about it. So what the hell did that mean? Was he losing his damn mind?

"Was a time they burned fourteen-foot logs in there," Kellen said. "Imagine that, right? Like cutting telephone poles in half and tossing them into the fireplace. You ought to get a shot of it."

Eric nodded, got the camera out but didn't put it on the tripod, just stood and held it up to his shoulder, turned and focused on the mural and watched the Sprudel figure fill the lens.

There was a piano not far from the bar, a full-size grand, and a man in a tuxedo was playing it. Eric swiveled to catch a shot of it, and the piano player saw him, looked back at the camera and winked. For some reason that made Eric turn away immediately, lower the camera and click it off and put it back in the bag. When he straightened from the bag he was dizzy, and squares of light floated in front of his eyes when he faced the rows of bottles behind the bar.

"Did that quick," Kellen said.

"Light's wrong," Eric muttered, reaching for his drink. He took a long swallow and blinked a few times, waiting for steadiness to return. It didn't.

The size of the rotunda was getting to him now, giving him a strange sense of vertigo even though he was standing at the bottom of it, feet firm on the floor. The place was just too damn open and too damn big. He and Kellen were standing at the short length of bar that extended into the atrium, but opposite them the bar was enclosed, secluded in a small room with wood paneling and dim lights. He suddenly wanted to get in there. Into the tighter space, into the dark.

But Kellen Cage was still talking, going on about the Waddy Hotel and a Negro League baseball team called the Plutos, so Eric put one hand on the bar and one foot on the brass rail to steady himself, had another long pull of the Grey Goose. Let the guy talk, don't freak out. There was no problem here. Everything was fine.

His mouth was dry despite the drink, and Kellen Cage's voice seemed to be coming from far away, with a trace of an echo to it. The lights in the atrium were growing brighter, slowly but obviously, as if someone had a hand on a dimmer switch and was rotating it gently, turning up the wattage. The headache was back, a faint throb down at the base of his skull, and that too-large buffet dinner was shifting in his stomach.

He put both hands on the bar, leaning onto the cold granite top, and was about to interrupt Kellen Cage to say he needed to step outside and get some air, when a new sound replaced that strange, echoing conversation around him. Music, a clear melody, pure and beautiful. Strings. A cello in the background, maybe, but at the forefront was a violin, a violin played as sweetly as anything Eric had ever heard. It was a soothing sound, a caress, and he felt the trapped air leave his lungs and the headache fade and his stomach settle. The cello hit on a low, long note and then the violin came back in over the top, soaring now, exuberant, and Eric was in awe of the beauty of it, turned to look for the source. It had to be live; he'd been around a lot of recording equipment and was certain they had yet to invent something that could capture sound this well.

The atrium was empty except for a few people in chairs, no band in sight, nothing but the piano player. He turned to look at him again then as the violin music dipped away, the song sad and sweet again. The piano player had his head bowed, and his hands were flying along, their motions completely out of sync with the strings. But the violin piece was coming from the piano. There wasn't any doubt about it. The thing was no more than thirty feet away and Eric, blessed with good ears and better vision, knew without question that the violin music was coming from beneath the lid of that grand piano.

"You dig the music, huh?" Kellen Cage said.

Eric was still staring, waiting for something that showed him he was wrong but finding nothing—the piano, somehow, was playing a strings melody. The most beautiful strings melody he'd ever heard. But the hands didn't match. The hands were not playing this song.

"What's this song?" he said. His voice was a rasp.

"Huh?" Cage said, leaning closer, smelling of cologne.

"What's the name of this song?"

Kellen Cage pulled his head back and gave Eric a curious smile. "You kidding me? It's the thing from *Casablanca,* man. Everybody knows this one. 'As Time Goes By.'"

That wasn't the song Eric was hearing, but he could tell that Kellen was right from the way the piano player's hands moved, locked in that gentle, familiar rhythm.

"I mean the violin thing," Eric said.

"Violin?" Kellen said, and then the piano player's tuxedo was gone and in its place he wore a rumpled suit and a bowler hat, and if Kellen said anything else, Eric did not hear it. He was staring at the piano player, whose face was hidden by the angle and by the bowler hat. Just over his shoulder, standing not five feet away, was a tall, thin boy with a violin at his shoulder, his eyes squeezed tightly shut. He wore ill-fitting clothes, his bony forearms protruding from the shirtsleeves and several inches of socks exposed. His blond hair had not been cut in many weeks. There was an open violin case at his feet with scattered bills and coins tossed inside.

For a moment they just played on in that soft duet, the boy

always with eyes shut, and then the man at the piano looked up. He lifted his head and looked Eric full in the face and smiled wide, and when he did, the beautiful, haunting strings melody shattered once again into a violent, urgent sawing, the notes frenzied and terrifying.

Eric opened his hand and the glass fell from it and hit the edge of the bar before dropping to the tile floor and breaking, sending splinters of glass sliding in all directions. The moment the glass broke, the music vanished. Cut off in midnote, like somebody had jerked out a stereo power cord. With it went the boy with the violin and the man in the bowler hat, replaced by the first piano player, who frowned but didn't stop playing, bowed his head again, and now Eric could hear the song — "You must remember this, a kiss is just a kiss..."

"As Time Goes By." Made famous by *Casablanca*. Kellen was right, everybody knew this one.

"Uh-oh, going to need a mop if you want to finish that drink," the bartender said, smiling, jocular. Eric felt Kellen's hand on his arm, the grip strong.

"You okay? Eric? You all right?"

He was now. On one level, at least. On another...

"You mind if we go somewhere else?" Eric said. "There's gotta be someplace to get a drink that isn't in this hotel."

Kellen Cage was watching him with raised eyebrows, but he gave a slow nod and set his drink down and released Eric's arm.

"Sure, man. There's places."

He felt better as soon as they were outside. It was still warm, had to be close to eighty, but some of the humidity had left with the sun, and the air outside the hotel was fresh and fragrant, pushed by a mild breeze.

"You didn't look so good back there," Kellen said as they went around the building and up toward the parking lot.

"Got a little dizzy," Eric said.

"What were you talking about with the violins, though?"

"Just confused."

Logical thing to do was shake Kellen's hand, tell him it had been good talking, and then go up to the room and get some sleep. Something seemed to be tugging him elsewhere, though. He wanted to be away from the hotel.

"Head up to the casino?" Kellen asked as they approached the parking lot.

Eric shook his head. "No, I'd rather find someplace"—*without so many lights*—"quieter. Smaller."

Kellen pursed his lips, thinking. "Be honest with you, there aren't many places around here. There's a little bar up the road that's decent, though. Called Rooster's. Went in there a couple times for lunch. Friendly woman behind the bar, if nothing else."

"That'll do."

Kellen lifted his hand and punched a button on his key chain and the lights of a car in front of them flicked on. A black Porsche Cayenne that looked brand-new.

"They must pay students better than they did when I was in school," Eric said.

"Nah, I bought this with my side venture. Sling a little bit of that crack."

"I'm sure you do."

Kellen smiled. "One of these days I'm going to get a white guy to believe that."

"Matter of time," Eric agreed, walking around to the passenger side, opening the door, and sliding into the leather seat. "It is a damn nice car, though."

"My brother gave it to me," Kellen said. "Twenty-fifth birthday present."

Eric raised his eyebrows. "That's one hell of a present. What's he do?"

"I'll show you in a while," Kellen said, and he didn't elaborate as he started the engine and drove them away from the hotel. Eric didn't question him. On another night, the remark might have caught his curiosity more. Tonight, all he wanted to do was press his head back against the seat, shut his eyes, and believe that when he opened them again, the only things he'd see would be of this world.

IO

JOSIAH BRADFORD WOULDN'T HAVE minded just sitting on the porch with his feet up and having a few beers in privacy that night, waiting on the heat to settle and letting a day's work ease out of his muscles. Danny Hastings had a wild hair in him, though, way Danny tended to on Fridays, and so Josiah found himself away from the porch and at the casino instead.

Danny was maybe the dumbest son of a bitch had ever learned to walk upright, but he still had more brains than money. Despite that, he found his way down to that casino about weekly. He was the sort of dumb that thought he was one pull of the slot lever away from rich, one righteous shuffle and deal away from flying first class to France.

Pathetic shit, if you asked Josiah.

Could've stayed home, of course, but once Danny called, Josiah relented pretty easy. That had nothing to do with Danny or the casino and more to do with the fact that Josiah's mood was darker than normal after working in that blistering sun and dodging Amos and watching the weekend crowd arrive at the hotel. A distraction seemed like a good choice. Josiah knew his own moods pretty well by now, saw 'em coming like storm clouds, and tried to get out of their way when he could. There'd be times, though, when he'd see them on the horizon and just not give a shit, let them come on and wash over him. And on those occasions, heaven help you if you got in his way.

He was inclined, as he often was, for a good screw. That was fortuitous, because the women did more drinking on a week-end night, a circumstance in his favor. He and Danny got to the casino around eight, and Josiah downed a few bourbons and watched Danny gamble away the forty bucks he had in cash — money that was supposed to get him through till next Thursday's paycheck — then go to the ATM and take out a fifty-dollar cash advance on the last credit card any bank would ever be fool enough to give him. Josiah left the blackjack table then, ordered another drink, and shot the shit with a few old boys he knew who were hanging around the bar waiting for Danny to get cleaned out one more time.

It was carrying on toward ten when he walked by the black-jack tables on his way to take a piss and saw Danny haggling with the dealer, two dollars in chips left in front of him. Couldn't do nothing but shake your head at that. Stupid bastard.

Josiah took a leak and came out and stared around the room, feeling the weight of his anger again, anger driven even deeper because he hadn't found a woman. Oh, there were some tens around, no mistake about that, but they were all hanging off some-body else's arm already, rich bitches come down for the weekend with their boyfriends. Wouldn't look at Josiah but would look through him, same as the hotel guests always did. There were people — Danny Hastings, for one — who were comfortable with that sort of thing, slipped into their anonymous little life like it was skin that fit them. Didn't fit Josiah, though. He wasn't the sort who could tolerate being an unknown. That was what he realized as he studied some of the men in the casino, men who controlled whatever crowd of assholes they'd arrived with. He didn't want their damn money or their slut wives or their ass-kissing buddies. What he wanted — deserved — was the role. People took notice of these pricks and treated Josiah like he was furniture.

Hell with it. He'd have one more drink and call it a night.

He was halfway back to the bar when he heard someone scream, a wild impression of a rebel yell that came out more like a little girl's sound, or maybe a pig's squeal, something that made the hair rise up along his arms and neck, not because it frightened him but because he knew the source — it was Danny.

Danny had won.

There were wild bells and chimes going off somewhere back among the slot machines, and Josiah fell in grudging step with a handful of other onlookers and walked toward the sound.

"*Josiah!* Josiah, where you at? You got to see this!"

Danny shouting for him even though Josiah was just five steps away now.

"*Josiah!*"

"Shut up, I'm right here." He shouldered up beside Danny to look at the display. Dollar slot machine, thing still buzzing and clattering, designed to draw a crowd of fools who'd want to rush off and shove their own cash into one of these glittering garbage disposals. It took him a second to find the figure — $2,500.

"You see that, Josiah? Twenty-five *hunnert!*" Danny gave another one of those damn squeals and slapped Josiah on the back. It took all Josiah had not to knock his ass to the ground.

"I put in a dollar, was all. One dollar, you believe that? Had myself some luck on over at the blackjack table, was starting to feel it 'cept for the last hand."

Except for the last hand. Brilliant. How many broke sons of bitches had said that?

"So I'd lost my money but I knew I had the luck going, right? Didn't have nothing but two dollars left, and I only played one of them here. Took a pull and won, took another and won, and then this one, this one was just the *third pull*."

Some stupid blond chick was clapping for him now, trying to get others involved, and Danny turned and grinned at them and held his hands up over his head, clasped them together like a boxing champ. Shit, but he was ugly. Josiah didn't know that he'd ever yet seen anyone uglier. Ugly breed, of course, red-headed men. Women could pull red hair off, but men? Damned disgusting.

Danny was heavy with beer weight, too, and freckled and sweaty. Looking at him now was almost too much to bear. Dancing around with his hands over his head like that, all over twenty-five hundred bucks. He'd give every cent back to the casino by next weekend, still be telling this story like it was some sort of accomplishment.

"I'll tell you one thing, hoss," Danny said, hitting the print button and watching his ticket come out, the blond girl still whistling and clapping. "Drinks is on me for the rest of the night."

"Better believe it," Josiah said, reaching out and — this took great effort — punching Danny in the shoulder, light, friendly. "Go on and cash that out, then come on back to the bar and spend it."

"I always said it, I *always* said it," Danny crowed, his voice thick with booze and excitement, "one day, the name Danny Hastings will be anonymous with success!"

Anonymous with success. Holy shit, he'd actually said that, and not on purpose.

"It already is," Josiah said, and Danny just grinned and slapped him on the shoulder again, still not getting it, as the rest of the onlookers snorted with laughter.

"Like I said, go on and cash that out. I'll be at the bar," Josiah said.

Danny was gibbering on enthusiastically as he went. Josiah let him get all the way up to the cashier before he circled around the slot machines and left the casino.

He found his Ford Ranger in the parking lot and fired it up, drove away from the casino, and then hesitated on 56, unsure of which way to turn. He sure as shit wasn't going to be able to sit in there and watch Danny carry on all night, not in this mood. Maybe if he'd been a little drunker. But he was still sober, and still angry. Could go home, but home was out in the hills between Orangeville and Orleans, and driving away from town now felt like cowardice, running off to sulk. No, go on to another bar.

By Monday — hell, maybe by Sunday — he'd feel some sense of regret for leaving like this. Mostly because Danny was going to be dumb enough to buy drinks all night; partially because the idiot had actually wanted Josiah around to share his windfall. Right now, though, there wasn't any way he could take it. It was only twenty-five hundred dollars, but it had fallen into Danny's fat, sweaty palm, not Josiah's.

He was at the parking lot exit, foot on the brake, waiting for a chance to pull out, not paying any of the passing cars a bit of attention except to look for a gap, until he saw a black Porsche Cayenne fly by.

That son-of-a-bitch student, still in town. The car incensed him, made him want to stamp on the Ranger's accelerator and ram right into the back of it, watch those taillights bust. He pulled out behind it and did hit the gas a touch, as much of a burnout as his worn tires would allow, then felt stupid for it. Peeling out in front of the casino on a Friday night was almost like yelling for the police on a bullhorn, asking to be arrested.

He drove more slowly but stayed behind the Porsche, followed it up the hill and out of town and then thought, *Oh, man, it's going to be hard to pass this one up,* when he saw its turn signal come on just in front of Rooster's, then watched it slow and pull into the bar's gravel parking lot. Just what he needed to tempt him tonight — some rich kid going into a local bar like it was a damn tourist attraction. Stare at the country folk, maybe take some pictures. Ask more questions about Josiah's own flesh and blood.

He pulled into the parking lot and watched the driver's door of the Porsche open and the kid step out, big as a damn barn. Josiah had him in the headlights, could see the muscled-up shoulders and chest. There was someone with him this time. The second guy was white, with short hair and one of those three-day beards that was supposed to make him look casual, indifferent. Older than the black kid, but not so old you'd have to feel bad about beating the shit out of him.

They disappeared inside and Josiah cut his ignition and shut off the lights. He'd been spoiling for a fight all day, and now he was going to get it. Size of that black kid, it was clear this one would be a sight. Wasn't nobody going to be talking about Danny Hastings and his twenty-five hundred bucks once Josiah finished this.

11

THE RAMSHACKLE JOINT Kellen drove them to had a neon rooster on its sign, but no name. Maybe the bar wasn't even called Rooster's. Could be they'd just taken a shine to that sign. Inside, it was a warm-looking place, old but clean. A handful of people were sitting in the booths that lined one wall, maybe six more scattered around the bar. Two guys tossing darts in a corner.

"You again!" the blond woman behind the bar said, squinting at Kellen. "Give me a minute, I'll remember it. Hmm...got a *K* in it. Kelvin?"

"Kellen."

"Darn! Should've had it. But you haven't been down here in a long time either, so it's really your fault."

"Can't argue with that," he said, and ordered a beer, asking for whatever was light and on draft. Eric held up two fingers, figuring it would be a good idea to shade on the light side for the rest of the evening anyhow, the way his mind was playing tricks.

"You need anything else, yell for Becky," the woman said, sliding the beers over.

Kellen nodded. "I'll remember it. Now, think you could find TNT on that TV?"

Becky tried the remote and didn't have any luck getting a response, tossed it down and stretched up on her toes to reach the TV. Good long legs, nice tan. Maybe forty-five. Older than Claire by a decade. Claire had great legs...

"Here we go," Kellen said. "Thank you."

He'd requested a basketball game, Timberwolves playing the Lakers. Eric despised the Lakers. He used to get dragged down to the games now and then by a producer friend who always considered it a business venture and spent the game with his back to the court, peering around the stands in search of A-listers. Eric, who'd been a pretty big basketball fan at one time, particularly of college ball, had hated the Hollywood aspect of the Lakers games, Jack Nicholson down there courtside in his damn sunglasses barking at the refs, other stars miraculously finding their way to the games only when they were on national TV.

"You wanted to know what my brother did," Kellen said, and nodded at the TV. "Number forty for Minnesota."

"No shit?" Eric said.

"None. I was recording this, hate to miss any, but what the hell."

Eric found number forty and saw the resemblance immediately. A few inches taller than Kellen and lankier, without the bulked-up muscle, but the head shape and the facial features were clear matches.

"What's his name?" Eric said.

"Darnell."

79

"Younger or older?"

Kellen hesitated for just a beat, and his eyes flicked sideways before he said, "Younger. Three years younger," in a voice that was softer than it had been.

They watched as the ball found its way to Darnell Cage. He took a kick-out behind the three-point line on a fast break, shot-faked and then drove to the foul line and put up a floater that caught the back of the rim and bounced long.

"Come on, D, come on," Kellen said. "Give that ball up. Had the cutter."

The teams went back and forth without Cage touching the ball. Then the Lakers scored and Minnesota ran a post set that didn't generate anything, threw it back out, and worked it around the perimeter. There were eight seconds left on the shot clock when the ball came to Darnell Cage on the left baseline, and Kellen laughed. It was a low, almost devious sound.

"Oh, they in trouble now," he said.

Darnell Cage faced up to his defender, ball held back on his hip, leaning forward.

"Crossover coming," Kellen said.

Darnell Cage gave a slight shoulder fake, then put the ball on the floor, moving left before shifting to the right, the defender sliding with him, not fooled by the fake. Then came the cross-over, a wickedly fast between-the-legs dribble back to his left hand, and Darnell Cage blew down the rest of the baseline in about two strides before going into the air and finishing with a tremendous one-handed dunk that brought the home crowd to its feet.

"Wow," Eric said.

Kellen was grinning. "He owns that left baseline, man. Owns it. He's a lefty, and you can give him some trouble if you force him to the right, but if he gets you off balance on that left baseline, you're done. Just too damn fast. He gets you rocked at all, then there's nothing to do but watch."

Kellen had turned to look at Eric but now his eyes drifted higher and his brow furrowed and he said, "You got to be kidding me."

"What?"

"You want to meet a relative of Campbell Bradford? *My* Campbell? He's standing back there by the pool table. This is the cat who threw the bottle at me. Josiah."

Eric turned and found himself staring into the dark eyes of a guy with shaggy brown hair and a black polo shirt who was standing beside the pool table, watching them.

"Appears he remembers you as well," Eric said.

"Uh-huh. I don't think I'll ask him any more questions about the family tree."

"I can't believe he's here."

"Small town," Kellen said. "Not many bars."

But he didn't seem confident about it.

"Well, there you go," Kellen said, turning back to the TV. "There's my brother, the family talent."

"You got one in the NBA and another getting a doctorate?" Eric said. "What are the rest of your siblings, astronauts?"

Kellen laughed. "Just the two of us."

There was someone beside them at the bar now, standing close and staring at Kellen. Josiah Bradford. He didn't so much as glance at Eric, and Kellen seemed well aware of his presence but did not turn to face him, choosing instead to continue to watch the game. After a while, Josiah Bradford reached across the bar and grabbed the remote and hit a button. It exasperated him when nothing happened.

"Becky, I want this channel changed," he hollered. "And bring me a Budweiser."

"Those guys are watching the game," she responded without looking back. "Come down here, change this one."

The man dropped his eyes to Kellen. "You don't mind, do you?"

"How you doing, Josiah?" Kellen said, finally looking at him. "Been a while."

The guy didn't respond, just stood there staring into Kellen's eyes. Becky seemed to sense the building tension when she set his Budweiser down and came over to talk to Kellen and Eric as if to diffuse it.

"You hear about the old guy whose wife makes him stop drinking, won't let him go up to his favorite neighborhood pub anymore?" she said.

"Can I get that channel changed?" Josiah said. "These boys don't mind at all."

"In a minute, maybe," Becky said, not even glancing at him as she continued with her joke. "Well, the wife keeps him from drinking, but she has to go out of town for a few days, visit her sister. Leaves him with clear instructions — you don't even *think* about going to the pub, buddy."

"I wouldn't last long with a woman like that," Josiah said, and then he turned away from the bar. When he did it, his shoulder collided with Kellen's. Hard. Too hard for accidental contact.

"Watch it, Josiah," Becky snapped, and Kellen just looked up at him and didn't say a word, didn't change his expression.

"Oh, he's big enough it didn't hurt him," Josiah said. "Ain't you big enough?"

Kellen held his eyes for a moment, then said, "Sure," and turned back to Becky. "Let's hear the rest of that joke."

Josiah seemed disappointed.

"Okay," Becky said. "So the old guy, he figures, how's she gonna know, right? First night she's gone, he heads up the street.

Place is only a block away. Goes in and has a few, then a few more, and a few more after that. By the end of the night it's catching up with him and the room's starting to spin. Decides he better head on home. So he stands up to pay the bill and almost falls on his face, has to hold on to the bar to keep himself up. Puts his money down, takes a few steps and, *whap,* he falls down, smack on the floor. Has a hard time getting up, and now he *knows* he's had too much. Good thing his wife won't know. So he crawls to the door, pulls himself up, and steps outside and falls over again."

Kellen was smiling, watching her, but Eric kept his eyes on Josiah. That shoulder move didn't promise good things.

"Old guy has to crawl on his belly whole way home," Becky was saying. "Drags his butt into bed. Next morning he's hardly awake when the phone rings. Wife calling. Starts yelling at him for going drinking and he says, 'How do you know?' And she tells him, 'Bartender called. Said you left your wheelchair down there again.'"

Kellen and Eric both gave it more of a laugh than it deserved and Josiah stood in silence. Waited until they'd stopped laughing before he said, "I got a joke."

Nobody reacted. Not even Becky. Eric didn't like the guy's tone at all, and he twisted his bar stool just a touch so he was facing him, then cleared his feet from the rail.

"Bunch of good ol' boys are down at their bar, gettin' lit up," Josiah said. "Big-ass bear comes into the parking lot, looking for food. Knocks the door open, goes inside. Shit's in the fan then, old boys running around, bear growling and knocking tables and chairs and shit over. Bear wrecks the place, then breaks the door down and goes away."

He paused for a long, dramatic drink of his beer.

"The drunk boys stand up, dust themselves off, and one says

to his buddy, 'Damn. Put a nigger in a fur coat and he acts like he owns the place.'"

Eric got to his feet and Becky said, "Shut your fool mouth, Josiah," as Josiah smiled, looking at Kellen.

"Get the hell out of here," Becky said. *"Now."*

Josiah flicked his dark eyes up to Eric, just a cursory glance, and then back down at Kellen.

"What? Don't like my joke?"

Eric moved another step away from his stool, sure now that a fight was coming. Kellen reached out, though, put up a warning hand.

"It's fine," he said. "We're all telling jokes, right? Just having some fun."

The look that crossed Josiah's face was disgusted and disappointed. He snorted.

"Oh, you like that joke? Well, I got a few more like it. Might enjoy them, too."

"Let me tell one first," Kellen said.

Josiah waited, feet spread, hands at belt level.

"You hear the one about the redneck with a hard-on who ran into a wall?" Kellen said. Paused one beat, then finished: "He broke his nose."

Josiah threw the first punch, but Eric was already coming at him, knocked him off balance so that the blow missed Kellen's head. Eric slammed him into the bar and then leaned back just enough to throw the uppercut he wanted to put into the son of a bitch's jaw. He didn't get it there, though. Caught a knee directly in his groin first and then his lungs turned to vacuums as bright, shining agony radiated through his abdomen and filled his chest. He took a stumbling step back and managed to get his head down to avoid Josiah's fist and catch the bottom of his forearm instead.

The blow landed flush on his nose, which promptly opened up and leaked blood over his lips and onto his chin as Josiah just missed with another punch, his fist sliding across Eric's face, a streak of his blood showing bright on Josiah's hand now. All this happening as Becky shouted at them from behind the bar and Kellen Cage slipped off his stool without a word.

Josiah seemed to have lost interest in Eric, turned from him back to Kellen with a wide grin on his face and said, "Come on, boy."

Kellen hit him. A flicking left that looked more like a snake-bite than a punch, and Josiah's head snapped back as Kellen easily deflected the return punch and then hit him again, this time in the stomach.

Josiah's knees sagged as he stumbled backward, but he took it better than most could have and was coming back for more as Kellen waited on him quietly and Eric straightened with an effort and Becky chambered a round into a shotgun with a ratcheting sound as loud as a bell choir.

Everybody stopped. For the first time Eric was aware that two men had risen from a booth and were advancing—toward Josiah. Now they stopped short, too.

"You want to wait on the police," Becky said, her voice soft and steady as she braced the Remington twelve-gauge on the bar, "that's fine by me. Otherwise, you better get the hell out of here, Josiah."

He gave her a sneer and then turned to the rest of the room, saw no support there. Looked back at Kellen and said, "We'll finish this'n later."

"If you do," said one of the men from the booth, "he'll have you swallowing your teeth, Josiah. Now listen to the lady and get your sorry ass out the door."

Josiah shoved past Eric, holding the stare with Kellen for a moment before turning to the door. He kicked it open with the heel of his boot and then stepped outside as the door banged off the wall and shuddered slowly back and Eric's blood dripped onto the floor.

12

Back in the Porsche, after getting Eric's nose to stop bleeding and then drinking one more beer to assure Becky that they were at peace with the bar, Kellen turned to him.

"Well, I'm sorry that happened, because that idiot is in no way representative of my experience in this town."

"Shouldn't have dragged you out to a place like that."

"No, man, that's what I'm saying — it wasn't the *place*. I've been in there before. In fact, I've been in this town a lot, and that's the first time I've ever had anything like that pulled. Which was, to be honest, against my expectation."

"Yeah?"

Kellen nodded as he started the engine. "Some racist history to this state, really. First hotel down here was built by a guy named William Bowles, who was tried for treason because he was involved with something called the Knights of the Golden Circle, which was pro-Confederacy and a forerunner to the

KKK. He was a real good guy — indicted for grave robbery, of all things. Wasn't all him, though. Back when the area was really booming, blacks weren't allowed to stay in these hotels. Joe Louis wasn't allowed to stay in these hotels. All the local tourism stuff uses his name today, brags on him being a frequent visitor, but the reality is, he always stayed at the Waddy."

They pulled out of the parking lot, Kellen driving with one wrist hooked over the wheel.

"So when I came down here, wanting to write the black history of the area, I maybe had a sour taste in my mouth from what I knew of the past. As long as I've been down here, though, people have been nothing but friendly — with the one exception being our buddy back there, Mr. Bradford. He would be the last of *my* Campbell's line. I hope you're right and you're looking for a different guy. Because Josiah isn't going to be a help to you."

"I'd say not," Eric agreed. "But you've got to figure my guy is related to him."

"I know it. And that's why I'll be interested to see what Edgar Hastings has to say. He's the only person I've found in town who has any clear memories of Campbell. But he's also something of a foster father to Josiah, so best not to mention what happened tonight, I guess. You free tomorrow if I get something set up with him?"

"Sure." Eric was touching his face with his fingertips, assessing damage. His lip would be a little swollen in the morning, but he'd kept a cool beer to it, so he wouldn't look too much the worse for wear.

"I've never heard of another Campbell Bradford," Kellen said. "It's strange."

"We'll figure it out," Eric said, thinking that the *least* strange thing in his day was confusion over the man's identity. That didn't come close to the black train or the leaves or that man in the bowler hat, no.

Kellen dropped him off with a handshake and a promise that he'd call Edgar Hastings the next day. Eric was almost nervous going back into the hotel alone and felt a childish desire to run back into the parking lot and flag Kellen down, ask him to have one more drink. *Just stay with me for twenty minutes, buddy, enough so I can look around and make sure the place is an ordinary hotel again and not the friggin' Overlook.*

For some reason, thinking of Stephen King's hotel horror story made him smile as he walked back into the atrium and looked around. Yeah, Kubrick would've salivated over shooting in this location. It had everything a filmmaker desired — beauty, grandeur, size, history, and, at least for Eric tonight, a King-size dose of creepy.

"Couldn't ask for anything more," he said under his breath. The hotel had quieted a bit, with just a handful of people left at the bar, the piano player gone, and the piano itself covered up. He didn't see anything out of place, didn't hear anything out of place. The hotel seemed sane again.

He headed upstairs to his room, where he put on every light and then immediately went around turning them back off when the brightness made his headache flare. It was past eleven now. The strangest day of his life was almost done. He felt a powerful need to call Claire, tell her every weird and frightening detail and hear her responses. No, the hell with calling Claire, he wanted to talk to her face-to-face, to see her in this bedroom. And the hell with *talking* to Claire, he wanted to take her right here on this large, luxurious bed. Wanted to be tugging her jeans off those long legs, wanted to feel them catch on the rise of her ass the way they always did.

Damn, but he missed her. Felt it the way old people feel arthritis in their bones, an unrelenting agony carried every day, every hour, every minute.

He'd met her at a deli in Evanston, where she was in her first year of law school at Northwestern and he was merely passing through after visiting a friend, this the summer before he'd moved to L.A. He had finished a sandwich and was sitting at the table with a newspaper, almost ready to go on his way, when she'd walked in with a friend and sat down across the room. He'd watched her cross the room — something about the way the girl moved that loosened his jaw, left him staring with his mouth half open — and she looked over and gave him the smallest of smiles, an awkward gesture more than anything, forced politeness in response to the unanticipated eye contact.

What he'd read in the newspaper over the next twenty minutes, he couldn't say. He kept his eyes on it only to avoid staring, and he sneaked looks as often as he dared, watching her talk and laugh and eat a Caesar salad, gesturing with her fork every now and then, waving bits of lettuce around in the air. She was facing him, caught his eye a few more times, gave him another cursory smile. She was eating too quickly, though, and so was her friend, and both were nearly finished with their food and ready to move on into the day before he ever said a word to her. He wanted so badly to say a word to her. He was not insecure with women, had no trouble asking for dates, but approaching a strange woman at a deli at noon on Tuesday was a hell of a lot different than approaching one in a bar at midnight on Friday. And with her friend there, there was that extra barrier of potential eye rolls and laughter.

Then the friend stood up and left the table, walking to the bathroom. Fate, Eric decided, it had to be fate, because the friend was the last excuse he was giving himself, and now she'd just checked out. He set the paper down and walked over to this dark-haired girl with the wry smile and the amused eyes and said, "My name is Eric, and I would love to buy you a drink."

What a breathtakingly original pickup line. She regarded him for a few seconds without speaking, then said, "It's a deli. They don't serve alcohol here."

To which Eric had responded, "Well, then, how do you feel about lemonade?"

They'd had the lemonade, and later that night the real drink, and a day later the first kiss and fifteen months after that the wedding vows and the honeymoon.

"Shit," he said now, lying on his back in a hotel room in Indiana, Claire a couple hundred miles away. He sat up and reached for the remote, seeking distraction. *Don't let this start. Don't let these thoughts be the cap to the kind of day you already had.*

He found the remote, then leaned back in bed again and kicked his shoes off and turned to look at TV. When he did, his eyes caught the bottle of Pluto Water on the desk. He frowned, stood up, and walked over to it. The damn thing was sweating. Covered in beads of moisture, a wet ring beneath it.

When he reached out and touched the bottle, he found it even colder than before. How was that possible? And while on that topic, how was it possible for the thing to be so wet, like a frosted mug of beer sitting in the sun? Could it be leaking? He ran his finger up the outside, collecting the moisture, then lifted his finger first to his nose and then to his lips and dabbed it against them. There was the same faint sweetness, almost like honey. Nothing close to the terrible foulness that had put him on his knees a few days earlier.

That had been the booze, though. Right? Wasn't that what he'd told himself? He loosened the old cap again, took a sniff and, yes, there was a touch of honey. It didn't smell anything like what he'd remembered.

"Don't even think about it," he said aloud, looking at the liquid inside. He'd read enough about the mineral water to understand that it was potent stuff, but nothing he'd read explained its behavior, particularly how it managed to stay so cold, let alone its shifting smells and flavors.

There was still a Pluto Water plant in town, directly across from the French Lick Springs Resort. Tomorrow he'd have to drop in and ask them for some details. That would be the second order of business if the visions kept up, though. If they did, a call to the doctor would come first.

The black kid had given Josiah something to remember him by, a left eye that was already going purple by the time he got home and studied himself in the mirror, holding a cold can of Keystone to his eye socket and burning with anger and shame.

He'd taken the only visible damage from the encounter, and that was as bullshit as bullshit got. He was supposed to put that guy on his big black ass. Instead, he hadn't even landed a real punch. Josiah had lost a fight or two along the way, but he'd never failed to do some damage.

Shit, he hadn't even gotten in the better insult. The black kid's line about Josiah's pecker was better than that dumb nigger joke. Funny thing was, Josiah wasn't even racist. Oh, he supposed he could be considered so, but he could be considered anything that was accompanied by a bad attitude and a chip on the shoulder. Didn't matter if you were white or black or Mexican or whatever. It was a disrespectful world, he'd seen that clear enough since he was a kid, and wasn't nobody disrespected the world better than Josiah Bradford.

He used to have some patience. He'd done a good job of waiting, went through each day knowing he'd leave his mark and trying to wait on the right opportunity. Today, though, the patience had slipped away, pulled from his soul by some unseen force the way the moon ebbed the tides back from the beach. It had started with the heat and been furthered by Amos before draining away altogether when Danny Dumb-shit Hastings hit a twenty-five-hundred-dollar jackpot and took to squealing and hollering and drawing a crowd of people who stared at his fat ass like he was somebody special.

No, Josiah Bradford didn't have any patience left. And something told him, something in the humid, black night, that it wasn't going to be coming back anytime soon either.

He still had the white guy's blood on his hand, he realized, as he went for another beer. A long streak of it, dried to a rust color. He went to the sink and ran warm water, scrubbed his hand with a bar of soap, and put it under the water to rinse it clean.

Strangest damn thing happened then — the water went cold. As the blood rinsed off his hand, the warm water went cold, then drove the blood down the drain in a pink-tinged swirl. Soon as the last trace of blood was gone, the water was warm again. It had been a quick thing, an instantaneous shift.

"Old pipes," Josiah muttered. Made sense that the plumbing, like everything else in this house, was turning to shit.

He went ahead and washed his hand a second time.

Anne McKinney woke just after two a.m., sat up in bed, and blinked against the darkness, short of breath, her chest tight. *Heart attack,* she thought. *Eighty-six years of good health and now death is going to steal in like the proverbial thief in the night, take me in my bed.*

But her breath came back then, and when she laid her palm beneath her left breast she felt her heart thumping along slow and steady. She pushed up on the pillows, wincing as her back howled in pain, and then swung her feet down to the cool floorboards, keeping both hands on the bed as she stood up. Out in public, Anne walked with her hands free as much as possible, but here at home it was different. Here she had to use a higher level of caution, because she'd lived alone since the heart attack that took Harold back in March of 'ninety-two, middle of that Duke ballgame with the Hoosiers, the refs making one more terrible call than Harold's poor sweet heart could take. That was almost twenty years past, and nobody but Anne had spent a night in the house since. She knew it would be a long time before anybody found her if she took a fall in here.

Originally her bedroom had been a library of sorts, or at least that had been the idea. Mostly, it had been used by the children for games and by Harold for storing odds and ends that Anne wouldn't tolerate in the living room. She'd stayed in their old bedroom until she was eighty-one, but then the daily back-and-forth on the stairs began to wear on her. She hadn't admitted it at the time — stubbornness was her most deeply ingrained trait — choosing instead to tell herself that it was simply time for a redecorating and, what the heck, might as well move downstairs for a change of scenery. Now she hadn't been upstairs in more than a month.

She stood with her hand resting on the desk beside the bed, giving her legs a few seconds to warm up. Just like a car in cold weather, that's how you had to look at it. Wasn't that the car was *done* if it did a bit of grumbling on a winter morning, it just needed some time. Once you gave it that, it would run as good as ever. Or close to it, at least. Well, it would run. That was the point. It would still run.

The surface of the little desk was empty except for the things she needed most: her pills, divided into one of those seven-day containers, a wicker basket for mail that was generally empty (nobody wrote Anne much these days), and one of her weather radios. This one wasn't but a scanner; the ham radio was down in the basement. There were times that she wished to have it upstairs, close at hand, but she wouldn't ever allow herself to seriously entertain such a notion. The shortwave needed to be in the most stormproof room of the house, and that was the basement. Concrete block walls and only two small windows up at the top of the western wall, right at ground level. When a big one blew in, the basement was the place to be, which meant that was where the radio needed to be.

Anne had been a weather spotter for decades now, and it was a job she took seriously. All the gauges in the world wouldn't mean a thing if you couldn't make contact, and in bad storms the phone lines went down. The radio in the cellar was nearly thirty years old, but it still worked just fine. It was an R. L. Drake TR-7, built by the first—and best—company that ever dealt with ham radio. Harold had bought it for her and set up a powerful antenna and showed her how to use it. He'd never been one who thought things like machinery and electronics were beyond the grasp of women, a trait that made him rare for a man of his time. It hadn't been long until she understood the Drake better than he did.

Her legs felt steady beneath her now, tingling with circulating blood, and she took her hand from the desk and moved for the door. The moonlight left a white streak across the floorboards, almost like a path in the darkness, and she followed it out of the bedroom and into the living room, crossed that, and opened the front door and stepped out onto the porch, still wondering what in the world had her up and wandering. Then she heard the chimes jingling, louder and faster than they had that evening, and she knew what had stirred her from sleep—the wind.

It had risen while she slept, was still blowing out of the southwest but was firmer now, really pushing. Had itself some confidence again.

Shuffling out to the end of the porch and taking the rail in her hands, she breathed the air in and shivered a little in its grasp. There was a barometer on the porch — there was a barometer in every room of the house — and it told her the pressure was 30.16. A rise from this afternoon.

The shift didn't make sense. Or maybe it did. Yesterday the gauges told her it would be another hot, peaceful day with steady pressure. But what her mind told her, a mind seasoned by eighty-six years of study and experience, was that it had been *too* hot and still, and for too long.

So maybe this made plenty of sense. She just didn't know what was coming next. The wind had blown up unexpectedly, and that was fine, but what was chasing on its heels?

13

THE SUN CAME INTO his room early, and it came in hot. Eric woke squinting against it, feeling the warmth on his face, and almost before he was fully coherent he knew the headache was back.

Back like a bastard, too, a motorcycle gang passing through town and revving engines. He groaned and covered his eyes with the heels of his hands, pressed hard into his temples with his fingertips. This was as bad as any hangover headache he'd ever had, and it wasn't from a hangover.

When he was on his feet, he took three Excedrin with a glass of water, not feeling overly optimistic — the Excedrin hadn't been effective yesterday — and then showered in the dark. Light seemed to be a problem. When he was out of the bathroom, he kept the lights off and the curtains pulled, then put on a pair of jeans and a short-sleeved button-down made from some sort of khaki-style material. It was a good-luck shirt. He'd worn it one afternoon in Mexico, where they were shooting a Western that flopped at the box office despite a terrific script and strong cast, and he'd gotten some of his all-time favorite film that day. The director on that one had been an absolute joy, one of the guys who was more focused on supervising the whole production than on telling his cinematographer how to do his job. Those were the directors of Eric's dreams, guys who trusted you and let you shoot, and he'd found far too few of them in Hollywood. Particularly after he'd broken Davis Vassar's nose.

Vassar was the biggest name Eric had ever worked with — and a man who'd made certain that he was also the *last* big name that Eric ever worked with. They'd hit it off well enough at the start, the project something Eric truly liked, an on-the-road thriller involving a hitchhiker who witnessed the execution-style killing of a journalist. It was a great story, gripping as hell, and the day Eric was hired, he bought four bottles of champagne and drove with Claire up to a beautiful inn near Napa and they had sex five times in the first twelve hours. Wild, playful, laughing, gasping sex. Victory sex.

There'd never been anything quite like that for them again.

You had heavy-handed directors and then you had Davis Vassar, who evidently hired a cinematographer just so he had someone else to bark orders at. Talent meant almost nothing to him, professional judgments even less. Eric fought through a month of it before the first blowup, and two days after that, his fist was connecting with Vassar's face and a waitress was screaming and Eric Shaw's Hollywood career was ending.

Temper, temper, temper. You have to watch your temper.

The moment it had started to go south with them was crystallized in his memory. Eric had come to the production company office for a meeting with Vassar and two of the producers.

They'd been sitting in a room that looked out onto Wilshire, and Vassar made the three of them wait on him for twenty minutes. There was a glass-topped coffee table in the middle of the room, and when he finally swaggered in, he plunked himself down in one of the black leather chairs and put his feet up on the table. Banged the heels of his shoes down on the glass with an unnecessarily loud flourish. The message: I'm a Big Fucking Deal.

They'd talked for nearly an hour, and Eric still couldn't remember what had been said. He was an image guy, and that image — Vassar's shining black shoes on that glass tabletop — wouldn't leave his mind. He stared at those shoes and listened and watched the producers cowering and sniveling with Vassar and thought, *This is bullshit. They're listening to you because of your damn name, not talent. Because you caught some breaks and rode somebody else's phenomenal acting performance into an Oscar nomination. You don't even see this story; you don't have the first damn clue how it should be told. I do. I should be directing this, not you, but I don't have the name. And so I have to sit here and watch you put your shoes up on somebody else's table and mouth off while looking at your BlackBerry every two minutes to remind us all how important you are.*

He'd made it out of that meeting peacefully. He didn't make it out of the film the same way.

"And this," Eric said aloud, "is how you ended up in Indiana. Well done."

He could shake the memory off for the morning, but not the headache. Food might help, or some black coffee at least, so he left the room and walked down the steps and out into the atrium again. Made it only twenty paces across before the light shining in through the dome brought him to a halt, and he turned on his heel, gritting his teeth, and retreated to the darker corridor that circled the atrium. Found his way to one of the dining rooms, took a table, and ordered an omelet and coffee. Hurry on the coffee, please.

He drank two cups and felt no effect, picked at the omelet and got maybe three bites down before giving up, tossing cash on the table, and returning to his room. This was bad. Headaches like this one, so sudden, so blinding in their pain...they were harbingers. Eric knew enough to understand that, and the possibilities chilled him. Brain tumor, blood clot, cancer. Aneurisms and strokes and heart attacks.

Time to call Dr. Sharp in Chicago. That was all there was to it.

He called from his cell phone. Only when he reached the robotic-voiced menu did he remember that it was a Saturday, and therefore getting the good Dr. Sharp on the line was going to be impossible. His office was closed weekends, and the monotone message suggested Eric visit the emergency room if his condition was serious.

It felt awfully serious to him, but it was also only a headache. You didn't walk into an emergency room with one of those. And where was a hospital around here anyhow?

He wasn't sure if he looked at the Pluto Water because he thought of it, or if he thought of it because he looked at it. The chain of logic wasn't clear, but somehow he found himself staring at the bottle on the desk and thinking, *Why the hell not?* It was supposed to cure headaches, wasn't it? He was sure he'd seen that on the lists of ailments the mineral water boasted it could handle. Granted, damn near every other affliction of the early twentieth century had been on those lists, but the stuff couldn't have gotten its reputation by being a pure placebo. It had to help *some* problems.

He walked over to the desk and reached for the bottle but

stopped with his hand about six inches away, tilted his head, and stared at it. There was a glaze over the bottle now. It looked almost like...

Frost. Son of a bitch, it was frost. He wiped some of it off with his thumb, found it just like wiping clear a streak on the window on an early winter morning in Chicago.

"I've got to figure you out," he said.

He wasn't going to figure anything out if he had to hole up in this room, sitting on the floor and chewing Excedrin like they were Skittles. So why not give the water a try?

He unfastened the cap and took a small, hesitant swallow.

Not bad. If anything, the sulfuric taste was down and more of the sugary flavor was present in its stead. He took a full swallow, and the taste drove him on for another and then a third, the stuff going down like nectar now. It took a conscious effort to stop, and when he lowered the bottle he saw that more than half of the contents were gone—the same liquid that had made him gag back in Chicago at the smallest of tastes.

The flavor might have improved, but it had no effect. The headache pounded on, that motorcycle gang still circling through town, racing one another.

Okay, the Pluto Water wasn't going to do the job. Dumb idea, fine, but he was willing to try a dumb idea if it meant he could go about his day.

He went back to the bed and stretched out on his stomach, slid his face under the pillows and held them to his head. Maybe he *should* go to the hospital. Probably was crazy not to. If Claire were here, it wouldn't even be an issue; they'd be driving these rural highways right now, looking for the telltale blue-and-white sign. She was a worrier. Protective of him, too. Would defend him to the end.

Well, almost to the end. She'd stuck with him through it all in

California, but once they were back in Chicago, back around her family and their judgmental whispers, her resolve had wavered. The questions started then, asking him what came next, saying that it was fine if he needed out of the movie business but what business was he going to find for the future, what would he do? He'd needed time, that was all, and she didn't have enough of it for him, evidently. Didn't have enough...

His thoughts left Claire, and, very slowly, he removed the pillows and lifted his head. Cocked it to the side, as if he were listening for something in the distance.

"It's going away," he said.

The damned headache was fading. Still present, but the biker gang was driving away now, heading uphill on the roads that led out of town.

14

HE DIDN'T TRUST IT at first, maybe didn't want to trust it. He went onto the balcony and sat overlooking the atrium for fifteen minutes as the headache continued to fade and then was gone. *No,* he thought, *it can't really be gone. You've just adapted to the light.*

So he went outside and walked the grounds for half an hour in the stark sunlight, waiting for the pain to return. It did not. The Pluto Water had done the job, done it with astonishing speed and efficiency.

He had to find out what the hell was in that stuff. And, why, if it was so incredibly effective, had the product vanished over the years? Did you build up a tolerance, or did it have unwelcome side effects? There had to be some problem, because anything that could obliterate a migraine like that would've been raking in billions a year by now.

The Pluto Water research would be a priority for the day, he decided as he walked back into the hotel and up to his room, feeling wonderful now, fit and energetic. But before he got to that, he had to call Alyssa Bradford.

He called from the balcony, looking down on a group of high school students on a tour, a man with a country drawl filling them in on the history of the hotel. Eric could catch pieces of his talk — "*The first West Baden hotel was destroyed by fire, and Lee Sinclair was bound and determined to replace it with something incredible.... They built this place in under a year, and that was in an era without modern construction equipment.... If you laid the glass in that dome end-to-end you'd have a path sixteen inches wide and nearly three miles long*" — as he located Alyssa's number and dialed.

"Well, Eric, what do you think?" she said. "Pretty amazing, isn't it?"

"It absolutely is," he said, and right now, free of headaches and troubling tricks of the mind, he was able to say that and mean it again, to really feel happy to be here. "I'd seen pictures, but it still took my breath away. Because it just doesn't seem to fit."

"It doesn't! That place belongs in Austria, not Indiana. Have you had much luck finding out about my father-in-law?"

"Only that there's some dispute over his age," Eric said. "Any chance he's really one hundred and sixteen?"

"What?" she said and laughed. "No, I don't think there's any chance of that. How did you arrive at that question?"

He told her about his first day in town — at least the research end of it. No need to enlighten her about the vanishing train or the violins in his head. Professional reputation to uphold and all that. Hate to lose out on future wedding videos over rumors of insanity.

"Campbell Bradford isn't a common name," she said. "The other one has to be a relative."

"That's what I was thinking," Eric said, "but my contact here assures me that the Campbell he knew of ran out on his family in nineteen twenty-nine. He left a son named William behind, but William stayed in town, and died in town."

"I have no idea what to think of that," she said, "only it can't be my father-in-law. The age is too far off."

"Right. Your father-in-law could have been a son this guy had after he left, but—"

"My father-in-law grew up in the town."

"Yeah. As an aside, I might have found a cousin for you. But I don't think he's a guy you'll be inviting to any family reunions."

He told her about Josiah and the fight with Kellen Cage.

"I certainly hope he's *not* family," she said. "But if you find out he is some distant relative, let's go ahead and leave him off the film."

"Don't worry, I won't be asking him for any interviews."

"Have you spent any time with the bottle yet?" Alyssa asked.

"Spent time with it?"

"Yes. Or, you know, tried to find anything out about it."

"No," Eric said slowly, "not yet."

He'd spent some time with it, certainly, but that level of research wasn't something he wanted to disclose.

"It seemed to upset him when I brought it to the hospital," he said.

"What? You went to the hospital?"

"Yeah. I didn't get your message until Thursday night. I went down to see him that evening, tried to talk with him. He got upset when I showed him the bottle, so I left."

There was a moment of silence and then she said, "Eric...the doctors told us he hasn't spoken a word since Monday. He hasn't been able to communicate with family, and the doctors don't think he will. He's very close to the end now. The mind is already gone, but the body is hanging on."

"Well, he talked to me. Showed a little of that sense of humor, too, tried to play a trick on me."

But even as he said it, he felt a cold shroud settle around him.

"A trick? I can't believe that. And you have it on video?"

"Yes," he said. Tried to say.

"What was that?"

"Yes," he said. "I should have it on video."

"That will be very special to us. I just can't believe it. Thursday night, you said? That was three days after he stopped speaking."

"I'm sorry to hear that," he said. "Hate to cut you off, Alyssa, but I'm going to have to go. I've got...one of my sources is calling. So I'll need to let you—"

"Of course, take it. Keep me updated, and enjoy your stay down there."

"I'm going to try real hard to do that," he said and disconnected. Below him the tour guide droned on. The kids in the group looked to be around sixteen, the classic bored-with-everything age, yet they were quiet, staring around almost in awe. Eric understood that. It was the kind of place that could grab your attention and hold it.

He stood up slowly and went into the room and got the camera out. It used miniature DVDs, and he'd put in a fresh one before he set out on foot the previous day. The DVD he'd removed from the camera then had been the one from his visit to Campbell Bradford. Now he took the West Baden DVD out and replaced it with the Bradford disc. He took a long, deep breath and looked up at the ceiling.

"He talked, and it's going to be on here," he said. "It is going to be on here."

He pressed play.

There was Campbell Bradford in the hospital bed. His face looked as Eric remembered — haggard, weary, fading. None of the spark in his eyes yet, but that had taken a moment. Eric turned up the audio volume, heard his own voice.

You going to talk to me?

On the screen, Campbell Bradford blinked slowly and took a hissed breath.

Are you going to talk to me tonight?

This was where he'd responded, right? Eric had dropped his eye to the viewfinder after asking that question, and Bradford had spoken for the first time.

But now as he watched, nothing happened. Bradford stayed silent. Okay, maybe Eric had the wrong spot. Maybe he'd talked for a while before the old man embarked on his game.

His own voice continued:

Great. Where would you like to start? What would you like to tell me?

Oh, shit. He was responding to Bradford now, wasn't he? Had to be. On the screen, though, the old man hadn't said a word, hadn't lifted his head or moved his lips.

Can I ask you something off topic?

Pause. No response from Bradford.

Are you going to talk to me only when I'm looking through the camera?

In his memory, clear as anything, Eric recalled the old man smiling here. On the screen, his mouth didn't so much as twitch.

That is one wicked sense of humor.

"No, no, no," Eric said. "He was talking. He was *talking*."

But he wasn't talking. Hadn't said a word, hadn't moved a muscle. And there in the background was Eric, gibbering along, carrying on a conversation with no one, sounding like...a crazy person.

"I'm not crazy," he said. "I'm not. You were talking, old man, you were talking and I'm sure of it, and I don't know why this piece-of-shit camera won't show it!"

He was half shouting now but through clenched teeth, and he got to his feet with the camera in his hands, his eyes still locked on the display. He could see himself on the screen now, the green bottle in his hand. This was when Campbell had gotten upset. When he'd moved, grabbed Eric's arm, and started to talk about the river.

What?

Well, I thought it was plenty cold. When I touched—

Eric's voice cut off on the audio then, and he remembered Campbell had interrupted him, but it didn't play that way. Instead, it sounded like he'd just cut himself off in midsentence. The man in the hospital bed had not moved or spoken.

What, then? What are you talking about?

"He talked about the river," Eric said. "The cold river."

But talk he did not. Only Eric spoke. Responding, according to the camera, to utter silence.

What river are you talking about?

What river? I don't understand what you're talking about, sir.

Mr. Bradford? I'm sorry I brought the bottle.

Mr. Bradford, I was hoping to talk to you about your life. If you don't want to talk about West Baden or your childhood, that's fine with me. Let's talk about your career, then. Your kids.

All Eric's voice. Not a single whispered word from Campbell Bradford. The video went blank then, the recording over, and

Eric was left standing there in the hotel room with the camera in his hands, staring at a blue screen.

Crazy, a voice whispered in Eric's mind, *you're going insane. Truly, literally, out of your mind. Seeing things that aren't there is one thing, but you had a* conversation *that wasn't there, buddy. That's the sort of thing that only happens to—*

"I didn't imagine shit," Eric said. "Didn't imagine a single damn thing. It was all real, and I don't know why this thing won't show it."

He rewound, played part of it again, saw the same thing he'd seen before, and now his heart was thundering.

"Bullshit," he said. "It happened, and the camera was on. So why didn't you record it, you piece of shit? Why didn't you *record it!*"

The video played on, no voice but Eric's audible.

"Fuck you," he told the camera, his voice shaking. "It's you. It's *your fault.*"

That had to be it—the camera. The thing was...not broken, but what? Evil, that was it. This camera was *evil.* Because Eric knew he'd had a conversation with Campbell Bradford, knew it as surely as he knew his own name, and he knew he'd seen the train and spinning leaves last night, and yet those things had not been recorded and that left no other option but that this shitty camera was corrupt, malevolent, evil...

He lifted it above his head and smashed it on the edge of the desk. A crack appeared on the casing but the rest of the camera stayed intact. Well-built, sturdy. Thanks, Paul. He lifted it and smashed it again. And again.

By now he was shouting, not words so much as guttural oaths as he lifted and smashed, lifted and smashed, lifted and smashed.

He didn't stop until the casing was shattered and the carpet was littered with plastic shards. Then he dropped it to the floor, breathing hard, and kicked it, sent the camera rolling across the floor, leaving a trail of broken pieces in its wake.

"There you go," he said softly, and then he fell back onto the bed, dropping his head to his hands as his chest rose and fell in deep, fear-fueled breaths.

Part Two

NIGHT TRAINS

15

THERE'D BEEN ELEVEN CANS of Keystone Ice in the fridge when Josiah got home Friday night, and he drank nine of them before falling asleep sometime in those silent hours before dawn. He fell asleep out on the porch, could remember that the wind had been starting to stir right toward the end and he'd had a notion that it was time to go inside, but alcohol-induced sleep crept on and held him down with heavy hands.

Dreams came for him then.

In the first one he was in a city, on some street of towering buildings unfamiliar to him. Everything was a dusty gray, like an old photograph, and the wind howled around the concrete corners and swirled dust into his eyes. The dust was painful, made him wince and turn away, and when he did, he saw that the cars lining the street were old-fashioned, every last one of them, roadsters with headlights the size of dinner plates and long, wide running boards.

There was no one on the sidewalks, no one in sight, but despite that, he had the sense that the place was bustling, busy. A powerful, impatient humming noise contributed to that impression, and then he heard a steam whistle ring out loud above it and he knew that a train was near. He turned back again, into the wind and the dust, and now he could see the train coming right down the sidewalk toward him. He stepped back as the locomotive roared up and went by in a blur that lifted more dust into his eyes and flapped his clothes against his body. The huge metal wheels were going right over the sidewalk, no rails beneath them, grinding off a fine layer of concrete, and Josiah knew then where all the dust was coming from.

He had his hands up, shielding his face, when he heard the locomotive slow, and the cars that had been flying by began to take shape, corrugated doors and iron ladders and couplers like clasped fists of steel. All a dirty gray; nothing in this world had color. Then he turned to his left, looked down at the long snake of train cars yet to come, and saw a splash of red on white. The red was in the shape of a devil, with pointed tail and pitchfork in hand, the word *Pluto* written above it, all this on the side of a clean white boxcar. As this car approached, he could see there was a man leaning from it, hanging out of the open door of the boxcar with just one hand to support him and waving with the other. Waving at Josiah. The man wasn't familiar but Josiah knew him all the same, knew him well.

The train was at a crawl now, and Josiah stepped closer to it as the Pluto boxcar approached. The man hanging from it wore a rumpled brown suit with frayed cuffs above scuffed shoes, a bowler hat tilted up on his head, thick dark hair showing underneath. He smiled at Josiah as the steam whistle cut loose with another shriek and the train shuddered to a halt.

"Time to be getting on," the man said. He was hanging out of the boxcar right above Josiah now, almost close enough to touch.

Josiah asked what he was talking about.

"Time to be getting on," the man said again, and then he removed his hat and waved it at the locomotive. "Won't be stopped here forever. You best hurry."

Josiah inquired where they were bound.

"South," the man told him. "Home."

Josiah admitted that he wouldn't mind heading home, didn't know this place, didn't like much about it. How was he to be sure the train was heading home, though? Home was a place called French Lick, he said, home was Indiana.

"This is the Monon line," the man said. "The *Indiana* line. 'Course we're going to French Lick. West Baden, too. Best be getting on now."

Josiah said, As he recollected the Monon hadn't carried a car in upwards of forty years. That got the man smiling as he set his hat back on his head and the whistle blew.

"Could be so," he said. "But if there's another way of getting home, I don't know it."

He shifted then, stepped back into the boxcar. Something splashed and Josiah looked down and saw the man was standing in water now, had soaked his shoes and those frayed pant cuffs.

"Best be getting on," the man said again, and the train began to move, water sloshing out of the boxcar and splattering the sidewalk. "I told you, we don't stop here forever."

Josiah asked whether the man was certain they'd be headed in his direction.

"Of course," the man said. "We're going home to take what's yours, Josiah."

The train was pulling away, and Josiah started walking after it and then broke into a jog and still wasn't fast enough, and then he was running all out, his breath coming in jerking gasps. He got too close to the train, though, and the force of the cars thundering by spun him and he stumbled, and then that dream was gone and he was into another.

Out in a field this time, a field of golden wheat turned blood red by sunset and bent double from a stiff wind. Shadows lay at the opposite end of the field, a row of trees there, and above them the dome of the West Baden Springs Hotel rose mighty and shining into the sky. It was time to head over there and get to work; Josiah knew that and knew he'd have to hustle because this was a mighty long field and that wind was pushing hard against him, making the walk difficult.

He leaned into it, walking hard, but the sun was sliding away fast and the moon was rising beside it at the exact same tempo, like someone pulling a clock chain that was attached to both. The dark fell fast and heavy and the hotel dome gleamed under the moon and the wind was colder now, so cold, and yet Josiah didn't appear to have gotten anywhere at all, had just as much of the wheat field ahead as he'd always had. As the dark gathered, he could make out a man at the tree line, the same man from the train, wearing his bowler hat and with hands jammed into his pants pockets. He was shaking his head at Josiah. Looked disgusted with him. Disgusted and angry.

The second dream faded and heat replaced it, an uncomfortable black warmth that eventually roused Josiah from sleep. When he opened his eyes, he saw that the sun was up and shining off the windshield of his pickup truck and right in his face.

He rose with a grunt, stumbled forward and leaned on the porch rail, felt the old paint flake under his palm. A dull throb came from his face, and only then did he remember the previous night, the white guy with the scruffy beard and the black kid with the blisteringly quick left hand. He felt around his eye with his fingertips, knew from touch alone how it must look, and felt the anger that had chased him into sleep return.

The beer had left his mouth dry, but his stomach was settled and his head was clear. Hell, he felt good. He'd taken a punch to the eye and then tied on a good drunk and slept sitting upright in a plastic chair, but somehow he felt good. Felt strong.

The phone started ringing, and he went inside, picked it up off the table, answered and heard Danny's voice.

"Josiah, what'n hell you'd take off for last night?"

"Wasn't feeling so hot. Needed some sleep."

"Bullshit. I heard you went to Rooster's and got knocked in the face by some—"

"Never mind that," Josiah said. "Look, you done crowing over your twenty-five hundred yet?"

"That what got you upset, that I had some luck? Downright shitty, Josiah."

"That wasn't it. I'm asking, though, you still feeling big about it?"

"Feeling happy is all. Took a little beating later on, lost about eight hundred, but I still got more than fifteen of it left. That ain't a bad night."

"No, it ain't. But is it a good enough night? It all you need?"

"What do you mean?"

Josiah turned and looked out the window, out into that sun-filled day.

"Time's come to make us some real money, Danny. Time's come."

16

A N HOUR AFTER ERIC played the video, he was still staring at the wreckage that remained from his camera, trying to understand what in the hell was going on, when his cell phone began to ring.

It was Claire. Calling him even though he'd told her he would not be available for a few weeks. He held the phone in his hand but didn't answer. He could not talk to her now, not in this state. A minute after it stopped ringing he checked the message, and the sound of her voice broke something loose inside him, made his shoulders sag and his eyes close.

"I know you're in Indiana," she said, "but I just wanted to check on you. I was thinking of you.... You can call if you want. If not, I understand. But I'd like to know you're all right."

A week ago, he'd have bristled. *Check on me? Like to know if I'm all right? Why would I not be? Just because you're not here, I'm not going to be okay?* Today, though, sitting on the hotel room floor surrounded by his broken camera, he couldn't muster that response. Instead, he called her back.

She answered. First ring.

"Hey," he said.

"Hey. You got my message?"

"Yes."

Silence.

"Well, I didn't want to bother you. It's just that you hadn't really said anything about where you were going or when you might be back, so—"

"It's fine. I should have explained more. I'm sorry."

She was quiet for a moment, as if the phrase had surprised her. Probably it had.

"Are you okay?" she said. "You sound a little off."

"I've been . . . Claire, I'm seeing things."

"What do you mean, you're—"

"Things that aren't there," he said, and there was something thick in the back of his throat.

Silence, and he braced himself for the scorn and the ridicule she'd have to levy now, the accusations. Instead he heard a door swing shut and latch and then a metallic clatter that he recognized so well—she'd tossed her car keys into the ceramic dish she kept on the table by the door. She'd been going out, and now she stopped.

"Tell me about it," she said.

He talked for about twenty minutes, gave her more detail than he'd planned, recalled every word Campbell Bradford had said about the cold river, described the train right down to the gravel vibrating under his feet and the furious storm cloud that came from its stack. Through it all, she listened.

"I know what you're going to say," he said when he was through recounting the story of the man in the boxcar. "But it's not booze and it's not pills and it's not—"

"I believe you."

He hesitated. Said, "What?"

"I believe that it's not booze or pills," she said. "Because this has happened before. You've had visions like this before."

"Not like this," he said. "You're thinking of that time in the mountains, but—"

"That's one of them, but there were others. Remember the Infiniti?"

That stopped him. Shit, how could he have forgotten about the Infiniti? Maybe because he'd wanted to.

They'd been looking for a new car for Claire, back in California when things were good and the job offers were rolling in, and had gone to an Infiniti dealership to test-drive a red G35 coupe she'd liked. The car was brand-new, and she hadn't wanted to spend that kind of money, but Eric was feeling cocky and flush and insisting cash wasn't an issue. So they'd taken the car out, the two of them in front and a paunchy salesman with effeminate hands wedged into the back, jabbering on about the car's amazing and apparently endless features: navigation, climate control, heated seats, pedicures, tranquilizers, a hand that came right out from under the dash and powdered your balls when you needed it. His voice was grating on Eric, but Claire was driving and it was her car to choose anyhow, so Eric had leaned back and closed his eyes for a moment.

He swore, even hours later, that he'd heard metal tear. He believed that in his heart. He'd heard the jagged, agonized rip of metal from metal, a sound that belonged at junkyards or disaster sites, and jerked up in his seat and opened his eyes to see the windshield splintered and spider-webbed, turned to Claire and saw ribbons of blood spreading across her forehead and over her lips and down her chin as her neck sagged lifelessly to the right.

He'd gotten out some sort of gasp or grunt or shout and Claire had hit the brakes and turned to him as the guy in back finally shut up, and then Eric had blinked and the freeway spun around him and then he focused again and could see that they were all fine, that the car was intact and the windshield was whole and Claire's face was smooth and tan and blood-free.

The excuse he manufactured at the time — something about a sudden stomach cramp — had satisfied the salesman but not Claire, and when they got back to the lot she pulled him aside and asked him what was wrong. All he'd said: *Don't you even* think *about buying this car.* He couldn't tell her any more than that, couldn't describe the way her face had looked in that terrible flash.

Five days later, she'd brought him a copy of the *Times* as he drank coffee at the kitchen table, dropped it in front of him and pointed to an article detailing how a music executive's daughter had wrapped her fresh-off-the-lot Infiniti G35 around a utility pole, doing about a hundred and ten. The car was red and had just been purchased from Martin Infiniti, the same dealership they'd visited. Eric had finally told her, told her what she already knew. Then he'd tried to convince her it could easily be a different car.

"I actually forgot about that," he told her now. "But even that can't touch what I've been seeing lately, Claire. That conversation with the old man, and then the train ... they felt real. During those moments, they were absolutely real."

"But in the past you've had psychic —"

"Oh, stop, I don't want to hear that word."

"In the past you've had *odd visions* — better? — that have been very real, too. You've been able to connect objects or places with things that had happened or were going to happen. So why wouldn't you believe this is similar?"

"This is so much more intense..."

"And those other experiences were from outside contact," she said. "You ingested that water, Eric. You put it inside you."

"The water."

"Of course. Don't you think that's what you're reacting to?"

Actually, I suspected your dad's camera. Had to beat the thing to death, in fact. How's that for a logical reaction?

"I haven't really had time to consider it yet," he said. "But that trip to see the old man in the hospital, that was days after I first tasted the water. Seems like a long time for a drug to stay in your system."

"It's not a drug, Eric. It's *you*."

"What?"

"You're connecting to it, just like you have to things before. The car, the old Indian camp in the mountains, things like that. And I'm not surprised you think this experience is stronger, more intense, because those were just things you *looked* at. This stuff, you consumed."

They talked for a while longer, and it was amazing how much better he felt after he finally hung up with her. Claire had not only accepted his version of what was going on but had also offered a memory that validated it. Sane once again. How lovely to be back.

He felt a mild tug of shame at the way he'd gone to her with this, and the way she'd listened. After all his recent coldness, he'd turned to her quickly in a moment of need, and she had allowed him to.

It was, he realized, the longest conversation they'd had since he left. The first long one, in fact, that hadn't involved heavy arguing or his shouting or her tears. They'd talked like companions once again. Almost like husband and wife.

That didn't change anything, of course. But she'd been there when he needed her, and that was no small thing. Not at all.

There when she was needed, that was Claire. Always and forever, that had been Claire. Until the return to Chicago, until he had no work and no clear prospects. Then where had she been?

There. In your home. And you walked out and never went back, and she's still there, she's still there and you're the one who left...

Hell with it. One phone call did not a marriage fix, but it had been good to talk with her and he felt far better now than he had before, shaken but relieved. It was the way you felt after getting sick to your stomach — unsteady, but glad *that* was over.

The water made sense. The water applied some element of logic to what had, an hour ago, seemed utterly illogical. And terrifying.

All right, then, time to move on into the day. There was research to be done, and he figured it would be a damn good idea to start with the mineral water. At any rate, he didn't need to stay in this room, cowering and questioning his own sanity. The headaches would be gone for a while now. Might as well get to work. Too bad he no longer had a camera with which to do his job.

Breaking it had felt good, though. Watching it shatter, throwing his full strength into those smashes against the edge of the desk, seeing something else pay a price for his own pain, his own fear. Yes sir, that had felt nice.

He wondered how Claire would respond to that notion. Something told him it wouldn't be with surprise.

*   *   *

The Pluto company was housed in a long stone building of a buttery color. There were two large holding tanks outside and banks of old-fashioned windows, some forty panes of glass in each one, a few of them opened outward to let the air circulate. The entrance led Eric to a flight of stairs, and at the top he found the office, went in, and explained what he wanted to a pretty, brown-haired woman behind one of the desks.

"You want to talk about the history of the company, your best bet is up at the hotel," she said.

"I'm interested in the history, yes, but I'm also interested in the actual water. What's in the water, and what it does."

"What it does?"

"I've seen some of the old promotional materials, things that claimed it would fix just about anything."

"There was only one thing that water ever fixed." She waited for a response and didn't get it, then leaned forward and said, "It made you shit, mister. That's all it did. Pluto Water was nothing but a laxative."

He smiled. "I understand that, but I'm trying to find out something about the legends that surrounded it, the folklore."

"Again, we're not going to be able to answer that. The only thing we've got in common with the original company is the name. We don't produce that water anymore."

"What do you produce, then?"

"Cleaning products," she said. "Things for Clorox." Then she smiled and added, "Well, I suppose that's got something in common, after all. Cleansers, right? Because the old stuff would clean out your—"

"I got it," he said. "Okay. Thanks for your time."

There was an older woman at a desk in the back of the room,

and she'd been listening and peering at Eric over her reading glasses. As he turned to go, she spoke up.

"You want to know about folklore, you should look up Anne McKinney."

He paused at the door. "Is she a historian?"

"No, she's not. Just a local woman, late eighties but with a mind better than most, and a memory that beats anybody's. Her father worked for Pluto. She'll answer every question you could think to ask and plenty more that you couldn't have."

"That sounds perfect. Where can I find her?"

"Well, you follow Larry Bird Boulevard—that's the street we're on—right on up the hill and keep going out of town, and you'll find her house. Nice-looking blue house, two stories with a big front porch, bunch of little windmills in the yard, wind chimes all over the porch. Thermometers and barometers, too. Can't miss that place."

Eric raised his eyebrows.

"Old Anne's waiting on a storm," the gray-haired woman said.

"I see. Think she'll mind me dropping in, or should I call first?"

"I don't think she'd mind, but if you don't want to bother her at home, you could go on by the West Baden Springs Hotel at about two. She goes there for a drink."

"A drink? Thought you said she was in her late eighties?"

"That's right," the gray-haired woman said with a smile.

17

AT NOON THE BAROMETER showed a pressure of 30.20, up a bit from morning. The temperature was at eighty-one but Anne didn't think it would touch quite so high today as yesterday, what with that light breeze and some cloud cover coming in out of the southwest. Thin white clouds, no storm. Not yet.

She spent the morning on laundry. Was a time when laundry was not an all-morning task, but the washer and dryer were in the basement, and those narrow wooden stairs gave her some trouble now. Oh, she could take them well enough, just a bit slower. That was true of so much these days. Just a bit slower.

She had the laundry done by eleven and then made some iced tea and went out onto the porch with the newspaper. The *New York Times,* which she'd taken for more years than she could count. It was important to know what was going on in the world, and last time she'd trusted TV was the last day Murrow had been on it.

At noon she got up and checked the temperature and wind direction and speed and the barometric pressure, wrote it all down in her notebook. She had logs going back more than six decades, five readings a day. Make a real interesting record, if anyone cared. She suspected not many would.

Her weather-watching habits had their roots in childhood. And in fear. She'd been petrified of storms when she was a young girl, would hide under her bed or in a closet when the thunder and lightning commenced. It had amused her father—she could still remember his soft, low laugh as he'd come in to fetch her from under the bed—but her mother had decided something needed to be done about it and had found a children's book about storms, one with illustrations of dark thunderheads, swirling tornadoes, tossing seas. Anne had been seven when she got the book, had the binding split from countless readings by the time she was eight.

"You can't be scared of them, because being scared of them won't change a thing," her mother had said. "Won't make 'em stop, won't make you any safer. You respect them and try to understand them. More you understand, less you'll be afraid."

So Anne had returned to the book for another reading and started forcing herself to stay at the window when storms blew in, watching the trees bend and the leaves whip through the air as rain lashed the house, drilling off the glass. She went to the library and found more books and kept studying. Had it been a different time, she'd have probably gone up to Purdue and studied meteorology. But that wasn't how things worked then. She had a sweetheart, got married right out of high school, and then the war was on and he was overseas and she had to get a job, and then he was back and they had children to raise. Children she'd put in the ground already, hardest thing she could imagine anyone bearing, her daughter gone at thirty with cancer, her son at forty-nine with a stroke. No grandchildren left behind.

She was thinking about her son when she first saw the car approaching slowly up the road, remembering the time he'd fallen off this very porch and landed on a flowerpot below, breaking his wrist. Five years old at the time, and he was trying to stand on the rail to impress his sister. Goodness, how that boy had cried. The car came to a stop then and turned in her drive, and her thoughts left the past and she got to her feet. The wind had freshened a touch just as the car pulled in, got the chimes jingling on the porch and lifted some dust off the floorboards. She swept the thing twice a day, but the world never would run out of dust.

The visitor got out, a man with short hair of a color that had gotten confused somewhere between blond and brown. He needed a shave but seemed clean enough.

"Anne McKinney? They gave me your name down in French Lick," he said, swinging the door shut and walking up the steps when she nodded. "I'm interested in Pluto Water. The old stories, the folklore. Think you'd be willing to talk about it?"

"Oh, I'm willing enough. Day I'm not willing to tell the old tales, you best call the grave digger — if nothing else just so he can hit me in the head with his shovel. Ought to issue a disclaimer before I get to it, though: time I get to storytelling, you best be comfortable. I've been known to go on."

He smiled. It was a nice smile, warm and genuine.

"Ma'am, I've got plenty of interest and time."

"Then come on up here and have a seat."

He walked up the steps and offered his hand. "Name's Eric Shaw. I'm down from Chicago."

"Oh, Chicago. Always loved that city. Haven't been there in years. I can remember riding the Monon up more than a few times, though. In fact, that's where my husband and I went on our honeymoon. Spring of 'thirty-nine. I was eighteen years old."

"When did the Monon stop making that run?"

"Monon stopped making any runs, period, in 'seventy-three."

Thirty-five years ago. She didn't consider dates all that much, but she'd just rattled two of them off, and they both sounded impossibly long ago. She remembered the day the Monon made its final run quite well, actually. She and Harold went up to the Greene County trestle and watched it thunder on across, waving good-bye as it went. Hadn't realized exactly all they'd been waving good-bye to. An era. A world.

"Each of the hotels here had its own train station for years," she said. "Doesn't that seem hard to believe now? But here I go — talking away from the topic before we even got started. What was it you wanted to know about Pluto Water?"

He sat down on the chair across from her and pulled out one of those tiny tape recorders and held it up, a question in his eyes.

"Oh, sure, if you actually want to listen to me go on about this a second time, you're more than welcome to it."

"Thank you. I was wondering if you could tell me what you'd heard about the ... more unusual effects of the water."

"Unusual?"

"I know that eventually people realized it was nothing more than a laxative, but in the early days the stuff had a reputation that went well beyond that."

She smiled. "It certainly did. For a time, Pluto Water was reputed to do just about anything short of put a man on the moon. The popular response to your question, of course, would be that as the years passed, people got smarter, learned more about science and health and figured out that all of that had been nothing more than snake oil sales. That the company survived for a time by toning down the claims, advertising it as a laxative, but the world's finest laxative. Then people saw through that, too, or found a better product, and Pluto Water went the way of a lot of old-fashioned things. Quickly forgotten, and then it disappeared entirely."

"You said that would be the popular response," Eric Shaw said. "Are you aware of a different one?"

That got her to grinning again, thinking about what her daddy's reaction to this man would be if he were still here. Why, he'd be coming up out of his chair by now, taking his pipe from his mouth and waving it around to emphasize his point. All the poor man had ever wanted was an audience for his Pluto Water theories.

"Well, sure, I've heard a few," she said. "My father worked for the company, understand. And the way he told it, the water changed over the years. Originally, they'd just bottle it fresh out of the springs and what you drank was essentially direct from the source. Problem they ran into with that was, the water didn't keep. They tried putting it into kegs and casks, but it went bad quickly. Unfit to drink. That wasn't any real dilemma until people realized how much money could be made from shipping the water all over. Then they had to do something about it."

"Pasteurization?"

"Of a sort. They boiled the water to get rid of some of the gasses that were in it and then added two different kinds of salt that fortified it, allowed it to keep. Once they had that process figured out, they bottled it and shipped it all over the world."

Eric Shaw nodded but didn't speak, waiting on more. She liked that. So many people were impatient these days, hurried.

"The company and most of the people involved with it swore up and down that nothing changed in the water during that boiling and salting."

"Your father disagreed," he said, and she chuckled.

"He suspected the preservation process changed what the water could do."

"You didn't believe him."

"I'd be willing to believe, maybe, that water fresh from the springs had more effect than the stuff they bottled and shipped. Isn't that true of most things? You eat a tomato from your own garden, it tastes different than the one you buy from the store."

"Sure."

"He also had a notion," she said, "that your standard-issue Pluto Water was a special thing, capable of startling healing powers, but that there were some springs in the area that went a touch beyond that. This area is filled with mineral springs. Some large, some small, but there's a lot of them."

"Did you ever hear rumors that the water caused hallucinations?"

That lifted her eyebrows. She shook her head. "I never heard that, no."

He looked positively disappointed but was trying to conceal it, nodding his head and rushing out another question.

"What about the temperature? I've, uh, I've heard that it would stay unusually cold. That there was some sort of...a chemical reaction, I guess, and you could leave the bottles out in a warm room but they'd stay cold, even get a little frost."

"Well," Anne said, "I don't know who you've been getting stories from, but they sound like a colorful source. I've never heard of anything like that."

He was silent for a moment, eyes concerned, and seemed to be groping for something.

"But you had the water that had been preserved or fortified, right?" he said eventually.

"Yes."

"What if it had been fresh water, bottled back before they did that process?"

"That would require the water being from before eighteen

ninety-three, I think," she said. "I really couldn't say much about that, but I never heard anything about any unusual coldness."

"What might happen if you drank Pluto Water that hadn't been preserved?"

"Well, the way I was always told, it simply wasn't fit for human consumption after much time had passed."

"And if someone *did* drink it?"

"If they could actually choke enough of it down," Anne said, "I do believe it would be fatal."

That seemed to rock him. He wet his lips and dropped his eyes to the porch floor and looked a little queasy. She frowned, watching him, wondering about all these questions now, about what exactly she had on her hands here.

"You mind my asking what you're working on?"

"A family history," he said.

"Someone that worked for Pluto?"

"No, but I'm trying to put as much area history into it as I can. I'll be making a film, eventually, but today I'm just doing some preliminary work."

"Who was it filled your head with all those ideas about the water?"

"An old man in Chicago," he said, and then, before she could respond to that, he asked, "Hey, is there a river around here?"

"A river? Well, not right here in town, no. There's the creek."

"I was told about a river."

"The White River's not far. And then there's the Lost River."

The wind kicked up then, set the chimes to work, a sound Anne would never tire of, and she tilted her head to look past Eric Shaw and out to the yard, where the blades were spinning on the windmills. Spinning pretty good, too, a decent breeze funneling through. Still nothing but sun and white clouds, though, no hint of a storm. Odd for the wind to be picking up like this with no storm...

"The Lost River?"

His question snapped her mind back. It was mildly embarrassing to be caught drifting off like that, but this wind was strange, grabbed her attention.

"Yes, sorry. I was listening to the chimes. It's called the Lost River because so much of it is underground. More than twenty miles of it, I believe. Shows itself here and there and then disappears again."

"That's pretty wild," Eric Shaw said, and Anne smiled.

"Everything that built these towns came up from underground. I walk into those hotels and just shake my head, because when it comes right down to it, they wouldn't be there except for a little bit of water that bubbles out of the ground around here. If you don't think there's a touch of magic to that, well, I don't know what to tell you."

"That's what Pluto was supposed to represent, right?"

"Right. He's the Roman version of Hades, which isn't all that pleasant a connotation to most folks now, but there's a difference between Hell and the underworld in the myths. My father did some studying on those myths. Way he understood it, Pluto wasn't the devil. He was the god of riches found in the earth, found underground. That's why they named the company after him, see? Thing my father always found amusing was that in the myths all Pluto was in charge of, really, was keeping the dead on the banks of the River Styx before they crossed it to be judged. So Pluto was essentially an innkeeper. And what followed the water in this town?"

She waved her hand out across her valley, the springs valley. "Inns. Beautiful, amazing inns."

She laughed and folded her hands, put them back in her lap. "Daddy probably overthought a lot of these things."

They were quiet for a time then. Her visitor seemed to have something else on his mind, and she was content to sit and watch the windmills spin, listen to the chimes.

"You said you were around the water a lot," he said eventually. "Think you could recognize a bottle if I brought one to you? Tell me when it might have been made?"

"I sure could. In fact, I've got a bunch of them upstairs, labeled with the years. Might be able to find a match. Where are you staying? French Lick or West Baden?"

"West Baden."

"I head down there in the afternoon and have myself a little sip. If you have the Pluto bottle, you can just bring it down. I'll be there in a half hour or so."

That seemed to please him, but he'd looked unsteady over the last few minutes, a fierce bit of worry clearly going on in his head, and she wondered what it was had him so concerned. Maybe he'd harbored hopes of using a lot of nonsense in his film, hallucinations and eerie cold bottles and such. Well, rare was the storyteller who got trapped by reality. She imagined he'd find his way around it easy enough.

He thanked her and got into his car and drove off down the hill, and she stayed on the porch with her hands folded in her lap. He'd come by and sparked memories on a day when they were already warm. She'd been thinking about her son, Henry, that tumble he'd taken off the porch. Then this Shaw fellow arrived and said he was from Chicago and her mind had jumped right off that porch and onto a passenger train. Harold had let her have the window seat and she'd sat with her hand wrapped in his and her eyes on the rolling countryside, the wheels on the track offering a soothing noise, light and steady, *clack-clack-clack-clack*.

He'd helped her to her feet when the train got to Chicago, pulled her into his arms, and kissed her long and hard, and someone on the train had whistled and she'd blushed red as the Monon car that carried them.

Spring of 'thirty-nine, she'd told Eric Shaw. Spring of 'thirty-nine.

Now she wanted to chase him down the road, pull him out of his car and shout, Yes, it was the spring of 'thirty-nine but it was also *yesterday*. It was an *hour ago,* don't you understand? It just happened, I just took that ride, just tasted those lips, just heard that whistle.

The train had seemed faster than anything to her that day, dazzling in its speed. There were race cars that went faster than the train, though, and planes that went faster than the cars, and rockets that went faster than the planes, but what still blew them all away was time itself, the days and months and the years, oh yes, the years. They went faster than anything man had the capacity to invent, so fast that for a while they fooled you into thinking they were slow, and was there any crueler trick than that?

The day Henry fell off the porch rail and broke his wrist, she'd scooped him into her arms and carried him up the steps and into the house before calling the doctor, doing it easily, without a thought. Today, though, she'd gone down the stairs one at a time, dragging the laundry basket behind her and clutching the railing.

She got to her feet and went inside in search of her car keys, ready to go to the hotel, a place that time had forgotten for a while and then remembered and returned to her.

18

I DO BELIEVE IT would be fatal.

Shit, what an encouraging statement that had been. Eric was past the casino parking lot and the old Pluto Water plant when his foot went heavy and hard to the brake pedal and a car behind him honked and swerved to avoid a collision. The driver shouted something as he went outside the double-yellow and passed, but Eric didn't turn. Instead, he pulled slowly to the side of the road and into a parking space, staring out of the driver's window.

Sitting there on a short rail spur in the middle of town was a white boxcar with a red Pluto devil painted on the side. According to the sign nearby, this was the French Lick Railway Museum, and as far as Eric could tell, it consisted of an old depot and a handful of decrepit train cars. Only one of which had caught his eye today.

He shut the engine off and got out. Might as well have a look. The wind came at him right away, warm and heavy, as he walked over to the station. When he entered, an elderly man wearing an engineer's cap and bifocals looked up.

"Welcome!"

"Hey," Eric said. "Yeah, look...I was just wondering..."

"Yes?"

"What's the story on that Pluto boxcar?"

"Good-looking devil, ain't it?" the man said and laughed as Eric felt a tide of liberation break through him. *This* train car was real.

"Sure is," Eric said. "You know how old it is?"

"Oh, fifty year, maybe. Not one of the originals."

"Okay. You mind if I take a look?"

"Shoot, no. Go on and climb inside if you'd like, but watch yourself. Them cars are taller than they look. Can fall right out of one. Say, you want to go on the next ride? Got a train runs up the valley, locomotive driven, just like the old days."

"Locomotive driven," Eric echoed. "They happen to run that in the evenings?"

"I'm sorry, no. Daytime only. Next ride in forty minutes. You want a ticket?"

"I don't think so. Don't really like trains."

The old man looked at him as if Eric had just called his daughter easy.

"I've had some bad experiences with them recently, that's all," Eric said. "Thanks a lot."

He closed the door and went back out into the heat and over to the Pluto car. The door was shoved most of the way shut and barely moved when he pushed on it. The size of the thing was impressive — they never looked that big from behind the wheel of a car. Had to be twelve feet tall, and the steel couplers on either side looked invincible, as if you could bang on them all day with a sledge and never do a bit of damage.

There was a ladder on either end of the car, as well as a few iron rungs on the front. He reached out and wrapped his fist around one of those, leaned on it, and that was when he saw the splotches. Glistening stains on the crushed stone beneath the car.

Water marks.

While he watched, another drop of water fell onto the stone, and he saw that it was coming from inside the car rather than from underneath it. When he stared through the door, though, there was nothing but old, dry dirt on the floor.

He tightened his grip around the rung of the ladder and hoisted himself up, swinging his left foot up and over the side. Hung there for a minute, peering into the shadowed interior, and then slid through.

The boxcar was heavy with trapped heat, the air smelling of rust. The car seemed far larger on the inside than on the outside, the opposite end lost in darkness. The rippled steel walls seemed to drink in the light, holding it all to the thin shaft in the center.

The floor beneath his feet was dry, but he could hear water now, a gentle sloshing sound. He took a hesitant step forward, out of the light, and felt cold moisture seep through his shoes and socks and find his skin.

He bent down and reached with his hand, dipped his fingertips into the water. About an inch deep, frigid.

Another step toward the sloshing sound, which had an even, constant beat. Water covered the floor throughout the dark portions of the boxcar, and he wanted to move back to the dry boards and the square of sunlight but kept shuffling forward into the darkness despite himself.

He was ten feet from the door and still moving when the silhouette took shape.

It was all the way at the back of the car, lost to the darkness except for the distinctive outline of a bowler hat.

Eric stopped where he was, the water like a winter creek on his feet, and stared down the remaining length of the boxcar, watching the silhouette take starker shape, first the shoulders and then the torso. The man was sitting in the water with his back against the wall and his knees drawn up, and he was tapping a slow, steady beat with the toe of his right shoe, slapping it into the water, which rose almost to his ankles.

"An elegy," he said, "is a song for the dead."

Eric couldn't speak. It wasn't just from fear or astonishment but from an almost physical thing, a limit he didn't understand and couldn't do anything about. He was a spectator in this car. Here to watch. To listen.

"I can barely hear it," the man said. His voice was a sandpaper whisper. "What about you?"

The violin music was back, soft as a breeze, as if it couldn't penetrate the walls of the boxcar.

"Been waiting a long time to get home," the man said. "Longer ride than I'd have liked."

Eric couldn't make out his face, couldn't see anything but the form of him.

"People 'round here seem to have forgotten it," the man said, "but this is *my* valley. Was once. Will be again."

His voice seemed to be gathering strength, and the features of his suit were now showing, along with his nose and mouth and shadowed eye sockets.

"Ain't but a trace of my blood left," he said, "but that's enough. That's enough."

The man dropped his hands into the water then, two soft splashes, and pushed off the floor. His silhouette rippled as he stood, like a water reflection pushed by wind, and something that had been unhooked in Eric's brain suddenly connected again and he knew that he had to move.

He turned and stumbled back for the streak of sun that represented the door, slid on the wet floor but righted himself, and then banged off the wall, groping with his hands. He got out of the water and onto dry floorboards and then had his hand around the edge of the door, shoved his shoulder through and lunged into the light.

His feet caught and he was free but falling, landing on his ass in the dirt and stone.

"Now, what did I tell you!" someone shouted, and Eric looked up to see the old man in the engineer's cap standing just outside the depot, shaking his head. "I said watch your step coming out of there!"

Eric didn't answer, just got to his feet and brushed the dirt from his jeans as he moved away from the train car. He took a few steps before turning to look back at it. After a few seconds he walked all the way back and dropped to one knee below the door.

The water marks were gone. The stones were pale and dry under the sun.

"You ain't hurt, are you?" the old man yelled, and Eric ignored him again and took hold of the edge of the big cargo door, leaned his shoulder into it, and grunted and got it moving. He slid it all the way back as the old man yelled at him to go easy on the equipment, then stepped aside and looked in.

The sun caught the corners now, and there was nothing in sight, neither man nor water. He leaned in and stared into the far end, stared at the emptiness. Then he bent and picked up a small stone and tossed it inside, listened to it skitter off the dry floor.

The wind picked up and blew hard at his back then, swirling dust around the old boxcar. There was a high, giddy whistling as it filled the car, as if it had been working on the door for a long time and was delighted to find someone had finally opened it the rest of the way.

19

He called Alyssa Bradford from the car, sitting with the air-conditioning blasting and the vents angled so the cold air blew directly into his face. The old man from the railway museum was leaning against the door frame, watching him with a frown.

"Alyssa, I did have a few follow-up questions I forgot to ask," Eric said when she answered. "The bottle of water you gave me.... Can you tell me anything about it at all?"

She was quiet for a moment. Then said, "Not really. That's why I wanted you—"

"I understand what you wanted. But I need a little help. It's the only thing you brought me that first day. The only artifact of any sort you gave me. No photos, no scrapbook, just that bottle. I guess I'm wondering why you thought it was so special."

He was staring at the Pluto boxcar, at the grinning red devil.

"It's strange," she said eventually. "Don't you think it's strange?

The way it stays cold, the way it...I don't know, *feels*. There's something off about it. And it is the only thing—and I mean the *only* thing—that he had from childhood. My husband told me that he kept it in a locked drawer in his bedside table, and said the bottle was a souvenir from his childhood and that no one was allowed to touch it. As you can see, it meant a lot to him for some reason. That's why I'm so curious."

"Yes," Eric said. "I'm curious, too."

"When I talked to you at Eve's memorial service," she said, "and I saw how you intuited the importance of that photograph, I knew I wanted to give you the bottle. I thought you might see something, feel something."

That damn photograph was why she had hired him, why she'd sent him here. He could have guessed it from the start but instead he'd chosen to believe her hollow assertions of being impressed by the film. Claire wouldn't have been fooled.

"I think I need to talk to your husband," he said.

"What? Why?"

"Because he's the one who's actually related to the guy, Alyssa. It's his family, and I need to ask him what the hell he really knows about his father. What he's heard, what he thinks. I need to ask—"

"Eric, the entire point of this film was that it would be a surprise for my husband and his family."

I don't care were the words that rose in his throat, but he needed to keep any touch of hysteria down, and he was close to shouting now, close to telling her that something was very deeply wrong with Campbell Bradford, and once he got started on that, it'd be rolling downhill faster than he could control, stories of phantom trains and whispering ghosts coming out, and then his reputation in Chicago would be crushed just as completely as the one he'd had in Hollywood.

"I'd like to ask you to rethink that," he said. "I believe I'm going to need to find out a little more from him to make any progress."

"I'll consider it," she said in a tone of voice that made it clear she would not. "But I'm heading out right now and I'm afraid I have to let you go."

"One more thing, Alyssa."

"Yes?"

"Is there any chance your father-in-law played the violin?"

"Yes, he played beautifully. Self-taught, too. I take it you're having some luck finding out about him, after all."

Eric said, "I'm learning some things, yes."

"Well, I'm amazed you learned *that,* because he hated to play in front of people."

"Really."

"Yes. As far as I know, he would only play when he was alone, with the door closed. Said he had stage fright and didn't like to be watched when he played. But he could play beautifully. And there was a quality to it…maybe it was because of the fact that I never saw him play and only heard it, but there was something about the sound that was absolutely haunting."

He drove back to the hotel then, leaving the Acura beneath one of the few trees in the parking lot for shade and avoiding the bright light of the rotunda, sticking to the perimeter hallway. The headache was showing itself again but not yet at full strength, a scout party sent ahead of the battalion.

The first thing he saw when he opened the door to his hotel room was the shattered camera on the floor. The cleaning people had been in here, but they'd left the camera on the floor, clearly unsure of what the hell to do with what was obviously expensive equipment, even if destroyed.

He'd never even wanted to use that damn camera, a gift that felt like a taunt from his father-in-law, a reminder that the days when he'd used first-rate studio equipment were long gone. A reminder of his failure.

"Claire tells me you're going to be doing something on your own," Paul Porter had said. "Thought this would help."

He'd emphasized the *something,* two unspoken questions — what and when? — clear in the word. And Eric had to thank him with false gratitude and put on a show of marveling at the camera, Claire standing beside him, watching it all with a smile.

She'd been on his ass for months, prodding him along when all he needed was some patience, and if she thought he missed the connection between all that and her father's gift, she was crazy. Ever since they'd left L.A. she'd been after him for his *plans,* and though he'd satisfied her with them at first — write a script himself, get some financial backing, direct his own indie film and use that as a springboard back to the big time — it wasn't long before she was dissatisfied with his efforts.

His efforts. In truth that wasn't the best phrase, maybe. He hadn't done all that much. Had not, for example, directed the film or sought financing or even written the script. Started the script, for that matter. It wasn't something you could rush right into, though, you had to have the right idea first, and it was going to need to be a big idea, with the right scope and ambition, and then you had to let it gestate for a time…

Yes, he'd been slow. Or totally stagnant. And gradually the gentle prodding turned to full-on accusations and demands and then things were spiraling down fast and deadly. They'd had one terrible blowup when she happened into a bar and grill downtown for lunch with a friend and found him camped out there with three whiskeys already gone, this at noon. It had been a sighting that led to an unfair conversation later that night, a conversation that quickly turned angry, and when Eric stormed out of the house with a string of expletives and an upended coffee table in his wake, he'd done so with an expectation of returning in a few hours. He'd ended up in a hotel room instead, though, refusing to give her the satisfaction of surrender and one night in the hotel quickly turned to ten and then he was looking for an apartment.

The bullshit "career" he was involved with now had been as much a guilt trip as anything. He'd wanted to find something so pathetic she had to feel the weight of it. Instead, she'd just told him how glad she was to hear he was working again. Oh, and she was happy to know he could make use of her father's camera.

"Made good use of it, Paulie," he said and let the door to the hotel room swing shut as he got down on his hands and knees and began cleaning up the mess.

It was no good to be without a video camera, not with these circumstances, when he needed something to tell him what the hell had been real and what hadn't. He still had the micro-recorder, though. He took that out when he had the camera cleaned up and played a few minutes of his talk with Anne McKinney, enough to verify that everything on the tape progressed as he'd experienced it. He was still listening to it when his phone rang, and he turned off the recorder and looked at the phone, hoping for Claire but instead finding a number he didn't recognize.

"Eric? It's Kellen. I got in touch with Edgar Hastings, the old guy who knew Campbell's family, and he's willing to see you. Should be able to straighten out this confusion."

"Great."

"I'm actually up in Bloomington right now, seeing my girl. Was going to stay overnight, but if I head on back down we can go together."

"You don't need to do that."

"No, it's cool. She'd just as soon throw me out anyhow."

Eric could hear a laugh in the background, a sweet female sound that cut him.

"That's your decision, Kellen. I'm not going anywhere."

"I'll give you a call when I get down there."

Eric hung up. The clock told him almost an hour had passed since he left Anne McKinney, which meant she'd probably be at the bar by now. He took a deep breath and picked up the bottle, felt its cold wetness against his skin.

"Okay," he said. "Routine sanity check coming right up."

She was in an armchair not far from the bar, with a short glass of ice and clear liquid in her hand, a lime perched on the rim. She'd added jewelry since he left her porch, two bracelets and a necklace, and her blouse was different. She'd gotten dressed up to head into town and have her cocktail, evidently. He was hardly into the atrium before she lifted a hand and waved. Good eyes. Eric's own mother was twenty years younger and wouldn't have noticed him from this far away if he'd been riding in on a camel.

The bottle sweated more once it was in his hand, and as he crossed the atrium, a few drops of water fell from it and slid down his wrist and dripped onto the rug beneath.

Anne's eyes were already fixed on the bottle as he pulled up a chair, and she set her drink on the table and said, "Well, let's have a look."

He passed her the bottle, and when she took it, her eyes first widened and then narrowed as she frowned, and she shifted it quickly from one hand to the other. A streak of moisture glistened on her wrinkled palm.

"You've been keeping it in ice?" she said, and Eric felt an explosion of relief, almost sagged with it.

"No," he said. "That's just how it is."

She stared at him. "What?"

"That bottle hasn't been anywhere other than the desk in the room since I got here. Before that, it was in my briefcase in the car. It hasn't been near a refrigerator, a freezer, or an ice bucket."

"Are you having me on? I don't understand the trick."

"It's no trick, Mrs. McKinney. This is why I asked about the cold. I thought it was very strange."

She was studying his face, looking for some sign that he was the sort of asshole who'd get a kick out of playing a game with an old woman's mind. Apparently she found none, because she gave an almost imperceptible nod and then dropped her eyes and looked at the bottle again, rolling it over in her hands.

"I've never seen anything like this," she said, her voice soft. "Or heard of it. Even Daddy never said anything like this, and he was full of stories about Pluto Water."

"Could it be so old that it never went through that boiling and salting?"

She shook her head. "No. This bottle isn't anywhere near that old."

She used her thumb to wipe some of the frosty condensation clear, then traced the etching of Pluto at the base.

"This one couldn't be any earlier than 'twenty-six or 'twenty-seven. I'll double-check, of course, but this color and this design...no, this would have to be from the late twenties. I've got a dozen like it. They made millions of them."

He didn't say anything, just watched her turn that bottle over again and again.

"I've never seen anything like it," she repeated, and then, without looking up at him, said, "You drank some of it, didn't you."

"Yes."

She nodded. "I thought maybe you had. You seemed so worried about what it would do. Looks like you've had a good deal of it, too."

Yes, by now he'd had at least two-thirds of the bottle.

"I think there's something else in here," she said. "That colored look, the sediment, that shouldn't be there."

"Go ahead and open it," he said, "and tell me if it smells like Pluto Water to you."

She opened it and held it to her nose and shook her head almost immediately.

"That's not Pluto Water. It would smell —"

"Terrible," he said. "Sulfuric."

"Yes."

"That's how it smelled when I opened it originally. Since then —"

"It's almost sweet."

"Yes," he said, again feeling that relief, this old woman confirming now with multiple senses what he'd feared was a trick of his mind.

"You asked about hallucinations," she said, speaking carefully and gently.

"I think I've had a few, all since tasting it."

"What do you see?"

"It's varied, but I imagined a conversation with a man in Chicago, and then I got down here and thought I saw an old steam train..."

"That's the kind they run for the tourists."

"It wasn't that train," he said. "It was the Monon, the same one you talked about, and it came out of a storm cloud of pure black, and there was a man in a hat hanging out of a boxcar filled with water..."

He spit all this out in a breath, hearing the lunacy in it but watching her eyes and seeing no judgment.

"And I've had headaches," he said, "awful headaches that go away quickly when I have another taste."

She looked down at the bottle. "Well, I wouldn't try any more of it."

"I don't intend to."

She fastened the cap again and then passed him the bottle. He didn't really want it back in his hands; it was nice to see somebody else handling it. He set it on the table beside her drink, and they both eyed it with a mix of wonder and distrust.

"I just don't know what to think," she said.

"Nor do I," Eric said. Then he reached into his pocket and withdrew the microrecorder, rewound it without comment, and pressed play. Their voices came back, discussing the water, repeating all of those things that had just been said. He played about thirty seconds of tape, then shut it off and put the recorder back in his pocket. Anne McKinney was watching him with both knowing and astonished eyes.

"That's why you're taping everything. You want to be sure you're not imagining it. You want to be sure it's real."

He managed a weak smile and a nod.

"Son," she said, "you must be scared to death."

20

Danny came by in midafternoon, and Josiah was feeling fine, having spent the day sanding and painting the porch rails, with a beer or three for company. Funny, too, because those porch rails had needed paint for years, and he'd never gotten around to it. He'd bought the paint damn near a year ago, figured on tackling the job the next day, but the next day got away from him and soon the paint cans were covered with dust and cobwebs and the porch rails looked worse than ever.

Today, though, he got to the job simply because he needed something to busy himself with. It was a fine day, warm and filled with promise, one that called for doing something beyond sitting on your ass. Most weekends, Josiah was more than content to sit on his ass; he spent Monday through Friday working for other people, figured he'd earned himself a couple days of doing jack shit. Something was different today, though, in his mind and in his body, as if that evening wind that blew up while he slept on the porch had carried some sort of energy right through his skin. Mark it on your calendars, folks — as of May 3, Josiah Bradford was no longer content to bide his time.

It was a shame to involve somebody like Danny Hastings in such a plan as this, but fact was, there were some things you couldn't do alone. Some things called for a bit of help, and though Danny wasn't ideal in a lot of ways, he was loyal to a fault. They'd been brought up near as family, though they weren't blood-related, and Josiah had spent much of his childhood kicking the shit out of Danny and then watching the little freckled bastard come ambling along for more, like a dog that doesn't know how to stop loving its master regardless of the whip. Danny was fire tested by now.

When Danny arrived in his Oldsmobile Cutlass with the mismatched door, Josiah was pacing the porch with paintbrush in hand, looking for places that needed a touch-up and not finding any. He'd done a thorough job. The house — if it could be called that — was a one-bedroom, cracked-slab-on-sloping-grade shit pile that Josiah never could figure why he'd purchased. It had been a bank repo, bought for a song but still overpriced, and there wasn't a thing desirable about it except for the fact that it was located within a sprint-car race of what had once been Bradford property. There had been a good-size parcel in Bradford hands once, and generation by generation, it got sold off in bits and pieces to keep the bill collectors at bay, pissed away until there wasn't anything left at all. Why he wanted to be close to those memories he didn't know, but somehow he'd found himself drawn back here.

"Hell," Danny said, walking up beside Josiah, cigarette dangling from his lips, "I was close to certain you wasn't never going to get that painted. What got into you?"

"Boredom," Josiah said. There was something about the

porch rails that offered him a surprising amount of satisfaction, his work shining clean and white and stark under the sun. It had the shine of achievement.

"Looks nice, though."

"Don't it?"

"Better'n you anyhow. That black boy poked you good, didn't he? Your eye looks like hell."

"It was a bullshit sucker punch," Josiah said and walked away. He went to the spigot that hung loose from the foundation—he'd been meaning to mortar it back in for years—and, turning on the water, put the brush under the stream and massaged it with his fingers, watching the white paint wash away from the bristles and waiting on his anger to do the same. Last thing he wanted to hear about was his damn eye.

"I got a funny story," Danny began, but Josiah lifted a hand to shut him up, not enough patience in him to listen to Danny carry on about some bullshit or another.

"You hear what I asked you earlier?" Josiah said.

"About making some money?"

"That's the one."

"I heard it, yeah."

"And you'd like to be in on that."

"You was to twist my arm enough, I'm sure I'd agree to it."

"Even if it was the sort of thing could get you in a piece of trouble if you were dumb enough to get caught."

Danny's florid face went grave and he took the cigarette from between his lips and tossed it down in the weed-riddled gravel drive, smashed it out with his boots. Wasn't like he could be shocked by the suggestion—he and Josiah had done some law breaking in their time—but he didn't look thrilled by it either.

"I hope you ain't talking about cooking crank," he said.

"Hell, no."

That seemed to put Danny's mind at ease. He'd had a buddy, a guy they all called Tommy Thunder for no reason Josiah could ever recall, who blew up his trailer and killed himself while attempting to fine-tune a batch of meth. Danny, who'd sampled the drug as a user and mover prior to that occasion, had steered clear of it since. Only took one explosion to get his attention.

"All right. Good. But what is it you're thinkin' of?"

Josiah went up the porch and into the kitchen, came back out with two Keystones and handed one to Danny and cracked the other open for himself.

"You ever lift your head up when you're pulling weeds down at that damn hotel?" he asked. Danny also worked on the grounds crew; he had, in fact, gotten Josiah the job.

"Every day," Danny said cautiously. He hadn't opened his beer yet.

"You noticed any signs up lately?"

"Always signs up."

"Uh-huh. I'm talking 'bout one in particular. List of things going on down there, conventions and tours and shit."

"I know it."

"You noticed what convention's heading in next month?"

Danny shook his head.

"Gemstones," Josiah said. "Gonna have an exhibit down in the lobby, cases of diamonds and rubies and shit. A pile of stones worth millions, Danny. Millions."

Danny's face went sour and he took a few steps to the side, started to lean on the railing, then remembered it was wet and stopped himself.

"A thing like that comes rolling into your town," Josiah said, "you'd be fool not to capitalize on it."

"You got to be kidding," Danny said.

"Kidding hell. We're going to get those stones. Won't be all that hard either. See, the way I got it figured, a fire clears that building out, and fast. With all the liabilities and shit they got to consider? Man, first flame goes up, that place empties out."

"Josiah . . . you don't think them guys who own the stones have thought of that?"

"They can think of it all they want, point is they can't *stop* it. You have any idea the sort of scene you'd have down there with a fire going? They call that chaos, son, and you know what happens during chaos? Shit gets lost."

"You think they're not going to notice—"

"'Course they're going to *notice,* numb nuts, what I'm saying is by the time they do, it'll be too late. We get a fire going, get the building empty and the sprinklers on and then hit those cases fast and get out. You don't got to worry about alarms because there'll already be a thousand going off, a few more ain't gonna mean a damn thing."

"All them stones is, like, registered or whatever," Danny said. "You can't sell them. Where we gonna sell them? Go on up to the pawnshop and sell stones like that?"

"We won't sell them here."

"Well, I know that, but where do you think we're going to do it? We could go all the way across the country—"

"Won't sell them in this country," Josiah said, voice soft, and that brought Danny up, his version of a thoughtful expression coming on.

"I'm getting out," Josiah said. "You can come or not, it ain't my concern. But I am getting *out* of this place."

"It's a dumb idea," Danny said, and the audacity of that blew Josiah away. Danny Hastings calling *him* dumb? He should've swung on him, knocked the red hair right off the top of his head. He didn't, though. Instead he just stood there and stared. Something was odd about what Danny had just said, and it took a minute but then Josiah figured out what the odd quality was—Danny had been *right*. It was a dumb idea.

Dumb, but not impossible. And Josiah Bradford was just about ready to take those odds, like one of the fools who went down to the casino on Friday night knowing they'd get cleaned out but not giving a shit. Worse came to worst, they'd remember Josiah in this town. They'd damn sure do that.

"It can be done," he said, but there wasn't much vigor in his voice. "If you don't have the balls, all right. But don't you tell me it can't be done."

Danny was quiet. After a time he opened his beer and then they drank in silence for a while, standing there awkwardly because they couldn't lean on the rail. Josiah went over and sat on one of the chairs and Danny followed and took the other.

"Story I had to tell you is that I spoke to my grandpa today. He said a man's in town asking about old Campbell."

Josiah frowned and lowered his beer. "That same son of a bitch I told you about?"

"The black kid? No. Said there's another one now. This one is doing some kind of movie. Black kid is helping him."

"A movie about *Campbell*?"

This was some kind of strange. Josiah's great-grandfather had been the subject of plenty of old Edgar's rants over the years, but who in the hell would want to make a movie about him?

"Edgar's addled," he said. "A *movie*?"

"What he told me," Danny said, "was that some guy was down from Chicago working on a movie and wanted to ask about Campbell today."

"Well, I don't know why anybody would want to waste their time on him. Campbell left a lot of nothing behind, and I'm still living off that today."

Danny said, "Well, that's what I was wondering. If what this

guy told Grandpa is true, and he's making a movie about somebody in your family, don't he owe you something?"

It was a fine question. A *fine* question. What right did strang-
ers have to go wandering around asking about Josiah's own
blood? Let alone turn a profit from it?

"You said these guys are headed down to see Edgar today?"

"That's right. I was going to go down there myself, make sure
they wasn't running some sort of scam like the ones you hear
about with older folks, but you'd told me to come by..."

Josiah finished his beer, crushed the can, and tossed it aside.

"We'll take my truck."

21

Eric left Anne in the rotunda when Kellen called to say he was nearing the hotel, took the bottle back to his room, and then went outside to wait. He was feeling better after having the elderly woman confirm all of the things he'd seen in the bottle.

Kellen pulled up outside the hotel in his Cayenne with the windows down and hip-hop music thumping from the speakers, old stuff, Gang Starr that had probably come out when Eric was in high school and Kellen was, what, seven? Eric had to suppress a smile as he got inside the car. A midthirties white guy like him sitting in a Porsche listening to rap—ah, this was almost like being back in L.A.

"You feeling all right?" Kellen asked when Eric climbed in.

"Yeah. Why?"

"Look pale."

"I'm white."

"Knew there was something funny about you." Kellen pulled away from the hotel. He was wearing jeans and a shiny white T-shirt made from one of those fabrics that were supposed to wick moisture, along with sunglasses and a silver watch.

"Are you close to your brother?" Eric asked, looking around the Porsche and thinking about the source of it.

"Oh, yeah. We talk about three, four times a week."

Eric nodded.

"You're wondering if it's hard," Kellen said. "Being his brother. Being the unfamous one."

"No, I wasn't," Eric lied.

"Man, everybody wonders. It's cool, don't worry about it."

Eric waited.

"I love my brother," Kellen said. "I'm proud of him." The fierceness in his voice seemed directed at himself, not Eric. "But the truth? No, it's not easy. Of course not."

"I wouldn't think so."

"I was supposed to be a professional basketball player. That was my destiny. I was certain of it. By the time I was in eighth grade, I was six four, and I was an *athlete,* you know? In AAU ball I had coaches coming to see me from the ACC, Big Ten, Big East, all of 'em. This at fourteen.

"I was a great student, too, reading books all the time. But you want to know why? This is the truth, man, I swear it — I was working on my image for when I joined the league. The NBA. I was going to be a paradox, you know, the professional athlete who was also a scholar. I had this plan for it, how in press conferences I was going to make comparisons between ball games and battles, coaches and generals, referees and diplomats. I would actually plan the interviews in my head, no lie. I would *hear* them, man, hear what these announcers would be saying about me, hear it like it was real."

Eric looked away, feeling embarrassment not for Kellen, but for himself. Kellen was describing a child's fantasy. He was also describing Eric's twenties. And, hell, most of his early thirties, when mythical movie reviewers had raved constantly about films he would now never make. Was just a matter of time, he'd known, until the fantasies became the facts. He'd been sure of that.

"When you're real young, all the coaches care about are tools," Kellen said. "And, brother, I had them. Size, speed, strength. Didn't have the feel for the game that some of the other kids had, but that comes with time, right? Well, it didn't come for me. Ever. I was hearing the word *focus* so much it should've been my name, but I just couldn't get into the flow the way I needed, could never lose myself in the rhythm of it. By high school, when other kids caught up in size, that was showing."

They were driving out through the hills south of the hotel now, winding country roads.

"My brother feels that game," Kellen said. "When he plays it, there isn't anything else there. *Nothing.* He sees it all before it happens; even as a kid he was like that. He'd come down the lane on a fast break, go right to left, then somebody would step out to cut him off, and he'd see it just before they committed, and then dish . . . he was slick. No question. But he was a kid, too, and scrawny as hell. So it was no big deal."

Eric was silent, waiting.

"My junior year of high school," Kellen said, "I had a game in front of some major coaches. And I just butchered it. Scored thirteen and had eight rebounds but damn near double figures in turnovers, too. They had this small, fast team that ran a press the whole time and just rattled the hell out of me. I couldn't handle it. Each time I'd make a decision on what to do with the ball, it was a half second too late. Just a disaster.

"So that's on a Friday night, and the next afternoon I go with my parents to watch my brother's eighth-grade game. And Darnell, he just ran on 'em. That's all. Not a soul on that court could even *imagine* playing at his level. He drove anytime he felt like it, got shots anytime he wanted them, made passes when he didn't, stole the ball from the other team like they'd left the doors unlocked and ladders at the windows. It was filthy. I went out on the court after the game and I congratulated him, but it was stiff."

He ran a palm over the back of his head, leaned forward, close to the steering wheel.

"That night, he's sitting in the living room watching TV, and I walked in and changed the channel without saying a word. He got pissed, naturally, and I just went after him. Tackled his ass over the couch and hit him and had my hands around his throat when my dad came in and dragged me off."

He gave a small, wry smile. "My father, he is not a small man. He took me out in the yard, and he just whipped my ass. Knocked me up one side and down the other and then kept coming, and the whole time he's doing it, he's saying, *Who you mad at? Who you mad at?* Over and over in this real soft voice, *Who you mad at?* Because he'd been at my game and then at my brother's, you know, and he understood what was going on. He understood it better than I did."

"Did you end up playing college ball?" Eric said.

"No. I had scholarship offers to small D-1 schools, but nowhere elite, and if I couldn't play at that level, I didn't want to play at all. Some people would call that quitting. I call it understanding. Because I never quit playing, I busted my ass right up until the last second of my high school career. But basketball, it was not my game. And I came to understand that. I had this real high grade point average, which was supposed to be like a complement to my game, right? Well, that changed. I refocused. Got an academic scholarship and then a degree and then a master's, and now I'm closing in on the doctorate. I am *good* at what I do, right? But it's not playing ball. That's not quitting, though. That's changing. That's growth."

"Good thing you're a likable guy," Eric said. "Because if there's anything more obnoxious than a wise old man, it's a wise young one."

"Man, it just sounds good 'cause I've had a lot of time to think on it," Kellen said with a laugh, and then he hit the brakes and twisted the wheel, taking a hard turn off the road and down onto a rutted gravel drive. "Damn. Almost missed it."

This was a far sight different from visiting Anne McKinney. Instead of the well-kept two-story home on the hill surrounded by windmills and weather vanes, there was a small house with warped and peeling siding and a front gutter that hung about a foot off the roof at one end. An old aerial antenna was mounted at the peak of the roof, tilting unnaturally and covered with rust. There was a trailer set on stone blocks no more than thirty feet from the house and only one gravel drive and one mailbox.

"You know which it is?" Eric said.

"He told me to come to the house."

Kellen parked in front of the trailer and they got out and closed the car doors. When they did, a dog with long golden fur rose from the tall weeds that grew alongside the block foundation. Eric tensed, thinking this was the sort of place where bite might precede bark, but then he saw the dog's tail wagging and he lowered his hand and snapped his fingers. The dog walked over with the stiff gait of arthritic hips and smelled Eric's hand, then shoved its muzzle against his leg, the tail picking up speed.

"You make friends fast," Kellen said.

It was a mutt, some blend of golden retriever and shepherd

probably, and was friendly as hell. Eric scratched its ears for a few seconds before moving on to the house, the dog following at his side like they'd been together forever. Only the screen door was closed, and when they got there, Kellen called out a loud hello instead of knocking.

"It's open," someone on the other side said.

Kellen pulled the screen door back and the dog immediately started through. Eric made a grab at its neck but found no collar, and then the thing was inside the house, nails clicking on the old wood floor.

"What in hell you go and let him in here for?" the voice inside shouted. "He'll wreck this place faster than a hurricane."

"Sorry," Kellen said, and then he stepped inside and Eric followed, seeing Edgar Hastings for the first time, an angular-faced, white-haired man in a blue flannel shirt, sitting in a chair in the corner of the room. The TV was on but the volume was off. He had a pack of cigarettes in the pocket of the flannel shirt, and a crossword puzzle on his lap. One word had been filled in. There were a half dozen juice glasses on the end tables around him, all of them partially filled with what looked like Coke that had gone flat.

"I'll get him out of here for you," Kellen said. The dog was off in the kitchen now, regarding them from behind the table, and something about his expression told Eric those arthritic hips were going to get a hell of a lot looser when the dog wanted to avoid being caught and put out of the house.

"Oh, don't worry about Riley. I'll get him out in time. Go on and sit on the davenport there."

Davenport. There was a term Eric hadn't heard in a while. He and Kellen sat on the couch Edgar had indicated, a spring popping beneath Kellen, and Riley, as if aware that the threat of imminent eviction had passed, came back over and dropped to his haunches at Eric's feet.

"Nice dog," Eric said.

"My grandson's, not mine. He lives in the trailer." Edgar was regarding Eric with a harsh squint, skeptical. His face was spider-webbed with wrinkles, even his lips, and whiskers were scattered on his chin. "Now tell me why in tarnation you want to know about Campbell Bradford?"

"Well, Eric here is interested in someone of the same name," Kellen said, "but we're not sure if it can be the same person. His Campbell is still alive."

The old man shook his head. "Not the right man, then. He'd have to be long dead. Who sent you down here to ask about him?"

"A woman in Chicago," Eric said. "She's a relative of Campbell's, but the one she knows is ninety-five now."

"Different man," Edgar said flatly. "Should've made a phone call."

"Well, my Campbell says he grew up in this town. Left when he was a teenager."

"He's lying," Edgar said.

"You claim to know everyone in the town?"

"I know everyone has the name Bradford, and I *absolutely* know everyone has the name Campbell Bradford! Hell, anybody from my time would. Wasn't never but one Campbell Bradford in this valley, so if somebody's telling you otherwise, they're lying. Why in hell they would want to do that, though, I have no idea. He wasn't the sort of man you'd want to pretend to be. Campbell went beyond bad."

"Excuse me?"

"He was worthless as worthless gets, ran around with every gambler and crook ever came to town, didn't pay any mind to his family at all. Used to keep a hotel room just for fornicating, drank all hours of the day, never met a truth he wouldn't rather turn into a lie. When he ran off, he left his wife without a cent, and then she died and my parents had to take in the child. Those days, that's what folks would do. My parents was Christian people and they believed that's what they ought do, so that's what they done."

He offered the last part like a challenge.

"He doesn't sound impressive, I'll grant you that," Eric said.

"Campbell even went beyond all that," Edgar answered. "Like I told you, that man went beyond bad. There was the devil in him."

"You're telling me he was evil?"

"You say that like it's funny, but it ain't. *Yes,* he was evil. He was, sure as I'm sitting here. It's been damn near eighty years since the man left. I was a boy. But I remember him like I remember my own wife, God rest her. He put the chill in your heart. My parents saw it; hell, everybody saw it. The man was evil. Came to town in the middle of the high times, started in with the gamblers and the whiskey runners, made the sort of money doesn't come from honest work."

Eric felt an unpleasant throb in his skull, the headache level jumping on him.

"You told me Campbell didn't have any family left but Josiah," Kellen said.

"That's right. Josiah is Campbell's great-grandson, last true member of Campbell's line that there is, least as far as anyone around here knows. I'm as good as a grandfather to him myself, I suppose, though there's plenty days when I wouldn't want to claim that. Josiah's got him a streak of difficult."

Kellen hid a laugh by coughing into his fist, looking at Eric with amusement.

"I mean, we was all like family, you know, even though I'm not blood relation to that side," Edgar Hastings said. "Josiah's mother, she called me Uncle Ed, and I thought of her as a niece. We was close, too. We was awful close."

The room seemed smaller to Eric now, as if the walls had sneaked in on him during a blink, and he was more aware of the heat, felt perspiration worming from his pores and sliding along his skin. How in the hell could Edgar Hastings possibly wear a flannel shirt in here? He took his hand away from the dog's head and got a whine in response, one that sounded less like a complaint and more like a question.

"Like I told you, I just don't know who'd want to bother with a man like that in some sort of movie," Edgar said. "Not that I think most movies are worth anything anyhow, I got that TV set on from sunrise to sunup and don't never find anything a normal person would want to watch."

That one seemed to amuse Kellen again, but the smile left his face when Edgar flicked his eyes over, and Kellen said, "Um, so there's just no way the Campbell who left this town could still be alive up in Chicago?"

"No. He left in fall of 'twenty-nine, and he was in his thirties then."

Eric said, "Could it be he had another son after he left? Gave the son his name?"

"Hell, anything's possible after he left."

"And is there any chance that he came back to town, or brought his son back . . . ?"

"None." Edgar gave an emphatic shake of his head.

"You met the man personally," Eric said. "Correct?"

"Yes. I was only a boy when he left, but I remember him, and I remember being scared to death of him. He'd come by and smile and talk to me, and there was something in that man's eyes like to turn your stomach."

"You told me he was involved with bootlegging," Kellen said.

"Oh, sure. Campbell was supposed to provide the best liquor in the valley, and the valley was waist-deep in liquor during Prohibition. My father didn't drink much, but he said Campbell's whiskey made a man feel like he could take on the world."

"They still make booze that will do that," Eric said with a grin that Edgar wouldn't match.

"I've seen liquor turn good men sour," he said. "I used to have a glass or two, but truth is, I stayed away from it much as I could. It takes things from a man. You look at my grandson, he's thirty year old and can't even get off my property. Good boy, means well, but he lets the liquor take him. Wasn't for me, who knows where he'd be now, though. My wife had the best luck with him but she passed nine years ago."

"So he was a bootlegger," Eric said. "Illegal, yes, but not *evil*. I don't see—"

"Campbell saw to it that the law in town stayed bought off to certain enterprises," Edgar said. "All the sorts that he was involved in. When they didn't, they died. Was a deputy in town back then who was a cousin of my father. Good man. He wanted to investigate Campbell for killing a man had tried to run out on some debts. Wanted to charge him, thought he had the evidence. Told people in town he was going to nail Campbell to the wall. It's a turn of phrase, you know. Figure of speech."

Nobody spoke when Edgar paused, staring at Eric with flat eyes.

"They found that deputy nailed to his own barn wall. Literally. Had ten-penny nails through his palms, wrists, and neck. One through his privates."

The dog whined again at Eric's feet. Kellen said, "Did anyone try to arrest Campbell for that one?"

Edgar gave a small, sad smile. "I don't believe so. Matter of fact, I believe it made things a little easier on Campbell. Those who had thoughts of crossing him, well, maybe they changed their minds."

At that moment, there came the sounds of an engine and tires plowing through gravel, and Eric and Kellen twisted to face the window as the dog barked and stood.

It was an old Ford Ranger, two men inside. Came to a stop just behind Kellen's Porsche and then the doors banged open and the men stepped out. A shorter, redheaded guy from the passenger side, and from the driver's side a lean, dark-haired...

"Oh, shit," Eric said. The driver was Josiah Bradford.

"Who is it?" Edgar said, pushing up from his chair and peering out the window. "Oh, hell, it's just my grandson and Josiah. You might as well meet Josiah. Like I said, he's the last of Campbell's line."

"We've met him," Kellen said softly, and he stayed on the couch while Eric stood and went to the door.

22

ERIC WATCHED THROUGH THE screen door as the redheaded man walked to the porch and Josiah Bradford hung back, standing in the driveway staring at the Porsche. He was still studying it when his companion came through the screen door without a knock. Edgar Hastings's grandson entered with his chest puffed out, swaggering in bold and tough, like a cowboy crashing through saloon doors, but the sight of Eric standing so close to the door gave him an awkward moment of hesitation, one that Edgar filled by saying, "Damn it, Danny, show some manners."

The redhead looked at his grandfather, then back at Eric, and grudgingly put out his hand.

"Danny Hastings," he said.

When Josiah Bradford left the Porsche he moved quickly, up the steps and across the porch and through the door in a flurry. The door banged off the wall and his eyes found Eric's and then went to Kellen on the couch. Kellen gave him a little wave and a wriggle of the eyebrows, Groucho Marx if Groucho had been six foot six and black.

"Edgar, these sons of bitches are asking about my family?" Josiah said.

Danny still had his hand out, and Eric shook it, said, "Good to meet you. I'm Eric Shaw."

Danny pulled his hand back like it had touched hot coals, then stepped away hurriedly and looked to Josiah for guidance. Josiah stood in the doorway with his feet spread wide. Kellen still hadn't moved from the couch. Now he leaned back against the cushion, stretched, and laced his fingers behind his head, watching them with a lack of interest, as if the scene were unfolding on the TV instead of five feet away.

"You know them?" Edgar asked Josiah. Then to Eric, "Thought you was from Chicago?"

"I am," Eric said. "Just got in yesterday. Haven't been here for twenty-four hours yet, but it was long enough to meet Josiah and have him take a swing at me."

"I believe we encountered that difficult streak you spoke of," Kellen told Edgar.

"I'd have beat the shit out of you last night and I'll do the same today," Josiah said as he stepped into the living room. The dog hurried away into the kitchen and placed himself behind the table and chairs. Evidently Riley was acquainted with Josiah.

Josiah pulled up with his face a few inches from Eric's. "Who are you, and what business is it of yours to come into my town asking about my family?"

Eric was looking into the other man's weathered face, burnt by the sun and seasoned by the wind. The skin beneath his right eye was swollen and discolored, streaked with purple and black, a souvenir of Kellen's left hand. Eric found himself staring at it, something about the color of the bruise reminding him of the storm cloud he'd seen coming with the train. Above the injury Josiah Bradford's eyes were a dark liquid brown that seemed familiar. Campbell's eyes? No. Eric had just seen Campbell on the tape that morning, remembered well that his eyes were blue. But he'd seen these eyes, too. They were the eyes of the man on the train, the man who'd played the piano.

"I asked you a question, dickhead," Josiah said.

"I've been hired to do a video history," Eric said, not wanting to stare at Josiah Bradford's eyes any longer but unable to stop himself. "My client wanted me to find out about Campbell Bradford. I didn't know a damn thing about you, your family, or anybody else here until I got down here yesterday. Sure as shit didn't expect to have you acting like an idiot the first night I got in town, begging for a fight."

The longer Eric looked into Josiah's eyes, the worse his headache became. It had swelled into a pain so intense and so demanding that even the conflict of this moment couldn't distract him from it, and he turned away from him and sucked air in through his mouth, wincing and lifting his hand involuntarily to the back of his head.

"You been fighting again?" Edgar said. "Josiah, I swear you're a lost cause."

"They was looking for trouble, Edgar."

"Bullshit."

"Ah, he was only joking around with us yesterday," Kellen said. "Say, Edgar, you ever hear the one about the nigger in the fur coat?"

Josiah lifted his arm and pointed at Kellen. "You watch your ass."

"You watch yours," Edgar shouted. "I won't have this carrying on in my house."

Josiah dropped his arm, ignoring the old man, and looked back at Eric. "I want to know why you're down here asking about my family."

"I already told you," Eric said, and he had to speak with his head turned sideways. He didn't like that body language; it suggested he was intimidated, but he also couldn't stand to look him in the eye, because when he did, the pain flared worse.

"You didn't tell me shit. Working on a movie, my ass. Where's the cameras?"

That made a smile creep over Eric's face.

"You think it's funny lying to me? I'll whip your ass right here."

"Like hell you will," Edgar said, and over by the door his grandson said, "Ease up, Josiah," in a voice that was near a whisper.

"Where's the cameras?" Josiah repeated.

"I had a little equipment malfunction this morning."

"I don't believe you."

Eric shrugged.

"Who's making the movie?" Josiah said. "And why?"

"I have no interest in answering that question," Eric said, and this time he got his head lifted and looked Josiah Bradford in the face, taking care to stare at the center of his nose and avoid a direct look into those liquid brown eyes.

"Well, boy, I'm about to give you the interest," Josiah said, stepping up and bumping his chest against Eric's. Eric held his ground as Edgar shouted at Josiah to back off and Danny Hastings shifted uneasily at the door. Kellen stretched his legs out and put his feet up on the coffee table and yawned.

"You got no right to be asking about my family," Josiah said, breath warm and reeking of beer. "You got questions? Then you'll pay for the answers. I got a financial right to anything you do that so much as mentions my family."

"No," Eric said, "you do not. Perhaps you've never heard the word *biography*. I wouldn't be surprised. Even if I want to make a movie about *you,* asshole, I'm legally entitled. The good news is, nobody in the world would be interested in seeing it. So rest assured, that won't be happening. Meantime, if you threaten me again or harass my friend or pull any more of your pathetic, childish shit, I'll have your ass thrown in jail."

"It's been there before," Edgar said from his chair. "Going to have to say something different than that to convince him."

"Shut up, Edgar," Josiah said, his eyes still on Eric.

"Hey," Danny Hastings said. "No call for that."

Eric said, "Thanks for your time, Edgar. You were a help."

He walked past Danny, then turned back when he had his hand on the door and watched Kellen get to his feet slowly, letting his full size unfold and fill the room.

"Get out," Josiah said.

Kellen smiled at him. Then he leaned across the coffee table and offered his hand to Edgar Hastings, passed very close to Josiah without touching him or looking at him, nodded at Danny, and joined Eric at the door. Eric pushed it open and they stepped outside. They were halfway to the car when Josiah followed to yell a parting line.

"You better forget you ever heard the name Campbell Bradford," he shouted. "All right? You better forget you ever heard his *name*."

Neither of them responded. Eric kept his eyes on the mirror as Kellen started the Porsche and backed around the pickup truck, but Josiah stayed on the porch.

"Well, that sure was fun," Kellen said as he backed out of the drive. "Made the trip down from Bloomington worth it."

"Sorry."

"No, no, I'm serious. I'd have driven an extra hour to see that.

You get a look at his eye?" He laughed. "Ah, that made my day. You notice he seemed a little less brave today? No punches, no jokes."

"I noticed."

"Yeah, well, black eye can do that."

There was a blue minivan pulled off on the side of the road not far from the house, and Kellen came dangerously close to sideswiping it, flying along at least twenty miles an hour over the limit.

Kellen looked over at Eric, eyes hidden by the sunglasses. "You mind my asking you something?"

"Go ahead."

"Seeing as how your Campbell doesn't seem to have existed in this town . . . have you stopped to consider that he might be a liar? Might have been pretending to be somebody else for his whole life?"

"Yeah."

"In which case, he's successful, rich, and has a family," Kellen said, "but he assumed the identity of an asshole from a small town in another state. Why in the hell would anyone do that?"

"I think that," Eric said, "is about to become a really important question. I got one other thing I could throw at you, too, but my guess is after you hear it, you'll probably want to kick me out of your car."

Kellen tilted his head, confused. "What?"

"It's going to sound crazy, man."

"I can dig crazy."

"See the thing is . . . I've seen Josiah's great-grandfather before. I've seen *that* Campbell. I'm almost sure of it. And he's not the same guy as the one I met in Chicago."

"Then, where did you see him?"

"In a vision," Eric said, and Kellen pursed his lips and gave a slow, thoughtful nod — *Oh, sure, in a vision, of course.*

"You don't have to believe that," Eric said, "but before you make any judgments, I've got a bottle of water I'd like to show you."

23

A T FIVE THE BAROMETER dropped a bit and the western sky began to fill with tendrils of clouds. They were cirrus, rode very high in the atmosphere, twenty, thirty, even forty thousand feet. The name was a Latin term for a lock of hair, and that's exactly what they looked like today, fine wisps of white up there against a backdrop of cobalt blue.

They seemed almost stationary, trapped near the western horizon, but Anne knew that in reality they were moving along just fine. Problem was, they were *so* high that their speed didn't show itself. They were serene clouds, looked still and peaceful, but they heralded a change, too. High cirrus clouds like that signaled a pending deterioration in the weather and stronger winds on the way. There was even an expression for it—*See in the sky the painter's brush, the winds around you soon will rush.* Interesting thing about today's clouds was that the wind was *already* rushing. Had been since yesterday. So if this meant something stronger was on the way...

She logged the changes in her notebook and then went inside and prepared a vegetable soup. The weather changes didn't hold her mind as they normally would. Her thoughts were on the strange man from Chicago, Eric Shaw, and that bizarre bottle of Pluto Water. She'd never seen anything like it. So cold. And the man himself, well, he was scared. That much had been obvious.

She'd heard plenty of folklore about Pluto Water, but even the wildest tales had always claimed it to be a cure, not a curse. She couldn't remember a single story about visions or premonitions. The town had its share of ghost stories, sure, but none connected to Pluto Water. She believed Shaw, though, believed at least that the visions hadn't come until he'd tasted the water. And she wasn't all that surprised.

This valley, her home for so many years, so many decades, was a strange place. It was a spot touched by magic, of that she was certain, but ill winds often followed the favorable ones here, ebbing flows of wealth and poverty, glory and tragedy. Everything about the valley seemed in a permanent state of flux unlike any other place she'd known. She had some ideas on it, too, but they weren't the sort you told people about. No, ideas like that would get you laughed at mighty quick.

She put the soup on the stove and then left the kitchen and faced the stairs that had stood for weeks without supporting so much as a footstep. Well, time to go up. She used the railing and went slowly and tried not to think about a fall, got to the top, and then walked into one of the empty bedrooms, the one that had once been home to her daughter, Alice, and pulled open the closet door. A stack of cardboard boxes faced her, musty and dust-covered and taped shut. A few years ago she'd have remembered which box held the bottles, but it had been a long time since she'd opened them and now she had no idea. Nothing to do but start at the top then. They were heavier than she'd expected, the sort of thing she had no business trying to move by herself, but she knew all the contents were carefully wrapped and would hold up to a little jostling. She dragged the first one off the top until it started to fall and then got her foot out of the way just in time. It hit the floor with a loud thump, dust rising. She got her sewing scissors and set to work on the tape.

The bottles didn't turn up until she'd reached the third box from the top, and by the time she got that one open, her joints were screaming and she felt exhausted and didn't think she'd even be able to eat the soup, wanting only to get off her feet and shut her eyes. Then she got the tape off the third box and her spirits lifted, success bringing some energy back. There were nearly thirty different bottles in the box, all protected by the Bubble Wrap and labeled with a date. It took her only a few minutes to find a match for the one Eric Shaw had shown her. There was a piece of masking tape stretched across the wrapping, the year *1929* written on it. She'd been right.

She unwrapped the bottle and held it in her hand. It felt cool, but naturally so, the way glass was supposed to feel. Inside, the water was a little cloudy, but not so grainy and discolored as what she'd seen in Eric Shaw's bottle.

She left the boxes on the floor. It was one thing to tug them down, another to lift them back up. With the bottle in hand she went back downstairs, checked on the soup, and then called the West Baden Springs Hotel and asked to be put through to Eric Shaw's room. The phone rang several times, and then she got a machine.

"This is Anne McKinney. I have an idea. . . . I'm not sure if it'll be any help, but I don't see where it could do any harm either.

I found a bottle that's the twin of yours. Only one I have from that year, and it's still full. Never been opened. I'll let you take it. My idea was that you could find a place to test the water. I don't know who'd be able to do it, but surely there's a laboratory somewhere that can. They could analyze both of them, and tell you what the difference is. There's something in your Pluto Water that's not in mine. It might be a help to you if you knew what that was."

She left her number, hung up the phone, and went out to the porch. Her back throbbed when she pushed open the door. Outside the windmills were turning fast and steady, and the cluster of cirrus clouds that had stood in the western horizon at her last check were now directly overhead. The air was fragrant with the smell of rhododendrons and the honeysuckle that grew along the side of the house. An absolutely gorgeous day, but still that wind blew, and those clouds, they were warnings.

24

KELLEN CAGE SAT IN the desk chair and stared at the green bottle, touched it gently with his fingertips, and then pulled them back and studied the traces of frost as they melted away, leaving a wet shimmer on his dark skin. Eric had told him all of it by now, and Kellen hadn't said much yet. He'd held Eric's eye contact throughout, though, and that was promising. One thing Eric had taken away from years of gradually deteriorating meetings with studio execs — when people questioned your judgment or believed you flat-out crazy, they began to find other places to look during a conversation.

"I can believe this shit would give you hallucinations," Kellen said. "What I *can't* believe is that you ever drank it in the first place. Looks nasty to me."

"It was," Eric said. "The first time, at least. The second time, it was fine. And that last time, this morning? Stuff was *good*."

Kellen took his hand off the bottle and scooted the chair back a few inches.

"Whole time we been talking, it just gets colder and colder."

"Uh-huh."

Kellen eyed the bottle distrustfully. "Good news is, maybe the visions will go away if you don't take any more of it."

That was probably true, but while the hallucinations were terrifying in their vividness, the other side of the coin was marked by what he'd come to think of as withdrawal symptoms, the headache and vertigo and dizziness. His head was throbbing as badly as it had all day, and even while Kellen sat there and told him how repulsive the Pluto Water looked, Eric found himself wanting another sip. Just something to take the edge off the blade that was turning slowly in his skull, a blade that seemed to have found its way to a whetstone in the past half hour. Withdrawal, indeed — he craved that infamous hair of the dog.

"Likely your mind is just spinning out from whatever's in the water," Kellen said.

"I'm telling you," Eric said, "that guy in the train, his eyes were a perfect match for Josiah Bradford's."

"I believe it. But you'd already seen Josiah's eyes. Got an intense look at them last night. So they were already in your brain, something for your mind to fool around with when the water took you on a trip."

Possible, but Eric wasn't convinced. That man on the train had been Campbell Bradford. He was sure of that in the same way that he'd been sure they had the wrong valley on that film about the Nez Perce, and in the same way he'd been sure of the importance of that photograph of the red cottage in Eve Harrelson's collection.

The phone on the desk began to ring. Kellen looked at him

questioningly, but Eric shook his head. Let it go to voice mail. Right now he didn't want an interruption.

"I guess if it's more than a drug effect, you'll know soon," Kellen said.

"What do you mean?"

"If it's a drug effect that gives you straight-up hallucinations, then they'll stay random, right? You'll start seeing dragons on the ceiling next. But if it's something else, if you're seeing... ghosts or something, well, it'll be more of the same guy, right?"

More of the same guy. Eric remembered him in the boxcar, saw that water splashing around his ankles and the bowler hat he'd tipped in Eric's direction. No, he did not want to see more of that guy.

"I'm having visions," he said, "not seeing ghosts. Maybe that shit sounds one and the same to you, but it's not. Trust me."

Kellen leaned back, one shoe braced against the edge of the desk. Looked like about a size sixteen. "You know what got me interested in this place to begin with?"

Eric shook his head.

"My great-grandfather was a porter at this hotel back in the glory days. He died when I was eleven, but until then his favorite thing to do was tell stories about his time down here. He talked about Shadrach Hunter a lot. Had a theory that Campbell Bradford murdered the man, like I said earlier, and that it was over a dispute concerning the whiskey Campbell ran through this town. He talked about the casinos and the baseball teams and the famous folks who came down. All those stories about what it was like to be a black man in this town in those times are what gave me my original interest. But those weren't the only tales he told."

Eric said, "Don't give me ghost stories."

"Don't know if you could call them ghost stories, really. The man did believe in spirits, though—he called them *haints*—and he thought there were plenty of them down here. An unusual number, according to him. And they weren't all bad. He thought there was a mix of both, and that there were a lot of them here. What he told me was that there was a supernatural charge in this valley."

"A charge?"

"That's right, just like electricity. Way he explained it to me was to think of it as a battery. He said every place holds a memory of the dead. It's just stronger in some than in others. A normal house, according to old Everett"—there was a smile on Kellen's lips but his eyes were serious—"was nothing more than a double-A battery, maybe. But some places, he said, it's more like they've got a generator going, working overtime."

"This hotel is one of those places?"

Kellen shook his head. "Not the hotel. The whole valley. He thought there was more supernatural energy in this place than anywhere else he'd ever been."

"That a place would hold a memory of the dead, I could believe," Eric said. "Hell, I have to believe it, with the experiences I've had. But the idea of a ghost, of anything that can actually affect things in the world, I cannot buy."

"This valley is a strange place in a lot of ways."

"So it is. But there's strange, and then there's the idea of active ghosts. You don't believe in the latter, do you?"

Kellen smiled. "I'm going to quote old Everett on this one, brother. 'I ain't a superstitious man, but I know better than to walk through a graveyard after dark.'"

Eric laughed. "It's a good line."

They looked at each other in silence for a while, as if neither one really knew how to redirect the conversation now that ghosts had become a focal point of it. At length, Kellen nodded at the phone, which was now blinking red.

"You got a message."

Eric picked up the phone and played the message. Anne McKinney. He was listening with half attention at first, but then her words clarified and he focused. What the old lady was suggesting was a hell of an idea, actually. He wrote her number on the pad beside the desk, deleted the message, and turned back to Kellen.

"Remember the woman I told you about who came by to see the bottle? She's got a match. Same bottle style, same year, never opened."

"Let me guess," Kellen said. "It ain't covered in frost."

"No. But her idea was that I could take that water and mine somewhere to have them compared. Chemically."

Kellen tilted his head and pursed his lips in a way Eric was beginning to recognize as one of his habits and nodded slowly. "That could be worth trying. And I might be able to help. Well, my girl might. She was a chemistry grad student at IU, spent the last semester studying for the MCATs. If there's somebody local who can run an analysis on it, she might know who."

"Fantastic," Eric said, and though this suggestion of Anne McKinney's was a small thing, it felt bigger, because it gave him some kind of action to take. Because it gave him some sense — or some illusion, maybe — of control.

"You might not have the need for it, running on ghost-water the way you are, but I could stand to get a meal," Kellen said.

"Actually, I need to eat. Haven't had a damn thing all day. But do you care if I run up to get the bottle from this woman first? I'd like to have it."

"Nah, man, I'll drive."

Eric called Anne McKinney back, thanked her for the offer, and said they'd be by to pick the bottle up. She told him that was fine, but she sounded different than she had that afternoon. Less spark. Tired.

The sun was low and obscured by the hills west of the hotel as they came outside and walked to the parking lot. There was a blue minivan beside Kellen's Porsche. Eric didn't pay it any mind until the driver's door opened and a man in a sweat-stained polo shirt stepped out and said, "Slow down, Mr. Shaw. I'd like to have a word."

The driver was a short but well-muscled guy of about forty, bald except for razor-thin sidewalls of dark hair above his ears. He stood ramrod straight and with his shoulders back, a military bearing. Cold blue eyes, a BlackBerry in a leather case clipped onto his belt.

"Should I know who you are?" Eric said, coming to a stop as Kellen walked on to his Porsche and leaned against the hood, watching them, curious. He had his sunglasses on, and when the stranger glanced in his direction, Eric could see his reflection on the golden lenses.

"Mr. Cage," the guy said, nodding.

"Wow," Kellen said, "he knows everybody."

"Just need to take a minute of your time if I could."

"Then you better tell us who you are," Eric said.

The bald man took out a business card and passed it to Eric. *Gavin Murray, Corporate Crisis Solutions,* it said. Three phone numbers and a Chicago street address.

"I don't have a corporation," Eric said, "or a crisis."

He moved toward Kellen's car and when he did, Gavin Murray held up a hand, palm out, and said, "You may be headed toward a crisis, though, and I'd like to help you avert that. We should have a quick talk about what you're doing for Alyssa Bradford."

Eric stopped short and looked back at him, got a cool stare in response. Kellen slid his sunglasses off and clipped them to the neck of his shirt and looked at Eric with raised eyebrows.

"Like I said, he knows everybody."

"I do, Mr. Cage. I'm awfully quick when it comes to getting to know people. Congratulations on your brother's success, by the way. Hell of a ballplayer. And your father-in-law, Mr. Shaw, why, he's sold a lot of books, hasn't he? Oh, I know you're separated from Claire, but until the divorce is final, he's still your father-in-law."

He gave them an empty smile. "Now, how about that talk?"

"All right," Eric said, reaching up to squeeze the back of his neck, the headache seeming to be lodged there now, driven toward his spine. "Let's hear it."

"Good. But much as I've enjoyed meeting Mr. Cage, this is a private discussion. So if he'll wait for you for a few minutes, let's take a walk down there to the gardens."

Eric hesitated, but Kellen said, "Go on, man. This boy's got a pretty clear plan. Hate to get in his way."

"Appreciate that," Gavin Murray said, and then he turned and walked away from the cars, leaving Eric to follow.

25

I WASN'T PLANNING ON grabbing you in the parking lot like
that," Gavin Murray said as they walked away from Kellen.
"Was going to go into the hotel and ask them to send you down,
but before I had a chance, you walked out. Figured now was as
good a time as later."

Eric said, "I'm guessing Alyssa didn't send you."

"No."

"Who, then?"

"I can't answer that question," Murray said. "I'm in a confi-
dential business."

"And what business is that?"

"CCS is an investigations and solutions firm. Think of us as
troubleshooters."

"Traveled all the way down here from Chicago instead of making a phone call. This must be some trouble you're shooting."

"We like to conduct business in person. The discussion I need to have with you is important, and it's actually to your benefit."

"Is that your opinion or your client's?"

"Both, in this case."

Eric was silent. They were walking into the gardens now, toward the fountain.

"I understand that you're down here working on a video history," Murray said. "Sounds like an interesting line of work. Must be fun. But this isn't the project for you."

"No?"

"No."

"I think that could stand some clarification. Like who sent you."

"I'm really not at liberty to disclose that. I'm sure you understand."

"Sure," Eric said. "You're doing your job. Respecting your client's wishes, fulfilling their requests."

"Exactly."

Eric stopped walking. They were beside the fountain now, and a strong wind pushed fine drops of spray across his skin.

"Well, that's what I'm doing, too," he said. "And it's what I'll keep doing, Gavin, old buddy. I've been paid, and I'll complete the job."

Gavin Murray didn't look up at him. He took a pack of American Spirits from his pocket and pulled one out, pausing to offer the pack to Eric, then sliding them back in his pocket when Eric shook his head. He lit the cigarette, took a deep drag, and exhaled smoke through his nose, gazing back up at the hotel.

"How much is she paying you?"

"That's both irrelevant and none of your business."

"I've been authorized to give you fifty thousand dollars to cease the endeavor."

"Hell," Eric said, "that's less than I'm making on it."

A lie, of course, but he was curious just how much this was worth to whoever was at the other end of Gavin Murray's puppet strings. Fifty grand was a hell of a starting point, one that put a prickle in his spine.

Murray smiled around his cigarette. "A negotiator. Well played. I can go as high as seventy-five while we stand here. You can ask for more than that, but you probably won't get it, and you know seventy-five is more than you could hope for."

"I'm not going to ask for more than that, and I don't *hope* for any of it. Go on home, Gavin. Sorry you wasted the trip."

"Give the self-righteous thing a rest, Shaw. I'm surprised at this. You were in the movie business for long enough that you should know how rare a sure-money offer is, and how fast they can go away."

"They go away fast," Eric agreed. "But you know what never does? Cocksuckers who try to use money as muscle. There seems to be an inexhaustible supply. Shit, L.A. alone has more than I ever cared to meet. But I met a lot of them, enough to get awfully tired of the act. So go on and call your client, tell him to roll his seventy-five or a hundred or two hundred grand up nice and tight and put it right up his ass."

He started away but Murray followed, saying, "You're too smart for this. You know how business works at this level. Money's a first attempt, and other leverage is found if it's needed."

Eric stopped walking and turned to face him. "What does that mean?"

Murray tapped ash out of his cigarette. "It's not a complex statement."

"It sure as hell better be. Because if it's as simple as it sounded, then you just threatened me, asshole."

Murray sighed and brought the cigarette back to his lips. "Guys like you are exhausting, you know that? There's no reason in the world—*none*—for you to be a stubborn bastard on this, but you still can't stop yourself."

"Must be nice to have a bank ledger where your ethics should be, Gavin. You'll probably go on to big things. Most people like that do."

"It would be a great idea to negotiate, Mr. Shaw. I can assure you of that."

"Negotiate with *who*? You offer me money, I damn well want to know where it's coming from." Eric studied him. "So which family member do you work for?"

"Excuse me?"

"The only person who'd be worried about what I'm doing would be somebody close to Campbell Bradford back in Chicago."

Gavin Murray smiled. "You would think that, wouldn't you?"

Eric waited but nothing else was offered. He said, "I'm done with you, Gavin. And tell whoever hired you that they can find me directly if they want to talk."

"I've got one more question," Murray said. "What exactly were you discussing with Josiah Bradford?"

Eric cocked his head. "You really do know everybody, don't you?"

That got a tight smile and a nod.

"What I told him was a private matter," Eric said. "But if you don't get the hell out of my sight, I'll go fill him in on some more things. Like the fact that somebody's in town waving seventy-five grand in my face. Wonder what they'd wave in his."

"Not a cent."

"I find that hard to believe. Looks to me like somebody's awfully concerned about the Bradford legacy. And probably the Bradford stock portfolio."

"Not true."

"No? Then what are you doing in beautiful French Lick, friend?"

Silence.

"Right," Eric said. "Well, enjoy your stay, buddy. And keep away from me."

This time, Murray let him go.

26

K ELLEN WAS WAITING IN the car with the windows down and music playing. He turned the volume down when Eric got in.

"So, who's that guy working for?"

"Someone who offered me seventy-five grand to go home."

Kellen leaned across the steering wheel, mouth agape. "What?"

Eric nodded. "Started with fifty, then bumped it up to seventy-five."

Kellen said, "What?" again as if the answer had never been offered.

"I know," Eric said. He was staring back down the hill, looking for Gavin Murray. He finally located him beside one of the gazebos, standing with a cell phone glued to his ear. Probably calling Chicago to provide the update and await instructions.

"Another family member would be my guess," Eric said. "Or

somebody from Campbell's legal team. The old man's dying, and he's worth a few hundred million. Could be worried about Josiah."

"You think?"

"Yeah. If Josiah's close blood to the old man in the hospital, he could make a compelling legal claim to compensation. Campbell abandoned the family. A few generations ago, maybe, but there would be plenty of lawyers who'd be happy to argue for reparations on Josiah's behalf."

"But you don't think the two Campbells are the same guy."

"No, I don't. Which makes this all the more interesting, don't you think?"

"Sure. Also makes me wonder what your client will have to say."

"Oh, yeah," Eric said. "She's getting a call. Right now."

Down by the gazebo, Gavin Murray lowered the phone and put it back in the case at his belt and lit another cigarette. He was leaning against the rail, staring up at them.

"Think that's a good idea?" Kellen said. "Telling her about this?"

"She has a better chance of understanding what the hell it's about than I do. How can it be a bad idea?"

Kellen shrugged, then waited while Eric dialed Alyssa Bradford's number. Cell first, then home. No answer. He left messages on both phones but no details, just a request to call him as soon as possible.

"Headache back?" Kellen said when he hung up, and Eric realized he'd been rubbing the back of his skull while he made the calls.

"Don't worry about it. Let's get moving. I told Anne we were on our way."

As they drove away from the hotel, Gavin Murray lifted a hand in recognition. He was on the phone again.

*　　*　　*

Josiah left Danny at his grandfather's and drove off without a word minutes after the Porsche pulled out of the drive. He considered following them, driving that polished piece of shit right off the road and hauling them out of it one at a time, administering the beating he should've issued at Edgar's house. They were out of sight, though, no car visible ahead except for a blue minivan pulled into the weeds.

Josiah blew past that and on into town, stopped at the gas station and put twenty dollars' worth into his empty tank and bought a six-pack, drank one down fast while he stood at the pump. Someone pulled in and tapped the horn, annoyed that Josiah was there blocking the pump while drinking a beer, but it only took one look to make the driver go on to the next available pump.

He threw his empty beer can into the trash and drove away from the station, heading home. His house was out in the wooded hills just east of Orangeville, surrounded by a few hundred acres of Amish farmland. They ran up and down the road in their buggies and sold vegetables in front of the farm, and early on, Josiah would hit the gas in his truck when he passed, let that oh-so-scary modern machinery roar at them. Made him laugh. Over time, though, he began to appreciate them despite himself. They were quiet neighbors, took care of their land, didn't bother him with noise or forced-friendly conversation or gossip. Minded their own, let him mind his. As it should be.

The porch looked clean and bright when he pulled into the drive, but it no longer satisfied him. He'd taken a hell of a one-two punch. Seeing those guys sitting in Edgar's living room was bad enough, but that had come right on the heels of Danny Hastings, old dumbass Danny, looking Josiah in the eye and telling him he thought Josiah's plan was stupid. And being right to say so.

Yes, this day was spinning away from him in an altogether unpleasant fashion. Hell, the whole weekend was. Had gone south fast and furious, starting last night. Things had been fine Friday morning, fine as they ever were, at least.

That was the problem, though—things never were fine and never were going to change. Not unless he took some action. He'd be sitting on the porch drinking piss-water beer and matching wits with Danny for the rest of his pathetic life, till his reflexes went and he could no longer handle the truck with booze in his veins and he put it off the highway and into the trees just like his worthless father had before him.

"Something's got to change," he whispered to himself, sitting there in the cab of the truck with sweat trickling along his neck and the beer warming in the sun while horses walked in circles at the Amish farm next door, turning some sort of mill wheel, their heads down the whole time, step after step after step. "Something has got to change."

He got out of the truck but didn't want to go in the house, didn't want to sit on the stained couch and look at the cracks in the wall and the sloped floor. The porch rail glinted under the sun, sure, but now he realized just how damn little the porch rail meant. The house was still a dump, with sagging gutters and a stain-streaked roof and mildew-covered siding. Sure, those things could be addressed, but it took money, and even then, what the hell was the point? Could only accomplish so much with polish on a turd.

Instead of going inside, he took the beer and set off on foot, walked through the backyard and into the field beyond, picking his way through the barbed-wire fence that separated the properties. He'd walk up into the wooded hills, have a few more beers.

He was halfway across the field, head bowed against the sun and the warm western wind, when he remembered the second half of his dream, the man waiting for him at the edge of the tree line. The thought was enough to make him look up, as if he'd see the old bastard standing out there. Wasn't anything in sight, but the memory chilled him just the same, thinking of the way the guy had been shaking his head at Josiah as the day faded away and the night came on. Weird damn dream. And that after the one on the train, the same man standing in the boxcar with water around his ankles.

We're going home to take what's yours.

There were those who believed dreams meant something. Josiah had never been of that breed, but today he couldn't help it, thinking about the man in the bowler hat. *Take what's yours,* he'd said. Wasn't much in the world that belonged to Josiah. Funny, though, him having a dream like that just when everyone was asking questions about his family. Who the hell would possibly care about Campbell at this point? Had been damn near eighty years since the thug hopped a train and disappeared.

Hopped a train. An old-fashioned train, with a steam loco- motive and a caboose, like the one in his dream.

"Was that you, Campbell?" Josiah said softly, tramping across the field, and he smiled. A bunch of crazy, stupid thoughts, that's what he was lost to today. Setting fires and stealing gems and see- ing his great-grandfather in dreams? He was coming unhinged.

The sun was hot and the beer cans clanged awkwardly against his leg as he walked, but he didn't mind. His shirt was soaked with sweat and gnats buzzed around his neck but that was fine, too. It felt good to be outside, good to be moving, good to be alone. He'd grown up in the woods and fields out here, spent more time in them than in his home. *Field runners,* Edgar used to call him and Danny. Old Edgar had done well by Josiah. Josiah's own family had been such a damned disaster that he'd as good as taken in with the Hastings instead. He and Danny had been close as brothers, and while Danny wasn't much in the brains department, Josiah had never minded that so much as he did lately. Fact was, he'd always liked Danny fine, just looked down on him a touch. Danny was a good man, but not one who was going to do anything with his life. Even when they'd dropped out of high school on the same day, it had felt like Danny was playing out his fate while Josiah was making a choice. Josiah was the half of the pair who would accomplish something, the half with ambition.

That had always been the notion in his head, at least. Now, though, he felt as if he'd sobered up and took a blink and realized there was nothing separating him from Danny at all, nothing that anybody else would see, at least, nothing tangible. They were both still in town, living in shitty houses and driving shitty cars and swinging weed eaters and hedge clippers and drinking too much. How in the hell had that happened?

The place he was headed today was a spot he'd found when he was a kid, twelve years old and hiking alone. Well, not hiking as much as running, with the sting of the old man's belt still on his back. They'd lived only two miles from where he did now, two miles separated by the fields he'd just come through.

That day he ran until his lungs were clenched tight as fists and his hamstrings were screaming, and then he'd slowed to a stumbling walk, moved through another field and into the woods, and found himself scrambling across the face of a steep hill. It was a difficult climb, overgrown and pockmarked with slabs of limestone. He'd heard a gurgling noise and frozen, listening and growing progressively creeped out because the sound was coming from *beneath* him. From right under his feet, he was sure of that, yet there wasn't so much as a puddle in sight.

He'd followed the sound, fought down through the trees, and found a cliff face, a good hundred feet of sheer rock leading to a strange pool of water below that had an eerie, aquamarine glow. The pool was still as a farm pond, but all around it the gurgling, churning noise of water in motion persisted. Birch trees had tumbled off the ridge and lay half in and half out of the water, their ghostly white limbs fading into green depths. All along the top of the cliff face, root systems dangled free, hanging across the stone like something out of one of those slasher movies set in the swamps.

The ridge ran around all sides of the pool, forming a giant bowl, and it took some effort for him to pick his way down to it. At the bottom the place seemed even more ominous than at the top, because here there was no getting out fast, and the wind picked leaves off the trees that rimmed the ridge and sent them tumbling down on you. Now and then one corner of the pool would seem to snarl, spitting water into more water, and beneath the rocks water trickled, always audible but invisible.

Josiah had never imagined such a place.

He'd risked another beating that night by telling his father about it, swearing the place was something magic, and the old man had laughed and told him it was the Wesley Chapel Gulf, or the Elrod Gulf if you were an old-timer, one of the spots where the Lost River broke the surface again, coughed up by the caves that held it.

"You stay away from there in flood season," the old man had warned. "You know where the water was today? Well, it'll rise up thirty feet or more along that cliff when the underground part of the river fills up, and it'll spin, just like a whirlpool. I've seen it, boy, and it's made for drowning. You go there in flood season and I'll tan your ass."

Naturally, Josiah had gone back to the gulf during the spring floods. And son of a bitch if the old man wasn't telling the truth for once—the water did climb the cliff face, and it did spin like a whirlpool. There was a shallow spot in the bowl-shaped ridge that held it, and the water broke through there and found a dry channel and filled it, rushing along for a piece and then disappearing into one of the swallow holes only to resurface a bit farther on.

It was one strange river, and it held Josiah's attention for most of his youth. He and Danny traced the dry channels and located the swallow holes, found more than a hundred of them, some drinking the water down in thirsty, roiling pools, others spitting it back to the surface as if disgusted. There were springs, too, some of them so small as to be missed unless you were standing beside them, springs that put off a potent odor of eggs gone bad. They even found traces of old dwellings scattered along the river and through the hills, rotted timbers and moss-covered slabs of stone.

The gulf became a regular spot for Josiah, but one he'd never hiked to with anybody but Danny until he was sixteen, when he brought a girl named Marie up to it one night. She'd bitched the whole way, said the place was creepy, then stopped him from putting his hand up her skirt and had been with another guy not a week later. After that, Josiah never took anybody else back.

Sometimes people came by and dumped trash down the slope and into the pool, and that incensed Josiah in a way few things ever could. He'd hauled countless beer cans and tires out of there, once an entire toilet. When he was in high school, the national forest claimed the property, realizing it was something special, and they cleaned it out and put up a sign and took to monitoring the place.

Today he climbed up to the east side of the ridge and picked his way down to a jutting limestone ledge that looked out over the pool below. He sat with his feet dangling off the ledge and cracked open a beer. It was lukewarm by now.

If he were on the opposite side of this same hill and the leaves were off the trees, he'd be able to look out to the house he'd grown up in, what was left of it, at least. Place had been vacant for ten years, and last spring a tree had come down and bashed a hole in the roof above the kitchen, letting the rain come in. He was surprised the county hadn't knocked the house down when they came to remove the tree.

The gulf was within walking distance of his childhood home, and within walking distance of his adult home. He was all of two miles from the place of his birth.

Two miles. That was how far he'd gotten in life. *Two fucking miles.*

He drank another beer as the sun sank behind the trees and the air began to cool. Down in the gulf, long trunks of fallen trees weathered to bone white faded into the shadows, the blue-green of the water edging toward black. Now and then there was a churlish splashing at the edge of the pool as the Lost River gave up more of its hidden water, and the wet whispering of it moving through the stone below ground was always present. He opened one more beer but didn't drink any, just set it beside him and stretched out on his back. He wanted to close his eyes for a piece. Try not to think about the man from Chicago or the one from the dream. Try not to think about anything.

27

ANNE McKINNEY ANSWERED THE door with bottle in hand. She smiled when Eric made introductions between her and Kellen but kept her hand on the door frame, too, looking less steady than she had earlier in the day.

"It's the same as yours, isn't it?" she said, offering Eric the bottle.

He turned the bottle over in his hand and nodded. Every detail was the same, but this one was dry and room temperature, felt natural against his skin.

"It's a perfect match."

"I don't know who you'd ask to compare them. Maybe it was a foolish idea."

"No, it's a great idea. Kellen knows somebody who should be able to help."

"Good."

"And you're sure you don't care? Because I'd hate to open this if I thought —"

She waved him off. "Oh, it doesn't matter. I've got more, and I doubt anybody will care much about them when I'm gone anyhow. I'll leave them to the historical society, but they're not going to miss one out of the lot."

"Thank you."

"How you feeling now?" she asked with what seemed to be genuine concern.

"I'm doing fine," he lied and then surprised himself by saying, "what about you?"

"Oh, I'm a little tired. Did more than I should have today probably."

"I'm sorry."

"Don't you worry about that. It's just been one of those days..." Her eyes drifted past him, out to the windmills that lined the yard and looked down on the town below like sentries. "Some strange weather coming in. If I were you two, I'd have an umbrella handy tomorrow."

"Really?" Kellen said, looking up at the blue sky. "Looks perfect to me."

"Going to change, though," she said. "Going to change."

They thanked her again and went down the porch steps and back to the car. The chimes were jingling, a beautiful sound in an evening that was going dark fast.

Kellen asked if he had a dinner preference, and when Eric said no, they ended up back at the buffet in the casino, because Kellen said he was "in a mood to put a hurting on some food." By the time they got inside, Eric's stomach was swirling and the headache had his vision a little cloudy, sensitive to the lights that surrounded them. All he needed to do was eat a little. Surely that was it.

When they entered the long, wide, and brightly lit dining room, the smell of the food was strong and immediate, and Eric had to hold his breath for a second to ward off the surge of nausea the odor brought. They followed the hostess to a table out in the middle of the room, and he wished she'd put them somewhere else, a corner maybe, or at least close to the wall. When she took their drink orders, he barked out, "Water's fine, thanks," just because he wanted her to go away, wanted everybody in the damn room to go away until he'd had a chance to get himself together. But Kellen was already heading toward the serving areas, so he followed.

The china plate felt heavy in his hands, and he grabbed at food without giving it much thought. He had a plate full of fruit and vegetables when he turned and found himself staring at the carving station, watching a heavyset man in a white apron work a massive knife through a roast. The knife bit into the meat and then the man leaned on it, using his weight to drive it through, and when he did, juice flowed from the meat and formed a pink pool on the cutting board and Eric's knees went unsteady and a hum filled his ears.

He turned fast, too fast, almost spilling the plate, and started for the table, which seemed miles away. His breath was coming in jagged hisses, and then the hum picked up in pitch and almost took his stomach with it. He got to the table, thinking that he just needed the chair, just needed to get off his feet for a moment.

For a few seconds, he thought that might actually do the trick. He leaned on the table with his forearms and concentrated on slowing his breathing, and he was just starting to feel a touch better when Kellen returned and sat before him with a steaming plate of food. Then the hum returned and his stomach went into the spin cycle.

Kellen was oblivious, chattering away while he set to work with a knife and fork, and Eric couldn't even speak, knowing only that he needed to get out of the room *fast*.

He lurched to his feet and bumped into his own chair but shoved past it, eyes on the exit and the hallway beyond, which seemed to be undulating, all the harsh white light in the room slipping into motion now as the hum in his ears turned to a roar. A warming sensation enveloped him and spread through his limbs and tingled along his skin as he passed the cashier's stand and kept moving toward the hallway, thinking, *I'm going to make it,* just before the warmth exploded into a scorching heat and the dancing lights went gray and then black and he fell to his knees and the room vanished around him.

A soft, sweet strings melody lifted him and guided him through the tunnel that led to consciousness. It was a beautiful sound, so soothing, and when it began to fade, he was racked with sorrow, hated to let it go.

He opened his eyes and stared directly into a glittering light fixture. Then a face floated down and blocked it, Kellen Cage's face, eyes grave. He was saying Eric's name, and Eric knew that he should answer but didn't want to yet, didn't want anyone to speak, because maybe if it was completely silent, he'd be able to hear that violin again.

The first coherent thought he had was of the cold. Where before the blackout his flesh had tingled with warmth there was now a deep cold, but it felt good. The warmth had been ominous, a harbinger of physical disaster, and the cold seemed to be his body's reassurance that it could handle the ailment on its own—*Don't worry, buddy, we got those boilers turned down for you.*

"Eric," Kellen said again.

"Yeah." Eric licked his lips and said it again. "Yeah."

"We got an ambulance on the way."

There were other faces over Kellen's shoulder, a security guard talking into a radio and then a cluster of curious onlookers. Eric closed his eyes, feeling the embarrassment of this now, realizing that he'd just fainted.

"No ambulance," he said with his eyes closed, and took a deep breath.

"You need to go to the hospital," said someone with a deep and unfamiliar voice.

"No." Eric opened his eyes again, then rose slowly, until he was sitting upright with his arms hooked around his knees for balance. "I just need some sugar, that's all. Hypoglycemic."

The security guard nodded, but Kellen's face said *bullshit*. A woman nearby murmured that her sister was hypoglycemic and then left to get him a cookie.

He was on his feet by the time she got back, and though the idea of food was sickening, he had to stick to the lie now, so he took the cookie and a glass of orange juice and got both of them down.

"You *sure* you don't want to go to the hospital?" the security guard said.

"I'm sure."

They called off the ambulance then, and Eric thanked the woman and the guard and made some lame joke to the rest of the onlookers about being happy to provide dinner theater. Then he told Kellen he wanted to head back to the hotel.

They went out and walked down the sidewalk in silence and crossed to the parking lot. When they were halfway out to the Porsche, Kellen said, "Hypoglycemic?"

"Sure. Didn't I mention that?"

"Um, no. Left that out."

They walked to the car and Eric stood with his hand on the passenger door handle for a few seconds before Kellen finally unlocked the doors. Once they were inside, Kellen turned to him.

"You really should be going to a hospital right now."

"I just need some rest."

"Just need some *rest*? Man, you don't even know what went on in there. One minute you were sitting at the table, next you were passed out in the hallway. Something like that happens, you don't rest, you talk to a doctor."

"Maybe I'll call somebody in the morning. Right now, I just want to lie down."

"So you can swallow your tongue or some shit in the middle of the night, die up in that room?"

"That's unlikely."

"Look, I'm just saying—"

"I *get it*," Eric said, and the force of his words brought Kellen up short. He studied Eric for a few seconds, then gave him a shrug and turned away.

"I appreciate the concern," Eric said, softer. "I really do. But I don't want to go to a hospital and tell them I'm having blackouts from Pluto Water, okay?"

"You think that was from the water?"

Eric nodded. "The headache came back and was getting worse. By the time we left Anne's, I was feeling bad. Thought maybe it would help if I just got some food."

"Didn't help."

"No. Sorry about your dinner, by the way. You were starving."

Kellen laughed. "Not a big deal, man. I can always eat. What you got going on, though . . . that's something needs to be figured out."

"Withdrawal symptoms," Eric said.

"You think?"

"Yeah. Definitely. The physical problems go away when I have more of the water and get worse the longer I go without it. Anne McKinney's right—I've got to figure out what's in that bottle."

"And until then?"

Eric was quiet.

"This is why I suggested a hospital," Kellen said. "I believe you—it's probably withdrawal from whatever is in that water. But if it's getting worse, you could be in real trouble. That act you pulled back there was scary, man."

"I could just take more of the water, if that'll relax you." It was supposed to be a joke, but Kellen tilted his head sideways, thoughtful.

"Wow, you'd be good in AA," Eric said. "That's not one of the ideas you're supposed to support."

"No, I was just thinking, what if you tried different water?"

"I drank about ten glasses of water today, trying to flush this out. Hasn't helped."

"Not regular water. Regular *Pluto* water." Kellen nodded at the bottle Anne McKinney had given him. "It's a thought, at least. Things get worse tonight, try her bottle before you go back to yours."

Kellen dropped Eric off at his hotel, and the look he had when Eric got out of the car was that of a parent watching a child wander toward traffic.

Eric's headache was whispering to him again by the time he got off the elevator, and the sense of defeat he had at that realization was heavy. He'd hoped that the episode during dinner had been punishment enough, that he'd earned a few hours of reprieve. Evidently not.

The message light on the room phone was dark and his cell

showed no missed calls. He felt a vague sense of apprehension over that, having expected Gavin Murray to try and make contact again, to put some other offer — or threat — on the table. He called Alyssa Bradford again and got voice mail. Annoyed, he waited ten minutes and called back, still with no success. This time he left a message. Call immediately, he said. There is a serious problem to discuss.

Serious problem seemed almost too light a phrase. Where was Gavin Murray now? The blue minivan hadn't been in sight when Kellen brought him back, but it seemed unlikely that Murray was driving back to Chicago already. Eric got his laptop out and logged onto the Internet, ran some searches under both Murray's name and the name of his company, Corporate Crisis Solutions. Didn't find much on Murray — his name on some roll of military personnel attending a reunion at Fort Bragg was the most noteworthy result. Bragg was home to the Special Ops boys.

Corporate Crisis Solutions didn't have much of a Web profile either. There was a company site, but it seemed intentionally vague. A few pages for private investigators offered links with CCS contact information. Hell, he should call Paul Porter, ask him what he knew. Paul had done twenty years as a criminal defense attorney before selling his first book and giving up the practice to write a series of best-selling novels about an intrepid crime-solving lawyer, no doubt some sort of pathetic wish fulfillment. Still, he was connected to the Chicago police and legal worlds both through his writing and his background, and he'd probably heard of the firm, and maybe even Gavin Murray.

"I won't give him the satisfaction," Eric muttered. That was just what Paul would want, wayward son-in-law calling for help. Son of a bitch had actually suggested once that he and Eric work together to shop the film rights for Paul's novels, which he'd been hanging on to all these years despite offers. *I could write, and you could direct,* Paul had said. Yeah, that would've been a hell of a pairing.

Eric had actually liked the guy all right at first. They'd gotten along just fine back when they were separated by a few thousand miles and Eric's career was on an upward trajectory. Paul hadn't displayed any less ego over his little series of detective novels back then, but it hadn't rankled Eric as much either. Probably because things were going well on his end. Gave him a layer of protection. It wasn't until they'd moved back to Chicago and Paul was underfoot at all times that it got really bad. All those damn suggestions of his, the ideas, story proposals—shit, they had never stopped.

He closed the laptop, beginning to suspect that staring at the screen was goosing his headache. He turned the lights off and put the TV on, tried again to distract himself from the pain. Over on the desk, Alyssa Bradford's bottle glittered and sweated, and Anne McKinney's stood beside it, dark and dry.

Let them sit, he told himself. *Let them sit there untouched. I know what's coming for me, and I can take it. I won't drink the water again, though.*

28

JOSIAH WAS BACK IN the gray city again, that colorless empire, and the wind blew through the alleys and whistled around the old-fashioned cars that lined the empty streets. A huffing noise filled his ears and he knew before he turned to look that it was the train coming on and thought, *I've had this dream before.*

But at least the train was coming back for him. Dream or no dream, he'd lost it last time, run after it and couldn't catch up and then found himself in that field walking hard against the dark. Yes, if the train came back around this time, he surely ought to take it.

He stood to the side and watched as it thundered toward him, stone dust rising from beneath its wheels, a funnel of black smoke pouring from the stack. All just as it had been. Good. Must be the same train.

It slowed as it passed, and again he could see the white car with the splash of red across its doors, the colors standing out so stark against all that gray. He walked toward it, eager now, as the locomotive whistle shrilled and the train lost momentum. This one was headed home. The man in the bowler hat had promised him that.

And there was the man, visible in the open boxcar door as he had been before. He wasn't leaning out of it this time but sitting with his arms resting on raised knees and his back pressed against the door frame. He lifted his head as Josiah approached, used one finger to push the hat up on his forehead.

"'Spect you want a ride," he said when they were close enough for words, and the smile was gone, the charm not present in his eyes this time.

Josiah said he'd be more than happy for a ride, provided they were still homeward bound. The man paused at that, considered Josiah through those dark eyes. Josiah could hear a gentle splashing from inside the car, saw drops of water coming out over the rim of the door frame and falling to the sidewalk below.

"Told you we was homeward bound last time through," the man said. "Told you there was a need to hurry should you want a ride."

The man seemed displeased, and that made Josiah's stomach tremble and his skin prickle as if from the touch of something cold. He told the man that he had desired a ride, indeed, and that he'd run in pursuit of the train, run as best as his legs could do, and still not caught up.

The man listened to that, then tilted his head and spit a plume of tobacco juice toward Josiah's feet.

"I was to tell you it's time to get aboard now, you'd take heed?" he said.

Josiah assured him that was a fact.

"You'd also understand," the man said, "I might be needing you for a piece of work when we get home."

Josiah asked what that work would entail.

"A good mind and a strong back," the man said. "And an ability to take direction. Might those be traits you possess?"

Josiah said they were, but he wasn't overly pleased at the prospect, and it must have shown in his face.

"You don't think that's a fair exchange?" the man asked, his eyes wide.

Josiah didn't answer that, and up ahead the steam whistle blew again and the engine began to chug. The man smiled at him and spread his hands.

"Well," he said, "you know another way of getting home, you're welcome to it."

Josiah was unaware of another way home, and he'd already missed this train once. Time came when you had to make a sacrifice or two in the pursuit of what you desired, and right now Josiah desired a ride home. He told the man he'd get aboard.

"About time," the man said, and then he rose to offer Josiah his hand and help him into the boxcar. When he stood, water streamed from his suit. Josiah edged closer to the train and leaned forward.

Took his hand.

Part Three

A SONG FOR THE DEAD

29

A N HOUR AFTER KELLEN dropped him off, Eric's headache
was back in full force, and he took more Excedrin and
drank a few glasses of water and turned the volume on the TV
louder, searching for distraction.

It didn't work.

By eleven he had the TV off and was holding a pillow over his
head.

I can beat it, he told himself. *I can wait this out. I will not drink
the water.*

The hum soon returned to his ears, quickly built to a bell-
clear ring. His mouth dried and when he blinked, it felt as if his
eyelids were lined with fine grains of sand.

*It's terrible, but it's real, too. These things are better than the alter-
natives. I am seeing nothing but the walls of this room and the furniture and the shadows, seeing no dead men in train cars filled with
water. This I can take. This I can bear.*

When the nausea caught him in full stride, he made it to the bathroom before vomiting, taking that as a comfort until the second wave hit and drove away what little strength he had left.

Let it come, he thought savagely as he lay with his cheek on the cool tile and a string of spit hanging from his lip. *Let it come with the best it has, because I'm not drinking that water, won't take a sip.*

The sickness returned, even though his body was empty, and then came again, and by the end, he could no longer lift himself from the floor, racked by vicious dry heaves that seemed to spread his ribs even while squeezing his organs, the headache a crescendo and his conviction a memory.

The visions were bad, yes, but these withdrawal effects, they could *kill* him.

His mind went to Kellen's suggestion, the words floating through his pain-fogged mind as he lay on the floor: *Things get worse tonight, try her bottle before you go back to yours.*

Anne's bottle was on the desk, looking as normal as could be. It had been when he last saw it, at least. That had been on his way to the bathroom, and who knew how much time had passed since then. Maybe five hours, maybe fifteen minutes. He really couldn't say.

He couldn't stand. Managed only to get to his hands and knees, wobbling and bumping against the door frame, spit hanging from his mouth, a human pantomime of a rabid dog. He crawled forward, felt the tile change to carpet under his hands, and went left, toward the desk. He blinked hard and his vision cleared and he became aware of a glow from the top of the desk, a pale white luminescence that seemed like a guiding light.

He pulled up then and came to an abrupt stop, the rabid dog told to heel.

The light was coming from the bottle. Alyssa Bradford's

bottle. It offered a faint glow that seemed to come not from within it so much as from an electricity that clung to the outside, a sort of Saint Elmo's fire.

Drink it.

No, no. Don't drink it. The whole point, the reason for this absurd suffering, was to avoid taking any more of that water.

Things get worse tonight, try her bottle before yours.

Yes, her bottle. It wasn't glowing, wasn't covered in frost, looked entirely normal. He pulled himself over to the desk and reached for it, and when he did, his hand went to the glowing bottle first, and some part of him wanted that one desperately. He stopped himself, though, shifted his hand to Anne McKinney's bottle, and got his fingers around it, brought it down. His breath was coming fast and uneven again, and he opened the bottle quickly and brought it to his mouth and drank.

It was hideous stuff. The sulfuric taste and smell were overpowering, and he got only two swallows down before he had to pull away. He gagged again, sagging back against the legs of the desk, and then he waited.

"Work," he mumbled, running the tip of his tongue over lips that had gone dry and cracked. *"Work."*

But he was sure it wouldn't. The water his body desired so desperately was in the other bottle, the one putting off that faint glow and gathering ice in a seventy-degree room. This version, this *sane* version, would do nothing.

Then his breathing began to steady. That was the first perceptible change; he could fill his lungs once again. A few minutes after that, he felt the nausea subside, and then the headache dulled and he was on his feet again, splashing cold water on his face from the bathroom sink. He stood there with hands braced on the counter and lifted his face and stared into the mirror.

It was working. Anne's water. What did that tell him? Well,

for one thing, the Pluto Water was involved in whatever was happening to him, was part of it. *Part.* He couldn't believe it was the sole cause, because Anne's water didn't have any of the same bizarre properties as Alyssa Bradford's. And yet it had quelled the agony that came from Alyssa's water. Whatever had been put into his system seemed satisfied now. Content.

As if it had just been fed.

How he'd slept so long on a rock ledge, Josiah couldn't imagine. No pillow for his head, even, and still he'd managed to sleep past sunset. When he opened his eyes, the treetops above him were a rustling mess of shadows, and when he sat up with a grunt, the pool of water far below was no longer visible. Full night.

Two of the beers remained warm and unopened at his side. The gulf gurgled down below, and he got to his feet stiffly, thinking about the dream and unsettled by it. Wasn't often that Josiah dreamed when he slept, and he couldn't recall ever having the same dream twice, or even a variation of it.

But this one had returned, this dream of the man aboard the train. Strange.

He'd ordinarily hike back the way he'd come, but he had no flashlight and it was a difficult trek in the darkness even if you knew where you were going. Too many roots to stumble over and holes to turn an ankle in. Taking the road would be longer but easier.

He left the ledge and climbed to the top of the ridge and found the trail that led to the gravel drive the state had put in. From there he came out to the county road as a dog barked in the distance and the moon and stars glittered and lit the pavement with a faint white glow. To the right he could see the white sides of Wesley Chapel gleaming against the dark, and a few pale orbs surrounding it, the stone fronts of the monuments in the old cemetery also catching the moonlight. He turned left, toward home.

Not a single car passed. He hiked south, open fields on each side of him for a spell, then into the woods of Toliver Hollow, and there the road curved away and he walked east for a time before leaving it for another road and moving south once more. A half mile farther and he left the paved road for a gravel one. Almost home. He'd taken no more than twenty steps on the gravel when he pulled up short and stared.

The moon was three-quarters full and bright in the periods between clouds, and it was glittering off something just down the road from Josiah's house.

A windshield.

A car.

Parked on the Amish farm property. Last time Josiah had checked, his Amish neighbors didn't have cars.

He hesitated for a moment and then left the road and went into the weeds as he continued on. As he got closer, he could tell it was a van. Funny place to leave a car, and funnier still was that it was parked in one of the few locations where Josiah's home showed in the gaps between the trees. He could see the outline of his house from here. The Amish barns were visible, but not their home. Just Josiah's.

Someone had run out of gas or had engine trouble, no doubt, pushed the thing off the road and left it till daylight. Nothing to trouble his mind over; Josiah couldn't give a shit whose car it was. Had nothing to do with him.

That was his thought for another fifty paces, until he saw the glow.

A brief square of blue light inside the rear of the van was visible for about five seconds and then extinguished. A cell phone. Someone was inside that van. In the back.

He felt something dark spread through him then, a feeling he knew well, his temper lifting its head on one of those occasions when it would not be denied, when fists would surely be swung and blood drawn.

Somebody was watching his house.

There was nothing else to see from there. Nothing but fields and trees and Josiah Bradford's own home.

A memory hit him then, a flash of something seen but ignored — the blue minivan that had been pulled off the road near Edgar's house when the man from Chicago and the black kid left. Josiah had driven right past it, had seen that it was parked off the shoulder and in the grass. Just like this one was now.

Son of a bitch was following him.

This would not be tolerated.

He dropped the beer cans he'd been carrying into the grass, then slipped down off the road and into the weed-covered ditch and picked his way along in a crouch. The van was parked facing the cattle gate, both sides exposed to the road, but its occupant was in the rear, and odds were he was watching the house and not the road.

It took him a long time to work his way down until he was directly across from the van. Twice the blue light appeared and disappeared, and he decided that whoever was inside was checking the time. Impatient, wondering where the hell Josiah was. Waiting on him.

Ideas tumbled through his mind, endless options. He could walk right up and knock on the door, call this son of a bitch outside. Could pick up one of the large loose stones from the ditch and use it to bash the windshield in. Could sneak home and get his shotgun. One way or another, he'd get this asshole out and answering questions.

That should have been his desire, at least. Find out who this was and what in the hell he was doing following Josiah. Funny thing was, Josiah was having trouble bringing himself to care. Those questions he should be asking, they didn't seem to matter anymore. All that mattered was the fact that someone was here watching his home. The hell with answers—Josiah wanted punishment. Wanted to crawl under the car, puncture the gas tank, set the thing on fire. Watch it blow this nameless son of a bitch sky high in a cloud of orange flame, teach him there were people to be fooled with and people not to be fooled with, and Josiah Bradford was absolutely of the latter set.

He dropped his hand into his pocket at the thought and wrapped his fingers around his cigarette lighter, actually tempted for a minute. But no, those answers were important, and if he blew up the van before the questions had been asked, he would surely regret it. So the dilemma was how to get the man inside the van out of it and willing to talk. Well, the cigarette lighter might help with that after all.

He pulled off his T-shirt and felt around the bottom edge of it until he found one of its holes. Worked his fingers in and tugged and then the cheap cotton tore, the sound loud. He went slower, quieter, tearing again and again until he had five separate strips of fabric. When he had the shirt torn up, he crammed the strips into his pockets, patted around the ditch with his hands until he found a large stone—felt like the broken-off corner of a cinder block—and then dropped to his belly, the weeds and gravel tearing at his skin as he crawled up onto the road and toward the van.

Slow, patient going, stopping occasionally to catch his breath and adjust his position. The ditch on the other side of the road was deeper, and it came to an end right where the van was parked, had a steel culvert that ran from one end of the dirt farm lane to the other. It was packed with dry leaves. Josiah waited for a moment, hearing nothing, and then he slid right under the van.

He left the cinder-block chunk behind, pushed across the gravel on his stomach until he was beneath the front of the van, and put his hand back in his pocket and took out the strips of T-shirt and the lighter. Then he sparked the lighter's wheel and got the flame going and held it to the end of one strip of cloth and then another. When he had them both going, he reached out and tossed them down into the ditch, which was filled with leaves and grass and was dry from days of sun and wind. Wouldn't do anything but burn itself out, but all it had to do was burn.

He had a third strip of shirt out, ready to light another, but the fire had already caught some fuel down in the ditch, so he dropped the cloth and slid backward, under the van again.

It was a good thing he'd moved when he did, because the man in the van spotted the fire when it was still in its infancy. Josiah heard a murmuring from inside and then the door slid open and someone stepped out, said, "What in the hell?" under his breath, and then walked down into the ditch and began stomping at the fire. When he did, Josiah slid out from under the van on the other side, screened from view, and crawled around to the back, kneeling and grabbing the chunk of cinder block.

He stood up just as he came around the back, maybe ten feet from the man, who was still stomping at the grass, the fire already gone. Josiah was intending to just bounce the chunk of stone in his hand and tell this boy it was time to talk. When he came around the van, though, he saw that the man had a gun in his hand, thought, *Well, good thing I didn't just knock on the door,* and then jumped into the ditch and swung the hand with the cinder block.

The guy was fast, got turned and had the gun half lifted before the stone caught him flush on the side of the head, caught him with an impact that jarred Josiah's shoulder and made a wet crunch in the silent night, and his knees buckled and he was down in the ditch with dark blood dripping into the grass and his gun loose at his side. It was over then, over, and Josiah knew it, but for some reason he jumped down there and hit him again, even harder this time, and the sound the stone made on the man's skull was terrible, a hard-to-soft shattering.

For a moment Josiah stayed where he was, crouched above the guy, who hadn't so much as twitched. Then he reached down and put his fingertips on the man's chin and turned his head to the side, and even in the shadows what he saw made him hiss in a breath between his teeth. He took his lighter from his pocket and flicked the wheel and lowered the flame toward the man's head and said, "Oh, shit, Josiah, oh, shit," and then he snapped the lighter off because he didn't want to look anymore.

30

Eric slept soon after drinking Anne McKinney's water. Slept deep and restful, stretched out on his back on top of the covers. When he woke, his first thought was one of relief, an immediate recognition that the terrible pain was past, that he was whole again.

It was cold in the room — he'd cranked up the air in an effort to combat the fever sweats — and he'd been above the covers and below the air vent. Too cold for sleep.

He swung his feet to the floor and sat on the bed for a moment, breathing deep and testing his physical sensations, looking for a chink in the armor. Nothing. His throat was a little raw, his lips dry, but other than that, he felt almost normal.

Over on the table, the Bradford bottle still glowed, though the glow seemed fainter to him, almost like a reflection from some light source he couldn't see. He got to his feet and went to the thermostat and turned the temperature up, then reached down and touched his toes and stretched his arms above his head, feeling liberation at the ability to move without pain.

The heavy curtains had been pulled to block out any trace of the lights that fueled his headaches, but now he crossed the room and shoved them back, looked down on the rotunda below. Beautiful. At night the massive pendulum that hung from the center of the dome was equipped with colored lights that shifted every few seconds. He unlocked the door to the balcony and stepped out, braced his hands on the railing, and looked down.

Empty and still. No one in the atrium or out on one of the other balconies. It was his world right now, his alone.

He knew he should go back to bed, that his body would demand plenty of sleep after the gauntlet he'd just run it through, but he didn't want to. Instead, he propped the door open and dragged the desk chair out onto the balcony, sat and put his feet up on the railing, and watched the colors change on that incredible ceiling. Purple, green, red, purple, green, red, purple, green...

The colors faded on him then, shifting to darkness broken by small points of white light, and then the ceiling and the hotel were gone and he was someplace else entirely.

It was a cloudless night, the sky a splendor of stars, and beneath a gleaming half-moon stood a shack that appeared unmeant for habitation. There were torn strips of cloth plugging holes in the shingles, and the front door was separated from its frame at the bottom, hanging from just the top hinge. Of the three windows in the front of the house only two panes of glass remained. Beyond the house was a tilting shed and an outhouse with no door.

Somewhere in the dark, soft but sweet, a violin played. There was no living thing in sight, neither man nor creature, just that sad, shivering song.

Another sound soon caught the violin and overran it, the strong purring of an engine, and headlights lit the filthy gray front of the house as a roadster with wide running boards appeared and pulled right up to the sagging edge of the front porch. The door to the shed banged open and a man stepped out and peered at the car. He was tall but stooped, a bare chest showing under his open shirt, tangled gray hair hanging down over his ears and along his neck. He had a cigar pinched in one corner of his mouth.

"That you, Campbell?" he hollered, squinting and shielding his eyes.

"You get many other visitors?" came the chill-voiced reply.

The old man grumbled and stepped farther out from the shed as Campbell Bradford advanced, pushing his bowler hat up on top of his head. He'd left the car running and its headlights on, and the light came up from behind him and spread his shadow large across the front of the shed.

"You's late," the old man muttered, but he extended his hand, friendly.

Campbell didn't move his own hands from his pockets.

"I don't want your handshake, I want your liquor. Step to it now. Don't want to spend any more time in this den than I have to."

The old man edged backward, grumbling but not raising his head. Maybe because he didn't want to look into the lights; maybe because he didn't want to look into Campbell's eyes. He turned and went in the shed. There was a lantern lit inside, casting flickering golden streaks about the walls. In the middle of the shed stood a rusting cistern. Then the door swung shut and it was hidden from view.

Campbell Bradford remained outside, shrouded by the headlight beams, shifting his weight impatiently and looking around the wooded hill with distaste. He took the bowler hat from his head and scratched at his scalp and then put it back on. Removed a pocket watch from inside his suit and flicked it open, twisting it to catch the light, and then his shoulders heaved with a sigh and he snapped the watch shut.

It had been quiet since his arrival, but now the violin began again. Softer even than before. Campbell looked once toward the house and then turned away, uninterested. The music played on, though, and at length he cocked his head to the side and stood stock still, listening.

The old man reappeared with a jug in each hand. He set them at Campbell's feet and turned to go back in but Campbell reached out and caught his arm.

"Who's that fiddling?"

"Oh, it's just my sister's boy. She passed with the fever a year back and I've had him at my damned heels ever since."

"Bring him out here."

The old man hesitated, but then he nodded and shuffled past Campbell and through the weeds and into the dark house. A moment later the music stopped and then the broken door pushed open again and the old man returned, a tall, thin boy behind him. He had pale blond hair that caught the moon glow, and a violin in his hands.

"What's your name, boy?" Campbell said.

"Lucas." The boy did not look up.

"How long you played?"

"I don't recall, sir. Long as I've known."

"How old are you?"

"Fourteen, sir."

"What was that song you were playing?"

The boy, Lucas, chanced a look up at Campbell and quickly dropped his head again.

"Well, it don't have a name. Just something I made up myself."

Campbell Bradford leaned back and tilted his head in surprise. When he did it, the headlights caught him full in the face, and his dark eyes seemed to swirl against the brightness like water pulled toward a drain.

"You wrote that song?"

"Didn't write nothing," the old man said. "He can't read no music, just plays it."

"I wasn't speaking to you," Campbell said, and Lucas tensed. "What kind of song is that? I ain't never heard the like of it, boy."

"It's what they call an elegy," he said.

"What's that mean?"

"It's a song for the dead."

It was quiet for a moment, the three of them standing there in the headlights, silhouettes painted across the weathered boards of the whiskey-still shed, a mild wind waving the treetops that surrounded them.

"Play it for me now," Campbell said.

"He don't play for nobody," the old man said, and Campbell turned on him fast.

"Am I speaking to you?"

The old man took a few quick steps backward, lifting his hands. "I ain't meaning to interrupt you, Campbell, I'm just warning you. He won't play in front of nobody. Won't play at all 'cept by himself."

"He'll play for me," Campbell said, and his voice was darker than the night woods.

The old man said, "Go on and play, Luke," in a jittery voice.

The boy didn't say anything. He fidgeted some with the violin but did not lift it.

"You listen to your uncle," Campbell said. "When I tell you to play, you best get to fiddling. Understand?"

Still the boy didn't move. There was a pause, five seconds at most, and then Campbell stepped forward and struck him in the face.

The old man shouted and moved forward to intercede, but Campbell whirled and struck again and then the old man was on his back in the trampled weeds. Campbell leaned into the boy, who now had a trickle of blood dripping from his lip, and said, "Let's try this again."

Down in the grass, the old man said, "Luke, just shut your eyes. It'll be like playing in the dark, nothing to it. *Shut your eyes and play, boy!*"

Lucas shut his eyes. He brought the violin to his shoulder and then the bow, which shook violently in his hand, and began to saw across the strings. At first it was a terrible wreck of a song, no note clear for the shaking, but then his hand steadied and the melody stepped forward and rang out into the night.

He played for a long time, and nobody said a word. The old man got to his hands and knees in the dirt and then crawled hesitantly to his feet, watching Campbell, who snapped his head in the direction of the shed. The old man went inside and came back out with more jugs, eight in total, and then he carried them down to the car and loaded them inside. All the while the boy played, eyes closed, facing away from the light.

When the old man had made his final trip, Campbell said, "Enough," and the boy stopped playing and lowered the instrument.

"How'd you like to make a dollar or two doing that?" Campbell said.

"Aw, Campbell," the old man said, "that really don't seem like a good idea."

Campbell turned and looked at the old man and whatever argument might have come died a quick and trembling death.

"I got a liking for that song," Campbell said, "and I'm going to bring him down in the valley to play it."

He reached into his vest pocket and pulled out a handful of money and passed it over to the old man.

"There. Five extra dollars in it for you. Satisfied?"

The old man rubbed the money with a greasy thumb and nodded and put it in his pocket.

"You play that song," Campbell said to the boy, "and you play it right, and there'll be some dollars for you, too. Go on and get in the car."

"When you bringing him back?" the old man asked.

"When I get tired of the song," Campbell said. "Why's he still standing there?"

"Listen to Mr. Bradford," the boy's uncle said to him. "Go get in the car."

The boy left them and went to the car without ever speaking a word. When he walked into the headlights, he took on a strange, shimmering glow, and there were colors in the light now, purple and then green and then red and . . .

The ceiling of the dome was back in front of Eric's eyes, and he was on the balcony. There was no more car or house in the woods or boy with a violin. No more angry blows from a man he'd just heard called Campbell. The past was gone from him now. He sat up slowly and looked around him. Twisted his head right and then left and saw the whole room was empty again, and quiet, and above him the dome changed colors, a beautiful silent sentry to it all.

31

THE WIND PICKED UP while Josiah crouched in the ditch over a man he knew was dead, watching the flow of blood from the wound slow, a thick pool of it all around now, spreading so much that Josiah had to move back to keep it from hitting his shoes.

It was dark and silent and no cars would come along the road at this hour, but all the same, decisions needed to be made, and fast, because this man was dead.

The stone was going to be a problem. It would have blood on it and maybe hair and flesh and for damn sure would have Josiah's fingerprints. He felt around in the ditch until he relocated the chunk of cinder block and then he held it and hesitated for a moment, considered tossing it into the field but decided against that. They'd bring dogs out here and find it no problem and then they'd have his fingerprints, and Josiah had been arrested enough times that matching those prints wasn't going to be a problem.

What to do, then? What to do?

Now that he thought about it, this whole ditch was filled with evidence—there were pieces of Josiah's shirt down there beside the dead man—and there wasn't any way in hell he'd get all of it cleaned up. He could load the man into the van and drive him off somewhere, but that didn't get rid of the blood in the ditch, and odds were somebody would've known his location anyhow.

Odds were, somebody would've known he was watching Josiah.

No good way to clean up this mess, then, but he could leave more of one behind. Burn this place, scorch it all, and let them sift through the ashes for evidence.

He wiped the rock down carefully on his pants and then set it on the edge of the road and, dropping onto his back, slid under the van and found the gas line and jammed his pocketknife into it. First few times it glanced off the metal, and once his hand slipped down and across the blade and opened his flesh up. First his fingerprints, now his blood. He drove the knife at the gas line again, drove it with the fury of fear and anger, and this time the blade popped through and gasoline spilled out and onto his bare chest.

The idea of trying to tip the van into the ditch and create an accident scene ran through his mind but he discarded it. There wasn't enough time, and it probably wouldn't work anyhow. He wrapped his hand in one of the torn pieces of shirt he still had and then opened the driver's door and climbed inside. There was a leather case on the passenger seat, and all the way in the back he found a digital camera. He took them both—after all this risk, might as well get something out of it, and maybe it would help if the scene had the look of a robbery. Then he went down into the ditch and patted through the dead man's pockets and found a wallet and took that, too, dropped it into the leather case as the gasoline ran through the gravel and dripped into the ditch behind him.

He tucked the camera into the case, set it aside, and pulled the two remaining strips of shirt from his pocket and held them in the pool of gasoline forming by the car. When they were damp, he got the lighter out and lit them, one at a time. The first flared too hot and burned his hand, the hand that was already bleeding, and then he tossed the strip down onto the dead man's body. For a moment it looked like the flame would go out, so he held the other strip of cloth over it and squeezed and the drops of gasoline got the blaze going again, and this time it caught the dead man's shirt and then he was burning.

Josiah lit the final strip of cloth and tossed it back up on the gravel, into the pool of gasoline, which went up like a bastard, three feet tall and brilliantly light before he'd even had a chance to move. He got to running then, grabbed the leather case in his bleeding hand and ran for his house as the fire spread behind him. He was no more than a hundred feet away when the gas tank blew, and he felt the shock of it in the ground, and the whole night was filled with orange light then and he knew his time was slim, indeed.

He hit the front yard at a dead run, dropped the case in the grass, got his keys out of his pocket and unlocked the door, ran inside in the dark, and went to his bedroom. Pulled a fresh shirt on, then opened the closet. There was a twelve-gauge pump shotgun inside, and he took that and a box of shells and ran into the yard. Tossed the shotgun and the shells into the bed of the truck and pulled a plastic tarp over them, then grabbed the leather case and threw it onto the passenger seat. His front yard was lit by the fire, but already the blaze was going down. He thought he could hear voices up at the Amish farm, but maybe that was his imagination.

He got into the truck and started it, thought about leaving the headlights off but then realized that would be begging for trouble and turned them on, pulled out of his driveway and sped down the gravel road, came out to the county road, and turned west. Sirens were audible by the time he reached the first stop sign. He drove on into the night.

Eric didn't expect to sleep again, but he did. Long after the vision had passed he was still on the balcony, waiting, willing it to return.

It did not.

Eventually, he rose and carried the chair back into the room and looked at the clock and saw it was four in the morning. Claire was in the central time zone, an hour behind, and it was too early to call. Kellen would be asleep. All sane people would be asleep.

He lay on the bed and stared at the bottles on the desk as the sounds of early-morning preparations carried on around him in the old hotel.

Campbell, the old man had called the one in the bowler hat. Campbell.

It was what Eric already knew, had known since he looked into Josiah Bradford's eyes and saw the similarity. The man in the bowler hat was Campbell Bradford, and he'd arrived in town yesterday on an all-black train. The boy, then? The boy who played the violin with his eyes squeezed shut to block his terrible stage fright?

He was Alyssa Bradford's father-in-law. Eric was sure of that in the way he'd been sure of Eve Harrelson's affair in the red cottage and of the Nez Perce camp in that valley in the Bear Paws. But the boy's name was Lucas, and he had not been a relative of Campbell's. So why had he claimed the man's name? Had he been adopted, removed from the care of his uncle and placed into Campbell's? Why take the name, though?

Amidst all the questions were two other confirmations: Anne McKinney's water both alleviated his withdrawal pains and brought back the visions. Only this time, the vision had been more like watching a movie. He had distance. Previously, Campbell had looked right at him, spoken to him. He'd been a participant, not a bystander. With Anne's water, what he'd experienced felt truly like a vision of the past, a glimpse into something that had happened long ago and could not affect anything in this world. What he'd seen from the Bradford bottle was hardly so tranquil. In those moments, Campbell had been *with* him.

He fell asleep sometime around six and woke to the phone ringing at nine-thirty. He fumbled for it with his eyes still closed, knocked the thing off the base, and then got it in his hand and gurgled out a sound that didn't even come close to *hello.*

Kellen said, "You made it through."

"Yeah." He sat up, rubbed at his eyes.

"No problems?"

"Wouldn't say that."

"Uh-oh."

Eric told him about it all, disclosing the depth of physical agony and the drinking of the water and the vision that had followed. It was odd he'd be willing to tell this stranger so much, but he was grateful that Kellen was willing to listen to it. He wasn't running yet, dismissing Eric as crazy. That meant something.

"This changes things," Kellen said. "It's not the specific bottle of water that hits you, it's Pluto Water in general."

"I don't think we can go quite that far. I'm getting visions from them both, yes, but there's still something different about that first bottle, the one that started it. Last night, after trying

Anne's water, it was like I was watching something out of the past. When I've had the Bradford water, everything I see is right here with me."

"So you still want to run the test."

"Absolutely."

"Well, I'll come by and get the bottles then, take them up to Bloomington."

Eric opened his mouth to say that was great, then stopped, realizing what it meant. If Kellen took both bottles to Bloomington, Eric would have nothing in his arsenal. It was a thought that chilled him.

"Do you know how fast they can test it?" he said.

"No idea. But it's Sunday, you know, so probably not today."

"If there's any way they could test it today...or at least tomorrow...I'm just thinking, the faster, the better. I'll pay whatever it takes."

"Well, you're talking to the wrong person, my man. I got no idea what the process entails. But I'll see what I can do once I'm up there."

Kellen said he'd come by the hotel in a few minutes and they hung up. Eric studied the bottles for a few seconds longer and then, hating himself for it, went into the bathroom and found one of the plastic cups and emptied a few ounces of Anne McKinney's bottle into the cup. He took a small taste. Just as bad as it had been hours earlier, no trace of sweetness or honey. Good. This one didn't change.

He took the plastic cup and carried it over to the bedside table and set it down. There if he needed it. He would try not to need it, but at least it would be there.

The Bradford bottle he left untouched.

He got in the shower, was hardly out when Kellen called from the lobby. He threw on clothes and grabbed the bottles, then almost dropped the Bradford bottle.

Cold was no longer an accurate assessment. The thing was *freezing,* gave his hand the sort of cold burn you could get from touching a metal railing on a Chicago winter night. The frost was dry now; he had to use a fingernail to scrape any off.

"I'm going to find out what's in you," he said. He carried the bottles down in the elevator and out into the lobby, shifting them from one hand to the other because the Bradford bottle was too cold to keep in one for a prolonged time. Kellen was waiting near the front doors. He looked at Eric with a critical eye as he approached.

"Looks like you *did* have a rough night." Kellen lifted a finger and indicated his own eye. "You ruptured some blood vessels, man. Across the bridge of your nose, too."

Eric had already seen that in the mirror.

"Like I said, it wasn't a whole lot of fun."

"Doesn't look like it, no." Kellen reached out and took the bottles from him, said, *"Damn!"* when he touched the Bradford bottle.

"Getting colder," Eric said.

"You ain't kidding. That's a big difference from yesterday."

Eric watched Kellen study the bottle, saw the awe in his eyes, and thought, *This is why he believes me.* The bottle was so insane it made Eric's story acceptable.

"I called Danielle," Kellen said.

"Danielle?"

"That's my girl, yeah. Told her we needed to get somebody to look at this thing fast, and she said she'd call around and see what she could do. No promises, though."

"I appreciate it. Tell her I'll pay —"

"Nobody's worried about that." Kellen was juggling the bottles from hand to hand now just as Eric had been. "She knows somebody to do it, that's all."

"You said she's going to med school?"

"Yeah."

Eric nodded, feeling a pang of guilt. Claire had been in law school when they'd met. Had dropped out when they got married to follow him to L.A. She had a good job now, working for the mayor's office, but it wasn't the career she'd had in mind for herself. She'd given that up for him.

"Well, you might ask her to have them run a specific test," he said. "If it's even possible. I've got an idea of what might be in it. We know Campbell was involved with bootlegging and moonshine, and in my vision last night I saw that whiskey still..."

"Old moonshine," Kellen said and gave a nod. "That would make some sense. Who knows what the hell they put in it or how potent it was back then, let alone now. It could be giving you fits, no question. I still think it might be worth talking to a doctor."

"I will if I need to," Eric said. "But I'm feeling all right now."

"Okay. I'll come back down this afternoon, catch up with you then."

Eric followed Kellen out the doors and onto the veranda overlooking the grounds. Out in front, at the end of the brick drive, a TV news van was parked.

"Something going on today?" Eric said.

"I don't know. Saw another one on my way here, somebody interviewing a cop on the sidewalk. Could be something happened last night."

"Casino robbery. *Ocean's Eleven* shit."

"There you go." Kellen laughed, then lifted the bottle and

held it up to the sun. The frost glittered. "All right, I'm off to Bloomington."

"Hey, thanks for helping with the water. I appreciate it, more than you know."

Kellen looked at him, serious, and said, "You take care today, all right?"

"Sure."

He left and then it was just Eric on the veranda, facing into a warm morning wind that was tinged with moisture. It was humid already, and though the sky was blue, it had a hazy quality. Maybe Anne McKinney had been right. Could be a storm brewing.

32

TIRED OF THIS TOWN as he was, Josiah still found himself grateful for familiarity in this situation. Figured he had to get himself hidden quick, because there wasn't going to be a whole lot of time passing before the police were looking for his truck. Hell, they'd do that on principle, something like that happening so near his home. He wasn't real eager to talk the matter over with them either.

Time to get off the roads and out of sight, then, and while the idea of flight was appealing, gassing up the truck and heading for the Ohio River line and points beyond, he wasn't foolish enough to do that. He had a grand total of twenty-four dollars in his wallet and maybe four hundred in the bank, and that wasn't going to get him far.

He drove about three miles west of his house, into the woods that climbed the hills between Martin and Orange counties, and turned into a gravel drive marked with a half dozen

NO TRESPASSING signs. Had been a timbering camp at one time, years ago, and now all that remained was a weathered barn and decrepit equipment shed. The place was isolated, though. Josiah had found the spot deer hunting one year — the property wasn't open to hunting, but hell if he cared — and filed it away in the back of his mind, knowing that such a location could prove useful to any of the handful of illegal ventures he experimented with from time to time. This wasn't the sort of use he'd hoped to require it for, but right now he was glad that he'd stumbled across the spot.

He stopped and then dug his toolbox out of the truck and found a stout pair of bolt cutters. Should've thought to grab a hacksaw, but he hadn't been exactly flush on time when he'd left the house. He left the lights on in the truck, used them to illuminate the sagging doors on the barn. Just as he'd recollected, there was a rusted chain with a padlock holding them closed, and the chain wasn't thick. It took him a few minutes of grunting and swearing — his burned and bleeding hand hurt like hell each time he squeezed the bolt cutters — but eventually he broke through half a link and then he slipped the chain apart and dropped the lock at his feet.

The doors swung open with a crack and groan, but they slid apart all right, and inside there was plenty of room for the truck. He pulled it inside, hearing a harsh scrape as he dragged past the door, then turned the engine off, and sat there in the dark.

What in the hell had he done? What in the *hell* had he just done?

The last fifteen minutes had been too full of action for much thought, but now, up here in the dark barn, hiding his truck from the police who'd soon be looking for it, he was forced to consider what had just occurred. That man was dead, and Josiah had killed him. Killed him, then lit his ass on fire. That wasn't just murder, that had to be some aggravated version of it. Sort that got you on death row.

It wasn't as if Josiah had never thought of killing a man before, he'd just never actually expected to do it. Figured if he ever did, it would come slow and calculated, the product of a great deal of provocation. Revenge for some grave offense. But tonight...tonight it had happened so damn fast.

"Was the gun that did it," he said. "Was his own fault for pulling that gun."

Surely that had been it. A self-defense move and nothing else. You see a man swinging a gun your way, what in the hell were you supposed to do?

Problem was, it hadn't been the first blow that killed him. Josiah was almost certain of that. Oh, it had knocked him out well enough, but the one that killed him had been that second strike, when the man in the ditch was already down and out and Josiah jumped down there and laid the cinder block to his head with every last ounce of strength he had in him. That wasn't Josiah's nature; he'd never been one for kicking a man he'd already put on the ground. But tonight he'd done that, and then some. And in that moment, that blink-quick moment, he hadn't even felt like himself. He'd felt like another man entirely, a man who'd enjoyed that deathblow a great deal.

Shit, what a mess. You killed someone, better have both good cause for it and a good plan for dealing with it, and Josiah had neither. Didn't even know who the son of a bitch was, just that he'd been watching the house. Why had he been watching the house?

He reached over to the passenger seat and got the case he'd stolen, a big leather bag with a shoulder strap, and felt around for the wallet. When he got his fingers around it, he flicked on the interior lights and opened it up. First thing he saw was a photo ID. *Licensed Private Investigator.*

A detective. That didn't make a bit of sense, and the name— Gavin Murray—didn't mean a thing to Josiah either. He studied the picture, confirmed that this man was a stranger. The address given on both the investigator's license and his driver's license, which was tucked in the same compartment, was Chicago.

Same city as the man who'd gone to see Edgar, pretending to be making a movie. Two of them in French Lick on the same day, one asking questions about Campbell, the other watching Josiah's house with a camera. What could these bastards be after? Hell, Josiah didn't have anything to take.

He removed the cash from the wallet and put it in his pocket, then felt around in the case and came across a fancy leather folder, took that out and opened it, and found himself studying a sheet of paper with his own name, date of birth, and Social Security number. Plus a list of addresses going back the better part of fifteen years, places *he'd* almost forgotten about. He thumbed past this sheet and saw that the next one detailed his arrest history, complete with case numbers and dates of arrest and charges. He flipped through a few more papers, then found one that said *Client Contact*. There were two phone numbers and a fax number and e-mail address, but Josiah was far more interested in the name itself:

Lucas G. Bradford.

This morning the humidity had arrived even ahead of the heat. It was a liquid breeze that came in through the screen as dawn rose, and Anne, expecting to see heavy clouds when she got out of bed and looked out the window, was surprised to find sun.

She showered, a process that now took too much time and too much energy, holding on to the metal railings with one hand at all times, and then dressed in slacks and a light cotton blouse and the sturdy white tennis shoes she wore every day. Had to wear them; balance was all that kept her from a hospital or a nursing home. She loathed those shoes, though. Hated them with a depth of passion that she'd rarely felt for anything. When she was young, she'd been a shoe fan. All right, that was an understatement and a half—she'd been *crazy* about shoes. And the shoes she loved had heels. They were tall and elegant and you had to know how to walk in them, you couldn't just clomp around, you had to walk like a *lady*. Anne McKinney had always known how to walk. Had earned her share of stares over the years because of that walk, had watched men's eyes drop to her hips all the time, long after she became a mother, even.

She took short, steady steps now in her flat, sturdy shoes. Hated the walk, hated the shoes. The past taunted with every step.

Once she was dressed, she went out onto the porch to take the day's first readings. The barometer was down to 29.80. Quite a drop overnight. The sun was out, but the lawn didn't sparkle under it, no heavy dew built up overnight the way there had been recently. She leaned out from under the porch roof and looked up and saw a cluster of swollen clouds in the west, pale on top but gray beneath. Cumulonimbus. Storm clouds.

All signs, from the clouds to the dry grass to the pressure drop, indicated a storm. It was confirmation of what she'd suspected yesterday, but she felt a vague sense of disappointment as she studied the clouds. They were storm makers, sure, but somehow she'd expected more. Still, it was early. Spring supercells developed quickly and often unpredictably, and it was tough to say what might find its way here by day's end.

She recorded all of the measurements in her notebook. It was a ritual that usually gave her pleasure but today, for some reason, did not. She felt out of sorts, grumpy. It happened when something of note occurred, like Eric Shaw's visit, and she had nobody to share it with. It was then that she felt the weight of the loneliness, then that the mocking of the empty house and the silent phone rose in pitch. She'd kept her mind all these years, her memory and logic, was proud of it. Mornings like this, though, she wondered if that was best. Maybe it was easier to be the doddering sort of old, maybe that dulled the sharp edges of the empty rooms that surrounded you.

"Oh, stop it, Annabelle," she said aloud. "Just stop it."

She would not sit around here feeling sorry for herself. You had to be grateful for every day, grateful for each moment the good Lord allowed you to have on this weird, wild earth. She knew that. She believed it.

Sometimes, though, believing it was easier than at other times.

She went back inside and fixed toast for breakfast and sat in her chair in the living room and tried to read the paper. It was tough to concentrate. Memories were leaping out at her this morning, nipping the heels of her mind. She wanted someone to talk to. The phone had been quiet all week but that was partially her own fault — she'd worked so hard to convince those at church and in town of her strong independence that they didn't worry about her much. And that was good, of course, she didn't want to give anyone cause to worry, but...but it wouldn't hurt if someone checked in now and again. Just to say hello. Just to make a little conversation.

Heavens, but Harold had loved to talk. There had been plenty of times when she'd said, *Harold, go outside and give my ears a break,* just because she couldn't take the unrelenting chatter. And the children...oh, but those were *his* children, sure as anything, because both of them caught the gift of gab like it was a fever. This house had been filled with talk from sunrise to sundown.

She set the paper down, stood up, and went to the phone,

ignoring, as she usually did, the cordless unit that sat beside her, because it was good to move around, good to stay active. She called the hotel and asked to be put through to Eric Shaw. It had occurred to her last night that she'd never asked what family he was researching. Maybe she could help. Maybe if he told her the family name, she'd remember some things about them, maybe she could tell him some stories.

It went to voice mail, though, and so she left a message. Anne McKinney calling, nothing urgent. Just wanted to check in.

33

Eric went into the dining room and ordered breakfast, realizing with relief that he was truly hungry again, sipping his coffee with a touch of impatience, eager to see the food brought out. That had to be a good sign.

He couldn't stop thinking about the effects of Anne's water. It had eased his physical suffering just as the Bradford bottle had, but the vision it brought on was so different, so much gentler. Like watching a film, really. He'd had distance, separation of space and time. If what he'd seen were real...

The possibilities there tempted him in a strange way. Maybe it was a hallucination the same as those experienced by drug users every day. If it wasn't, though, if he was really seeing the past, then the water provided him something far different from pain. Provided him with power, really. A gift.

"French toast with bacon," a female voice behind him said, and then the waitress set a plate before him that intensified his hunger. "And you need more coffee. Hang on and I'll get a refill. Sorry about that. I stopped to watch the TV people for a few minutes."

"Uh-huh," Eric muttered, putting the first forkful of French toast into his mouth even before she was gone. It tasted fantastic.

"They were filming right in the lobby," she said. "I was hoping they'd come in here and I could make the news. You know, fifteen seconds of fame."

Eric swallowed, wiped his mouth with the napkin, and said, "Oh, right, I saw the TV vans. What's the deal?"

"Someone was *murdered*," she said, dropping her voice to a grim whisper as she leaned over him to fill his coffee cup. "Blown up in his van, can you believe it?"

"Really? So much for this being a peaceful place. If people find out the locals are blowing one another up, it might hurt business."

"Oh, it wasn't a local. Was some man from Chicago. And he was a detective, too. So it's even more interesting, you know? Because who knows what he was doing down here. I don't remember his name, but they said that—"

"Gavin," Eric said, feeling his body temperature drop and his breathing slow, the food in front of him no longer so appealing. "His name was Gavin Murray."

It was a hell of a long hike, particularly going through the woods to avoid the road, but Josiah didn't trust his cell phone, figured they could track it. He turned it off and took the battery out to be sure it wasn't transmitting any signal, and then he set off through the woods and toward town. He hated to involve Danny Hastings in this mess, but there was work to be done now that he couldn't do alone, and Danny was the only person he trusted to keep his mouth shut no matter what happened. Oh, Danny would stand a good chance of getting caught at it, but he'd never tell the cops a thing. They'd gotten into plenty of scrapes with the police over the years, and if there was one thing Danny knew how to do in those situations, it was keep his mouth shut.

The hike into town took more than an hour, and then he had to chance being seen, come out into the open for at least a little while. There was a pay phone at the gas station, one of the last pay phones in town, and he called and told Danny where to meet him. The whole time he felt a prickle in the middle of his back, expecting a police car to come swerving around the corner at any minute, cops boiling out of it, guns drawn. Nothing happened, though. Nobody so much as blinked at him.

As soon as he hung up, he went back into the woods and climbed out of sight. Sat on an overturned log and waited. Fifteen minutes later, Danny's Oldsmobile appeared, driving slow, Danny craning his head and looking for him. Shit, way to avoid attention.

Josiah hustled down the hill and came out of the woods and lifted a hand. He jerked open the passenger door when the car pulled up, and said, "Drive, damn it."

Danny took them up the hill, the transmission double-clutching and shivering.

"What in the hell is going on, Josiah?"

"I got powerful problems is what's going on. You willing to help a friend out?"

"Well, of course, but I'd like to know what I'm getting into."

"It ain't good," Josiah said, and then, softer, "and I'll try to keep you out of it much as possible. I will."

It was that remark, the show of concern for someone other than himself, that seemed to tell Danny the gravity of the situation. He turned, frowning, and waited.

"I got into a scrape last night," Josiah said. "Man pulled a gun on me. I had a rock in my hand, and I used it on him. Hit him once more than I needed to."

"Oh, shit," Danny said. "I ain't helping you bury no body, Josiah. I ain't doing it."

"Don't need to bury a body."

"So you didn't kill him?"

Josiah was quiet.

"You *did* kill him?" Danny almost missed a curve. "You *murdered* somebody?"

"It was self-defense," Josiah said. "But he's dead, yeah. And you know what the police around here will do to somebody like me in a case like that. Self-defense ain't going to mean shit. The prosecutor will pull out all my old charges and tell the jury I'm nothing but trash, *dangerous* trash, and I'll be up in Terre Haute or Pendleton."

Danny's fat tongue slid out, moistened his lips. "It wasn't that guy in the van?"

"How'd you know about that?"

"Whole town knows about it, Josiah! Grandpa dragged my ass up to church today, was all anybody was talking about. Oh, hell, it was you?"

"He pulled a gun on me, damn it! I told you that."

They'd reached the logging road, and Josiah instructed him to turn in. He explained everything except the odd dreams of the black train and the man in the bowler hat.

"I don't understand what everybody's interested in Campbell for," Danny said.

"I don't either. But somebody named Lucas Bradford sent this guy down from Chicago to watch me, and old Lucas has himself some dollars. I found a bill in that dead guy's papers, Danny—he'd been paid fifteen thousand as a *retainer*. And there's a note in there says he was authorized to spend up to a hundred to resolve the situation. That's what it said — *resolve the situation*. A hundred thousand dollars."

Danny reached up and scratched the back of his neck. He was still in his church clothes, had on a starched white shirt that was showing sweat stains under the arms.

"Something going on, that's for sure," he said. "But the way you're handling it ain't right. You're just making things worse. You said he pulled a gun on you? Shit, call the police and tell them that. Get yourself a lawyer —"

"Danny," Josiah said, "I set the man on fire. You understand that? Think about that, and about the reputation I got in this town, and you tell me what's going to happen."

Danny was frozen for a moment, but eventually he gave a small nod. Then, in a whisper, he said, "What in the hell did you set him on fire for?"

"I don't know," Josiah said. "I don't even know why I hit him the second time. Didn't feel like myself. But I did it, and now I got to figure something out fast."

"What are you thinking?"

"This fella Lucas Bradford has money to spare. And I'm in need of it. But first I got to understand some things — who he is, and why he's asking about me. I'm going to need your help to do that. I'm asking you, please, to help."

Danny sighed, reached out and wrapped his hands around the steering wheel, squeezed it tight.

"Danny?"

He nodded. "I'll do what I can."

"Good. Thank you. First thing I want you to do is find that son of a bitch who came down to Edgar's and told us that bullshit about making a movie. He'll be staying at one of the hotels. You find him, and you follow him."

34

Alyssa Bradford didn't answer her phone. Eric called without even leaving the table, speaking into the cell phone in a hushed but hostile voice as he left yet another message, and demanded that she call him back, and this time he *would* be talking to her husband, thanks. Someone was dead, damn it, and he needed to know what the hell was going on.

The phone didn't ring. He sat there for a while, waiting and thinking of Gavin Murray with his sunglasses and cigarettes and smug voice. Blown up in a van.

The waitress came by and said, "Is there a problem with the food?" as she eyed his practically untouched plate.

"No," he said. "No problem. Just...thinking."

He ate the meal without tasting it, paid, and went back up to the room. He hadn't gotten the door open before the phone began to ring. *Alyssa,* he thought, *it damn well better be you.*

It wasn't her. Rather, the manager of the hotel, wishing to inform him that the police were looking for him.

"Tell them I'll be down in five minutes," he said, and then he hung up and called Claire.

"Are you home?" he said when she answered.

"Yes. Why?"

"I'd like you to leave."

"Excuse me?"

"I need you to bear with me for a minute, and I need you to believe that I'm not crazy. You still believe that?"

"Eric, what's going on?"

"Somebody followed me down here from Chicago," he said. "A man named Gavin Murray. Write that name down, or at least remember it, would you? Gavin Murray. This guy was a PI from Chicago, with a group called Corporate Crisis Solutions."

"All right."

He heard a sheet of paper tear loose, then a rattling sound as she looked for a pen.

"He showed up at the hotel yesterday," Eric said, "and he knew all about me. He mentioned you by name. He knew that we were separated and that the divorce hadn't gone through yet."

"What?"

"Yeah — pretty detailed, right? He'd done his research, but that's the sort of thing those guys can do quickly and easily. So I wasn't too concerned. Now I'm starting to be."

"You think I should be afraid of him?"

"Oh, not of him. He's dead."

"He's *what?*"

"Somebody killed him last night," Eric said. "Murdered him, blew up his van. I don't know the details yet. I'm on my way to meet with the police. What I do know is that the guy followed me down here, offered me seventy-five grand to stop asking about Campbell Bradford, and then he was killed. I don't have any idea what that means, but I do need to tell you that he essentially threatened me last night. He said other sorts of leverage could be used if I ignored the money."

"Eric..."

"I'm sure this is an undue precaution," he said, "but all the same, I'd like you to stay away from the house for a while. Until we understand a little more about this, I think that would be a good plan. It would give me some peace of mind, at least."

"Eric," she repeated, voice lower, "did you drink any more of that water?"

"That's irrelevant right now, because we've got—"

"You did."

"So what if I did?"

"I'm just wondering...are you sure this happened? Are you sure that man—"

"Was real?" he said, and gave a wild laugh. "Is that what you're asking me? Shit, Claire, that's just what I need, to have you questioning my sanity. *Yes,* the man was real and yes, he is *really dead* now, okay? He is dead. Somebody killed him, and I'm going to talk to the police about it now, and if you don't believe that, then get on the damn computer and look it up, look him up, do whatever the hell you need to do to convince yourself—"

"All right," she said, "okay, okay, calm down. I just had to ask, that's all."

It was quiet for a few moments.

"I'll leave," she said. "If that's what you want, I'll leave. Okay?"

"Thank you."

"Don't get upset when I ask you this, but why did you drink the water again?"

So he answered that as the room phone began to ring again — probably the police wanting to know what the hell was keeping him — and told her about the terrible night he'd had and the way Anne McKinney's water had quelled it, and about the vision of Campbell Bradford and the boy with the violin.

"The only thing I'm worried about right now," she said, "is what that water is doing to you. Physically, and mentally. All the rest of this — it's scary and it's weird, but it can be dealt with. But that water . . . that's more frightening, Eric. Your body is dependent on it now. Your brain, too. That's not a safe situation."

"We don't know if I'm dependent yet," he said, but the headache was back and his mouth was dry.

"You need medicine," she said, but then there was a knock on the door and he knew the police had decided not to wait for him to come down.

"I've got to go, Claire. I've got to talk to the cops. Will you please get out of the house for a while? At least until I know what's going on."

She said that she would. She told him to be careful. She told him not to drink any more of the water.

35

THE COP WHO TOOK the lead in talking with him was with the Indiana State Police, a guy named Roger Brewer. He drove Eric down to the little police station in the middle of French Lick, didn't speak much on the way, didn't say hardly anything at all until they were seated and he had a tape recorder going. He was a grave man with a focused stare.

"Isn't a whole lot I can tell you at this time," he said, "or at least that I can *disclose* to you, that's the better word, but for right now it'll suffice to say that Gavin Murray was killed last night. I was wondering what you could tell me about that."

"What I can tell you?" Eric echoed. The headache had dialed up a notch as soon as they were under the fluorescent lights. In addition to the tape recorder on the table between them, there was a video camera showing near the corner of the ceiling. "I can't tell you anything about that."

"Then tell me about him," Brewer said, "and about you. Curious as to what brought everybody down to Indiana."

Eric started to speak, then caught himself and hesitated for a moment while Brewer arched a questioning eyebrow.

"Something wrong?"

"Just thinking it might behoove me to ask whether you consider me a suspect."

"Behoove?" Brewer's face seemed lost between angry and amused.

"That's right." Maybe it was a mistake to ask — Eric's previous dealings with the police had been few, and he had a natural instinct to just roll with Brewer's authority — but the hissing wheels of the tape recorder had put his guard up. Eric understood better than most the potential for manipulation of film and tape.

"Well, Mr. Shaw, as is generally the case when we have the discovery of a homicide victim, the suspect pool is initially deep and wide. Are you in it? Sure. So are plenty of others, though. Right now, you're looking like one who can maybe provide some answers. Hate to think you're unwilling to do that."

"It's not a matter of being unwilling, it's a matter of understanding the situation. I'd like to know how you got my name."

Brewer was silent.

"Look," Eric said, "I'd like to talk to you. It's my preference, in fact. But I'm also not going to treat this as a one-way exchange. I'm worried, and I feel like there are some things I deserve to know. If you want to have a conversation, great. If this is an interrogation, though, I'll ask you to hold on until I get a lawyer in the room."

Brewer sighed at the mention of the word.

"Hey," Eric said, "it's your call."

"We have a homicide to solve," Brewer said eventually, "and

unless you were directly involved, I'd hate to think you'd voluntarily slow us down."

"Detective, yesterday that man surprised me in a parking lot, discussed details of my personal life, and then made a clear threat. You want to know about it, I'll be happy to share, but like I said, I have some other things to consider. Like protecting my family."

He'd hoped a little tease of information would improve Brewer's cooperation, and it seemed to. The cop's eyes lit at the disclosure, and he pulled his chair closer.

"I'll do what's within reason for you, if you do the same for me, Mr. Shaw. And that's going to require a full explanation, quickly."

"I'll give it. Just tell me, please, how you got my name. I need to know that."

"Gavin Murray's company."

"They told you he'd come down here after me?"

Brewer nodded. "They said that you were the target of his investigation."

"Well, who hired him?"

"We don't know."

Now it was Eric's turn to sigh, but Brewer lifted a hand.

"No, really, Mr. Shaw, we do not know. That's all his company would tell us. They're balking at more disclosures right now, claiming attorney-client privilege."

"Private investigators have attorney-client privilege?"

"They do when they've been hired by an attorney. At that point, they're part of the attorney's legal team. It's legit, if a pain in the ass. They seem eager to cooperate, but refuse to provide the client's name. We'll work on it, but for now that's where we stand."

Brewer leaned back and spread his hands. "So as you can

imagine, it is pretty damn important for us to hear what you have to say, Mr. Shaw. All we know now is that the man came down from Chicago to follow you. Or, apparently, to speak with you. The same night he arrived, he was killed. We'd like to know why."

"So would I," Eric said, and then he hesitated briefly, wondering again if a lawyer was in his best interests, because in the scenario Brewer had just recounted, Eric seemed not only like a suspect, but like a good one.

"The faster we move on this," Brewer said, "the faster we can put your mind at ease for your family and yourself."

"Okay," Eric said. "Okay."

He had Murray's business card in his wallet, and he gave it to Brewer and then gave him Kellen's name and number, and explained he was a witness to the initial encounter.

"But not to the conversation," Brewer said. His tone was soft and unchallenging but it still stopped Eric short, gave him a tingle of warning.

"No," he said. "There were no witnesses to the conversation. But I came back from it and told Kellen what had been said, immediately. That's the best I can do."

Brewer nodded, placating, and asked him to go on. Eric explained everything he could as Brewer sat quietly with his eyes locked on Eric's, the tape recorder's wheels turning steadily. Brewer's face didn't change throughout, didn't react even when Eric spoke of the payment offer or the suggestion that he could be convinced to go home through other means if he passed on the money.

"He was talking on the phone when we left. You want to know who his client is, you should probably check the phone records."

"We'll be checking those, don't worry." Brewer looked down

at the recorder, thoughtful, and said, "And this was both the first and last time you saw Gavin Murray?"

"Yes. You want to talk to someone, I'd look for Josiah Bradford. He was the last person Murray asked me about, and in my opinion, he's probably the core of the reason Murray came down here."

"Can you elaborate on that theory?"

"Have you talked to Josiah?"

Brewer looked pained, but he said, "We're going to, don't worry. It's a matter of locating him, same as with you."

"So he's missing?"

"He's not home, that's all, Mr. Shaw. I'd hardly term him missing yet." There was something in Brewer's eyes that hinted at a deeper level of dissatisfaction, though, something that told Eric they were indeed interested in Josiah Bradford. "Now, could you please elaborate on the suggestion you just made?"

"Well, it's a pretty simple idea. I came down here to do a movie about this rich guy in Chicago, about his childhood here. As soon as I get here, somebody offers me a decent amount of money to go home. Felt like a protective move to me, somebody maneuvering to head a problem off at the pass."

A plausible explanation, but the details it omitted, like Eric's growing confidence that the old man in the hospital was not the same Campbell Bradford of local infamy, were not minor. How in the hell could he be expected to explain it all, though? It was too damn strange. He'd sound like a lunatic.

"You said you're making a movie," Brewer said. "A documentary."

"Yes."

"Fascinating. So you tape interviews, things like that."

"Yes."

"Great. If we could have a look at the film you have from yesterday..."

"I don't have any. Well, I've got audio. I can give you audio."

But the audiotapes were going to introduce a new element to all this. Eric didn't like the idea of Brewer and a roomful of additional cops sitting around listening to him tell Anne McKinney about his visions. No, that didn't seem like a good choice at all.

"You don't use a camera? Seems tough to make a movie without a camera."

"I use them."

"So you have one with you?"

"No. I mean, I brought one down, yeah. But it...it broke."

Shit, that couldn't sound more like a lie. Maybe he could find some wreckage from the camera to back him up, but that would require an accompanying explanation of how he'd come to beat an expensive camera into pieces on the hotel desk. Not the sort of story you wanted to tell a cop who was investigating a rage homicide.

"It broke," Brewer said in a bland voice. "I see. Now, could you describe what your night looked like after your talk with Gavin Murray?"

"What it looked like?" Eric echoed, trying to focus. His head was pounding steadily now, and his stomach clenched and unclenched. He tried to will it all away, or at least down. Now was not the time for another collapse.

"Yes, what you did, who saw you, things of that nature."

He should tell the truth, of course. But telling the truth would take them to Anne McKinney, and that would take them to his talk of visions and headaches. Of course, he'd already given them Kellen, who would have to say the same thing...

"Mr. Shaw?" Brewer prompted, and Eric lifted his head and

looked at him and then the vertical hold went out in his eyes. It was like watching old reel-to-reel tape that had been damaged; the scene in front of him began to shake up and down, as if Brewer were sitting on a pogo stick instead of a chair. He had to reach out and grip the underside of his chair to steady himself.

Oh, shit, he thought, *it's coming back. It's coming back already, I didn't even get a day out of it this time.*

The shaking stopped then, but double vision came in its place, two of Brewer across the table from him now, two sets of skeptical eyes regarding him, and there was a buzzing in his ears.

"I think," Eric said, "I'm going to need to take a break."

"Excuse me?"

"I'm not feeling well. It's got to be nerves. I'm worried about my wife."

"Mr. Shaw, I assure you there's no reason to think your wife is in any danger. Unless *you* have a reason beyond what you've said…"

"I just need a break," Eric said.

Yes, a break. That's what he needed. A long-enough break to let him get back to his hotel room, let him get back to that plastic cup he'd filled with water from Anne McKinney's bottle. It was the only thing that could save him now.

"I can get you some water," Brewer said, and that produced an almost hysterical urge to laugh. *Yes, water, that's* exactly *what I need!*

"I'd actually… I need to step out for a while," Eric said, and the suspicion was building in Brewer's face like a flush.

"Well, go on outside," Brewer said. "But we do need to finish this talk."

"No, I'm going to need to go. I can come back later. I need to lie down, though."

"Excuse me?"

"Unless you're arresting me, I'm going to need to lie down. Just for a while."

He'd expected resistance, but instead Brewer gave him a very cool, skeptical nod and said, "Well, you do what you have to do, Mr. Shaw. But we're going to need to talk again."

"Of course." Eric lurched to his feet as the buzzing intensified. He felt as if he were moving through water as he went to the door. "I'm sorry, I really am, but all of a sudden I'm feeling very bad."

Brewer stood, and the sound of his chair sliding back on the floor went off in Eric's brain like a power grinder applied to the edge of a blade, sparks coming off in showers.

"I'll drive you back to the hotel," the detective said, moving around the table, and Eric raised a hand and waved him off.

"No, no. I've got it. Could use the exercise. Thanks."

"You really don't look so good, Mr. Shaw. Maybe you should let me drive you."

"I'll be fine."

"I hope you are," Brewer said. "And I hope the recovery is quick. Because we're not done talking."

"Right," Eric said, but he had his back to Brewer now. His double vision had persisted upon rising, and there were two doors floating in front of him, with two door handles. *Better grab the right one.* He reached out and fumbled, his hand sliding across the door, and then he had the handle and twisted it down and stepped out into the hallway, crossed through the front of the station and made it through the next set of doors, and then he was outside.

The fresh air was bracing and comforting, but it was accompanied by glaring sunlight that almost brought him to his knees. He staggered like a drunk and lifted a hand to shield his eyes and kept on going, plowing ahead the way he had in the dining room the night before, hoping this trip would have a better ending.

He got to the sidewalk and turned toward the hotel. There were white squares at the edges of his vision now, and he was certain he couldn't continue, but then the sun fell behind a bank of clouds. They came in quickly, pushed by a strong, warm wind, and the white squares went gray and then faded and the headache seemed to lose steam.

On he walked, sucking in the deep, grateful breaths of a man just saved from drowning. When he crossed the street he looked back at the police station, saw Brewer standing in front of the building with his hands in his pockets, watching.

This could not have been timed worse. The last place he needed to have a breakdown was inside a police station while answering questions about his whereabouts during a murder. He probably couldn't have looked guiltier if he'd been setting off three lie detectors at once. What could be done, though? It was remarkable he'd made it out as calmly as he had. The only choice was to go back to the hotel and drink what was left of the water and then call Brewer and apologize, tell him he was feeling better and ready to finish the interview. Maybe he'd even try to explain the whole crazy story. All that could be sorted out in time — right now, he needed the Pluto Water.

When he was halfway back to the hotel, the clouds lifted from the sun and the harsh white light was back, bouncing off the pavement and into his eyes, a searing, penetrating brightness that lifted the headache to a gleeful roar. He held his hands cupped over his eyes and stumbled along, walking quickly but unevenly, aware of the occasional slowing of cars beside him as passersby stared.

He'd forgotten to go through the casino parking lot and take the back way to the West Baden hotel and had walked instead all the way through town. For a long time he concentrated on his breathing, trying to keep a steady rhythm, but then his stomach got into the act, that swirling nausea, and he couldn't keep count anymore. He was soaked with sweat, but it sat cold on the surface of his skin. At one point he felt his knees wobble and he almost went down, had to pull up short and bend over and brace his hands on his thighs. A white Oldsmobile pulled up slowly when he did that, and he was afraid the driver was going to offer help, but then the car pulled away again. Nobody wanted to get out for a stranger who was bent over on the sidewalk like some sort of derelict.

The sun disappeared while he was standing there, and a minute later his legs steadied and he straightened and began to walk again. About twenty steps after that, the wind picked up swiftly and then a few drops of rain began to fall.

The rain saved him. As it opened up and began to fall harder, the wind whistling in behind him, his head cleared and the nausea subsided. Not much, just the slightest change, but it was enough to keep him upright, keep him going. As the clouds went from pale gray to a dark, deep mass that covered the street in shadows, he lifted his head and let the rain fall on his face, water running into his eyes and his mouth.

It'll keep raining, and you'll keep walking. You'll keep walking, and you'll get there and get the water. It's not that far.

It was raining hard by the time he reached the hotel, and there were short, soft rolls of thunder. The brick drive seemed impossibly long, miles upon miles, but he kept his head down and his stride as long as he could manage and he made it to the end.

Made it. I actually made it.

It was too early for a victory celebration, though — as soon as he stepped inside and the cooling rain vanished, hotel lights in its place, the sickness came galloping back out of the gates, digging the spurs in. He stumbled on his way to the elevator, turning heads and bringing silence to a group of women talking in the hall. Once he was in the elevator, the damn thing wouldn't go up, and it took him a minute before he finally remembered it required a keycard. The rapid motion when it rose was enough to make him lean over and clutch the wall, but then the doors were open again and he was out in the hallway, just paces from the room, from salvation.

He opened the door and stepped in, awash with bone-deep relief, made it halfway to the table before his brain finally caught up to what his eyes were showing him.

The room had been cleaned — carefully and completely. And there beside the freshly made bed was an empty table, the half-filled water glass discarded.

36

THIS WAS TERROR, as true and as deep as he'd ever felt it.

He dropped to his knees, driven not by physical pain but by anguish.

"You bitches," he said, speaking to the long-departed cleaning team that had removed the water. "Do you know what you did? Do you know?"

He knew. The withdrawal was going to return now in full glory, and this time there was nothing he could do to stop it, nothing he could take.

Call Kellen. Make him bring it back.

Yes, Kellen. That was the best chance he had. He got the phone out of his pocket, still on the floor, and dialed the number, held his breath while it rang.

And rang. And rang.

Then voice mail, and for several seconds he couldn't even think of words to say, too awash in the sick sense of defeat. Eventually he mumbled out his name and asked for a call back. He had no way of knowing where Kellen was, though, or if he even still had the bottle. He could have passed it off to someone by now.

All he needed was a sip, damn it. Just a few swallows, enough to hold the monster at bay, but there was nowhere to find even that much because he'd given up both the Bradford bottle and Anne McKinney's...

Anne McKinney. She was right up the road, with bottles and bottles of the water — old, unopened bottles.

All he had to do was make it there.

He stood again, shaky, dropping a palm to the bed to hold himself upright. He got in a few breaths, squinting against the pain and the nausea, and then went to the door and opened it and went out into the hall. He was alone in the elevator again, and that was good, because this time, holding the wall wasn't enough — he had to kneel, one knee on the floor of the elevator, his shoulder and the side of his head leaned against the wall. It was a glass elevator, open on the back, looking down at the hotel atrium below, and he saw a young girl with braids spot him and tug her father's sleeve and point. Then he was on the ground floor and the doors were open. He shoved upward, got out, and turned the corner and broke into a wavering jog. Speed was going to be key now. He could feel that.

He'd parked the Acura in the lower lot, closest to the hotel, and he ran for it now through the rain, which was coming down in gusting torrents, no trace of the sun remaining in the sky. Behind the hotel the trees shook and trembled.

He had his keys out by the time he got to the car, opened the door, and fell into the seat. The warmth inside the car made the nausea worse, so he put down the windows and let the rain pour in and soak the leather upholstery. He drove in a fog of pain, didn't even realize the windshield wipers were off until he was out of the parking lot. He flicked them on then, but the slapping motion made him dizzy and clouded his vision even worse than the rain itself, so he turned them back off and drove with his right hand only, leaning out the window and squinting into the rain.

As he looped through the casino lots and into French Lick, each passing car seemed to have three windshields and six headlights. At some point he must have edged across the center line, because he heard a horn and jerked the wheel to the right and hit the curb, felt the front right tire pop up onto it and then drop back to the road with a jarring bang. The thunder was on top of the town now, harsh crackles of it, and occasionally lightning flashed in front of him, leaving behind a fleeting white film over his eyes.

The tires spun as he turned onto the uphill road that led to Anne McKinney's house, but then the car corrected and he was almost there. A moment later he could see lights on in the windows, and out in the yard the windmills spun in silver flashes.

He missed the drive when he pulled in, felt the tires churn through wet soil instead, slammed on the brakes and brought the car to a stop and then threw it into park and popped the door open with the engine still running. He ran through the rain to the front door, and when he got to the steps, his shoe caught and he tripped and fell to his hands and knees on the porch. Then the door opened and Anne McKinney looked out at him, her face knit with fear, and said, "What's wrong?"

"I need some water," he said. "I need some of your water, fast."

"Pluto Water?" she said, and she pushed the door back until it was open only a few inches, allowing her to peer out, as if she were afraid of him.

"Please. I'm sorry, but I need it. I'm getting sick. I'm getting very sick."

She hesitated only a moment, then swung the door open, blinking against the rain that blew in her face, and said, "Get in here, then."

Most days she'd have been down at the hotel at this time, but it was a Sunday, and on Sunday afternoons she stayed home. The rain that blew in made her glad of that, because it came down in gales, and she was no longer fond of driving in foul weather.

She'd been studying the skies when he arrived. What thunder there was had some courage to it, and the lightning flashes were brilliant, but beyond the quantity of rain it seemed a very ordinary storm, which both surprised and on some level disappointed her. The weather radio — or *weather box,* as her husband had always called it, a small brown cube that broadcast only the National Weather Service updates — crackled with the usual warnings, but there was no mention of tornadoes or even severe storms or supercells, no spotter activation. She kept watch on the clouds all the same — she never had required spotter activation, thank you — and didn't see anything of note.

She'd been expecting more, and probably that was why the crashing arrival of Eric Shaw on her porch didn't surprise her as much as it should have.

She left him on the floor and went to the stairs, and when she took the first step, pain flared in her back and her hip. Then she looked back at Eric Shaw and saw the anguish in his eyes, blended pain and terror, and she bit down against her own aches and got moving up the steps, going just as fast as she could.

The box with the water bottles was still out in the middle of the floor because she wasn't strong enough to replace it, and now she was grateful for that. It took but a few seconds to grab a full bottle and remove the wrappings and start back down the stairs, clutching the rail with her free hand and taking careful steps, getting her foot down firm and flat each time. Eric had crawled back to the door, was sitting with his back against it and his head in his hands.

"Here you go," she said, and she was almost scared to hand him the bottle, scared to touch him. Whatever was going on in his body and mind wasn't right. Wasn't natural.

He took the bottle from her and opened his eyes to thin slits, just enough to let him see the top. He was mumbling something, but she couldn't make it out.

"What's that?"

"Lights," he said.

"Excuse me?"

"Turn them off, please."

She leaned over him and hit the wall switch and plunged the room into darkness. That seemed to give him some relief as he drank from the bottle. Years she'd saved those bottles, unopened, some of the only original Pluto Water in the valley, and now he'd gone through two in two days. Oh, well, wasn't Christian to worry about a thing like that, sort of condition he was in.

There was still a light on in the kitchen, so she walked over and turned it off, too, and now the whole house was dark. She came back into the living room and stood with her hand on the back of a chair and watched him as the rain hammered the windows and another bolt of lightning lit the room briefly. He was sitting with his knees pulled up and his head down, and after a moment's pause he drank again, just a few swallows.

I should call a doctor, she thought. *He's sick with something fierce, and the last thing that's going to cure it is Pluto Water. I've got to call him a doctor.*

But he was coming back. It was astonishing, really, the speed of it. He was recovering while she watched, his breathing easing back to normal patterns and color returning to his face and the tremors ceasing in his hands and legs. Across the room the grandfather clock Harold had made back in 'fifty-nine began to chime, and Eric Shaw lifted his head and looked at the source of the sound, and then he turned and looked at her. Smiled. Weak, but it was a smile.

"Thanks," he said.

"You're feeling better," she said. "That fast."

He nodded.

"I mean to tell you, I've never seen anything like it," she said. "Shape you were in...I was standing here thinking I'd have to call for the ambulance, and then I took but a blink and you looked better."

"It works quick when I get it."

"And when you don't?"

He closed his eyes again. "Gets pretty bad."

"I could see that. Go on and finish it."

"Don't need to," he said. "Doesn't take much."

He put the top back on the bottle, which was now about two-thirds full, and added, "I'm sorry. First of all to come crashing in your house in the rain like this; second for ruining more of your water."

"Don't you worry about that." She went over to the hall closet and got a couple kitchen towels out, brought them over and handed them to him. "Go on and dry off."

He dried his face, neck, and arms and then used the towels to mop up some of the water from the floor. While he was doing that, she noticed that his car was still running out in the yard, lights on and driver's door open. She went outside and down the steps into the wet yard. The storm was dying down now, but the thunder still had a menacing crackle to it, like a dog snarling and snapping its jaws as it retreats. Thing about a dog like that—it always comes back.

When she got to the car, she leaned in and turned it off and took the keys in her hand. The interior was soaked, water pooled on the leather seat. She closed the door and then went back into the house and handed him the keys. When he finally stood, his legs looked steady. Anne told him to take the wooden rocker and she sat on the sofa.

"I've come across plenty of stories about that water," she said, "but I never did hear of anyone needing it like you did. It's almost like you're addicted to it."

"A lot like that."

"Well, it doesn't make any sense. I don't know what would be in it that would—"

She stopped talking when she saw his eyes. They had shifted suddenly, warped into something flat and unfocused.

She said, "Mr. Shaw? Eric?"

He didn't answer. Didn't seem to have heard her, even, was staring at the old grandfather clock, but she wasn't certain he was seeing that.

"You all right?" she asked, her voice a whisper now. He was in some sort of trance. Could be a seizure, could be something for that ambulance she'd considered a few minutes ago, but for some reason she didn't think it was, didn't think she ought to go for the phone.

Give him a minute, she thought.

And so, as the thunder continued to roll, softer now, pushing east, and a light, fading rain pattered off the porch and the windows, she sat there in the dark living room and watched him slip off into a place where she could not follow.

37

It was twilight, the treetops lit by a gray gloom, and long shadows beneath, and the shack on the hilltop was creaking under the force of a strong wind. Stray raindrops splattered the ragged boards of the porch and plinked off the big roadster parked in front. Both doors opened and the two occupants stepped out — Campbell Bradford and the boy.

"Hold on there," Campbell snapped, and then he took the violin case from the boy's hand and flicked up the latches and opened it, lifted the instrument out. He handled the violin roughly, and the boy winced. Inside the case were a few handfuls of bills and coins. Campbell took all of the bills, folded them, and put them in his pocket. Then he dropped the violin back in on top of the coins and latched the case.

"There. What's left is yours. Now go on and get your uncle. I need a word."

Lucas took the case and went to the front door, stepping

carefully around one gaping hole in the porch floor. A moment after he went inside, the door opened again and the old man stepped out, clothed in the same dirty overalls and with a hat on his head. The hat had holes in the brim.

"I don't got no liquor for you tonight," he said.

"I know it. Now come on down here so I can speak without shouting."

The old man didn't seem to like that idea, but after a hesitation he walked slowly down the steps and out into the yard.

"I wish you wouldn't drag the boy down there with his fiddle," he said. "He don't like playing in front of folks."

"He makes some money at it, and so do you," Campbell said. "So kindly keep any more such thoughts unspoken. I like the sound of his playing."

The old man frowned and shifted his weight but didn't answer.

"I got a business dilemma," Campbell said, "and you're the cause of it. You ain't given me but eight jugs in a month. That's not enough."

"It's alls I had."

"That's the problem. What you have is not enough."

"There's other places for 'shine, Campbell. Lars has a still not two mile from here. Then there's them boys from Chicago, they'd bring you down booze in barrels if you was to want it."

"I don't want their damn swill," Campbell said. "Ain't none of it the same as yours, and you know that."

The old man wet his lips and looked away.

"How do you make it?" Campbell said, voice softer. "What's the difference?"

"Make it same as anybody, I suppose."

Campbell shook his head. "There's something different about it, and you know what it is."

"Figure it's the spring water, maybe," the old man said, shying away from Campbell's stare. "I found me a good spring. Small one, but good. Strange. Water don't look right coming out of it, don't smell right either, but it's got a ... *quality*."

"Well, I want more of it. And I want it fast, hear?"

"Thing is"—the old man shifted again, moving away from Campbell—"I'm not going to be able to help you much longer."

"What?"

"I'm fixin' to move. The boy needs to be somewhere else. I got a sister—not his mother, but another one—who got married and moved out east. Pennsylvania. Wrote and said he should be somewhere he could get music schooling. I don't know about that, but this place ... this place ain't fit for raising a child. I ain't fit."

Campbell didn't speak. Night was coming on quickly, shadows lengthening, and the wind howled around the home and the shed that housed the whiskey still.

"This valley's drying up," the old man said. "I've heard the talk, everybody losing their savings, banks closing. Won't be anybody down here spending money on gambling and liquor anymore, Campbell. You ought to think about getting out yourself."

"I ought to think about getting out," Campbell echoed, his voice a thousand-pound whisper.

"Well, I don't know what your plans are, but I'm going to try to get the boy east. Get him to somebody will see to him in the right way. Figure I'll probably come back, this is the only home I know. But—"

"This is *my* valley," Campbell said. "You understand that, you old shit-heel? I don't give the first damn about what's happening to banks and stocks, and I don't give the first damn about what's happening with your bastard nephew and your whore sister. This here is *mine,* and if I tell you to keep on making liquor, you damn well better take heed."

The old man kept shuffling backward, but he lifted his head and dared to meet Campbell's eye.

"That ain't how it works," he said. "You ain't my master, Campbell. Run people all over here like you was, but the truth is, you're just another greed-soaked son of a bitch. I've made money selling liquor to you, but you've made it back tenfold at least, so don't tell me that I owe you a damn thing."

"That's how you see it?" Campbell said.

"That's how it *is.*"

Campbell reached into his jacket, pulled out a revolver, cocked it, and shot the old man in the chest.

The gun was small but the sound large, and the old man's eyes widened and his hands went to his stomach even though the bullet had entered high on his chest. His tattered hat fell from his head and landed in the grass a half second before he did. Blood ran thick and dark from the wound and coated the backs of his hands.

Campbell switched the gun to his left hand and walked over to him. His stride was brisk. He looked down at the body and spat a stream of tobacco juice onto the wound. The old man gurgled and stared.

"This world breaks many a man," Campbell said. "I'm not one of them, old-timer. It's a matter of the strength of your will. You ain't never seen any strong as mine."

The door to the shack banged open and the boy stood there, hands at his side, hair tousled. Campbell gazed at him without reaction. The boy looked at the body, and then at the gun in Campbell's hand, and he did not move.

"Get down here," Campbell called.

The boy made no response.

"Son," Campbell said, "you best think about your future right now. You best think fast and hard. Ain't going to be but this one chance to make the decision."

The boy, Lucas, came slowly down the steps. He walked across the grass toward his uncle's body. There was no motion from it now, no trace of breath. When he reached the body, he looked up at Campbell. He said not a word.

"You are facing," Campbell said, "a key moment in your life, boy. *Seminal* is the word. Now look down at your uncle."

Lucas gave the body a flick of the eyes. His knees were shaking and he'd squeezed his fingernails into his palms.

"Look," Campbell said.

This time he turned his face down, stared right at the corpse. There was blood in the grass on both sides of it now, and the muscles of the dead man's face looked stricken and taut.

"What you see there," Campbell said, "is a man who had no appreciation for strength. For power. A man who could not take heed of ambition. What you have to decide now is, are you such a man?"

Lucas looked up. The wind was blowing hard and steady, bending the treetops and whipping his hair back from his forehead. He did not meet Campbell's eyes, but he shook his head. He shook it slowly but emphatically.

"I thought not," Campbell said. "You been up here for a good while. You've seen him at work. Do you know how to make that moonshine?"

Lucas nodded, but it was hesitant.

"Whatever you've forgotten about it," Campbell said, "you'd be advised to start remembering."

He put the gun away and then dropped his hands into his pockets, hunching against the wind.

"Time for you to find a shovel, boy. I'd hurry, too. Feels like rain."

Eric's hearing returned before his sight. He was dimly aware of the chiming grandfather clock before the room appeared around him, vaporous at first and then hard edged, and he found himself looking into Anne McKinney's fascinated and fearful eyes.

"You see me again," she said. It was not a question.

"Yeah." His voice was a croak. She went into the kitchen and poured him a glass of iced tea and brought it back and watched silently as he drank the whole thing down.

"You had me a little nervous," she said.

He choked out a laugh. "Sorry about that."

"It was plain to see you'd gone somewhere else," she said, and then, leaning forward, added, "Tell me — what were you seeing?"

"The past," he said.

"The past?"

He nodded. "That's the best I can describe it. I'm seeing things from another time.... They're from this place, and they are not from this time."

"This place," she said. "You mean my home?"

There was something so excited in her voice, so *hopeful,* that he was taken aback.

"No. I mean the town. The area, I guess. But not your house."

"Oh," she said, disappointment clear. "Is it scary, what you're seeing?"

"Sometimes. Other times ... just like watching a movie."

"You always have the visions when you drink the water?"

"I seem to," he said. "They're different when I have your water. Then I'm nothing but a spectator. When I drank from the other bottle...then it was more like seeing a ghost right here with me. I wasn't seeing the past, I was seeing something out of it that had joined the present."

She was quiet, considering what he'd said.

"Do you know the name Campbell Bradford?" he asked.

She rocked back. "That's not who you're seeing?"

He nodded.

"Oh, my. Yes, I know the name. Haven't heard it in years, but he was the talk of the town when I was a girl. There's plenty of folks who thought he was evil, you know. Or became evil, that's the way I remember my daddy telling it. He said Campbell was just another mean man at first, but then something dark took hold of him and pushed him beyond mean. Pushed him until he wasn't even himself anymore."

"Something dark?"

"You know, a spirit. A lot of folks believed that sort of thing in those days."

"You remember Kellen, the guy I brought over?" Eric said, and she nodded. "Well, his grandfather worked down here in the twenties and had some idea that the area was...not necessarily haunted, but—"

"Charged." The word left their mouths simultaneously, and Eric pulled his head back and stared at her.

"He talked to you about this?"

"No," she said softly, "it's just the right word."

"So you believe there are ghosts here?"

She frowned and looked at the window. "I've always connected it more to the weather myself. That's what I study, you know. And there's something different in this valley.... You can feel it in the wind now and again, and on the edge of a summer storm, or maybe just before ice comes down in the wintertime. There's something different. And *charge* is the best word for it. There's a charge, all right."

"Does that mean you believe there are ghosts here or not?"

"There's something in this area that's close to magic," she said. "You call it supernatural if you want; I've always called it magic. But there's something in the place itself—in the earth, in the water, in the wind—that has power. You know, with weather there are cold fronts and warm fronts, and when they collide, something special is going to happen. I think there's something about Springs Valley that's similar. It feels the same way to me as the air does right before those fronts collide. That probably doesn't make sense to you but it's the only way I know to explain it. A special kind of energy in the air, maybe energy beyond the natural. Could there be ghosts here? Certainly. Not everyone sees them, though. That much I'm sure of. But those who do, well, I imagine it has a mighty powerful influence."

Eric was staring at her, silent.

"Thing you need to remember?" she said. "You can't be sure what hides behind the wind."

"I don't know what that means."

She smiled. "You're too worried about figuring out what you can believe about all of this, and then figuring out how to control it. That's how most people approach their lives. Way I feel, though, after a lot of years of living? Not much of what matters in the world is under your control. You don't dictate, you adapt. That's all. So stop trying to control this, and start trying to listen to what it's telling you."

His reaction made her frown and tilt her head. "What?"

"If there's a single point to these visions," he said slowly, "I haven't been able to understand it yet. Except the first one, with the train, when he tipped his hat at me. I understood that. Campbell was thanking me."

"Thanking you? For what?"

"For bringing him home."

38

ONCE DANNY LEFT AND it was just Josiah up at the old timber camp, time slowed to a lame man's crawl, the heat baking him as he sat outside the old barn and swatted at mosquitoes that approached with a mind for feasting.

He wished he'd thought to ask Danny to bring him some food and water, but he hadn't, and now his tongue was thick from thirst and his belly knotted with hunger. Eventually the heat and mosquitoes conspired to send him into the barn.

It was a dusty wreck of a place, lined with discarded equipment and broken crates and pallets, two chipmunks coming and going through a torn board near the floor. It should have been dark, but the light bled in from a thousand cracks and holes and gaps and formed crisscrossing beams through the shimmering dust in the air that reminded him of the laser security systems you saw in heist movies.

He wandered, shoving pallets and barrels around, searching

the place because it offered a distraction to ease the painful passage of time. There was a chain saw in one corner, but it was rusted and worthless. Beside it was a long metal box, padlocked shut. That struck his curiosity — anything in a lockbox might have value. He gave the lock a tug but it held. The hasp around it was rusted, though, and the metal looked thin.

There was a crowbar in the bed of the truck, and he went for it now and returned to the box and gave it a gentle tap near the hasp. The sound of metal on metal banged loudly in the barn, and the box held. It was damn foolish to be hammering away up here, risking attention, but he was curious, so he gave it another whack, harder this time. Then a third, and a fourth, and on the fifth, the edge of the crowbar bit through the metal above the hasp. Success in sight now, he swung it in again, punching a hole in the box, and then levered the crowbar up and down, working it like a water pump handle, until the hasp had split from the box and the lock was now meaningless. He dropped the crowbar onto the dusty floor and lifted the lid.

Whatever the hell was inside certainly hadn't been cause for all that effort. A weird tangle of rubber hosing, all connected but crimped in intervals of about sixteen or eighteen inches. Looked like something you'd see in a butcher shop, a long string of sausages waiting to be cut into individual links.

He reached in and grabbed one end, then hauled the stuff up close so he could see better in the dark. There was some fine print written along the casing, and he squinted and read it: *DynoSplit*. *"Shit!"*

He dropped the stuff back into the box and took a stumbling step backward. It was dynamite, a form of it, at least. He'd been around a construction site or two, had worked for about six months at a quarry up near Bedford, knew enough to understand that dynamite wasn't made of red sticks with wicks at the end like in some cartoon. But he hadn't seen a long, continuous tube like that either. And here he'd been, hammering away at the damn box with a crowbar....Maybe you couldn't set the shit off without a detonator, but that wasn't an experiment he wanted to try.

He closed the lid carefully and stepped back from the box, wiping sweat from his face. Best not to smoke a cigarette in this place, that was for sure. He wondered how old the stuff was. Ten years? Fifteen? More? Probably wasn't even usable at this point. There was a shelf life to explosives, and the way he recollected, it wasn't long. Again, something he'd just as soon not find out in person, though.

He went back to the truck and dropped the crowbar into the bed and leaned on it with his forearms, looking around the dim, dank barn and feeling the sweat drip off his face and down his spine. He felt alone, as alone as he ever had in his whole life. Wanted to check in with Danny, see what the word was down in town, but he didn't trust the cell phone anymore. Maybe the radio would give him a sense of the situation. He got in and turned the battery to life, having no desire to start the ignition with a boxful of old dynamite not fifteen feet behind him.

There was a partial expectation in his head of hearing an "all-points bulletin," like something out of an old gangster movie, calling him armed and dangerous. Instead, he listened to fifteen minutes of shitty country music and never heard so much as a mention of the murder. He gave up then and waited until it was on the hour, when they always did a short news update, and tried again. This time they mentioned it, but said only that a man from Chicago had been killed in a van explosion in French Lick and that homicide was suspected.

It was stuffy as hell, even with the windows down, and the heat made him sluggish. After a while he felt his chin dip and his eyelids went weighted and his breathing slowed.

Good, he thought, *you need the sleep. Been a while since you had any. Last you did, in fact, was at the gulf, laying there on the rock with no reason to hide from the police, no blood on your hands...*

The shadow-streaked barn faded from view and darkness replaced it, and he prepared to ease gratefully into sleep. Just as he neared the threshold, though, something held him up. Some warning tingle deep in his brain. A vague sense of discomfort slid through him and shook loose the shrouds of sleep and he lifted his head and opened his eyes. Ahead of him the closed barn doors looked just as they had, but when he exhaled, his breath formed a white fog. It was pushing on ninety degrees in here, he had sweat dripping along his spine, but his breath fogged out like it was a February morning. What in the hell was that about?

He felt something at his shoulder then, turned to the right, and saw he was no longer alone in the truck.

The man in the bowler hat was beside him, wearing his rumpled dark suit and regarding Josiah with a tight-lipped smile.

"We're getting there," he said.

Josiah didn't say a word. Couldn't.

"We ain't home yet," the man said, "but we're getting on to it, don't you worry. Like I told you, there's a piece of work to be done first. And you made a bargain to do it. Made an agreement."

Josiah glanced down toward the door but didn't go for the handle, knowing on some instinctive level that he couldn't get out of this truck now and that it wouldn't matter even if he did. He turned back to the man in the hat, whose face seemed to be coated with the same shimmer Josiah had noticed in the dust motes caught by the streaks of sunlight in the barn. Only the man's eyes were dark.

"You don't look grateful," the man said. "You ought to be, boy. Didn't have to be you that I selected for the task. Nothing requires it. I'm bound by no laws, bound by nothing your sorry mind can even comprehend. But I came back for you, didn't I? Because you're my own blood. All that's left of it. This valley was mine once, and will be again. You're the one who's going to see to it. Time to start showing gratitude, because ain't a man alive can help you now but me."

The man turned from Josiah and gazed around the barn, shook his head and let out a long, low whistle.

"It's a fix you got yourself in now, ain't it? There's a way out of it, though. All you got to do is listen, Josiah. All you got to do is listen to me. You can count on me, yes, you can. Ask anybody in this valley, they'll tell you the same. They'll tell you that you can count on Campbell. Consistent as clockworks, boy. That's me."

His head swiveled again, dark eyes locking on Josiah's.

"You ready to listen?"

Wasn't nothing Josiah could do but nod.

The rain had stopped but the clouds were still winning the bulk of a struggle with the sun, allowing the occasional insurgency but then stomping it out quick, when Eric left Anne McKinney's house to go back to the hotel. She followed him out onto the porch and pressed the bottle of Pluto Water into his hand.

"Thank you," he said.

"Of course. Doesn't take much brains to see you need it bad. But it isn't going to work forever. So..."

"I've got to figure something out before you run out of bottles. Because then there's none of it left."

"Sure there is," she said. "Hotel's got it coming in through pipes."

"What? I thought they stopped making the stuff decades ago."

"Stopped *bottling* it, not making it. Shoot, never was something you *made*. Comes out of the ground, nothing else to it. There's still springs all over the area. They got one piped into the hotel, use it for the mineral baths."

"You can still take a mineral bath?"

She nodded. "One hundred percent pure Pluto Water."

"Maybe I'll sneak some gallon jugs in there, fill them up, and go the hell home. Pardon my language."

"Son," she said, "I was having your sort of week, I'd be saying a lot worse."

"You saved me today," he said.

"Held it off. You ain't saved yet."

That was true enough. He thanked her again and went to the car, felt the water soak instantly into his jeans when he sat. The seat and dashboard were drenched, but his cell phone, dropped onto the passenger seat and forgotten, was dry. He picked it up and saw nine missed calls, ignored them all, and called Alyssa Bradford. Got no answer. Hung up and dialed again, and then a third time, and this time she picked up on the first ring.

"I'm sorry," she said. Her voice was hushed, and he was so surprised that she'd actually answered that for a moment he said nothing.

"Sorry," he got out at last. "You're sorry. Do you understand that I've spent my day with police because a man is *dead?*"

"I don't know anything about that," she said, and now it was clear that she was whispering intentionally. Someone was probably in the room with her or nearby, and she didn't want this conversation to be overheard. "Listen, I can't talk to you. But I'm sorry, and I don't know what to say except that you should leave that place —"

"Why did you hire me?"

"What?"

"You didn't send me down here to make a happy little memory film, damn it. The bottle was part of it, but I want to know what you really were hoping to find out."

"I was tired of the secrets." She hissed it.

"What does that mean? What secrets?"

"It doesn't matter anymore. Not to you. Just—"

"Don't tell me it doesn't matter to me! I'm the one down here dealing with murders, not to mention the effects of that fucking water! Someone from your family knows the truth, and you need to find it out. I don't care if you have to go into that hospital and electroshock your father-in-law back into coherence, I want to know—"

"My father-in-law is dead."

He stopped. Said, "What?"

"This morning, Eric. About four hours ago. He's dead, and I need to be with my family. I don't know what else to tell you. I'm sorry about everything, but let it go. Leave that place and get rid of that bottle and good luck."

She disconnected, and he was sitting with a dead phone at his ear and Anne McKinney watching him from the door. He lowered the phone and started the car and gave her a wave, tried to put some cheer into it.

The old man was dead. Not that it mattered—he'd been as good as dead anyhow, but, still...

He thought of Anne's words about the supernatural being just like the weather, ebbing and flowing, fronts colliding, one side winning at least a temporary victory. When that old man in the hospital died, the one who'd been keeper of the bizarre damn bottle for so many years, what did it mean? Would it have any significance? Did it matter?

Stop thinking like that, Eric thought. *Stop buying into the idea that whatever is happening down here is real. You're seeing visions, but the people in them can't affect this world. They just can't do it.*

"They can't." He said it aloud this time, hoping the sound of his voice would add strength of conviction in his mind. It did not.

39

THE MAN IN THE bowler hat disappeared in a blink. Just that fast. He was in the passenger seat at Josiah's side, real as the truck beneath him, and then he was a memory. A memory that had every muscle in Josiah's back tight as winch cables.

He actually put his hand out and waved it around the cab. Caught nothing but air. Then he puffed out a deep breath and waited to see if it would fog again. It did not.

The man in the hat, that's how Josiah still thought of him. But this time he'd identified himself. Had called himself Campbell, had told Josiah that he was all that remained of the family blood.

Didn't have to be you that I selected.... Nothing requires it.... All you got to do is listen, Josiah. All you got to do is listen to me.

It had been another dream, that was all. Just yesterday Josiah had wondered if the man in the dream could be Campbell, and his heat-addled brain had grabbed on to that and worked it into this latest dream. Odd thing was that all his life Josiah had been a man of deep, dreamless sleep. What had changed?

Hadn't been a thing strange going on until the men from Chicago had shown up in town. The first of the strange moments had been the dream he'd had yesterday morning after the fight the night before...

No, it hadn't been then. The *first* strange thing had been what happened when he went to wash Eric Shaw's blood off his hand. The way the water had gone from hot to ice cold when it touched the blood. He'd never felt anything like that before. The house was still on a well, had an electric pump bringing in water from the same ground that produced the springs and the Lost River and the Wesley Chapel Gulf, and Josiah had always liked it that way. Didn't need any treated city water.

But, still...that had been strange. Then the dreams began, culminating in this last experience which should have been a dream but absolutely was *not*. It was like the man in the bowler hat snuck up on him only when Josiah let his conscious mind down a bit, when he was asleep or close to it. And strange as it was, the man felt familiar. Felt connected, the way old friends did. The way family did.

He popped the door handle and crawled down, his legs numb from the long stretch of sitting, looked all around the dark barn and saw nothing but shadows. Even the streaks of sun were gone, and that realization unnerved him, sent him toward the doors. When he slid them back, he saw the sky had gone the color of coal and rain was beginning to fall. There was even thunder, and how in the hell he'd missed that, he couldn't guess. Maybe this was proof that he had fallen asleep, that it had been another dream.

As he stood in the open barn door and let the rain strike his face, though, he knew that wasn't it. He'd had dreams with the man before, and this had not been one of them. This time, the man had been here. He'd been real.

He stepped out into the rain, heedless of the storm, and walked toward the trees. He felt strange, off-kilter. As if some worries had been lifted, not from his memory but from his ability to care. The rain and the thrashing trees and the lightning didn't bother him, for example. Neither did the murder warrant they were probably filing for him right now. That was strange. He should have been concerned as hell about that.

But he wasn't.

The rain soaked his clothes and made a flat wet sheet out of his hair, but he figured, what the hell, he'd needed a shower anyhow. He walked on into the woods, moving along the top of the ridge, the saturated ground sucking at his boots. He was out of sight of the timber camp and Danny was due back at any time, but the hell with Danny. He could wait for Josiah.

He came out to the edge of the ridge and stood in the open, looking out over the wooded hills that stretched away from it, a few cleared fields in the distance, the towns of French Lick and West Baden somewhere beyond. There was a sturdy sapling near the steep side, and he wrapped his hand around it and then leaned out over the drop.

"My valley," he said. His voice sounded strange.

His priority, just hours ago, had been escape. He'd need some money to do it, but if he could pull that off, he was going to get the hell out of Dodge. Now, hanging here above the stormy landscape, he didn't much want to leave. This was home. This was his.

But that didn't mean he intended to let go of the money. Lucas G. Bradford's money, a man who bore Josiah's name and had some tie to old Campbell himself. Could be Campbell had left this valley and made himself a dollar or two, then left it to Lucas

G.; could be Lucas G. had made it for himself. Josiah figured it was the former. He was feeling a strange sense of loyalty to Campbell, the great-grandfather he'd never seen. Poor old bastard had become a figure of infamy in this valley over the years, but time was when he ran it, too. He'd been a big man here once, and people liked to forget that. Would be nice to offer a reminder.

The rain was gusting into his face, no trees shielding him from the west wind now, but he was enjoying the water. Felt good to be in it. Funny, because most times he hated to get caught out in the rain.

No, he wasn't feeling like himself at all.

There were five messages on Eric's phone. One from Detective Roger Brewer, who said he was wondering when they might be able to finish their talk. The edge in his voice wasn't anything as casual as his words. Three from Claire, each with a sense of growing urgency. One from Kellen. "Heard from the police," he said. "This is no good, is it? I'd like to hear what you think."

Was there suspicion in his voice? Couldn't fault him if there was. Eric called Claire first, and the relief-fueled anger he heard in her voice when she answered warmed him in an odd way.

"Where are you? I've called that hotel fifteen times. They're probably going to throw you out of there if I call again."

"I was talking to the police," he said. "And then I, uh, I had a rough spell."

Her voice dropped, softened. "Rough spell?"

"Yeah." He gave her the update.

"You left the police station? Walked out in the middle of an interview?"

"Wasn't much else I could do, Claire. You don't have any idea what these spells are like. I barely made it to the door."

"You could have tried to explain—"

"That I'm having drug reactions to *mineral water?* That I'm seeing *dead men?* I should explain these things to a cop who's questioning me about a murder?"

It was a terrible moment of déjà vu, a return to so many instances over the past few years, him shouting at her for her inability to understand, for just not *getting it,* and her responding with silence.

A few seconds passed, and when she spoke again, it was with the careful, measured tone that he'd always found infuriating because it made him feel so small. Damn her composure, her constant control.

"I understand that might be a little difficult," she said. "But I'm worried that if you didn't offer *some* explanation, you're going to create problems for yourself."

"I'm not short on problems, Claire. Let's add more to the pile, what the hell."

"All right," she said. "That's one approach."

He rubbed his temples again, but this time there was no headache. Why was he snapping at her? Why did he always resort to this, no matter the situation?

"Where are you?" he said.

"With my parents."

Oh, how he wished she'd said a hotel. Now Paulie could step in and protect her, clean up yet another of Eric's messes. He was probably enjoying the hell out of it.

"I don't know if that's such a good place. If anybody's looking for you, that will be near the top of the list."

"They have good security here."

Indeed they did. They were twenty-six floors up in a restricted-access, luxury condo building overlooking Lake Michigan. Was going to take a damn long grappling hook to get up there.

"Dad's been making calls," she said.

"What? Why in the hell is *he* making calls?"

"To find out about the man who was murdered. Gavin Murray."

"Damn it, Claire, the last thing I need is your father stirring up more trouble."

"Really? Because it seems to me what you need is some *help*, Eric. It seems to me you need some answers. Who hired this guy, and why?"

Grudging silence. She was certainly right on the need for answers, and Paul was well connected in the Chicago legal community. He just might be able to get some.

"Tell him to start with the Bradford family," he said finally. "Start with Alyssa, and then see who surrounds her. She shut me down today, and it wasn't her decision. She was following instructions. Her only advice for me was to leave. Real insight, huh? Oh, and she said the old man is dead. Campbell. Or some version or impersonation of Campbell. Whatever the hell he was, he's dead."

"What? How?"

"Died today in the hospital, I think. She hung up without offering details."

"Wonderful. One more person who can't verify what you've told the police."

"He couldn't talk anyhow," Eric said, thinking, *except to me. He could talk to me, no problem at all. But let's not share* that *with the police just yet.*

"Have you heard back on the water test?" she said.

"Not yet. I need to call Kellen back. Then the police."

"I don't think you should do that. My father said you shouldn't."

"I can't just blow them off, Claire, you just said that yourself."

"I didn't say blow them off. But Dad said that under the circumstances you absolutely should not talk to them again without a lawyer in the room."

"But I'm just a witness."

"You've told them what you know, right?"

"But he said he had more questions and I —"

"Here are some of his questions, Eric — he wants to know if you have a history of drug or alcohol abuse or violent episodes."

"What?"

"Those were high on the list of questions when he called me, which was what I was going to explain before, but you cut me off. He seemed disappointed when I told him we were still on good terms. In other words, never say I can't lie for you."

Nice shot.

"I can't believe he called you," Eric said.

"Well, he did. And when I told my dad what was said, his response was that you need to get a lawyer. Your background isn't relevant unless they consider you a suspect."

"He doesn't think I should talk to them at all?" Eric said, hating to give any credence to Paul Porter's advice, but recognizing that the man had been a criminal attorney for many years.

"Not if you've already given a statement. He said he'll get a lawyer if you —"

"I can find a lawyer."

"All right. Great. You need to do that, and then you need to come home. You can't stay down there anymore. You *can't.*"

His response came without any thought: "But the water's here."

"The *water?* Well, take the bottle you have and come home and go to see a doctor! That's what you need to be doing."

"I don't know," he said, still taken aback by his own strange response. The water's here? It had left his mouth as if of its own accord.

"What's not to know? Have you even heard yourself tell me what's been happening? You're sick. That water is making you very, very sick."

The idea was logical enough, sure, but it felt wrong. Leaving felt wrong.

"Anne's water is different," he said. "When I drink that, Campbell stays in the past. Stays where he belongs. As long as I don't drink any more of the original bottle — and I don't even have that one right now — I'll be fine."

"Listen," Claire said, "either you come back here, or I go down there."

"That's probably not a good idea."

"It's a hell of a lot better idea than you staying down there alone, Eric. You really want to do that? With everything that's happening to your body and to your mind, you want to be down there alone?"

No, he didn't. And the idea of seeing her . . . that was an idea he'd been trying to keep out of his head for weeks. *Stop wanting her,* he'd told himself, *stop needing her.*

"I'm coming down," she said, firm with conviction now. "I'm going to drive down in the morning, and we're coming back together."

He was thinking of the weeks of silence, the way he always waited her out, lasted until she called him so he wouldn't have to show need or desire. Now here she came again, ready to get in the car and come after him while the incomplete divorce paperwork *he* had requested floated between them. *Why,* he wanted to ask, *why are you still willing to do this? Why do you want to?*

"I don't know if you should be here," he said. "Until we understand —"

"I'm going to leave in the morning," she said. "And I don't give a shit what we understand until then."

That actually made him smile. She rarely swore, only when she got fired up about something, and he'd always made fun of her for both that restraint and the periods when she cast it aside. The Super Bowl when the Bears had lost to the Colts, for example.

"I'll call you when I get close," she said. "And until I do, can you please just stay around the hotel? Please?"

"All right," he said, and he was fascinated and ashamed by the way their separation did not cast even a shadow over the conversations they'd had today, by the way she'd slipped so easily and completely back into the role of his wife. There when he needed her. Why?

"Good," she said. "Stay there, and stay safe."

40

He took Claire's advice and ignored Brewer's messages, called Kellen instead.

"You in town?" he asked.

"Yeah. Think you could come fill me in on this? I've had cops calling me."

"I'm hanging tight to this hotel," Eric said. "Preferably with witnesses present."

It was supposed to be a joke, but Kellen's silence confirmed that it was a bad one.

"Why don't you come down here and meet me at the bar," Eric said.

He agreed to that, and twenty minutes later Eric was sitting in the dark, contained side of the hotel bar when Kellen stepped through the door.

"My brother's game is on now," he said when he got to the

table, "and I don't miss those games. But this is a unique circumstance."

"Sorry. If it helps, they got it on the TVs here. You heard anything on the water?"

Kellen shook his head, sliding into the chair across from Eric, then rotating it so he could see a TV. It was late in the first quarter and Minnesota was down six. Darnell Cage had gone to the bench. Eric hadn't seen him hit a shot yet.

"So the cop wanted to know about you and that guy who stopped us in the parking lot," Kellen said. "You can imagine my surprise when they told me he was dead."

"You can imagine *mine*," Eric said.

Kellen nodded, his eyes on Eric's, and then said, "Did you kill him?"

"No. You don't know me well, don't have any reason to believe that, but I assure you, the answer is no."

"I don't think you did."

"I did see a murder today, though."

Kellen raised his eyebrows.

"Campbell Bradford committed it," Eric said. "He killed the boy's uncle. The boy with the violin. His uncle was a moonshiner, and Campbell murdered him."

"You've gathered all this through your visions."

"I know it sounds crazy, but you've seen that bottle, you've been around for everything's that happened and—"

"Whoa," Kellen said. "Slow down, man. Slow down. All I did was ask a question. Didn't make a single accusation that I can recall."

"All right," Eric said. "Sorry. I just hear how it sounds when it leaves my mouth, and I know what you must think."

"A lot of what I'd usually think has changed in the last day or two, hanging around your weird ass. So while I'm not dismissing one crazy word that comes out of your mouth, I'd also like to hear you tell me what the hell's been happening down here."

It took them almost an hour, Eric explaining what he knew and Kellen offering the same, arriving at a total that was just as empty as its parts. Kellen said Brewer had told him that while Josiah Bradford was "historically fond of trouble, but not the murdering sort of trouble," detectives were indeed looking for him. Eric knew he should care more about that, but it was hard to right now. Ever since the latest vision, it was hard to keep his mind on the present, in fact. Strange.

"I've got a question for you," Eric said.

"Shoot."

"You're the student of the area, you're the one who knows so much about the history of this place. Do you believe that the moments I've seen after drinking Anne's water have been real? Those scenes with Campbell and the boy?"

Kellen thought on it for a long time, and then he nodded. "Yes," he said. "I do. Obviously, I can't speak to the details you're seeing. But in general terms, they fit with history. Could be you're making the whole thing up, of course. I can't imagine a reason you'd do that, though, and after seeing you collapse in the dining room the other day, I'm pretty damn convinced that whatever is happening to you is real."

"Okay," Eric said. "That's what I think, too. That the moments I've seen are real. And I've started to think about ways to utilize it."

"Utilize it?"

"Think about it, Kellen — I'm seeing an untold story, but a true one. If I can keep seeing it . . . if I can get a sense of the whole, then we can try to document it, right? Document it and tell it."

"Right," Kellen said slowly.

"You're thinking that the average person would write it off as crazy," Eric said. "People love this sort of shit, though. If I could make a film out of this? Oh, man. We could be on every talk show there is, telling this story."

Kellen gave a slow nod, no response showing, and Eric had to swallow his annoyance. *Get excited,* he wanted to shout, *don't you see what this could do? It could bring me* back, *Kellen. It could give me my career back.*

There was no need to push that idea yet, though. He could take it slow. There was plenty of water.

"Anyhow," he said, "I'm just thinking out loud, sorry. I really would like to try to find that spring, though. The one they used for the alcohol. If the boy's uncle was really murdered, there must be some record of it, right? Some way to put a name with him, to identify him."

"Probably. I've been wondering about that spring, though. You said Campbell claimed it was different from the rest, and that's the same thing Edgar told us about Campbell's liquor. Remember? He said it made a man feel like he could take on the world."

"You're thinking that's what is in my bottle?" Eric said.

"Could be."

"And there might be a whole spring of that shit somewhere out in the woods around here?" Eric laughed. "Who knows what would happen if I tasted that one."

"Yeah," Kellen said. "Who knows."

The rain returned about an hour after Eric Shaw left Anne's house, but it was gentler and without the theatrics. Hardly any wind at all, but she remembered that fading thunder that had reminded her of a retreating dog and she knew that it would be back. Probably these were lines of storms coming in from the plains, a prelude to a cold front. It wasn't an unpleasant prelude to her, though. This was what she watched for. What she did, now that there was no job and no children to raise, no husband to care for. She watched over the valley instead. They didn't know she was there, maybe, didn't pay her any mind as she sat up here with an eye to the skies, but still she watched for them.

She had a card taped to the refrigerator with a few handwritten excerpts from the National Weather Service's advanced spotter's field guide.

As a trained spotter, you perform an invaluable service for the NWS. Your real-time observations of tornadoes, hail, wind, and significant cloud formations provide a truly reliable information base for severe weather detection and verification. By providing observations, you are assisting NWS staff members in their warning decisions and enabling the NWS to fulfill its mission of protecting life and property. You are helping to provide the citizens of your community with potentially life-saving information.

And below that, written larger and underlined:

The most important tool for observing thunderstorms is the trained eye of the storm spotter.

This claim made in an era of Doppler radars and high-tech satellites. They were the experts, too. So if they said it, she figured it was true. Besides, that statement was the sort of thing that had always made sense to her. It gave science its due while warning that humans hadn't yet developed a science that could understand, encompass, or predict all the tricks of this wild world. Nor, she knew, would they ever.

She turned the television on and saw they still had a thunderstorm warning active for Orange County. Well, they could pull that down. The storm was gone now and wouldn't be back for a bit. They might want to keep the flash flood warnings handy, though, because if this rain fell all night, the creeks would be high come tomorrow, when the thunderstorms returned.

There was nothing on TV worth watching. A basketball game, but while she'd been raised on basketball, she didn't care for the pro game. Still followed the Hoosiers, of course, and went to the high school sectional, but that had never been the same since they broke the legendary tournament into classes. Thank heaven Harold had been gone before that happened.

The phone rang just as she was making dinner, startled her, and she went to it, wondering if it was Eric Shaw, fearful he was having trouble again. Instead it was Molly Thurman, a young woman — well, forty — from church who was calling to tell Anne she'd been right about the weather again. Anne had guaranteed a storm after the service this morning, and it was nice to see somebody had remembered and thought to call. Molly had two boys, five and seven, and it wasn't but a minute after she called that she had to hang up to tend to some crisis with them.

The phone was silent then, as was the house around it, just the hissing of the gas flame on the stove and the dripping of water down the gutters and off the porch roof to keep her company. She was glad the phone call hadn't been Eric Shaw, having another spell, but she also would have been interested to know what was happening with him. If he were to be believed, things would remain normal for a few hours, at least. Then the pain would come back, and then he'd need some more of her water, and then he'd take to seeing things...seeing the past.

That's what he'd said this afternoon, at least. *What were you seeing?* she had asked, and he'd said, *The past.* Moments from the valley's history. And people from it. He'd seen the hotel in its glory, and then some old whiskey still up in the hills, seen it just as vividly as if it were real, seen the people as if they were in the room with him.

She thought on that while she ate her dinner and cleaned up, and when she was done, she went to the stairs again, sighed, and took the railing and started up.

When she got up to the empty bedroom, she unwrapped another bottle—her supply was dwindling fast this weekend—and held it in her hand. She hadn't tasted the stuff in years. Decades. Surely nothing would happen, though. Whatever Eric Shaw was experiencing had to be unique, or unrelated to the water at all.

But she'd *seen* him react to it. She'd sat there in the living room and watched his eyes leave this world and find another, and in that world was this town in a way she ached to see it, with people she missed, people she loved.

He'd told her it appeared to be sometime in the twenties in the visions. Her mother and father would have been young people then. Her grandmother would have been alive. Now, that would be something to see again.

There was no telling the water would land her in the same place as him, either. It could take her fifty years back instead, to a time of Harold and her children...

"Why not, Annie," she said. No one had referred to her by that name since she was a child, but sometimes she said it aloud to herself. Now she unfastened the wires and lifted the stopper from the bottle, smelling the sulfur immediately. What she'd told Eric Shaw on his first visit was true enough—this water was probably dangerous. But then, he didn't seem to drink much of it. Just a taste. And that taste took him back.

She tried a nip. Horrible stuff, made her head pound and her stomach churn, but she got it down. One thing she'd never lacked was willpower. She took a minute to settle herself and then tried another swallow, smaller this time, and then she replaced the stopper and wrapped the bottle again and put it away.

Now she would wait. Wait and, hopefully, see.

41

TIME SLID AWAY FROM Josiah while he was out in the wet woods. He'd walked all the way to the far end of the ridge and then down the slope, moving aimlessly but enjoying the feel of the water running over his skin and saturating his clothes, savoring the way he sometimes had to blink it out of his eyes just to see. The lightning stopped and the thunder softened and then faded away, and it surprised him when he realized that the western sky was no longer dark from storm clouds but from sunset.

He started back up the ridge then, mud and wet leaves stuck to his boots, everything smelling of damp wood. He caught himself spitting often, which was odd as it wasn't a habit he'd practiced before. Stranger still was the mild taste of chewing tobacco in his mouth.

The long stretch of summer twilight that should have guided him back wasn't present beneath tonight's overcast sky. He came back to the timber camp in almost total darkness and didn't make out the shape of the car until he was almost upon it. He gave a start at first and shrank back into the woods but then recognized it as Danny's Oldsmobile. When he came up behind it, the driver's door swung open and Danny stepped out with a face twisted with consternation.

"Where in the hell you been? I swear, Josiah, I was ten minutes from leaving."

"My truck was in the barn."

"I seen it, else I would've been gone an hour ago." He frowned. "You been walking around in the rain?"

"I have." Josiah leaned past him, looked into the car. "That a pizza?"

"Figured you'd need some grub. Cold by now, of course."

"Hell if I care."

They pushed the barn door open a few feet and sat just inside while Josiah ate some pizza and drank a bottle of water. It took the edge off the powerful thirst that had built in him, but neither food nor water removed that faint taste of tobacco.

While he ate, Danny gave him the update from town. Talk of the murder was common, but credible theories were not.

"You find out if the one who called himself Shaw is still in town?" Josiah said.

"He is. I had a hell of a time finding him, but then I got lucky."

"Yeah?"

"I called both hotels and asked for him. French Lick said he wasn't registered, but West Baden put me through to a room. I hung up soon as it rang."

"That's a hell of a hard time?"

"No. But just because he had a room doesn't mean he was still in it, and besides, you told me to follow him. But I don't know what kind of car he has. Car they were in yesterday was the black guy's."

"Right." Josiah caught Danny frowning at him. "What are you staring at?"

"Why do you keep spitting?" Danny said. Josiah was surprised; he hadn't even realized he was doing it again.

"No reason," he said. "Get back to the story."

"Well, I went through the parking lot, looking for Illinois plates, but there was quite a few of them, so I didn't know what to wait on. It started to rain then and I decided I'd drive back up here and ask what you thought. I was halfway through town when I seen him walking down the sidewalk."

"You did."

"Uh-huh. Wouldn't have even noticed him but he was all bent over like he was about to be sick. He walked all the way back up to the hotel, stumbling like a drunk. Wasn't but five minutes later he came out and got in a car. Acura SUV. Then he drove to Anne McKinney's house."

"Anne McKinney?" Josiah said, incredulous.

"You know who she is, right?"

"Got that house with all the windmills and shit. Comes to the hotel every day."

"Yeah."

"What would he be doing up there?"

"I'm not sure," Danny said, "but he looked awful strange going inside. Left the door open and the engine running. She had to come out and turn it off."

"She did? Well, how long did he stay?"

"A long time. Then he went back to the hotel. Didn't see him come out again, so I left to come up here. Something else — what he told Grandpa is that some woman from Chicago hired him."

"A *woman?*"

"That's what he said."

"Bullshit. He's working for Lucas."

"I got to say I don't know what we're doing, following this guy around," Danny said. "You're in a shit-ton of trouble. You ask me—"

"I didn't ask you."

Danny shut his mouth and stared at Josiah, then spoke again, his voice lower.

"Maybe not. But *if* you did ask, I'd say you only got two options. First is to turn yourself in. I know you don't want to do that, but I think it's smartest. That guy pulled a gun on you, right? You did what you had to."

"Not going to happen," Josiah said. "I got no interest in trusting the local law."

"Fine," Danny said. "Then you best get out of town. You said you need money to do it, but I don't know how you're getting any from these people from Chicago. I'll give you what I got left from the casino, be enough to get you out of here, at least."

Josiah shook his head. "Again, not an option that I favor. I'm disinclined to leave a place I've known for so long as home. It's more mine than theirs, Danny, more mine than theirs."

Danny tilted his head and squinted at him. "Why you talking like that?"

"Way I always talk."

"No, it's not."

Josiah shrugged. "Well, you never know how a man might progress, Danny, in conversation and conduct."

"I got no idea what you're talking about."

"Here's all you need to know—they aren't going to take me from this valley again, aren't going to take me from my home."

"Again?"

"My blood kin, Danny. Campbell."

"*Campbell?* What the hell? The man's been dead for eighty years! You'd never have so much as known his name if it weren't for Grandpa."

"And there's the dilemma, Danny, my boy. Isn't hardly anybody remembers his name anymore, and those that do, well, they got no word but a harsh word. In his time, Campbell did plenty for these people. Why's the man faulted just for having some ambition? Can you answer that?"

"He ran out on his family. What are you talking about, ambition?"

"That's the thing—weren't his choice to leave. He never had a mind to go."

Danny stared at him. Out beyond the barn, the dark trees were starting to weave again in a mild breeze.

"Why you using that voice?"

"Only one I got."

"Don't sound normal. Don't sound anything like you."

"Boy, you are one critical son of a bitch today, aren't you? Pardon my voice, Danny, pardon my manner of speaking, and pardon my occasional desire to spit. Sorry such qualities don't find your favor this evening."

"Whatever, man."

"You had enough of helping me? Going to leave me to handle this on my own?"

"I didn't say that. I just don't understand what I'm supposed to do that can help."

"Good thing I do, then. I got a real clear sense of your role, Danny, and it won't be a difficult task. All I'll require now is that you go on down to the gas station and buy two of those prepaid cell phones. I have some cash for you to use. Bring them back up here. I'll wait before I make my call. Seems like the sort of call you make in the middle of the night."

* * *

The pain held off until evening. Eric lingered with Kellen at the bar, drank a few more beers and even ate a meal and felt fine through all of it, actually had himself thinking maybe it was done.

It wasn't.

The first headache came about an hour after he'd eaten. The nausea settled in soon after the headache, and when he looked up at the bartender and saw the vertical hold go again, that rapid shuddering of the scene in front of him, Eric knew it was time to go.

"Feeling bad again?" Kellen said when Eric got to his feet.

"Not great. Probably just need to lie down."

He wasn't sure why he said that; they both knew it was bullshit.

"You want me to hang around or..."

Eric shook his head. "No, no. You don't need to worry about it, man. If it gets bad, I'll do what I've got to do."

"And see what you have to see," Kellen said, face grave, studying him. He put out his hand. "All right, my man. Good luck to you. And I'll be in town tonight. So anything gets away from you..."

"I'll be fine. Guarantee it. By the time we talk tomorrow, you'll see."

There was an odd ghosting to the door as he walked out of the bar, a hint of double vision returning, and the lights in the hallway burned in his skull, but somehow neither occurrence struck quite the same the chord of fear that it had before. Bad things were coming for him, yes, but he could hold them at bay now. He knew that.

He'd just take some more of the water, that was all. Every day.

Have some bad moments, sure, maybe deal with some effects that weren't ideal, but it would keep the real demons away, too. Even though it had given birth to them, it could now keep them away. Wasn't that a hell of a thing? So he'd stay on the cycle, that was all, protect himself with the same thing that threatened him.

Up to the fourth floor, hand on the elevator wall for balance, then out into the hall, smiling and nodding past a middle-aged couple who went by without a second look. He was getting the hang of this now, learning how to hide the symptoms, knowing that he no longer had to cope with them — the water would do that for him.

There was a rapid tremor working deep within him and his vision was blurred and unsteady, but he found himself laughing at it as he took the keycard from his pocket, whistling as he opened the door, cheerful as hell. *Can't touch me, can't touch me, can't touch me.* Not anymore, it couldn't. He had the cure, and who gave a shit if it was also the cause? Important part was that it worked. Control was his again.

He'd left the bottle in the room, but this time he'd taken a precaution. The room had one of those traveler's safes in the closet, the sort people used for jewelry or wallets. He'd put a bottle of water in his. Now he punched in the code — the number of Claire's old apartment in Evanston — popped the door open, and found the bottle.

Cool but not cold to the touch, completely normal in fact, and he found himself almost missing the Bradford bottle as he opened this one and drank. The taste of Anne's water was so unpleasant, fetid and harsh, with none of that honey flavor that had developed over time in the Bradford bottle. It would do the job, though, and that was enough.

Only this time it didn't do the job. Not as quickly, at least.

Five minutes later, his nausea was worse and the headache still present. Odd. He gave it another five and then drank again. Full swallows this time, steeling himself against the sulfuric taste.

Finally, success. A few minutes after this second dose, the throbbing in his temples diminished and his stomach settled and his vision steadied. His old friend was coming through again. He'd just needed a touch more this time, that was all.

He was still in the chair when the violin called to him. Whisper-soft at first, but he raised his head like a dog hearing a whistle. Man, it was beautiful. An elegy, the boy had called it. A song for the dead. The more Eric heard of it, the more he liked it.

He got to his feet and went to the balcony, where the music seemed to be originating. He opened the doors softly and stepped out and the rotunda below was gone, vacant gray space stretching on beneath the balcony instead, falling away like an endless canyon. Even the smells of the hotel were missing, replaced by dead leaves and wood smoke. Two points of light showed somewhere down in the gray canyon, and he turned to watch them. As they approached, the hotel and his memory of it faded away.

He was with the lights now and saw that they were the cold white eyes of Campbell's roadster, which had pulled to a stop outside a long wooden building with a wide front porch. Rain was pouring down, finding holes in the porch roof here and there. A few black men sat on the porch in the dry areas, smoking and talking in voices that went soft when the car door opened and Campbell stepped out into the puddles beside the car. A moment later the passenger door opened and there was Lucas, with the violin case in hand. It seemed always to be in hand.

"Gentlemen," Campbell said. "Enjoying the porch on a rainy evening, I see."

None of the black men responded.

"Shadrach's indoors?" Campbell said, unbothered.

"Downstairs," one said after a long pause, and Campbell tipped his hat and went to the door, opened it, and held it for the boy to step through. Now they were in a dark room with round tables and a long wooden bar with a brass rail. The bar and all of the tables were empty. Stacks of cards and chips stood on one of the tables. Everything was covered with a fine layer of dust.

The two of them walked through the empty room to a dark staircase in the back, went down the steep, shadowed steps. At the base of the stairs was a closed door, and Campbell opened it without knocking and stepped inside.

"Easy there," he said. A short but muscular black man was standing just inside the door and had lifted a gun when Campbell intruded. There was another man, much larger, probably close to three hundred pounds, hulking on a stool on the other side of the door, and a third, rail-thin and very dark-skinned, seated behind a wooden desk. He leaned back in the chair with his feet propped on the desk, enormous feet, a pair of equally large hands folded over his stomach. He didn't speak or move when Campbell and the boy entered, just flicked his eyes over and studied them without a change in expression. The man with the gun lowered it slowly and moved a step back from Campbell.

"Shadrach," Campbell said.

"Mr. Hunter is what I'm called by those who aren't friends," the man behind the desk said.

"Shadrach," Campbell said again, no change of tone at all.

Shadrach Hunter gave that a wry curling of the lip that seemed to pass for amusement, and then he looked past Campbell to Lucas.

"This is Thomas Granger's boy?"

"His nephew."

"What in hell's he carrying the fiddle for?"

"He likes to have it with him," Campbell said. "You've heard him play."

"I have." Shadrach Hunter was regarding Lucas with a distrustful squint. "Plays like no boy should."

It sounded like a reprimand. Lucas had kept his eyes on the floor since entering the room, and they stayed there now.

"I've got the car out front," Campbell said, "and it's raining mighty strong. Best be stepping to it."

"Might not be the best night for a long drive, then."

"It ain't far. Just out beyond the gulf. You've been out there, and don't tell me otherwise, you lying son of a bitch. You've been looking for it on your own. I'm here to tell you that as of now, that spring is *mine*. You want a piece, you're going through me to get it."

Shadrach gave him a dour stare. "I still don't know why you think I'd be fool enough to partner with you, Bradford."

"Sure, you do. There's money to be made. You're a man, like myself, who appreciates his money."

"So you've told me. But I'm also a man has made his money by staying away from those of your sort as much as possible."

"Hell, Shadrach, I don't care about the color of your damn skin, I care about the size of your capital."

"You the only one talking about color," Shadrach Hunter said in a soft voice.

Campbell went quiet and stared at him. Just outside the wall, water streamed through a gutter and exited in noisy splatters. The wind was blowing hard.

"You might have some dollars saved," Campbell said, "but there are no more coming your way, Shadrach. With the way white folks around here are hurting, how you think your people will fare? Now, I got an offer that's been made, and you can take it or leave it. You've tasted the whiskey. You know what it's worth."

"There's whiskey all over."

"You find any matches that? Shit, Old Number Seven ain't nothing but piss water compared to that. I got connections in Chicago who'll be ready to pay prices you ain't even imagined for it."

"Then why you down here looking for me?"

"Because," Campbell Bradford said, "some projects require a piece of assistance. And I've been told you're the only man in this valley got a heart as black as mine."

Shadrach Hunter showed his teeth in a grin, then said softly, "Oh, there ain't nobody in this valley comes close to that, Bradford. And that's a known fact."

Campbell spread his hands. "Car's out front, Shadrach. I'm getting back in it."

There was a moment of hesitation, and then Shadrach Hunter nodded and dropped his feet to the floor and stood up. His two companions moved toward the door with him, but Campbell shook his head.

"No. You ride with me, you ride alone, Shadrach."

Shadrach stopped cold at that, looking displeased, but after a long pause he nodded. Then he opened a drawer of his desk and took out a pistol and slid it into his belt. He took a long jacket, still streaked from rain, off a peg on the wall and put that on, and then he reached back in the desk drawer and took out another gun, a small automatic, and put it in the jacket pocket. He kept his hand in the pocket.

Campbell smiled. "Brave enough yet?"

Shadrach didn't answer as he walked for the door. He went out and up the stairs, followed by Campbell, Lucas in the rear. The top of the stairs was utterly black, and as Shadrach Hunter stepped into it, he disappeared. Then Campbell did the same, and finally there was nothing left but a pale square from the back of Lucas's white shirt. Then that was gone, too, and there were voices and sounds of people moving in the hotel and Eric realized he was sitting on the balcony with an empty bottle of water in his hand.

Empty.

He'd had every drop.

42

For the first time, he did not feel relief when the vision passed. Instead, he felt almost disappointed. Cheated.

It had been too abrupt, like a film cut off in midscene. Yes, that was exactly what it was like — always before he'd gotten a full scene, and this time it had ended without closure.

"I got the name," he said aloud, recalling all that he'd seen. "He said the damn name. Granger. Thomas Granger. Lucas is his nephew."

The realization was exciting; the disappointment that countered was that the men had been bound for the spring when he lost the vision. If he could have stayed there longer, remained in the past, he might have seen the way to it. He was seeing the *story,* seeing more than random images, but now it was gone. Lucas and Campbell and Shadrach Hunter had been replaced by the reality of the hotel once again, and he held an empty bottle in his hand, which was astounding, because he didn't remember drinking it. And troubling, because this meant he was out.

The effective dose had, in the space of forty-eight hours, increased dramatically.

"Tolerance," he said. "You're building a tolerance."

Disconcerting, maybe, but not drastic. He'd just have to keep tweaking it, that was all. Surely, his need would plateau at some point. He wasn't going to run out of the stuff. Springs abounded in the area, filled pipes and poured from faucets down in the spa.

Poured from faucets. Indeed it did.

There was no need for another drink. Not now. His headache was gone; the sickness had been avoided.

But he could see the story again if he had more water.

He looked at the empty bottle in his hand and thought about the conversation he'd had with Claire, her insistence that he'd always been prone toward psychic tendencies. Hell, he knew that. He'd lived through the moments, after all, from the valley in the Bear Paws to the Infiniti to the snapshot of the red cottage for the Harrelson video.

The ability had always been there. The gift, if you wanted to call it that. The only change now was that the water gave him some control over it. He'd been scared of the stuff initially, but was that the right response? Should he fear it, or should he embrace it?

"You've got to shoot this," he said softly. "Document it and shoot it."

Kellen's response to the idea had been less than enthusiastic. The look he'd given Eric had been more doubtful than any of the looks he'd offered after discussions of ghosts and visions and the rest, and what in the hell kind of sense did that make? Oh, well,

Kellen didn't have to be involved. He didn't appreciate the possibility the way Eric did. It was the sort of thing that was so damn strange, people wouldn't be able to get enough of it. He could imagine the interviews already—Larry King's jaw dropping as Eric sat there and calmly explained the circumstances that had led to the film. *The gift was always there...always with me. It just took me a long time to get control of it. To learn how to use it.*

He got to his feet and went back inside the room. There was an extension number for the spa listed on the card beside the phone. He called.

The girl who answered told him the spa was closing in thirty minutes. There wasn't enough time for a session, she explained. A session? All he wanted was to see the damn mineral bath. He told her as much, and was met with polite but firm resistance.

"Sessions in the mineral bath run for half an hour or an hour. There's not enough time for that, sorry. We can schedule you tomorrow."

"Look," he said, "I'll pay for a full session."

"I'm sorry, sir, we just can't—"

"And tip you a hundred dollars," he said, the situation suddenly feeling urgent to him as he looked at the empty bottle in his hand. "I'll be out by nine, when you close."

"All right," she said after a long pause. "But you're going to want to hurry down here, or you won't get much time at all."

"That's all right. Say, do you have any plastic water bottles down there?"

"Um, yes."

He said he was glad to hear that they did.

The spa was beautiful, filled with high-grade stone and ornate trim, fireplaces crackling. He'd routinely mocked men he knew in California who frequented such places, too much of the Missouri farm-town boyhood still in him to sample that lifestyle. Yet here he stood in a white robe and slippers, padding along behind an attractive blond girl who was opening a frosted door that led to the mineral bath.

"It's a complete re-creation of the originals," she said, pausing with the door half open. "But most people these days do add aromatherapy. Are you sure you don't—"

"I want the natural water," he said. "Nothing else."

"Okay," she said, and opened the door. The potent stench of sulfur was immediately present, and the blond girl grimaced, clearly horrified that he hadn't elected to go with the scent of vanilla or lavender or butterfly wings or whatever the hell it was that you were supposed to use.

"You might feel a little light-headed at first," she said. "Kind of giddy. That's from all the gases that are released by the water, lithium and such. There's a complete list of the chemical content there on the counter if you're int—"

"Thanks," he said. "I'll be all set."

She'd been on the verge of a full introductory speech, he could tell, and he didn't want to waste time. He wanted to get to work emptying the two plastic water bottles she'd given him and filling them with Pluto Water.

She left then, and he was alone in the green-tiled room that stank of sulfur. The tub was still filling, pouring out of the hot-water faucet only. There were two faucets, the girl had told him, both depositing mineral water directly from the spring, with the only difference being that one carried water that had been heated to one hundred and two degrees.

There was a sink across from the tub, and he poured the water from his bottles into that, shook them as dry as possible, and returned to the tub. He turned on the cold-water faucet, cupped his hand, and caught some of the water. Lifted it to his mouth and sampled, frowning and licking his lips like some asshole wine connoisseur. It tasted different from Anne McKinney's, crisper and cleaner. Of course, it hadn't been in a glass bottle for eighty years. Just because it tasted different didn't mean it wouldn't work. He hoped.

He filled one bottle about a third and then pulled it back from the faucet and stared at it, thinking of the last vision he'd had, of the boy vanishing up the stairs beside Campbell Bradford and Shadrach Hunter. Where had they gone? What had happened next?

The idea that had slipped into his mind was growing legs now: if he could find ways to document this, if he could tell a tale that had been hidden from historians, hidden from the eyes of ordinary men, well, the result would be extraordinary. In the past, he'd never discussed his rare and brief flashes with anyone but Claire, because a man who claimed psychic tendencies would quickly be dismissed as a lunatic. It was the way of the world. But suppose he could *prove* what he'd seen as the truth. And suppose, with the water as his aid, he could do it again, on another story. A self-proclaimed psychic was the subject of ridicule, but a proven entity, a film director whose exclusive ability allowed him to shatter secrets and expose the unknown, would be something else entirely. He'd be a star. Beyond that. A legend. Famous as famous got.

It was a fantasy. But there was also a possibility, perhaps a stronger one than he dared admit, that it could become a reality. See the story, document it, and turn to the Hollywood connections he had left. There were publicists and agents who'd salivate at the very idea. And once the buzz began . . .

But first he had to see the rest of it. First he had to know what had happened. The water would provide that for him.

In a soft voice, he said, "Show me. Show me what happened," and drank. Drank it all. That done, he leaned back to the faucet.

Once both bottles were filled, he put them in the pocket of the big robe, then looked around the room and watched the water cascade into that old-fashioned tub. What the hell, he'd come down here, and he'd paid for it.

He took off the robe and his underwear and stepped down into the water, finding it the perfect temperature for soaking sore muscles. He probably had only ten minutes left, but that was all he'd need. He'd never been one for hot tubs, really.

But this one did feel good. Felt incredible, really, like it was finding kinks and knots in his muscles and lifting them away, lifting him a little bit, too. That must be the gas from the mineral blend. It did make you a little giddy, at that.

He flicked his eyes open and inhaled deeply, breathing in those mellowing fumes. The ceiling looked different. For a moment he was confused, unsure of the change, but then he realized — there was a fan overhead now, wide blades paddling lazily through the air. That hadn't been there before, had it? He rolled his head sideways then, back toward the door, and saw he was no longer alone.

There was a second tub in the room now. A long, narrow white bowl resting on claw feet. There was a man inside. He had his head laid back as Eric had a minute ago, face to the ceiling, eyes closed. He was clean-shaven and had thick dark hair, damp and glistening. His chest rose and fell in the slow rhythm of sleep.

He is another vision, Eric thought, not moving at all, afraid a single ripple in the water would cause the man to raise his head. *It's just like the others.*

It wasn't like the others, though. Not like watching a movie, everything distant. This time, it was here with him. As it had been with Campbell in the train car.

He heard a click then, and the door pushed open, nothing but blackness on the other side, and Campbell Bradford stepped into the room.

His eyes were straight ahead, on Eric. Maybe it *was* going to be like the one in the train car, when Campbell had spoken directly to him, when he'd had to run for the door because Campbell was on his feet and walking toward him...

Campbell turned away, though. He flicked his eyes away from Eric and to the sleeping man in the other tub, and then he walked toward him. He moved quietly, his shoes sliding over the tile floor, his suit barely rustling. When he reached the man in the tub, he stood over him silently, looking down. Then he slid his suit coat off his shoulders and laid it over the back of a chair. Once the jacket was off, Campbell unfastened his cuff links and set them on top of the coat. Then he rolled both sleeves up past the elbows. Still the man in the tub didn't move, lost to sleep.

Warn him, Eric thought. *Say something.*

But of course he couldn't. He wasn't part of this scene, he just felt like he was. Campbell couldn't see him; Campbell was not real. Eric hadn't taken any of the Bradford water, none of that dangerous stuff that brought Campbell out of the past and into the present. All he had to do was watch and wait for it to go away. It would end in time. He knew that it would end in time.

For a long moment, Campbell stood above the man in the tub and watched him, almost serenely. When he finally moved, it was with sudden and violent speed. He lunged out and dropped the palm of one hand on top of the man's head and put the other on his chest, near the collarbone, and then slammed his weight behind them and drove the man into the water.

The tub exploded into a frenzy of water and both of the man's feet appeared in the air, flailing. His hands clenched first on the edges of the tub and then grappled backward at his antagonist. Campbell appeared not to notice.

He held him down for a long time, and then straightened and hauled back. His right fist was wrapped in the man's hair now. Once he cleared the water, gurgling and gasping, Campbell slammed him down again. This time he held him even longer. Held him until the frantic motions slowed and almost ceased. When the man's hands had lost their grip on Campbell's jacket and drifted back toward the water, he let him up again.

They do not see you. Cannot see you. It was a frantic mantra, the desperate reassurance of someone in a plane hurtling toward the earth — *the pilot will fix this.*

Campbell had released the man in the tub and stepped aside and was only a few feet from Eric now. The man hung on to the side of the tub, gasping and choking, water streaming from his hair to the tile floor.

"There are debts to be paid," Campbell said. His voice was eerily calm. "I've established this with you in the past. Yet they remain unpaid."

The man looked at him with disbelieving eyes, chest heaving. His face was wet with water and tears, and there was a smear of blood-tinged mucus beneath his nose.

"I don't have any money!" he gasped, pulling back to the edge of the tub, dragging his knees up as if to protect himself. "Who does right now, Campbell? I lost my savings. You see how empty this hotel is? That's because nobody has any money!"

"You seem to think that your circumstances affect your debt," Campbell said. "That is not an idea which I share."

"You're crazy, trying to collect now. Not just from me — from anybody. There's no money left in this valley. The whole thing's going to disappear in a blink. Don't you read the papers? Listen to the radio? This country is going to hell, man."

"I'm not concerned with this country," Campbell said. "I'm concerned with what's owed me."

"They're not even going to be able to keep this hotel open, I can promise you that." The man was babbling now, his voice nearly hysterical. "Ballard might try to force it along, but it'll close and they'll be broke, too. Everyone will be. Everyone in this whole country will be broke soon, you wait and see. It'll come for us all."

Campbell used his index finger to push his hat up on his head, and then he reached into his pocket and came out with a chaw of tobacco, worked it in behind his lower lip. The man in the tub watched warily, but Campbell's silence and cool demeanor seemed to have soothed his panic. When the man spoke again, his voice was steadier.

"Hand me that robe, will you? You could've killed me earlier. All to try and get money that I don't have. Now what would the point of that have been?"

"The point?" Campbell said. "I don't understand your confusion. There's nothing difficult to this situation. The world breaks some men. Others, it uses for the breaking."

He tilted his head and smiled. "Which one do you figure I am?"

The man in the tub didn't answer. When Campbell walked toward him, he did not speak or cry out in alarm. Instead he watched, silent, until he saw Campbell's hand dip into his pocket and come out with a knife. Words left his mouth then, left in a harsh whisper of terror, just two of them: "Campbell, no—"

Campbell's hands flashed. One caught the man's sopping wet hair and jerked backward, exposing the throat; the other dropped the blade and cut a ribbon through it. Blood poured into the water.

Eric's body seized at the sight. He couldn't get a breath, couldn't do anything except watch the blood drip into the tub, the sound like a water glass being refilled from a pitcher. *They can't see me,* he thought. Had to remember that. Had to remember...

Campbell turned and looked at him. Those watery brown eyes found his, and when they did, the wild thoughts died in Eric's brain and even the sound of the blood seemed to disappear.

"You wanted me to show you," Campbell said. "Now you've been shown. There's plenty more on the way for you, too. I'm getting stronger, and you can't stop it. All the water in the world ain't going to hold me back now."

Then he pulled his lips back, the gesture a cross between a smile and the warning of a dog showing his fangs, and spit through his teeth. A stream of tobacco juice landed in the mineral bath, splattering Eric's stomach and chest with brown drops.

Eric shouted, the moment having just cost him any slight faith that what was happening in this room was not real. He scrambled to get out of the tub, moving to the far end, away from Campbell, and as he turned his head, Campbell laughed, a low whispering snicker of delight. Eric's knee caught the faucet and his shin smacked off the ceramic edge of the tub and then he was over the side and on the tile floor, naked and dripping and helpless as Campbell advanced. Eric twisted to face him, thinking he'd do what little he could to defend himself.

Campbell was gone. The second tub was gone, and the bleeding man.

Eric sat there on the floor in a puddle of water and gasped for breath, and then the door banged again. He tried to jump to his feet but slid in the water, his heels going out from under him and dropping him back against the edge of the tub with a painful impact as a female voice floated in from the other side of the door.

"Mr. Shaw? Are you—"

"I'm fine!" he yelled. "I'm fine."

"I thought I heard you shout," she said.

He reached for the robe and dragged it down to cover himself.

"No, no. I'm done, though. I'm going to be coming out."

He got unsteadily to his feet and slipped into the robe. The pockets banged off his hips, weighed down by the two plastic water bottles he'd filled.

"Just another vision," he said to himself. "Harmless as the others. You'll get used to them."

He turned to lift the plug from the tub and froze with his arm extended.

There, on the surface, floated a cloud of brown liquid. Tobacco juice.

He stared at it for a long time. Closed his eyes and reopened them and it was still there. Straightened and stood above the tub and studied it from an angle, then turned in a full circle, making sure the rest of the room was as it had been when he entered, before looking at the tobacco juice again. Still there. Disintegrating in the water now, thinning and separating, but still there.

How?

It had come from Campbell's mouth, and Campbell had been a vision, was gone completely now, just as had happened with all the previous visions. Never before had a trace lingered, never before had the visions left any mark on reality.

"Mr. Shaw?"

"Coming out!" he shouted, and then he opened the drain and

let the tub of mineral water begin to empty. He stood there until the tobacco juice found the drain, and when it did a shiver rode high on his spine.

For a moment, just as it swirled out of sight, it had looked exactly like blood.

Part Four

COLD BLACK CLOUD

43

It took Danny about forty minutes to return with the cell phones. At first Josiah waited on the floor of the barn near the open door. As time passed, though, he found himself outside in the rain, leaning up against the barn wall, the weathered boards rough on his back. There was a tree that hung over the barn at this edge and kept the rain from falling on him. It was a light rain now, a gentle touch on his flesh, so he moved away from the tree and found a spot where he could sit against the barn wall and let the rain come down unobstructed. He was there when he saw the headlights of an approaching car, and though he knew he should move into the woods until confirming it was Danny, he did not. For some reason, he wasn't all that concerned about who it was.

The car was the Oldsmobile, though, and Danny pulled it up close to the barn and pushed his door open while the engine was still running.

"What are you doing sitting in the rain?"

"Passing time," Josiah said, rankled by both the question and Danny's expression, the way he was staring at Josiah like he was crazy. "You get the phones?"

"I did."

"Well, bring them here. And shut the damn headlights off."

They went back into the barn and Danny set up one of those battery lanterns, filled the room with a white light.

"Figured you could use this," he said. He also had a few bottles of water and a bag of beef jerky, and all Josiah did was grunt a thank-you, but he didn't like the lantern. He'd grown used to dark — almost to the point of fondness, really.

Danny had purchased, as instructed, two prepaid cell phones and a battery charger that Josiah could plug into the truck's cigarette lighter. He got the first phone out of the package now and started charging it.

"I don't understand why you needed two of them."

"If I'm going to be calling these people in Chicago, you think it'd be a real good idea to call you from the same number?"

"Oh," Danny said. "That's good thinking. This guy you're going to call, his number was in the briefcase you stole?"

"Yes."

"I still don't understand how you're going to get any money out of him."

"Fact is," Josiah said, "a man can get awful lost in details if he dwells too much on them. I don't intend to have such a hindrance. The man paid someone thousands of dollars to drive down here and sit outside my home, Danny. Paid another man to come down and talk to Edgar. Hell, might have been paying that one that told me he was a student. But the paperwork I got suggests something about me was worth a dime or two to this old boy. If it was worth something last night, it still will be tonight."

"Last night his detective wasn't dead."

"Now, that is a fair observation."

"Josiah, why don't you just take the money I got and get—"

"You gone down to the hotel yet to check on Shaw?"

"No. You told me to get the phone first."

"Right. Well, now I got it."

Danny frowned. "All right. I'll go. You just want to know if he's there?"

"And where he goes if he leaves, yes. You got the numbers off the phones you bought, right?"

"Yes."

"Well, use the first one. Don't even think about calling the second one, just the first, got it? Call if you see him move."

Danny hesitated and then gave a short nod and moved toward the door. He stopped when he was just on the other side, turned back, and looked at Josiah, his face a pale moon in the lantern light.

"So you're going to call this guy and ask for money? Like that's all there is to it?"

"That's all there'll be to the start of it," Josiah said. "I figure there could be a twist or two along the way."

Evening came on and settled and the rain fell soundlessly but unrelenting. Anne sat in the living room with a book in her lap but didn't read. The depth of her desire was surprising to her, the sense of urgent anticipation she had as she watched the clock tick minutes off the day and waited for the water to take effect.

Come on, she thought, *let me see what he is seeing. Let me go back to those times I never appreciated enough when I was in them, let me see those faces and hear those voices again.*

Nothing happened. The short hand found seven and then eight and then nine, and she saw nothing but the achingly familiar walls of the house. She considered going for more water, but the stairs seemed so steep and the results so uncertain that she stayed in her chair. She'd seen how much Eric Shaw had to drink before the visions came for him and was sure she'd had at least an equal amount. Why, then, was he allowed to see the past and she was not?

She went to bed after taking her last round of readings, turned off the light, and watched the shadows shift as the moon struggled for a space amidst the clouds. The water had not worked for her. She'd felt vaguely nauseated since taking it, but she had seen nothing. A wasted risk. How could she have allowed herself to do such a thing? The water could have poisoned her. Or, worse, wreaked the sort of havoc it had with Eric Shaw, putting her into the throes of pain and addiction.

Logical as all those thoughts might be, she couldn't make herself care about them. She'd understood the risk well enough at the start, but the reward had seemed so tantalizing...and still did.

Maybe it started with his bottle, the bottle he claimed came from Campbell Bradford. Maybe you wouldn't see anything until you'd tried some of that. She'd have to call him in the morning, see if he'd gotten the Bradford bottle back yet, hope it would work with her as it had with him. It seemed worth a try.

She had a sense, though, that it would not work. She could drink his water and still see nothing, still be trapped here in the present, the lonely present of this empty house, and the ones she'd loved would continue to exist merely as memories and fading photographs. Why was Eric Shaw allowed to see the past and she was not? Why was some of the world's magic presented to only a few and hidden from others?

The visions would not come to her, no matter how much of the water she drank. She would wait for them without reward, just as she'd waited for the big storm, waited with faith and patience and a confidence of purpose that she would be needed, that there was a reason she remained here. They'd need her someday; they'd need her knowledge and her trained eye and her shortwave radio. She had been certain of it.

But maybe not. Maybe it was all a charade, a silly girl's notion that she'd never let die. Maybe the storm was never coming.

"Enough," she whispered to herself. "Enough of this, Annie."

Sleep swept over her then, descending with the speed and weight of a long day filled with unusual activity. She had a dim realization, just before it took her, of a light whistling sound.

The wind was coming back.

44

I'M GETTING STRONGER, and you can't stop it. All the water in the world ain't going to hold me back now.

The memory chased Eric up the stairs and back to his room, the words echoing through his brain.

He'd been real again. Without so much as a drop of the Bradford water passing through Eric's lips, Campbell had been made real again. This time the vision had been a sort of hybrid, actually — a moment from the past again, yes, but this time Eric had been a participant as well as a spectator.

What in the hell had happened? What had changed?

He called Kellen. The first thing he said was, "He spoke to me again."

"Campbell?"

"That's right."

"He spoke to you in a vision?"

"Well, it wasn't on the elevator."

Quiet again. Eric said, "Sorry, man. I'm just a little—"

"Forget it. What did you see?"

Eric told him about the murder of the nameless man in the mineral bath. He was sitting in the desk chair in the room, hair still damp, muscles still tight and stomach trembling from what he had seen.

"At first it was like they have been recently, you know, a scene from the past. Only there wasn't any distance; I was right there for it. It didn't involve me, though. Not in the beginning. When it was done, after he'd killed that guy . . . he turned and spoke to me. He spoke directly to me and spit tobacco juice into the water, and the tobacco juice was still there after he was gone. It was real, damn it. It was—"

"Okay," Kellen said, his voice soft, calming. "I get it."

"I don't know why it changed," Eric said. "I can't figure out why it would have changed. Maybe because I was in the water, you know, immersed? But the only times I've seen him like that before were after drinking from the original bottle, and that thing's nowhere near me now."

"He said he was getting stronger?"

"Yeah. And that all the water in the world wasn't going to stop him."

"So the water's been helping you."

"Helping me?"

"You know, protecting you."

From what? Eric thought. *What in the hell is going to happen if I stop drinking the water? And what if he wasn't lying—what if he is getting stronger? Does that mean the water won't work anymore?*

"You said that was your second vision," Kellen said. "What was the first?"

So he told him about the Shadrach vision, realizing halfway

through that he'd completely forgotten that he'd been given the name of the boy's uncle. Somehow such details seemed insignificant after the scene in the spa.

"Let me ask you something," Kellen said. "What did Shadrach Hunter look like?"

Eric gave as much detail as he could and then described the bar.

"I'll be damned," Kellen said, voice soft. "It's real. What you're seeing is real."

"Yeah?"

"I've found a few pictures of Shadrach. Very few. Aren't many that exist anymore. You just described him to a T. And that bar, that's one of the old black clubs, the one they called Whiskeytown. That's Shadrach's club."

"I've got to find that spring, Kellen."

"Why?"

"I think it matters," Eric said. "Check that—I *know* it matters. You were right with what you said earlier. Anne's water hasn't been causing problems; it's been preventing them. Showing me the truth but keeping Campbell at bay. I need to find the spring that mattered so much to all of them, though. There's a point to these visions, Kellen, and they're all headed in that direction. I need to follow them."

Kellen was silent.

"Can we find it?" Eric said.

"The uncle's name is a start, but I don't know how much of a help it will be. There's nothing else that we can go on? Nothing else you saw or heard?"

"No," Eric said. "Just that his name was Thomas Granger, and—. Wait. There was something else. Campbell told Shadrach he knew he'd already been out in the hills, looking for the spring. He said it was by the gulf. But what in the hell would that mean? The only gulfs I know are in the ocean."

"Wesley Chapel Gulf," Kellen said. "You've got to be shitting me."

"What?"

"It's part of the Lost River. A spot where it rises from underground and fills this weird stone sinkhole and then sinks again. One side of the sinkhole is like a cliff, must be a hundred feet high at least. I've been there once. It's a very strange spot. It's also where Shadrach Hunter's body was found."

"You're kidding."

"Nope. His body was found in the woods on the ridge above the gulf. That's why I went out there. I just wanted to see the place and, like I said, it's strange."

"Well, maybe I should see it, too."

"Yeah," Kellen said, and there was unconcealed fascination in his voice. "You're really seeing it, man. The truth. Everybody thought Campbell murdered Shadrach, but it's never been proven, you know? What you just saw, with the two of them heading out there...that's the truth, Eric."

I knew it was, he thought, *and maybe now you'll see the potential in this.*

"You can get me there, then?"

"Absolutely."

"We'll go tomorrow," Eric said. "First thing."

"All right," Kellen said. "But before you hang up, there's something I wanted to tell you. I talked to Danielle, and she said the bottle's getting warmer."

"Warmer?"

"Yeah. The Bradford bottle, the original. I thought it had warmed up a little during the drive, but she said it's almost normal now."

"Weird," Eric said. He didn't know what else to say.

"Yeah. I was just thinking that suggests whatever's happening has a lot to do with its proximity to this place."

"Maybe," Eric said, thinking that it had been cold back in Chicago, though, and that was miles farther away. "I'll call you in the morning, all right?"

He hung up and went out onto the balcony, stood and looked down over the hotel. The bottle could be affected by its proximity to this valley. Eric had consumed its contents, and the effects had changed dramatically once he left Chicago and came here. Perhaps if he left, they would lessen. Stop altogether, even.

But then I wouldn't be able to see it, he thought. *I want to keep on seeing it.*

He'd stay, then. There was no other choice. He couldn't leave now.

I'm getting stronger, Campbell had said.

Never mind that. He was a figment, nothing more. He had no real power in this world.

None.

Josiah waited until midnight to call. Originally, he'd planned to do it later but he was impatient and there was something about the hour of midnight that attracted him.

Both phones had full charges by then, and he used the second one and didn't worry about trying to block the number. It was an anonymous phone, paid for in cash, and even if they could trace it to the gas station where Danny had bought it, Josiah didn't much care. Anything coming from that sort of detective work took time, and he wasn't too worried about long-term plans. More concerned with getting what was owed to him. He didn't know what that was yet, but his gut said that Lucas G. Bradford did.

He called the number that was listed as residence on the paperwork he'd taken from the detective, listened to it ring. After five rings it kicked over to a message. He disconnected, waited a few minutes, and tried again. This time, it was answered. A male with a husky voice, speaking low, as if he didn't want to be overheard.

"Lucas, my boy," Josiah said.

"Excuse me?"

"I'm sure you've heard the unfortunate news of your friend in French Lick."

The silence that followed brought a smile to Josiah's lips.

"Who is this?" Lucas Bradford said.

"Campbell Bradford," Josiah said. Hadn't even planned on that; it just left his lips, natural as a breath. Once it was said, he liked it, too. Campbell. That felt right. Hell, felt almost like the truth. He wasn't Campbell, of course, but he was a representative. Yes, these days, he was the next best thing.

"You think that's funny?"

"I think it's true."

"Is this Eric Shaw? You better believe I'm calling the police to report this."

Eric Shaw? Now what the hell was that supposed to mean? Shaw was working for the guy…unless the story he'd told Edgar about working for a woman in Chicago had been true. But then who was the woman?

"The police will be called—"

"Really?" Josiah said. "That's what you'd like? Because I have some interesting documents in my possession, Lucas. And your detective, he had some interesting things to say before he died."

That last bit was improvisation, but it silenced the prick's tirade, seemed to take a little of his heat away.

"I'm not worried about that," he said, but there was no strength in his voice.

"Here's what I understand," Josiah said. "Some funds have

been authorized to resolve what you perceive as a crisis. One hundred thousand dollars, I believe."

"If you think you're getting that now, you are out of your mind."

"I'll get what's owed to me."

"There's nothing owed to you."

"I disagree, Lucas. I firmly and vehemently disagree."

As he heard the words leaving his mouth, Josiah frowned. Danny was right—he was starting to talk funny. Not like himself, at all. That probably wasn't a bad thing on a call like this, though. A disguise of sorts, albeit unintentional.

"I'm not interested in the hundred grand," he said. "I don't find that sum to be satisfactory. In fact, I haven't determined what will be satisfactory. I'm still considering."

"If you think we're in a negotiation, you're mistaken. I know my wife had no idea what she was doing when she hired you, but she regrets it now, and any further contact you have with this family will be done through attorneys. I encourage you to find a good one. My recommendation is that it be one with criminal defense experience, too."

When my wife hired you? This was interesting. This was different.

"Never call this house again," Lucas Bradford said.

"Now, Lucas," Josiah began, but the line had clicked and gone dead. He switched to the other cell phone and called Danny.

"What happened?" Danny said, his voice choked with either alcohol or sleep or both. Hell of a guy to have working for you on a stakeout. "What's going on?"

"I think you best get your eyes open," Josiah said. "I do believe there may be a police appearance at the hotel shortly."

"Why? What are you talking about?"

"Eric Shaw should be getting some visitors," Josiah said, and then he hung up and sat in the dark with a grin spreading across his face. Shaw would buy him some time, and that was good, but moreover he'd enjoyed this first brush with Lucas G. Bradford. He liked the rich bastard's tone, the sense of control, the belief that he could run this world and everyone in it. He thought he was strong, and Josiah was pleased by that. Let it turn into a battle of will, Lucas, let us see who breaks first.

45

FOR A LONG TIME Eric sat on the balcony, sipping the water he'd taken from the faucet in the spa and waiting for visions, but none came. Eventually, he went back inside and pulled the curtains shut and turned off every light before he got into bed. Around him the room existed in shadows and silhouettes and nothing changed within it or entered from outside. At some point consciousness slid away from him, folded beneath sleep.

The thumping on the door woke him.

He let out a grunt and sat up, blinking at the dark room and trying to get his bearings. Just when he thought he'd imagined the sound, he heard it again. A knock.

The clock beside the bed said it was twenty past one.

He sat in bed, supported by the heels of his hands, and stared at the door. *It's Campbell,* he thought, and then he turned and looked at the door to the balcony, as if he could run out there and hide like a child or fling himself from it and sail down to the floor below and escape.

Another knock then, louder this time.

"Shit," he said under his breath, and then he got to his feet, wishing for a weapon. He'd never had any interest in guns as an adult, though he'd hunted as a boy, but he wanted one now. He ignored the peephole because he was afraid to peer out and see what waited, chose instead to unfasten the lock quickly and jerk the door open.

Claire stood in front of him.

"I didn't think it was a good idea to wait until morning," she said, and then she stepped past him and into the room.

He closed the door and locked it, then pulled on jeans and a T-shirt while she sat on the edge of the bed, regarding him like an engineer inspecting a building's structural integrity, searching for cracks. He had not seen her in more than a month. Her beauty struck him now just as it always had, or maybe even harder because it had been so long. She was wearing jeans and a black tank top over a white one, no jewelry and no makeup, and her hair was tousled in the way it often was after a drive because she liked to have the windows down. He'd always loved that about her, had always liked a woman who didn't mind being windblown. There were laugh lines around her mouth, and he remembered telling her he was proud of them when they began to show because he could take credit for plenty of them. There were also lines on her forehead now, though, creases of frowns, of sorrow and pain. He could take credit for plenty of those, as well.

"What are you doing here, Claire?"

"Like I said, I didn't think it was good to wait until morning. The conversations we had today were getting progressively worse. Scarier."

"What did you do, climb out the window and rappel down from Paul's penthouse? There's no way he would've wanted you to be a part of this."

"Actually," she said, "he encouraged it. He thought it was a dangerous idea for you to be alone. Medically, and legally."

He grunted.

"Can I see it?" she said.

"See what?"

"The bottle."

"I don't have it, remember? Kellen took it up to Bloomington to have it tested."

"I didn't realize you sent the whole thing. I thought maybe he just took a sample. I wanted to see it."

"Well, it's gone."

She'd given him an odd look when he told her the bottle was gone, and he wondered if she was searching for proof, looking for some sort of sanity test.

"You've stayed here tonight?" she said. "Haven't left the hotel?"

"That's right."

"I looked for your car in the parking lot. If you were gone, I was going to hunt you down and kick your ass."

He couldn't find anything to say. It felt so out of place to be in the room with her, to be looking her in the eye again. She sensed the response.

"You may not want me here. I understand that. But I'm worried. If you come back to Chicago, if you go to see doctors and lawyers and people who can help, I will step aside. But I want to make sure you do that."

"Thank you."

"Hey, don't worry about it. Just protecting my reputation. Reflects poorly on me if my husband gets arrested for murder or locked up in a hospital for the insane."

He smiled. "People would gossip about you."

"Point their fingers and whisper. I couldn't bear that shame. Just taking social precautions, that's all."

Say, "I miss you," he thought. *Say it, you dumb shit, it's all you want to tell her, so just put the words in your mouth and let them go.*

"How long was the drive?" he said.

She gave him a look that was both amused and sad. "That's what we should be talking about?"

"Sorry."

"No, I understand. It's strange to see me, and you don't even really want me here, but there are things —"

"Stop," he said. "It's good to see you. The fact that you came down...I appreciate it more than you know."

"You can mail me a formal thank-you next week. Use nice stationery. But until then, we've got to figure out what to do. I still think you need to go home. It's why I came. To bring you home."

"Right," he said. "Go home." Home. Away from here, away from the story that had wrapped him in its eerie embrace. Away from the water.

"So you're agreed? We can leave in the morning?"

He got to his feet and walked over to the balcony door, pushed back the heavy draperies, and waved his hand out at the dome and the expansive rotunda.

"It's a hell of a place, isn't it?"

"Gorgeous," she said. "So we're leaving in the morning?"

He looked out at the hotel for a long time in silence, then turned back to face her.

"Claire, the things I'm seeing...the story that's there, it's powerful."

"What does that have to do with staying or going?"

"I'm getting the story because I'm *here,* Claire. Because I'm here, with the water. I'm seeing it almost like a narrative now, I'm seeing the story moving forward, and—"

"What are you talking about?"

"I'm beginning to realize that there's a purpose to it, that I need to *tell* this story. This is the movie, Claire, this is the one I've been waiting for, the one I couldn't find. If I stay down here for a while—long enough for me to get the whole thing down—I can turn this into something special, I can use this to get back in the game. Wouldn't that be amazing? To use something like this as a way to get back what I've lost? But I'm starting to feel like that's what it was all about, like I've been given a shot here, a chance at redemption and I just had to see that it was there."

She was watching him in disbelief, lips parted. Now she said, "Are you kidding me? You want to keep having these visions? To keep drinking that water? The water that almost *killed*—"

"That was when I *didn't* take it. The water has been nothing but good for me."

"Nothing but good for you! Eric, are you hearing yourself?"

"This story needs to be told, and I've been looking desperately for something that would give me a chance to get back. There's a *purpose* to this, Claire."

She shook her head in exasperation and turned away from him.

"You can stay with me," he said. "Give me some time."

"No. I will not *stay*. I came to get you, Eric, damn it, I came to bring you home because I was afraid for you. But I will not stay here with you!"

She shouted so rarely—that had always been his job, a self-appointed task, of course—that this outburst stunned him silent. After a moment, he nodded and held his hands up, palms out.

"Trust me, Claire, there's nobody more concerned than me. I'm the one who's going through it. But I'm also trying very hard not to panic. So can you back me on that? Can we throttle down on the planning and wait to see what tomorrow brings?"

"How long, though, Eric? How much time do we give it?"

It was a frighteningly familiar question to hear issued in her voice. One that had been offered in response to so many of his explanations and rationalizations over the past two years. He'd work again, he just needed time. He'd write a screenplay, he just needed a while to think of the idea. He'd be in a good mood again, he just needed a few days to get through this bad spell....*How long, Eric? How much time?*

"Let's talk it out in the morning," he said. "Let's see where we are then, okay? We'll get some sleep, and then see where we are."

She nodded. It was a grudging, fatigued gesture. Like she was going along with somebody else's practical joke even though she understood she was the target, even though she'd seen the joke before and knew it wasn't a damn bit funny.

He walked toward the bed. He wanted to reach for her, wanted to push her down onto that soft mattress and cover her body with his own, but instead he picked up one of the pillows and stepped away.

"What are you doing?" she said.

"I'll crash on the floor. You should have the bed."

She gave a sad laugh and shook her head. "I'm sure we can sleep in the same bed without touching each other. In fact, I thought it was an art we'd perfected by now."

He didn't respond to that, just turned off the light. He heard two soft thumps as she kicked her shoes off, and then she slid back on the bed and stretched out and put her head on a pillow. He crawled stiffly in on the other side and lay on his back beside her, no part of them touching.

It was quiet for a while, and then he said, "Thank you for coming."

When she answered, her voice sounded choked, and all she said was, "Oh, Eric."

The rain let up sometime after midnight and the clouds thinned, showed the moon again. Josiah left his position by the old barn and paced the woods, waiting. Every now and then he checked the cell phone to see if there was a signal. It claimed there was, but he was surprised Danny hadn't called yet. Surprised there'd been no word.

He went through a bottle of water, rinsing and spitting with it more than drinking, still unable to rid himself of the odd tobacco taste that had taken to his mouth. It wasn't an unpleasant taste, though. Matter of fact, he was growing to like it.

He wondered what the scene was like down at the hotel. Must be taking a while if Danny hadn't reported back in yet. Would the cops stay down there to talk to Shaw or haul him off to the police station? Couldn't arrest him for anything, but maybe they'd bring him in for questioning. Maybe he already *had* been in for questioning, if Lucas Bradford was so convinced he'd done Josiah's killing. It was a strange circumstance, no question, and one that begged for exploitation.

By one-thirty his enthusiasm was gone. There should have been word by now. Josiah called, fearing the lack of answer that would tell him Danny had run into trouble and Josiah was now in this thing without any help at all.

Danny answered, though. Said, "Josiah? That you?" in a hushed voice.

"Yes, it's me, but if you're not sure, then don't use my damn name when you answer the phone, you jackass. What if it had been a cop?"

"Sorry."

"Why in the hell haven't you called? What's going on with the police?"

"Haven't been any police."

"What?"

"Not a one, Josiah. I'm parked where I can see the back of the hotel and the front drive, and there's not been a cop car up here yet."

More than an hour had passed since he'd hung up with Lucas Bradford. If the man were going to call the police, he'd have done it by now. This was both surprising and encouraging. Whatever had kept Lucas from phoning the police once probably would again. Now it was just a matter of getting his sorry ass engaged in conversation, keeping the son of a bitch from hanging up on Josiah and acting like he could avoid the hell storm that was headed into his life.

"Josiah? You there?"

"Yeah, I'm here. Just thinking."

"Well, there ain't been cops. But somebody else might've come to see Shaw."

"Who?"

"A woman. See, I got a place where I can look down at his car, that Acura. Well not fifteen minutes ago this woman drives up real slow through the parking lot, like she's looking for a car. Then she pulls in and parks right by his. When she got out, she put her hand on the hood. Like she wanted to see if it was warm, if it had been driven."

"Could be a coincidence."

"Could be. But the car has Illinois plates."

No coincidence. The woman had come to see him, a woman from Illinois.

When my wife hired you...

"Oh, Lucas," Josiah breathed. "You dumb bastard, you're in trouble now."

46

H E LAY IN THE DARK in bed with his wife of fourteen years and he could not sleep. They had not spoken in more than an hour now. He was no longer sure if she was awake. Her chest rose and fell slowly as if in sleep but there was a rigidity to her body that suggested she was not.

Six weeks since he'd last seen her. And then it had been tense and angry, as was always the case since they'd separated. Since he'd moved out of the home they shared, moved out because she dared to question the indulgence of self-pity that he was still riding after two years.

You are a child, Eric thought, *a petulant boy, not a man. And still she is here now. Still she came for you.*

He wasn't surprised either. Despite everything that had happened, he'd believed she would be there when he needed her. She'd gotten into the car and driven six hours through the night, and that very act defined the question he'd never been able to answer, one that had been in his head for years—why was she still with him?

He understood the possibilities she'd originally seen; theirs had been a truly passionate romance from the start, and the future they had planned to share was full of promise. Had been, at least, until his failure.

And that was it—*failure*—no other word applied, though Claire had sure as hell tried plenty of them out. There'd been talk of obstacles, setbacks, hindrances, delays, tests, interruptions, and holdups, but never talk of the one cold truth. Eric had failed. Had gone out to California expecting to be directing films within a few years, expecting to be a figure of fame and acclaim soon after that. It hadn't happened. The goal had been clear, the results equally so, and the verdict couldn't be argued: failure.

It was in her calm acceptance of that, in her unyielding patience, that Eric's frustration grew. *Don't you get it?* he'd wanted to scream at her, *it's over. I didn't make it. What are you still doing here? Why haven't you left?*

He'd never have blamed her. Hell, he was *expecting* it. After the broken dreams in California, followed by the two-year tantrum in Chicago, how had she *not* left him? It was the right thing to do, so he'd waited for her to go, waited and waited and still she was there, so finally he'd left himself. It had to happen. The circle had to be completed, the whole package of Eric's once-bright future, professional and personal, had to be sealed and stamped with one bold black word: **FAILED**.

He was merely trying to complete the fall, but she kept interrupting it, kept trying to lift him up again. Why?

Because she loves you. And you love her, love her more than you've ever loved anything in this world except for yourself, you stupid, selfish bastard, and if you can learn to deal with that, *maybe it would be a start.*

She was asleep now. Hadn't stirred or changed her breathing in a long time, and he thought that it would be safe to touch her, very lightly. He wanted to touch her. He turned onto his shoulder and reached out with his left hand and lowered it, gently as he could, onto her stomach. He felt the fabric of her shirt under his palm and felt the heat of her and the slight rise and fall of each breath. He was sure that she was asleep until she lifted her own hand and wrapped her fingers over his. For some reason when she did it, he held his breath.

Neither of them spoke. For a long time, they just lay there in the dark with their hands joined across her flat stomach.

"I should tell you that you are a bastard," she whispered. "Do you know that?"

"Yes."

"But that's exactly what I shouldn't say, too. Because it's all you really believe."

"I love you," he said.

It was quiet. After a long time, she took his hand and lifted it to her face, held his palm over her eyes. She did not speak. Soon he felt moisture on his hand. Tears. She did not make a sound.

"I love you," he said again, sliding toward her. "I'm sorry, and I love —"

"Shut up," she said, and she let go of his hand and grabbed the back of his head instead, pulled it down roughly and kissed him hard on the mouth. She tightened her fingers in his hair as she held the kiss, his scalp alight with wonderful pain.

They shed their clothes in an awkward, frantic tangle, trying to help each other but then having to finish alone, graceless and hurried and needy. When she was naked, he rolled on top of her, still kicking his underwear from his feet, and he tried to force himself to slow down, ran a palm along her side and up her thigh in a deliberate, measured stroke as he lowered his mouth to her breast.

"No," she whispered, and for a terrible moment he thought she was calling him off entirely, but then she tugged on his shoulders and pulled him upward and he understood that she wanted to move quickly, perhaps because she thought it was a mistake. He was afraid of that, but then her hand was on him and guiding him and all the thoughts in his mind faded and there was only her. When he entered her, she let out a soft gasp and he dropped his face to her neck, her hair tangled about him, and for a moment he lay completely still and breathed in the smell of her hair. Then she lifted her hips and urged him forward, and though he began to move, he kept his face pressed close to hers, where he could hear her and smell her and taste her.

They were done quickly the first time, lay breathing heavily but not speaking for a while and then began again, this time with a different pace, the slow savoring of one encountering something once feared lost. They spoke in breaths and kisses but not words, and it was quite a while before they were finished again, the sheets now damp with sweat.

"Your hands are shaking," she said. Her cheek was on his chest, and she was holding his right hand close to her face.

"All of me is shaking," he said. "It's a good thing."

Truth was, he seemed to have developed a muscle tremor in his hands, and the headache was returning already. He didn't want to think about that.

"It won't always feel this easy," she said.

"I know it."

"Do you? Because if you want to keep running, let's be clear on that now, and not let tonight slow you down."

"I don't want to run, Claire. I want to be with you."

"And you want it to be easy," she said. "Easy, and as planned.

You want everything to fit into the plan, *your* plan. Some of us try so hard to fit into that for you. It doesn't matter. You still can't handle the fact that the entire world does not."

Her voice was weary when she said it, and he lifted his head to look down at her.

"You sound like you've given up," he said.

"On you? On us? Oh, please, Eric. I'm the only one who never will."

"Then we can make it work. I know it will not be easy, or as planned. But we can make it work."

"You left," she said. "*You* left. Don't you remember that? And now I'm supposed to be thrilled with the idea of you coming back?"

"You don't me want to?"

She snorted out a laugh of exasperation. "I didn't want you to *leave,* Eric. But you did. So when you talk about making this work, forgive me if I'm a little hesitant."

"I love you, Claire."

"I know that," she said. "The problem is, you're going to have to figure out how to like Eric a little bit, too. Or at least be at peace with him. Until the two of you can sort that out, I'm afraid I'll be lost in the middle."

She fell asleep soon, her head on his chest and her hand curled around his side, and he watched her, feeling a sense of hope and possibility that had been absent for far too long. They would fix this. They would fix it all.

Though she did not yet know it, the water had saved him. It was the water that had returned her to him, that had her at his side right now. Without the water, he'd been alone. With it, here she was. It had revived his marriage and it would revive his career.

The thought returned his mind to Campbell and Lucas and Shadrach, to the story that could lift him to success. He was bothered that the water he'd bottled at the spa had not produced a vision or stopped the withdrawal pains, bothered that he'd required so much from Anne's last bottle to achieve so little. What he needed was the original. The Bradford bottle. There'd been something different about it, and while the regular Pluto Water had fed the need for a while, it was not doing the job now.

It's that spring, he thought, *the spring that the boy's uncle used for the moonshine. There was something different about it, and if I could find that spring...*

If he could find it, the possibilities were damn near endless. If he could find that spring, the world would just about curl up in his palm.

But he could not find it tonight, and the headache was building and his hands were shaking and he needed to try to hold the dragon at bay if he could. He moved Claire gently, slipped out from beneath her, and went for the plastic bottle he'd filled at the spa. He'd had only a little before falling asleep the first time, and it had not been enough. He'd have to adjust, that was all. A little more, bit by bit, until he found the amount that worked. As the dark hours moved toward the light ones, he drank the water and watched his beautiful wife.

The planning took longer than it should have, wasted more time than Josiah would have liked. But he didn't know much of the enemy, had only limited information to work with, and that slowed him.

He'd hung up on Danny after instructing him to continue

to watch the hotel, and then he returned to pacing the woods around the old timber camp and thinking.

Lucas himself had confirmed that his wife had hired Shaw. Now a woman from Illinois had arrived in the middle of the night, and Lucas had chosen not to send the police after Shaw. Why not? There would be layers to that answer, Josiah was sure, but one of them had just landed at the West Baden Springs Hotel, Carlsbad of North America, Eighth Wonder of the Friggin' World.

How to leverage that, though? The simple answer was that Josiah needed control of the situation, and that meant he needed control of both Shaw and Lucas's wife. He went back to the dead detective's briefcase and riffled through the papers until he came up with a name. Alyssa. Alyssa Bradford. Pretty name. Probably was a pretty girl. According to the detective's files, she was thirty-six and Lucas was fifty-nine. Trophy wife.

The next step was getting control of Eric Shaw and Alyssa Bradford. It wasn't something he could accomplish with them in that hotel, but luring them out of that hotel and into a place more suitable for his needs was going to be a difficult task. The only person he knew who had any ties to them was that big black kid.

Wait a second. Wait just one moment, Josiah, use that head on your shoulders.

He called Danny back.

"Anything happening?"

"Nope. Nobody's come. I wrote down the license plate of that—"

"Great," Josiah interrupted. "Now tell me, Danny, you said when you followed him earlier today, he went to Anne McKinney's house. Right?"

"Right. Got out of his car and left the engine running and the door open and..."

Josiah tuned him out, thinking now of the old woman's house, that lonely, isolated place on the hill outside of town, no neighbors for a half mile in any direction.

"Okay," he said. "Just needed verification. You stay awake and watching, hear? I'll be in touch."

He hung up in the middle of a question from Danny, feeling a tingle in his limbs now, puzzle pieces fitting into place, giving him a sense of the whole. He had the crucial next step, and it was time to get moving. Dawn would be on him soon, and the less of daylight he saw, the better.

It would be a long hike, and there was a temptation to try and avoid that, but in the end Josiah relented. He didn't want to run the risk of taking his truck out on the roads, not even for a short drive. He filled his pockets with shells and took his shotgun, was just out of the barn when he stopped and went back and opened the door to the truck and tossed the wad of cash he'd stolen from the detective onto the driver's seat. He'd tell Danny to come get it. Danny'd earned that much, no question. Josiah didn't feel any great sense of loss, handing the cash over. Funny thing, but the more consumed he became with the concept of debt, the less concerned he was with money itself. Now, what kind of sense did that make?

It was beginning to rain again when he left the timber camp and walked into the woods. Gently so far, but with thick drops and an uncommon humidity for these hours opposite the sun. He hiked up to the highway and then pushed back into the trees, keeping about forty feet from the road. All told, it was probably six miles of solid hiking to Anne McKinney's, which would take at least two hours going through the brush. If he was at her home by dawn, that would be good enough.

What Josiah wanted out of this was only what was owed to him. There was a dollar figure to it, and he'd settle upon one eventually, but it started with answers. He was damn sure owed some answers, and he had a feeling—no, an assurance by now—that they weren't the sort of answers got offered up in conversation. They were the sort of answers got offered up when you had a gun barrel to someone's head.

He worked his tongue around his mouth and spat, that taste of tobacco growing. No cars passed on the dark, empty highway, and though the shotgun was awkward to carry, he was making good enough time, tramping along through the wet underbrush and working up a sweat. He'd spent years bitching about this place, promising himself he'd get out of the town someday and never look back. But out here in the woods, no other people around, no buildings or houses or hotels, he could appreciate what it had. It was beautiful land, really, rich and filled with strange gifts. It was the valley of his birth, the valley of his ancestors. Wouldn't be so terrible if it ended up being the valley of his death, too. No, that wouldn't be so bad at all.

The whole place was supposed to be coming alive again, was supposed to be on the threshold of a grand return. There were those who doubted it would happen, but the groundwork had been laid, and those hotels shone beside their casino, and through it all nobody remembered the Bradfords, nobody recalled that Campbell had been the man that made it work for years. Hell with Taggart and Ballard and Sinclair. Some men had visions, others had deeds.

"They forgot you, Campbell," Josiah whispered as he ducked under a branch and came up into a wind-whipped burst of rain. "You loved this valley more than any of them. Still do."

He should have felt strange to be talking to his dead ancestor, maybe, but he didn't. Felt close to him, in fact, felt the meaning of *blood kin* in a way he never had before. They were shared people, he and Campbell. Different versions of the same blood. Now, that was heavy stuff.

"I'll make 'em remember you," he said. "Might have to burn this whole town down to do it, but I'll make 'em remember you, and I'll get what's owed to us."

That last notion — of burning the town to the ground in order to see Campbell get his due — lingered in his mind. He envisioned those damn hotels going up in the same way the private eye's van had, a burst of white-to-orange heat, and he smiled. That would be fucking gorgeous. See the shining dome of the West Baden hotel exploding into a cloud of flame? Yes, that would be as sweet a sight as he'd ever happened across. Wouldn't be as easy as blowing that van up had been, though. It would require a good bit more than a pocketknife and a cigarette lighter, would require time and high-grade explosives and . . .

He stopped walking. The wind had died momentarily but now it returned in an irritable gust, blowing a squall line of rain into his face. It hit hard, the water like pebbles on his flesh, but he didn't so much as blink. Just stood there staring into the dark.

High-grade explosives.

He'd just walked a few miles away from an abandoned timber camp where a box of explosives sat, those strange sausage-looking dynamite strands. It was old stuff, probably not even potent enough to blow. Certainly not worth the walk back, because even if he had the shit, what in the hell was he going to do with it? The shotgun would be all the assistance he required. And yet . . .

It had been there for him. A box of dynamite, sitting in a barn that had stood empty for as long as he could remember. It felt almost planned, felt almost . . . promised.

All you got to do is listen, Josiah. All you got to do is listen to me.

Yes, that was a promise. *Consistent as clockworks,* that's what Campbell had called himself, and who cared that he was a dead man — he was a stronger friend than Josiah had left among the living.

He wiped the rainwater from his face and turned his head and spat and looked up at the hill he'd just climbed down, a slow, painstaking climb. No way he could carry that box of explosives all the way to Anne McKinney's house. Not if he had all day, and he didn't. He'd have to take the truck, and that was one hell of a risk.

"That shit won't even be good anymore," he said. "No way it's still good."

And yet it was there. As if it had been waiting for him. And all he had to do was listen...

He was halfway back up the hill before the rain started again in earnest.

47

THERE WERE NO VISIONS.

Eric couldn't believe it after the first hour — and half of the bottle — had passed, went back and drank the rest down, waited thirty minutes, and started on the second bottle.

Nothing.

The headache might have faded. *Might have.* It didn't worsen, but didn't disappear either, and his hands shook unless he held them clenched together. A tremor had taken hold in his left eyelid, too, made it hard to watch Claire, the damn thing fluttering constantly, twitching. This was not good.

He got back into bed as dawn rose, lay behind Claire's tightly curled body and stroked her arms and smelled her hair. Her presence was comforting, but still the water's lack of impact nagged at him. He could go for Anne's water in a few hours. Maybe that would help. But he was no longer sure that it would, and he *was* sure that it wouldn't be enough. Not after the way he'd gone through it tonight.

So it was the spring, then. The source itself. He had to find it.

He did not sleep. About an hour after he got back into the bed, Claire woke slowly, letting out a soft groan before stretching and rolling over to face him, and he leaned over and kissed her. When he did that, her eyes opened for the first time and he saw a flicker in them, a trace of anger. *What am I doing in bed with you?* her eyes seemed to say. *You left. Why am I here with you again?*

It would be that way, though. It would have to be. A smooth return wasn't reasonable; too much had happened, there would have to be awkward, painful moments. But he could minimize them. He could try to do that.

"Morning," she said, and he had a feeling she was thinking the same thoughts.

"Morning."

She sat up, pulling the sheet up to cover herself, and ran both hands through her hair, then held them to her face, eyes lost in thought.

"Is that a *What have I done?* look or a *What do we do now?* look?" Eric said.

"Neither," she said, and then, "both."

But she smiled, and that was enough. He kissed her again and this time she returned it without the same flicker in the eyes.

"What we do now," she said, "is the simple part. Today, at least."

"Yeah?"

"We go home."

He looked away.

"Eric?"

"You said we would talk it out in the morning," he said. He

had his hands pushed hard against the mattress, to still the shaking lest she notice.

"I also said that I *would not* stay."

"There's something I need to do," he said. "Something I need to resolve first. Once it's resolved, I'll leave with you. I promise I will leave with you. But first there are a few things I need to know. Document who the boy's uncle was, for one. That will be a *legal* help, Claire, maybe an important one."

She didn't respond. He felt desperation creeping on.

"I need you to understand, Claire, that what I'm going through, what's happening to me, it's powerful. It is *strong*. So I'm just struggling to deal with it, figure it out."

"I know that."

"Twelve hours, then. Give me that much. Give me *one day*."

"What can possibly be accomplished in a day?"

"I can try to get the answers I just told you I needed," he said. "If I can't do it by then, we'll leave, go home, and figure the rest of it out from there."

I can find that spring in twelve hours. I better. I sure as shit better.

"My preference," she said slowly, "would be to get in the car and head north. No pausing for loose ends, breakfast, even a shower. Just go. That would be my preference."

He waited.

"But if you need the day, take the day," she said. "We'll leave tonight, though?"

"Yes. We will leave tonight."

She stared into his eyes for a long time before nodding. "All right. In that case, I guess I'll go ahead and take the shower."

She slipped out of the bed naked and walked into the bathroom, beautiful and elegant as she moved through the dim light, always comfortable in her own skin. He watched her go, thought, *my wife,* savoring the sound of it.

She'd just closed the door when the phone rang.

He rolled onto his side and lifted the phone, said, "Yeah?"

"Eric. How you holding up, son?"

"Hello, Paul," Eric said, voice flat, and the bathroom door opened and Claire peered out.

"I've heard that you ran into some trouble down there."

Ran into some trouble, yes. Just like I did in California, just like you're sure I'll do again, and you want to play the role of the protector for your daughter now, prove to her yet again that I was a mistake, you passive-aggressive prick. He wanted to shout it all, but Claire was standing there at the bathroom door, watching him as if he were taking a test, and he said only, "It hasn't been a real good week."

"So I've gathered. Claire is with you?"

"Yes." *And she's going to* stay *with me, Paul, and I will stay with her, your influence be damned.*

"Good. Listen, I've been trying to help. I've been trying to find out who hired this man Murray, the one who was killed."

"Uh-huh."

"The investigations firm has been hiding behind attorney-client privilege so far, but when I called them, I said I'd be representing you—"

"You did *what?* I haven't asked you to—" Claire stepped out of the bathroom, a towel wrapped around her now, and Eric stuttered for just a moment, interrupted by her return. It was all the gap Paul needed to plunge ahead.

"I thought it was imperative that you know who hired this man before you made any decisions on how to act, so I pointed out that their client might be protected by his attorneys but that they had to disclose said attorneys, if nothing else. If anyone was going to stonewall, it had to be the law firm. They didn't like that but I mentioned a district attorney friend who'd be happy to call them and clarify the issue and possible repercussions, and they gave me the name of the firm: Clemens and Cooper."

"Terrific," Eric said. "But if all they're going to do is keep up the secrecy—"

"Well, the thing is, I have a few friends at Clemens and Cooper. I put in a call to one and said, without any explanation, that I understood they represented a man named Campbell Bradford and I needed to know which partner handled his interests. He just called me back this morning to tell me I was wrong—they don't represent Campbell, but they do represent his son."

His son. Alyssa's husband.

"His full name," Paul said, "is Lucas Granger Bradford. Does that mean anything to you?"

Claire was at Eric's side now, her hand on his arm. Her touch seemed hot on his skin, a cold shiver rippling through him.

"Yes," he said. "Yes, it does."

"He's married to the woman who hired you, correct?"

"Yeah," Eric said, but that wasn't the point of interest—the first and middle names were far, far more fascinating.

"Okay. Well, I called Lucas this morning. He told me you had called him last night and threatened him?"

"What? Paul, that's insane. I've never spoken to the man. And Claire was with me, she was here the whole—"

"I believe you, son. Of course, I believe you. I told Lucas he had some issues he was going to need to respond to, explained the criminal charges that could be brought his way if any withholdings put you or my daughter in jeopardy or sent undue police pressure your way. He was resistant. I was persistent."

Eric almost grinned despite himself. About damn time Paul's abrasive personality worked for him instead of against him.

"Did he tell you anything?"

"Not much. But he did say that the reason he hired a detective involved a letter written by his father, who is now deceased. The letter made some unusual claims, and he wanted to have it checked out before it hit the legal system. Evidently, the old man wanted this letter attached to his will, part of his estate order."

"What did it say?"

"He won't disclose that. He just said that he was sure the letter was the ravings of senility and that's what he intended to prove with the detective. He told me that he had not informed his wife of the situation, and he was unaware of her hiring you. When he found out she had, he asked his investigator to call you off."

"There's a hell of a lot more to it than that," Eric said. "He didn't try to call me off, he tried to *pay* me off. It's not so innocent, Paul."

"I'm sure it isn't. This is all that I've got so far, though. I'm trying to help."

"You have helped," Eric said. "Paul, you absolutely have helped."

Lucas Granger Bradford.

Yes, this was help, indeed. Paul was still talking, but Eric could no longer focus on his words. He was carrying on about the need for an attorney and people he could recommend, and Eric cut him off.

"Look, Claire really would like to talk to you. I'm going to pass the phone over to her. But Paul...I appreciate this. Okay? I want you to know that I appreciate this."

"Of course," Paul said, and there was a sense of genuine surprise in his voice, like he didn't understand why he'd be thanked, like he'd forgotten the conflict that had existed between the two of them for years. He and Claire were good at that sort of thing.

Eric passed the phone over to his wife and then got to his feet and went into the bathroom, closing the door to mute the sound of her voice. The headache was nudging around again, and enough nausea that he had no appetite, but right now those things didn't matter. He'd been given a gift, a piece of understanding. He used his cell phone to call Kellen.

"I was right," he said. "We were right. The old man in Chicago who was calling himself Campbell Bradford was actually named Lucas. And he was the nephew of the moonshiner, Thomas Granger."

"How'd you determine that?"

"My father-in-law just called. He found out that the PI firm was retained by my client's husband and gave me his name. It's Lucas Granger Bradford. He gave his son his own real name, and that middle name was his uncle's last name. You think we can find the spot where he lived?"

"We're damn sure going to try," Kellen said.

48

ANNE McKINNEY WOKE EARLY, as was her custom the last few years. Her body just didn't tolerate long stretches of sleep anymore. For three seasons of the year that wasn't such a problem, but the winter mornings, when darkness lingered long after she rose, were a burden on the heart.

She stayed in bed longer than she ordinarily would, let the clock pass seven and carry on till eight and then she sighed and got out of bed and went into the bathroom. She washed and dressed and came out into a living room filled with strange gray light. Not the light of predawn but the light of a cloud-riddled sky. It was long past sunrise but still the house was painted with shadows and silhouettes. Stormy.

There was no rain now, but it had evidently come down hard throughout the night, because her yard was filled with puddles and the tree branches hung heavy. The wind had not fallen off in the way that it typically did after a front passed through, but continued to blow, the porch a choir of chimes as she moved toward the front door. She felt the force of it as soon as she got the door open, an unusually warm wet wind for dawn. Where was all that wind coming from? She put it at just below twenty miles an hour.

She was wrong. According to the wind gauges, it was blowing twenty-two, this after the storm had finished its work. The barometer was still falling, but the temperature had risen overnight. That and the wet, rain-soaked earth would give this new front lots to work with. There'd be storms aplenty today, and some of them might be fierce.

Down at the end of the porch a flash of white caught her eye, and she took a few shuffling steps and leaned over the rail and stared into her own backyard. Way down by the tree line, parked close to the woods but carefully positioned behind her house, was an old pickup truck. Now, who in the world could that belong to? It had come in during the night, clearly, but there was no one behind the wheel.

"Get the license and call the police," she said softly, but the truck was a long way off across the muddy yard, and suddenly she didn't feel like being exposed out there, wanted to get back inside with the doors locked and the phone in her hand.

Her hearing wasn't what it used to be, and the yard was noisy with the wind and the chimes, but still the man must have moved silent as a deer because she was absolutely unaware of his presence until she turned back to face the door. He was standing in front of it with a shotgun hooked over his forearm. He looked familiar, but she couldn't place him just yet. She gave a start, as anyone would, took a small step backward. He gave a cold smile, and it was then that she recognized him.

Josiah Bradford.

A local ne'er-do-well, not one she'd have troubled her mind

over in the past, but he was more than that to her today. He was Campbell's last descendant, and something mighty strange was going on with Campbell.

"Josiah," she said, trying to put a stern touch in her voice even though she was standing with her hand at her heart, "what on earth do you think you're doing?"

"You have a reputation for unrivaled hospitality," he said, and his voice raised a chill in her because it did not fit the man, did not fit even the time. "For offering housing and help. I'm seeking both."

"I never opened my door to a man with a gun before. And I won't start now. So go on your way, Josiah. Please go on your way."

He shook his head slowly. Then he shifted the gun from one arm to the other. When he did it, the muzzle passed right over her.

"Mrs. McKinney," he said. "Anne. I'm going to need you to open that door."

She didn't speak. He reached out and twisted the knob and opened the door.

"Would you look at that." He turned back, the artificial smile gone from his face, and pointed the gun at her. "After you, ma'am. After you."

There wasn't a neighbor in view of the house, and Anne's voice would have been lost to that wind. Her car was in the carport on the other side of the porch, and the road stretched beyond that, kind neighbors in either direction, but Anne McKinney's days of running were many years past. Those much-loathed, sturdy tennis shoes on her feet might help get her up the stairs, but they wouldn't get her to the road. She took another look at the gun, and then she walked past Josiah Bradford and into her empty house.

He came in behind her and closed the door and locked it. She was walking away from him, toward the living room, but he said, "Slow down there," and she came to a stop. He walked into the kitchen, took the phone down and put it to his ear and smiled.

"You seem to be having some trouble with your service. Going to need to get a repair crew out for that."

She said, "What do you want? Why are you in my home?"

He frowned, wandering out of the kitchen and into the living room and settling into her rocking chair. He waved at the couch, and she walked over and sat. There was a phone right beside her hand, but that wouldn't be any help now.

"It wasn't my desire to end up here," he said, "just the unfortunate way of the world. Circumstance, Mrs. McKinney. Circumstance conspired to bring me here, and now I must take some measure to gain control of that circumstance. Understand?"

She could hardly take in his words for the sheer sound of his voice, that unsettling timbre it held, a quality of belonging to another person.

"Yesterday," he said, "a man paid you a visit in the afternoon. Came running in out of a rainstorm. I'm going to need you to tell me what was said. What transpired."

She told him. Didn't seem a wise idea not to, with him holding a gun. She started with his first visit, explained what he'd said about making the movie, which Josiah Bradford dismissed with a curt wave of his hand.

"How'd he hear of my family? What lie did he tell you, at least?"

"A woman in Chicago hired him. And she gave him a bottle of Pluto Water. That's why he came to see me."

"To ask about it?"

She nodded.

"Then why'd he come back yesterday?"

"For my water. I've kept some Pluto bottles over the years. He needed one."

"Needed one?"

"To drink."

"To *drink*?" he said, and the gun sagged in his hand as he leaned forward.

"That's right."

"You let him drink that old shit?"

"He said he needed it, and I believed that he did. It gives him some...unusual reactions."

"What in the hell are you talking about?"

She liked seeing him confused and unsteady. It dulled the fear a little.

"It takes away his headaches, but it gives him visions."

"Visions? Are you senile, you old bitch?" His voice sounded closer to normal now, the snapping anger of a young man, none of the eerie formality he'd shown before.

"He sees your great-grandfather," she said. "He sees Campbell."

His forehead bunched into wrinkles above those strange eyes he had, eyes like oil.

"That man told you he's seeing visions of *Campbell*."

"Yes."

"Either you are without your senses, or whatever scam this son of a bitch is running is more interesting that I had imagined. Can't be a thing about it sorted out without him, though, can there?"

Anne didn't answer.

"So we'll need a meeting," Josiah said. "A powwow, as our red brothers called it. You don't mind your house being the location, do you? I didn't expect that you would."

He looked at the grandfather clock. "Too early for you to call, so we'll have to enjoy each other's company for a spell."

She stayed silent, and he said, "Now, there's no cause to be unfriendly, Mrs. McKinney. I'm a local, after all. Called this valley home for all my life. You just think of me as a visiting neighbor and we'll be just fine."

"If you're a visiting neighbor," she said, "you'd be willing to do me a favor."

"I suspect you're going to request something unreasonable."

"I'd just like those curtains pushed back. I like to watch the sky."

He hesitated but then got to his feet and pulled them back. Outside, the trees continued to sway with the wind, and though it was past sunrise now, the sky was a tapestry of gray clouds. The day had dawned dark.

49

CLAIRE WANTED TO COME along. She said he shouldn't be alone, and when he told her that he wouldn't be, she said that Kellen was a stranger and as far as she was concerned, being with a stranger was as good as being alone.

"Look," he said, "you're safe here, and you're also here if I need you."

"Yes. I'll be here when you need me *there*. Wherever there might be."

"We're just going to look for a mineral spring. That's all. Maybe take two hours. It could tell me something. Being there could tell me something."

"And if it doesn't?"

"If it doesn't, then we go home," he said, although the idea left him uneasy, this place having wrapped him in its embrace now, made him feel like he belonged here.

She studied him, then echoed, "We go home."

"Yes. Please, Claire. Let me leave to do this one thing."

"Fine," she said. "It's not like I'm unused to you leaving."

He was silent, and she said, softly, "I'm sorry."

"You're honest."

She ran her hands over her face and through her hair and turned from him. "Go, then. And hurry, so we can go home."

He kissed her. She was stiff, returned it with an uncomfortable formality. Tense with the effort of hiding those things she hid so well—anger, betrayal. She felt them now, and he knew it and still he was heading for the door. What did that make him?

"I'll be right back," he said. "Quicker than you think, I promise."

She nodded, and then after an awkward silence, he went to the door and opened it and said, "Good-bye." She didn't answer, and then he was in the hallway, the door shutting softly behind him and hiding her from sight.

Kellen was waiting in the parking lot, the Porsche at idle. He had the windows down and his eyes shielded by the sunglasses even though the morning was dark with heavy cloud cover.

"Something tells me that ain't Dasani," he said, eying the bottle of water in Eric's hand. It was only half full now, maybe a little less. The headache was whispering to him, the pain like a soft, malevolent chuckle.

"No," Eric said, fitting the bottle into a cup holder. "It's not Dasani."

Kellen nodded and put the car into drive. "A word of warning, my man—this might be the definition of a goose chase we're embarking on here."

"I thought you knew where the spot was?"

"I know where the *gulf* is. That's all. There's a lot of fields and woods around it, and how in the hell we're supposed to find a spring, I don't know."

"We'll give it a shot, at least," Eric said. "Think we can beat the rain?" he asked, eyeing the darkening sky.

"I drive fast," Kellen said.

They were on their way out of town when Eric said, "Can I ask you something?"

"Go ahead."

"Why are you hanging in the game?"

"What do you mean?"

"If I were you, I'd probably have driven back to Bloomington by now and stopped taking calls from the crazy white guy. Why haven't you?"

There was a brief silence, and then Kellen said, "All those stories my great-grandfather told me about this place? All those crazy-sounding stories? Well, Everett Cage was a talker, I'll admit that. He liked to captivate his audience. But, Eric? He also wasn't a liar. He was an honest man, and I'm sure of one thing—whatever he said, well, he believed it. I guess I've always wondered how he could believe things like that."

It was quiet again, and then he said, "I'm starting to understand."

Josiah found himself watching the clouds. At first he'd taken to gazing out the window just because he wanted to be sure the old woman wasn't up to something, that there was no way she could signal for help once those drapes were pulled back. But the window showed only a field and a view of the western sky. The clouds were massing, unsettled and swirling, layers seeming to shift from bottom to top and then back. The sky over the yard was pale gray, but out in the west it looked like a bruise, and the wind pushed hard at the house and whistled with occasional gusts. Something about the turbulent sky pleased him, made him smile, and he pulled his lips back and spat tobacco juice onto the window, watched it slide down the glass in a brown smear. Funny he couldn't even remember putting a chaw in. Hadn't ever taken to the habit, threw up when he sampled his first dip at fourteen and never went back to the stuff, but there it was.

He waited until nearly nine before kneeling beside Anne McKinney and passing her his cell phone. Late enough that Shaw and the woman would be awake; early enough that they probably weren't ready to check out. He had Danny watching in case they did, and the phone had been silent.

"Time for your part in this," he said. "It's a most minor role, Mrs. McKinney, but critical nonetheless. In other words, it is a role that I cannot allow you to . . . what's the phrase I'm looking for? *Fuck up.* That's it. I cannot allow you to fuck this up."

She held his eyes and didn't so much as blink. She was scared of him — she *had* to be — but she wasn't allowing herself to show it, and there was a part of Josiah that admired that. Not a large enough part to *tolerate* it, though.

"If you're fixing to hurt people," she said, "I won't have a part in it."

"You don't have the faintest idea what I'm *fixing* to do. Remember that. But here's what I can tell you — this call doesn't go through, people will begin to get hurt. And there's only one person nearby for me to start with, too."

"You'd threaten a woman of my years. That's the kind of man you —"

"You ain't got the first idea the kind of man I am. But I'll give you a start: you picture the darkest soul you ever seen, and then, old woman, you add a little more black."

He hovered over her, the phone extended, his eyes locked on hers. "Now, all you got to do is make a phone call and say a handful of words, and say them right. That happens, I got a feeling

I'll find my way out of that front door of yours, and you'll be sitting here watching your damn sky as you like. But if it *doesn't* happen?"

He pursed his lips and shook his head. "I'm a man of ambition. Not of patience."

She tried to keep her gaze steady but her mouth was trembling a bit, and when he pressed the phone into her wrinkled palm, he felt a fearful jolt travel through her.

"You call that hotel," he said. "You said he wanted that water? Well, tell him now's the time to come get it. You'll give it all to him, but he's got to hurry up and get out here, because you're going to be leaving town for a few days."

"He won't believe that."

"Well, you best *make* him believe it. Because if he doesn't? We're going to have to find ourselves a whole new tactic. And with the mood I've found myself in, I don't believe anyone would like to see what happens should I be required to get creative."

He slid the shotgun over and leaned it against the edge of the couch so the muzzle was looking her in the face.

"Anne, you old bitch," he said, "it's got nothing to do with you. Don't change the way I feel on that front."

"All right," she said. "I'll call. But whatever you think is going to happen, I can assure you it won't work out as you've planned. Things never do."

"Don't you worry about me. I'm a man who's capable of adjusting."

She dialed, but he took the phone from her hand and put it to his ear to be certain she wasn't calling anybody else. The voice that answered said, "West Baden Springs," and Josiah, in a voice thick with easy charm, said, "I'm calling for a guest. Mr. Eric Shaw, please."

"One moment," the woman answered, and Josiah passed the

phone back to Anne McKinney. Then he dropped to one knee on the floor in front of the couch and rested his hand around the stock of the shotgun, curled one finger around the trigger guard.

"Hello," Anne said, and there was too much fluster in her voice. He shifted the gun as inspiration as she said, "I was, well, I was trying to reach Mr. Shaw."

"Oh," she said. A pause during which Josiah could hear a female voice, and then Anne said, "Oh, yes. Well...a message? I, um—"

Josiah gave an emphatic nod.

"Yes, I'd like to leave a message. My name is Anne McKinney. I've only just met...oh, he mentioned me? Well, you see, he wanted something from me. Some old bottles of Pluto Water. And I want him to have them but I need him to come get them soon because I have to go out of town."

She was talking too fast, and Josiah moved the gun so the barrel was just inches from her chin.

"That's all. Just tell him to come see Anne McKinney if he can. He knows where I live. Please tell him. Thank you."

She shoved the phone away and Josiah took it and disconnected, regarding her with a sour expression. It hadn't been the performance he'd needed. She was too shaky, too strange. He wanted to release some of the anger, but fear was already clear in her wrinkled old face and he didn't have the energy for shouting, so he turned away instead and went to the window with gun in hand and looked out at those oncoming dark clouds.

"She said he was gone?" He spoke with his back to her.

"Yes. She told me she'd see that he got the message."

"Ain't that just dandy news," Josiah said, thinking that Danny was even more worthless than assumed, had let Shaw walk right out of that hotel. Son of a bitch. Wasn't nobody could be counted on in this world except himself...

He called Danny. Exploded on him before a word had been said, asking what in the hell he was doing up there, because Shaw was gone, damn it, and Danny hadn't seen a thing because he was a useless piece of shit and—

"I'm *following* him, Josiah! Give me a break, I'm following him."

"Why the hell didn't you call and tell me that?"

"He didn't leave but five minutes ago! I'm just trying to keep up, see where's he going."

Josiah reached up and squeezed the bridge of his nose, took a breath. "Well, damn it, next time tell me when they start moving, then call back. Where *are* they going?"

"Headed toward Paoli. The black kid picked him up in the Porsche. It was good work that I saw him go, since he didn't take his own car."

"Just follow them," Josiah said, in no mood to offer Danny praise. "Hang back far enough that they don't notice you, but don't you lose them neither."

"I'm doing best as I can but that black kid, he drives like—"

"Just stay behind them and let me know where they end up."

They hadn't made it more than a few miles out of town before Eric's cell phone rang—Claire.

"Hey," he said. "What's up?"

"That old lady called. She wants you to get her Pluto Water."

"Okay. I'll call her back in a while. I don't really have time to—"

"She said she's leaving for a few days, and if you want the bottles, you have to get them now. She sounded upset."

Leaving for a few days? It was odd that she hadn't mentioned it.

"She say where she was going?"

"Nope. Just that if you want the water, today's the day to get it."

Damn it. He didn't have time for a delay like this, but he also couldn't afford to let the last supply of original Pluto Water he had access to close off. Not right now, not when his hands were shaking and his head was throbbing and even full bottles of the hotel water didn't do a damn thing to help. By now Anne's water might not help either, but it was better to have at least the *chance* of a net under your tightrope.

"Hang on," he said and then lowered the phone and said to Kellen, "Hey, are we going to pass by Anne McKinney's on our way to this place?"

"That's the exact opposite direction. But we can turn around."

He didn't want to turn around. He wanted to see the site of the old Granger cabin, and the sky was turning forbidding, more storms certainly on the way. But it was worth a delay if he could get his hands on a few more bottles...

"I'll go see her," Eric told Claire. "I hate to slow down for it now, because I want to find this spot I told you about and it looks like rain."

"I had the TV on. They're predicting bad storms all day."

"Great. I'd love to get caught out in the woods in those. But if she's leaving—"

"I could go get them," Claire said.

He hesitated. "No. We agreed that it was safest for you to stay—"

"She's an elderly woman, Eric. I think I can handle her."

"I don't really like that idea."

"Well, I'd like to see one of these bottles, honestly."

He remembered the way she'd inquired about the bottle as soon as she got to the hotel, as if testing him, searching for tangible proof of his wild stories.

"Fine," he said. "Let me give you directions to the house."

50

ANNE SAT ON THE COUCH with her hands folded in her lap and watched Josiah Bradford pace and mutter and thought that it was clear he was no longer in his own mind. He still managed lucid exchanges, but whenever he drifted away from the moment, his head was taking him far from this house. It was almost like watching Eric Shaw the other day. Like that but different, because with Eric it had been obvious that his mind was traveling somewhere else. With Josiah, it seemed something was paying *him* a visit. He was holding entire under-the-breath conversations, grumbling about a strong back and a valley that needed to be reminded of a few things, other bits and pieces that seemed just as nonsensical. His eyes were bloodshot and rimmed by puffy, purple rings, the picture of exhaustion. She wondered if he was using the strange, terrible drug that did so much harm in this area, meth. She'd only read of it, had no sense of the symptoms, but surely something had invaded his body and mind.

When he wasn't whispering to himself, he was spitting tobacco juice into an empty fruit cocktail can he'd dug out of the kitchen. He'd carry on in a whisper for a while, staring out the window, and then he'd peel his lips back from his teeth and —*ping*— spit into the can. Over and over he did that, and while watching a man spit tobacco was far more loathsome than fascinating, she found herself enthralled by it. Because, as far as she could tell, there was no tobacco in his mouth.

He'd never put any in his mouth, at least, and though she'd studied him hard, she could see no bulge in his cheek or lower lip. When he spoke, to her or to himself, he didn't seem to be talking around anything either. Yet his supply of amber-colored spittle never seemed to run dry, and she could smell the tobacco, dusky and cloying, from where she sat.

Bizarre. But at least he was distracted from her. Whatever he had planned for Eric Shaw couldn't be good, though she didn't know what she could do to prevent it, or if she even should try. Perhaps it was best to wait him out. Maybe he'd leave eventually, or maybe he'd burn himself out and fall asleep. If he did that, she could get to the R. L. Drake. He'd felt awful good about himself for cutting the phone line, but he hadn't counted on her having a shortwave. All she needed was the opportunity, but getting down those steep stairs into the cellar wasn't something she could do quickly. Quietly, maybe, but not quickly.

At least she was still free to move. He'd carried a roll of duct tape inside with him and she'd expected from the start that he'd use it to bind her hands and, God forbid, seal her mouth. She had enough trouble taking calm breaths right now. Close off her mouth and she shuddered to think what it would be like. He never used it, though, never even tied her hands, as if he'd taken stock and determined her too old and feeble to do harm.

A crazy man pacing the living room should have held her

attention, but after a time she found it drifting from Josiah Bradford to the big picture window and the tumultuous clouds blowing in from the west.

Today was going to be special. And not just because of the man with the gun who'd taken up residence in her home. No, today would have been special even without that. The air mass headed this way was unstable, and the ground wet and warm. That meant that as the day built and the heat rose with it, there'd be something called differential heating. A boring term, unless you understood what it did. Differential heating provided *lift,* allowing that moist, unstable air mass to take on an updraft. And once that started? Storms followed. Yes, they did.

All the basics were in play already today, but the clouds were showing Anne that another variable looked ready to join: wind shear. Specifically, the vertical sort. The stronger that was, the longer the storm front had access to the updraft, and that meant trouble. The banks of dark clouds to the west had an obvious tilt to them, seemed to be leaning forward from the top, a look that indicated high wind shear. Most anyone would notice that tilt, but few would see the secondary motion — a mild, almost undetectable clockwise shifting of the cloud layers. At first she hadn't been sure because she was distracted by Josiah's carrying-on, but then she squinted and focused and saw that she was right. The clouds in the lowest level of the atmosphere were turning with those at the bottom of the upper level, and the direction was clockwise. That was called veering. That was not good.

Veering was a form of rotation, and rotation was a hallmark of the supercell storm, the sort Anne had been watching for years. She wished she had the TV or the weather radio on. Ordinarily, she'd have not only reports from the surrounding area but readings on pressure and humidity. Now she was left with only the clouds. That was fine, though — they'd tell her plenty. They'd show her the storm's development, and the trees in the yard would tell her the wind speed, and through those things alone she'd have a better sense of what was about to happen than most. Right now there were large limbs in motion on the trees and a clear whistling sound as the wind went through the branches and the power lines, which meant the speed was somewhere between twenty-five and thirty, up a bit from early morning. The way that cloud front looked, it wasn't going to end there.

They passed cattle farms and a group of Amish men working beside a barn. The countryside here was rolling as if tossed by an unseen ocean, no flat fields as there were in Illinois and the northern half of Indiana. The terrain here was closer to what you'd find on the south side of the Ohio River, where Kentucky's rolling bluegrass fields edged into foothills and then became mountains.

Kellen was doing about seventy down the county road, and he jerked his head to the left and said, "That's where your buddy was killed."

"This road?"

"Next one down, I think. That's where his van was set on fire. I drove past it yesterday on my way back into town. I was...curious."

Something about this knowledge made Eric uncomfortable. Not just considering the man's death, but that it had occurred so close to where they were headed now. They were driving past low-lying fields and scattered homes and trailers, but in the distance the hills rose blanketed with centuries-old forests. They came into view of an old white church with a graveyard beside it, and Kellen hit the brakes hard. The Porsche skidded on the barely wet surface and they slid past the turn, so Kellen had to throw it in reverse.

"You always drive like this, then it's a good thing your girlfriend is going to be a doctor," Eric said. "You're going to need one."

Kellen smiled, backing up to the church and then making a left turn. They'd gone just far enough for him to build up his speed again when a sign and a gravel drive appeared to their left and he had to hammer the brakes again. This time he made the turn on one try, bounced them along the gravel until it ended in a circular turnaround.

"Now we got to walk."

"Where in the hell are we?"

"Orangeville. Population around eleven, but double that if you count the cows. This spot is Wesley Chapel Gulf. We have to hike to get to it."

They got out of the car and stepped into the brush. There was a trail of sorts leading away from the gravel drive, and they followed that. Fields showed on the high side to their left, and on the low side to the right, the woods were dense and pieces of limestone jutted out of the earth. It was evident that the slope fell off abruptly just past the tree line, but through all the green thickets Eric couldn't see what lay beyond. He was trying to fit the place in with what he'd seen in his visions but so far could not.

They walked for about five minutes before the trail forked and Kellen, after a moment's hesitation, went to the right, where the trail seemed to wind downward. They left the ridge and walked down into a sunken valley that was filled with waist-high grasses and reeds.

"Looks like this floods sometimes," Eric said.

"When the gulf gets high enough."

They followed the trail as it wrapped through the bottoms. Down here between the heavily wooded ridges any sun would have been screened, and on a morning like this there was a shadow-shrouded dark that felt almost like twilight, the day coming to a close instead of a start. At length the trail opened out of the weeds and thickets and they were standing at the top of a sandy, tree-lined slope facing a pool of water that was bordered on the far edge by a jagged stone cliff rising a good eighty or ninety feet above the water. The pool was of a shade Eric had never seen before—a bizarre aquamarine blend of deep green with streaks of blue, water that seemed to belong in a jungle river somewhere. There was a roiling spot in the far corner where water met rock, and out beyond that the pool seemed to swirl. All around them the sound of rushing water could be heard, but nothing flowed from the pool.

"Damn," Eric said. "This place is crazy."

"Yeah," Kellen said. He'd come to a stop and was staring down at the water, entranced. "Water must be rising. It starts to swirl like that if it's rising after a strong rain. Way it came down yesterday was enough, I guess."

Long white limbs of fallen trees slid in and out of the water in places, and on the low ends of the surrounding slope other trees lay on their sides, uprooted but snagged before they'd tumbled all the way into the pool.

"They have some sort of windstorm go through here?" Eric said.

Kellen shook his head. "That's from the water. It rises high enough to reach the trees, and then when it gets to swirling the force is strong enough to bring them down."

Some of the downed trees were a good twenty feet above the current waterline.

"See that ridge?" Kellen said, pointing at the woods to the west of them. "That's where they found Shadrach's body."

They'd begun walking again, circling toward the opposite end of the pool, where the best access seemed to be, and Eric pointed at his feet.

"It's been up here before. That's sand that got pushed up."

He was right. The soil here was soft silt, clearly carried high above the waterline during some flood or another. They walked through it and then began to work their way down, using trees for handholds and turning their feet sideways to avoid slipping. As they got closer to the bottom, Eric looked up at the cliffs and saw the root systems of the trees dangling off the stone face like Spanish moss. The wind scattered leaves that fell around them in a whispering rush.

"If there isn't a ghost down here," Kellen said, "there should be."

He laughed, but Eric was thinking that he was right. There was something strange about this place that went beyond the visual, an eerie vibe that seemed to rise from the water and meet the wind. That charge Kellen's great-grandfather and Anne McKinney had agreed about.

"You can hear the water moving underground," Eric said. "It's flowing right under us."

There was a steep, muddy slope between them and the water and no good way to get down to it. Beyond, the cliffs rose with jagged pieces of stone scattered in loose piles and dark crevasses looming, testaments to the cave that had collapsed here. Some of its passages clearly lived on.

Kellen came to a stop about ten feet above the waterline, but Eric kept going, attempting a careful climb that turned into a barely controlled slide, his shoes plowing through thick, slippery mud that coated the hill above the water. In the far corner the pool bubbled and churned.

"Is that a spring?" Eric called over his shoulder.

"I believe so. But it's a well-known spring. My guess is the one we're looking for is not, right?"

"I'm sure it's not," Eric said, but he picked his way over the slippery stones and down to the spring. Just as he neared it, some water shot forward, splattering off the rock and soaking his pants. He knelt and extended a hand and took a palmful of water and lifted it to his lips. Cool and muddy and with a whisper of sulfur. On the top of the ridge—which suddenly seemed a long way up—the wind gusted and sent a shower of leaves into a gentle downward spiral, scattering across the surface of the slowly spinning pool.

"So, uh, what am I supposed to do?" Kellen said. He was still standing on the hill above Eric. "You need me to leave, or say some sort of ghost chant, or . . ."

"No," Eric said, his voice barely loud enough to carry. "You don't need to do anything. This isn't the right spring."

"You know that?" Kellen said.

No, he didn't. He assumed the water in the right spring would taste the way the Bradford bottle had, though, with that faint trace of honey. And Kellen was right—Granger's spring wouldn't have been well known. Still, there was something about this place that had power. As if they had the wrong spring, but not the wrong spot.

This is where Shadrach died. You're close.

"So we keep looking?" Kellen said.

Eric gave a distracted nod, staring into the pool. A river coming from rock. Carrying along underground for miles, then surfacing abruptly in a strange whirlpool, then vanishing again. The Lost River. It would show you what it wanted to, and nothing more. A tease, a torment. *Here I am; here I am not. The rest is up to you. Got to dig, friend, got to look deeper, got to see the parts*

I've hidden away because they are all that really matter, and in that way I am damn near human, don't you think?

"If we climb back up and go into the woods, maybe you'll get an idea or something," Kellen said. "I've never heard of another spring near here, but there are dry channels—places the Lost River fills only during flood seasons. Some of the springs are dependent on high groundwater, I know."

"If we can find the site of the old cabin, maybe we can work back from that," Eric said.

"Think you'll recognize it?"

Eric nodded. He was trying to imagine the cabin as he'd seen it in his mind, to picture it coming into view from behind the wheel of an old roadster with large domed headlights, but his mind wouldn't cooperate, wouldn't let him get into the image. His headache was a constant cackling menace, and he was sitting with his hands pressed against his legs to still the shaking. His left eyelid was doing that damned twitch again, as if it were trying to blink out a grain of dust, and his mouth was dry and chalky.

The spring beneath him churned into life again, spitting more water out as if angry about it, and Eric lifted his head and looked out to the deep portion of the pool, watched that gentle swirl and felt his eyes come unfocused. His hands began to shake violently then, and this time Kellen noticed.

"Hey, man, you all right?"

"Yeah." Eric straightened abruptly, feeling a swift sense of dizziness overtake him and then pass. "Just getting a little...edgy."

Kellen took a few steps farther down the hill, frowning. "Maybe we shouldn't have you out in the woods right now. Anything happens—you have another one of those seizures or something—it'll be a bad place for it."

"I'm fine. Let's find this thing before the storm hits."

Back up the hill and away from the cliff, back in the direction from which they'd come. Just before they entered the trees again, Eric took one long look back at the gulf, blinked hard, and stared. He could've sworn the water was higher already.

51

TIME AND PLACE PLAYED tricks on Josiah's mind, as they had a few times up at the timber camp. He'd been staring out at the incoming storm clouds for a long time before the light changed enough that he caught a glimpse of his own shadow in the window and saw that there was a figure behind him. He whirled and found himself facing old Anne McKinney. Of course that's who it was. But for a moment there, he'd lost any memory of where he was or who he was with. For a moment there, he could've sworn he heard music, some sort of old-time strings number. He'd been sitting at a bar with a whiskey glass in his hand, laughing with some fat son of a bitch in a tuxedo, explaining that the economic shifts weren't going to bring a thing to this country that couldn't be solved with a bit of ambition...

A dream. But he'd been on his feet. He'd fallen asleep on his damn feet? What in the hell was going on? He was here to wait for Eric Shaw. Shaw would be coming for the water eventually, and when he did, Josiah would have him, and then the woman, and then he'd have answers. That's what he needed to focus on. He was here to get answers. Why was that so hard to remember?

He shook his head, blinked, then mustered a glare and held it on Anne McKinney for a few seconds, enough to show her that he was still in control. It wouldn't do to let his mind drift like that again, not with so many decisions to be made.

He turned back from Anne, thinking he'd steal another glance at that crazy damn cloud, but this time when he looked at the window, what he saw froze him.

Campbell was sitting where Anne McKinney had just been. He was staring dead on into the window, his face reflected clear as a bell, his dark eyes shimmering like the rain that splattered the glass.

You was told to listen, Josiah, he said. *Said you wanted to go home and take what was yours, and when a ride was offered in exchange for a piece of work, you agreed to it. But you failed to listen, boy. Needs to be a day of reckoning come upon this valley. It was mine once, should've been yours, and they* took *it from us. Took it from me, took it from you. You going to let that stand, boy? Are you going to let that stand?*

Josiah didn't answer. He just stared into the glass, into Campbell's reflected eyes.

I could've chose anyone for this task, Campbell said. *Could've chose Eric Shaw, or his black friend, or Danny Hastings. You question my strength, boy, question the power of my influence? That's foolish. It didn't have to be you. But you were here, my own blood, and that meant something to me. Doesn't mean a damn thing to you, though.*

"It does," Josiah said. "It does."

Then listen, *damn it. Do what needs to be done.*

Josiah turned to him then, anxious to say that he was more than willing to do what needed to be done, that he was just having some trouble understanding what in the hell it *was* exactly. When he turned, though, Campbell was gone, the old woman there in his place, looking at Josiah with fearful eyes.

He looked back at the window. Campbell was there again, but he was silent.

"I'll do your work," Josiah said. "I'll do it. Just show me what needs done."

Anne's fear had grown as the morning went on and Josiah Bradford's ravings turned stronger and stranger. Those muttered conversations had become something else, and now she could tell that Josiah was no longer imagining an exchange with someone, he was *seeing* someone, speaking directly to him as if he were in the room with him. Wasn't a soul in sight but Anne, and he sure wasn't talking to her.

When he got to the last bit and said *I'll do your work* in a voice that seemed untethered to his person, she squeezed her hands tightly together and looked away from him. He'd whirled on her once and she'd been afraid he might do something, but then he'd just turned back to the window and carried on with his conversation.

She wouldn't watch him anymore. Better to pretend she wasn't seeing or hearing any of this, better to pretend she wasn't even in the room.

He took to pacing again, in and out of the room, and each time he came back, he'd look from her to the window, do it suspiciously, as if trying to catch her at something he thought he saw her doing in the reflection. Then he went all the way into the kitchen and began to rattle around, and when he stepped back into the living room, she stole a glance and felt her heart seize.

There was a knife in his hand now. One of her kitchen knives, with a five-inch blade, plenty sharp. She pulled back, fearing harm, but he just carried on past her like she wasn't there and returned to the window.

Don't look at him, she thought, *don't make eye contact. He's as close to a rabid dog as anything now, and worst thing you can do with a dog like that is make eye contact.*

So she kept her head turned and tried not to make a sound that would attract his attention, tried not to so much as breathe too loud.

She didn't look at him again until she heard the squeaking noise. Even then she hesitated, but it kept up, sounding like he was polishing something with a damp cloth, and finally she turned to see what it was.

He was drawing on the window with his own blood.

The knife was on the end table beside him, and she could see that he'd cut his right index finger to draw blood and had then begun to smear it around the glass. His face was screwed into an intense frown, not from pain but from concentration, and he was moving his finger carefully, tilting his head from side to side occasionally to change the angle. It looked as if he was tracing something. Once he looked over his shoulder and then swore at himself and paused for a long time before beginning again, as if he'd ruined his image. She couldn't see what he was drawing at first, but then he stepped to the side and leaned over and she got a glimpse.

It was the outline of a man. The head and shoulders of a man, at least, etched in blood over her window. The man was wearing a hat, and Josiah Bradford appeared to have spent most of his time on the hat — and the eyes. The outline of the face and shoulders looked like a child's scribbling, but the hat and eyes were clear. He'd drawn a nice, smooth almond shape for the eyes and now, as she watched, he took his finger off the glass and stood there squeezing it to raise more blood. He was patient, waiting for a full, thick bead of it. When he was satisfied, he reached out with infinite care and touched his fingertip to the center of the eye, filled it in with blood.

He repeated the act for the second eye. Anne could hardly draw a breath, watching him.

When he had the second eye filled in with blood, he stepped back like a painter studying his canvas, cocked his head, and looked judiciously at the window.

"You see him now?" he said.

Anne didn't speak, keeping that vow of silence she'd made for her own safety. He turned on her then, though, looked right at her with a hard stare and said, "Do you see him now?" and she knew that she had to answer.

"Yes," she said. "I can see him."

He nodded, pleased, and then turned back to the window, sidestepping so that he was out of the way of the blood drawing. Anne sat trembling on the couch and stared at the liquid crimson eyes and, beyond them, the storm.

They found what appeared to be an old road about a half mile from the gulf, overgrown with weeds but absent of trees, maybe eight feet across. In the distance, off to the east and west, farm buildings were visible, but then the old track curved away from the fields and roped back into the trees. There was an old barbed-wire fence lining the edge of the field, and from that point they could see for miles in three directions. Every direction except the one they were facing, southeast, into the trees.

Eric tried to pick his way through the barbed wire, promptly got snagged and tore his shirt, then felt an idiot's flush of shame when he turned and watched Kellen step easily off the top of a stump and over the fence. Oh, well, he probably would've just jumped over it if the stump hadn't been there. Guy that size wasn't going *under* it.

On the other side of the fence the old track became even more overgrown, harder to follow, and it climbed gently but steadily. One of those hills that didn't feel like so much until you were a ways up it and began to feel a tight burning in your calves. After about ten minutes the slope fell off abruptly and they went downhill for a bit and then came to a rounded ditch packed with old leaves, slabs of limestone protruding here and there. Water flowed through it, no more than a foot deep but moving swiftly.

"One of the dry channels?" Eric said.

"I'd say so."

They slid down into the ditch and used one of the limestone pieces to cross the water, then got back to climbing. It was about five minutes before the ground flattened out and it was clear they'd reached the top. By now Eric was breathing hard—Kellen didn't seem to be breathing at all—and if not for the sudden absence of slope, it wouldn't have felt like much of an arrival. Everything up here looked pretty much the same as the hill had—thick with trees, tangled with brush and weeds, dark with shadows. Insects buzzed around them, and a pair of crows shrieked in discontent. The humidity seemed twice as high as when they'd started, and Eric lifted his shirt and used it to dry sweat from his face. When he lowered the shirt, he felt an odd tingle, like a ping of static electricity. The crows shrieked again and he winced at the sound.

"I feel like we're just wandering now," Kellen said. "We've got no idea where we should be looking."

"I know it," Eric said. A gust of wind blew up, and a thin branch from one of the young trees whipped into his face. When he lifted his arm to ward it off, his hand passed through a spider web, which stuck to him with wispy, sticky threads. He swore and wiped his hand off on his jeans and continued on as Kellen fell in behind him. They'd gone no more than twenty feet before Kellen's phone began to ring. Eric didn't turn at first, but when Kellen began to speak, his voice was low and serious in a way that brought Eric to a stop. When he looked back, he saw Kellen's face knotted in an expression of disbelief.

"You're sure?" he was saying, voice hushed. He was turned sideways, as if trying to retreat from Eric, attain privacy. "Thanks. Yeah, I know. Crazy. All right, baby. I'll talk to you. . . . Look, yeah, I got to go. I'll talk to you soon. Thank you. Okay? Thank you."

He disconnected and slid the phone into his pocket, a thoughtful look on his face.

"Your girlfriend?" Eric said.

"Yeah." He was looking at Eric with a frown of scrutiny.

"Why are you looking at me like I'm a test subject?"

"Danielle just got results on your water."

"Really." Eric's eyelid twitched and fluttered again. "Were we right? Is there something in it besides the mineral water?"

Kellen nodded.

"Alcohol?" Eric asked. "Some sort of whiskey?"

Now Kellen shook his head. "Not even a trace of alcohol. It was, according to Danielle, a mixture of mineral water and blood."

"Blood."

"Yeah."

"Just . . . blood. She has no idea where it might—?"

"Human blood," Kellen said. "Type A human blood."

Eric thought of the bottle, and his senses seemed to slam him right back into contact with it—he had a flash of the cold touch in his palm, the honey-tinged odor, the sickening-sweet taste . . .

"I feel like I should get sick," he said.

"Brother," Kellen said, "you already are. And there isn't a doctor alive that's going to know how to treat it, either."

"What about the other bottle? Anne's bottle."

"Typical mineral content. Nothing special at all."

"Not that shows up in a lab test, at least," Eric said.

A few drops of rain fell around them as they stood and looked at each other.

"Wonder whose blood it was," Eric said.

"Yeah," Kellen said. "I'm a bit curious about that myself."

52

JOSIAH WAS STANDING WITH his nose almost to the glass, staring out at the storm like a child. When he stepped back and looked at it from the right angle he could still see Campbell sitting there watching him, his face perfectly aligned with the silhouette Josiah had drawn in his blood. Campbell hadn't spoken in some time, but Josiah hoped he'd been pleased by the gesture, the only thing Josiah had been able to think of that would show his loyalty, show that he would indeed listen, would indeed do the necessary work. He'd brought Campbell into this world, at least to the point that the old woman could see him, and he'd done it with his own blood. Surely Campbell saw that as indicative of respect. Of loyalty.

Now he couldn't see Campbell, though, because he'd stepped too close to the glass. Couldn't help himself—the storm was doing something strange. There was a massive cloud taking shape ahead of them now, shaped almost exactly like an anvil.

It advanced slowly but steadily and seemed to carry both threat and calm at the same time. Like you could flip a coin and if it came up heads, the cloud would pass on by, or maybe offer a gentle shower. Came up tails, though, and God help you. God help you.

"You see the bubble?"

He twisted and stared back at the old woman, baffled both that she'd spoken at all and by what she'd said.

"Top of that big cloud," she said, nodding, "the one you're looking at that's shaped like an anvil? It's all flat across the top except for one part. You see it there? Looks like a little bubble up on top?"

He didn't know why he would bother with this talk, but he couldn't help himself. He said, "Yeah, I see it."

"That's called an overshooting top."

Great, he wanted to say, *now pardon me, but I don't give two shits, old woman,* but no words left his lips. He was staring at the cloud and thinking she was wrong. That aberration across the top of the anvil didn't look like a bubble. It looked like a dome.

"What's it mean?" he said.

"Will take a few minutes for me to know. But it'll be the part that tells the tale. You see how the rest of that cloud is all hard-edged? Could be some serious weather in there. But that bubble just formed. If it goes away soon, this one's no real bother. If it stays on for more than ten minutes, then we could have a gully-washer headed our way."

"How many minutes has it been?"

"Six," she said. "Six so far."

Anne wished Josiah would stand back from the window, stop blocking her view. This thing rolling in was on the verge of being something special, something dangerous, and she needed to see it clearly. Instead he just stood there with his face to the window as the minutes ticked by and the storm front advanced.

She leaned to the left and looked around him, studying the cloud and trying to remember all of the signs she needed to remember. The bubble on top of the anvil formation was holding steady. That meant the updraft was strong. The storm was being fed. The body of the cloud had a soft cauliflower appearance but its edges were firm and distinct and that meant...

A shrill ringing broke the silence that had grown in the house, and Josiah gave a startled jerk before reaching into his pocket and retrieving a cell phone.

"Yeah, I'm here," he said. "Speak loud, boy. Where in hell you been? You didn't lose them, did you?"

Josiah bristled at the response, and when he said, "They looking 'round my property?" his voice was softer than it had been and drove a chill through Anne. She willed herself to try and ignore the words, focus on the storm again.

Josiah shifted away from his spot at the window then, and when he did, Anne saw what she'd been missing, knew that the cloud edges were no longer important. Josiah's body had blocked the development of a new feature from her eyes. A lower formation, trailing beneath that bubble, long tapering wisps like an old man's beard. It was called a —

"What do they think they're doing?" Josiah hissed. "What are they doing in those woods?"

— wall cloud, and it was pulling in the rain-cooled surface air, sucking in that moisture and feeding it to the updraft. The tips were spinning, as if unseen hands were twisting the end of the beard. Behind the wall cloud —

"You got a knife on you? Then go back down there and put

an end to that Porsche's tires, Danny. All of them. Then you sit tight. I'm headed your way."

—amidst all that purple and gray was a slot of bright white. Downdraft. It slid out of the dark clouds and dropped toward the earth, cutting right through the blood silhouette Josiah Bradford had drawn on her window. The white light seemed to turn those dark red eyes into a shimmering black.

Josiah Bradford disconnected the phone and lowered it slowly, put it back in his pocket. He'd just removed his hand again when the air split into a wailing all around them. At the sound, he lunged for his gun.

"Don't need that," Anne said. "It's not the police. It's the tornado siren."

Part Five

THE GULF

53

Eric stood in silence and stared back at Kellen as the wind bent the treetops and tore leaves loose and spun them into the air.

"If your experience has more to do with the blood and less with the water," Kellen said, "maybe we're wasting our time up here."

He didn't answer. Kellen said, "Maybe finding that spring isn't worth anything, is what I'm saying. If there's nothing about the water itself—"

"There's something special about the water," Eric said. "I think it was the balance to his blood. The counter."

A steady rain was falling now, and he wiped the moisture off his forehead and turned away from Kellen, looked into the wind-swept trees. His head throbbed and his hands shook. The agony was approaching again, the fruit of poisoned water, of a dead man's wrath, and he had nothing left to fight it with. The hell of it was that the sorrowful sense of defeat had little to do with fear of what was coming. No, it was the understanding of what would *not* be coming: a continuation of the story, an eerie insight into that hidden world, and the glory it could have brought him. He could see the foolishness of his idea now. All thoughts of the fame that would surround his strange gifts were bullshit; he'd have been a fifteen-minute tabloid freak show, a washed-up almost-was who drank a bottle of old blood and fancied himself a psychic.

"A counter?" Kellen said.

Eric nodded. "Everything changed with Anne's water, with the water that didn't have blood in it. The story it was showing me was a warning."

"Of what?"

"Of what I did," Eric said. "I brought him back."

Campbell Bradford. His spirit, his ghost, his evil — pick your term, Eric Shaw had returned it to the valley, and the water allowed him to see that, caught his body with agonized cravings and forced him to drink more so it could force him to see more. He hadn't understood in time, though. Somewhere along the line he'd lost all sense of purpose entirely, had begun to fantasize about what the water could do for him, to think of it as a gift instead of what it really was: a warning.

"Now they've stopped," Kellen said. "Right? The visions are done."

"Yeah. They've stopped." Eric was thinking of the blood in the bottle and the way Campbell Bradford had looked right at him last night and said, *I'm getting stronger.*

There *was* a reason the visions had stopped. The past was not where it belonged anymore. The past was here.

Josiah needed that siren to stop. Damn thing was chewing into his brain, disrupting his focus, which needed to be on Danny's message.

Wesley Chapel Gulf. That's where Shaw was right now. In the sacred spot of Josiah's boyhood. It made not a lick of sense but still felt as purely right as anything he'd ever heard. Of course that's where they'd gone. Of course. There'd been something at work here for a while, something he couldn't get his head around, and now he understood that it was time to stop trying. Let the chips fall. Stop trying to figure out the house rules — there were none, at least not any he'd ever understand. Wasn't his place to lay plans now, was his place to listen to those that had been laid for him.

All you got to do is listen . . .

Yes, that was all. He was told that hours ago and still he'd been fighting it, making his own plans, trusting himself. Just listen, that was all he needed to do. He had a guide now, a hand in the darkness, and he wanted to listen but that frigging siren kept shrieking and screaming . . .

"Shut up!" he howled, tightening his hand on the gun as if he could put a few shells into the air and silence it all, silence the whole damn world.

"Won't stop till the cloud passes over," Anne McKinney said. "There's rotation in that cloud. Could touch down."

"A tornado?" he said. "A tornado's coming *here*?"

"Won't be here. Going to be well over our heads if it touches down. But it may hit the towns. It may hit the hotels."

She said this as if it were the very definition of horror.

Josiah said, "I hope the son of a bitch does. I hope it spins right into the damned dome and leaves nothing but a pile of glass and stone behind."

The idea thrilled him, drew him to the window. He looked off to the east as if he might actually be able to see the place.

I ought to be the one to take it down, he thought. *No damn storm — me.*

"You don't think I could do it, do you?" he said. "Well, I got a truck full of dynamite parked out back would do the job. Bet your ass it'd do the job."

Anne didn't answer, and he blinked and shook his head and tried to get his mind back to the task before him. He had to force his mind back to that fact time and time again, like a man trying to cross the deck of a ship that was forever tilting him in one direction and then another. Never mind this pissing contest with some old bitch, he had to get moving. That required a decision on what to do with her, though. He stared at her and pondered as the window glass rattled in its frame beside him. Best tie her up. Problem with that was she was in front of the big window, visible to anyone who stopped by. There was a basement in the house. With no phone to use, she could holler her lungs out down there and never be heard. Tie her up and stick her ass down there.

He crossed the living room and pulled open one door, found it went to a bathroom, then tried a second and saw the steep wooden steps leading down into the dark, smelled the moisture. Yes, that would do fine. He'd get her to walk down there before he bound her, make things easier to handle.

He was just about to tell her to stand up when he heard a car door slam.

He crossed to the window fast, stared out into the rain, and saw the car that had pulled in. Not police, but a Toyota sedan, unfamiliar to him. The driver's door opened and a tall, dark-haired woman stepped out, holding her arms up to shield herself from the rain. She ran out of sight, headed for the porch. For the front door.

"Who's here?" Anne McKinney said.

"Not a word, bitch," Josiah said. "Not a word. You speak, our visitor gets shot. It'll be your choice." Then he lifted the shotgun and walked out of the living room and down to the front door. He hadn't even made it there before the doorbell rang. He pulled the door open, keeping the gun in his left hand and using the door to screen it from sight.

The woman didn't give any real start or indication that she was expecting someone other than Josiah. She just said, "I hope I have the right address. I'm looking for Anne McKinney?"

She was even better-looking up close, the sort of woman Josiah wouldn't be able to hit on until he was at least ten beers into the night because the odds were so great she'd shoot him down, and Josiah didn't take rejection well. Raven-colored hair with some shine to it, damn near flawless face, body that would catch plenty of looks despite being a little on the skinny side. While Josiah studied her, she turned and looked over her shoulder at the howling storm and said, "Is that a tornado siren?"

"Yes," Josiah said. "And you best come inside quick."

"You don't think I can make it back to the hotel if I hurry? I just stopped by to pick up a few bottles of water from Anne."

A few bottles of water. He hadn't been certain of her relevance until now, but this brought a smile to his face that was no longer forced, as authentic and genuine a grin as he'd had in some time, and he said, "Oh, you're picking them up for Mr. Shaw?"

"That's right."

"I'll get them for you, but come inside and visit with Mrs. McKinney until the siren stops. It's the only safe thing to do. I insist."

She took one last, hesitant look back at her car, and right then a good-size branch pulled down from one of the trees in the yard and broke into pieces on the ground. She turned away, said, "I guess I'd better," and then stepped inside.

He had the door closed before she noticed the gun.

54

Anne couldn't see the front door from where she sat, and the wind and siren kept her from making out the words, but the sound of the unknown woman's voice, gentle and kind, put a sickness through her so powerful she moved her hands to her stomach. It was a feeling she'd had only a time or two in her life, the last coming when they swung the ambulance doors shut with Harold inside and assured her that it wasn't over yet, even though everybody knew that it was.

A minute later the stranger was standing there in the living room, a beautiful dark-haired woman with panicked eyes. Anne tried to meet those eyes and convey some sort of apology, but Josiah was shoving her over to the chair by the window and telling her there were two barrels to his gun, plenty to go around.

He had her sit in the old straight-backed sewing chair that Anne had upholstered herself some years back, then grabbed the duct tape he'd carried in originally and cut off a strip. She started to resist but he lifted the shotgun and pointed it at Anne and said, "You fight, that old bitch gets shot. Go on and test me. Go on."

The woman gave Anne a long look, one that lifted tears to Anne's eyes, and then she let Josiah tape her wrists together. Anne just stared back helplessly. The panic she'd done such a fine job of fighting when she'd been alone with Josiah was coming on strong, and she could feel it in her heart and stomach and nerves, everything going fast and jangly now, the way the wind chimes blew in a strong storm.

"Old Lucas will be answering phone calls now," Josiah was saying as he cut off more tape and wrapped it in circles around her forearms, pinning them together. "Yes, he'll take caution in his tone this time around."

Lucas? Who on earth was Lucas? "I don't know Lucas," the new woman said.

"Bullshit! You're his whore of a wife, sent people down here to spy on my home and ask questions of my family—"

"That's not who I am."

He struck her. It was an open-handed slap that raised a white imprint on her check but no blood, and the sound of flesh on flesh took Anne's breath from her lungs and sent the tears spilling free. *Not in my home,* she thought. *Oh, no, not in my home …*

"There won't be any more lies!" Josiah bellowed. Anne was mentally begging the other woman for silence—Josiah had been peaceable enough when he was agreed with—but instead she ignored the slap and objected again.

"I'm not who you think I—"

There was a second slap, and Anne gave a little shout, but the new woman was not moved to silence.

"I'm Eric's wife—Eric Shaw's. That's who I am! I don't know anything about Lucas Bradford. Neither does he. We're both just trying to—"

This time he passed on the slap, choosing instead to take the woman's hair in his fist and jerk it sideways. She gave a cry of pain and then the chair had overbalanced and she was on her side on the floor, still talking.

"We're just trying to get away from here while the police figure out what's going on. *I don't know Lucas Bradford!* Do you understand that? I don't know him and he doesn't know me. He doesn't care about me. I'm nothing to him."

Josiah dipped sideways and came up with Anne's kitchen knife in his hand, snatched it from her end table and held it at waist level with the blade pointed out.

"Josiah, no!" Anne shouted. "Not in my home, don't you harm anyone in my home."

He froze. She was taken aback, hadn't expected any reaction, but he stopped his assault completely and swiveled his head to face her.

"I'll ask you not to use that name any longer," he said. "If you'd like my attention, you can call for Campbell. Understand?"

Anne didn't know what to say. She just stared at him with her mouth agape, and he turned from her, dropped to one knee, and took a handful of the woman's hair again and used it to lift her head, moved the blade toward her throat, and Anne could look no more, squeezed her eyes shut as warm tears beaded over the lids and chased wrinkles down her cheeks.

"Look in my purse," the woman on the floor said in a ragged voice. "If you're going to kill me, you ought to at least know who I am."

For a long moment Anne didn't hear a sound, and she was fleetingly afraid that he'd made a silent slice with the knife, leaving the poor woman bleeding her life out on Anne's living room floor. Then she heard the boards creak as he rose and opened her eyes to see him crossing the floor to where a leather purse lay on its side, a lipstick and cell phone dumped out of it already. Josiah grabbed it and turned it upside down and a cloud of papers, coins, and cosmetics fluttered out and clattered onto the floor. In the center, landing with a dull, heavy thump, was a wallet. Josiah flung the purse at the wall and scooped the wallet up, tore the clasp open and flicked through it. For a long time, he stood staring in silence. Then he snapped the wallet shut and stared at the woman in the overturned chair.

"Claire Shaw," he said.

"I told you."

He seemed almost calm as he gazed at her, but somehow Anne was more afraid now than ever.

"You're his wife," he said. "Eric Shaw's wife."

"Yes. And we don't know Lucas Bradford. We have nothing to do with the Bradfords. If you want money, I can get you money, but you have to believe that we have nothing to do with the Bradfords!"

"I can get you money," she said again. "My family...my father...I can get..."

Her voice trailed off as he walked back to her. He still had the knife in his hand but now he knelt and picked up the roll of duct tape, pulled out a short strip and cut it free with the knife. She was trying to say more when he bent at the waist and smashed the tape roughly over her mouth, running his fist over it to make sure it was secure.

"Don't hurt her," Anne said softly. "Josiah, please, there's no cause to hurt anybody. You heard what she said, they have no idea—"

"What?" he said. "What did you just say?"

It took her a second to realize he was upset about the use of his name. He actually wanted to be referred to as Campbell. He was standing there in front of the bloody drawing he'd left on her window, asking to be identified as a dead man. She'd never heard of anything so mad.

"Don't hurt her," she said in a whisper. "Campbell? Please don't hurt her."

He grinned. Showed his teeth in a wide smile, as if the use of Campbell's name was something delicious to him, and Anne felt a bead of chilled sweat glide down her spine.

He turned from her, still smiling, to stare out the window. A moment later Anne realized he wasn't staring out of it but *at* it, at the blood silhouette he'd drawn there that had now gone dry on the glass.

"Well," he said, "what now? You told me to listen. I've tried. And this bitch isn't worth a thing to me. Not a thing. I'm standing here holding a handful of nothing, same as I always was. But I'm ready to listen. I'm trying to listen."

The wind rattled the glass against the old wood frame as he stood there and stared at it, stared as if there were something in it that could offer help. Down on the floor, Claire Shaw was silent, watching in obvious astonishment and horror.

"You're right," Josiah told the window. "You're right. 'Course she's not worth anything to me — none of them ever was. That isn't what it's about. I don't need the dollars. I need the blood."

Anne's mouth had gone chalky and her heart was fluttering again.

"I'll deal with them first," Josiah said, voice softer now, thoughtful, musing. "Finish what needs to be finished, and then I'll come back to that hotel. They'll remember me when it's done, won't they? They'll remember *us* when it's done."

He swiveled his head back and locked his gaze on Anne.

"Get up."

"What? I don't —"

"Get up and go down into the basement. *Now.*"

"Don't hurt her," Anne said. "Don't you hurt that woman in my home."

Josiah dropped the knife to the floor, stepped over it, and collected his shotgun. Lifted that and swung the barrel to face Anne.

"Go down into the damn basement. I ain't got time to waste tying your wrinkled old ass up."

It was only then, the second time that he said it, that she realized exactly what was being offered—the shortwave, the dear old R. L. Drake. A lifeline.

She stood up, legs unsteady after sitting for so long, and, with one hand braced on the wall, went to the basement door and opened it and started down the steps. There was a light switch mounted just beside the door but she didn't reach for it, preferring to walk down into the dark rather than chance his seeing the old desk with the radio.

He didn't even wait till she'd reached the bottom of the steps before slamming the door shut. That plunged her into *real* darkness, and she stopped and gripped the railing. She heard some banging around and then something smashed into the door and the knob rattled. He was blocking the door, locking her in.

She slid her hand along the railing and took a careful step down into the blackness, then another. A splinter bit into her palm and she gasped and stopped. Upstairs Josiah was saying something she couldn't understand, and then she heard footsteps, too many to be just him. The front door opened and then banged shut. She stood still and listened and when she heard the motor of his truck start, she thought, *Oh, no.*

They were on the move. He was leaving, and he was taking that woman with him.

Anne had to hurry now.

She took another step, down into the dark.

55

KELLEN AND ERIC WERE still standing in the same spot in the woods when they saw the cloud. The rain was coming down in furious gales and the wind was howling now, sounded like something alive, like something wounded and angry, and it was Kellen who pointed up at a bank of purple clouds that seemed to be separating and joining and separating again, partners in some strange turbulent dance.

"I don't like that," he said. "We got to get out of here, man."

"I need to find that spring," Eric said, feeling numb as he watched the clouds. "I'm going to need that water, Kellen. It might be the only thing that will work."

"Then we're going to have to come back for it," Kellen said. "We've got to leave now."

Eric stared at the clouds but didn't move or speak.

"Come on," Kellen said, and when he pulled Eric away by the arm, it was with the ease of a grown man moving a child.

Only when he realized Eric was finally cooperating and running alongside him did he loosen his grip.

"Gonna be slick!" he shouted in Eric's ear. "Watch your ass. We run fast enough, we'll be back at the car in a few minutes."

They ran down the hill and found the dry channel and splashed through it. It was a dry channel no longer—the slab they had used to cross was a foot underwater now. The Lost River filling it from beneath even as the rain attempted to do the same from above.

Eric's legs didn't feel steady, seemed to be operating more out of momentum than muscle control, but he kept up with Kellen as best he could and kept moving. Finally the edge of the tree line was in sight, and from there it was maybe a half mile through a field of short scrub pine to get back to the car.

They broke out of the trees into a roar of wind and ran right up to the barbed-wire fence. Eric was ducking to his hands and knees again, thinking, the hell with looking graceful, he just wanted to be on the other side, when Kellen reached down and grabbed the back of his shirt and spoke in a hiss of awe.

"Look at that. *Look at it.*"

Eric straightened and followed his stare and felt his own breath catch.

From here they had a view out across open fields, and to the west, a ways off but not so far as to feel comfortable about it, a funnel cloud was lowering to the earth. The mass above it was black and purple but the funnel cloud was stark white. It eased to the ground almost peacefully, as if settling down for a rest, and then its color began to change, the white turning gray as it blew through the fields and gathered dirt, sucking soil and debris into its vortex. The air around them vibrated with the distant roar.

"Is it going to come this way?" Eric shouted.

"I think so."

They stood without speaking for a moment and watched as the cloud churned through the field. The tight funnel shape morphed into something less distinct as it went, circles of debris ringing the base. It crossed the field with apparent leisure. There was a row of power lines just ahead of the road, and when the tornado reached them, the poles lifted from the earth and the lines snapped. When it crossed the road and went into the next field, something lifted it into the air, almost like a bounce. For a moment the base of the cloud seemed to hesitate, as if it might retreat altogether, but then it dropped again and there was another burst of dark gray when it tore back into the land.

"It's definitely coming this way," Kellen shouted. "We got to run!"

"We can make the car?"

"Hell, no. Can't outrun a tornado, man! We got to get down in that gulf. It's the only place low enough!"

He bent and grabbed the top strand of the rusted barbed wire and lifted, tugged it up and waved at Eric to climb through. Eric scrambled under, then turned to hold the wire for Kellen but saw that he was already across. He really could jump the damn thing.

The gulf was close and it was a downhill run, but the roar around them was getting louder, too. Out of the trees the wind was a stronger force, and Eric realized with a mixture of astonishment and fear that it was actually pushing him off course. They were running in a mad sprint now, and for a moment Eric didn't even realize that Kellen had hold of his shirt again, was dragging him along. By the time they hit the ridge above the gulf, the horizon line across from them was a wall of black sky.

"Got to get down!" Kellen shouted, and then he put his hand in the middle of Eric's back and shoved.

The drop-off was sheer and lined with trees, the sort of place you'd walk around carefully on a normal day. Today, Kellen just pushed Eric right out over the top of it and jumped after him.

For a moment Eric was airborne. Then his feet caught the hillside and his momentum sent him into a pinwheel down the slope, branches whipping at him. He was thinking that he'd fall all the way down into the water when he tumbled into the side of a tree. The impact exploded his vision into a burst of white light, but it also stopped him. He gasped and blinked and then he could see where he was — two-thirds of the way down the slope, a good sixty feet from the top of the ridge.

He looked for Kellen and found him fifteen feet farther down, covered in mud and leaves. He was crawling toward the stone cliffs, away from the trees. Trying to get lower. Eric followed, not even bothering to attempt getting to his feet, just sliding on his ass and using his hands and heels to push himself along.

They got most of the way down the slope, about five feet from the waterline, and pushed up against the loose stone wall, where there was an indentation that allowed them to pull back and find greater protection. There was no point in attempting to talk now; the roar had reached a thundering crescendo. It sounded exactly like the train that had blown past Eric on his first day in this place.

They didn't have to wait long. Thirty seconds, maybe a minute. It *felt* longer, though, felt like a damn eternity, the way time passed when you were sitting in a hospital watching an ER surgeon approach from down the hall to provide the status of a loved one. Then the storm finally caught them, and the world exploded.

A full-size birch, fifty feet tall at least and with a wide spread of branches, tore out of the earth on top of the ridge and shot into space. It didn't fall straight down, bound by the laws of gravity, but blew forward before catching on another tree and splashing into the swirling, roiling pool. The water sprayed up and showered them and then another tree was sliding down the cliff face, scattering loose stones in its wake. The woods were crackling with the sound of thick, powerful limbs and trunks snapping in two, and the wind was such that Eric could no longer hold his eyes open against it. He covered his face with his arms and pressed his body back into the indentation Kellen had found in the limestone wall and above them the world screamed in fury.

Then it was gone.

That something so terrible could pass so swiftly seemed impossible. There were still rumblings in the woods as uprooted trees and fallen branches slid down the hillsides and found resting places, but the raging wind was gone and the roar faded at its heels. Eric lowered his arms and stared out at the gulf. The water tossed and spun and in its midst were a half dozen trees now. When he looked up, he could see a line carved through the treetops on the east side of the ridge, as if trimmers had come through and topped them and then had gone on, leaving the limbs behind in careless piles. On level ground, the damage had been devastating. Would have been deadly. But they'd gotten down here into what was essentially a pit, ninety or a hundred feet below the surface, and the tornado had not been able to find them there.

"That would have killed us," he said. "If we'd been on level ground, that would have killed us."

Kellen nodded. "Yeah. We might still be airborne. In pieces."

His voice was as tight as if someone had a hold of his throat, and Eric finally turned and looked at him. Kellen's face and neck and arms were a mass of tiny cuts, and there was one good-size gash above his left eye that oozed a thick band of blood that ran along his jaw and curled out toward his chin like a sideburn, and Eric knew *he* couldn't look any better. Kellen's face was locked into a grimace, though, and he was rocking back and forth, hands squeezed into fists.

"You okay?" Eric said, and then he followed Kellen's eyes down his leg to his foot and whispered, *"Oh, shit."*

Kellen's right foot hung unnaturally beneath the leg, twisted almost backward, and there was a distended bulge just above his shoe, pushing at his skin. The ankle was clearly broken. Not just broken, he realized after a closer study—destroyed. The bone had snapped, but clearly some ligaments had torn loose as well to let his foot hang like that.

Kellen's face had drained to a gray pallor and he kept up that gentle rocking, but he didn't moan or gasp or shout with pain.

"You're hurt bad," Eric said. "We've got to get you out of here."

"Shoe off," Kellen said through gritted teeth.

"What?"

"Get the shoe off. It's swelling so fast... I don't think it should be in the shoe."

Eric slid down the slick rock and reached for the laces of Kellen's shoe. When he gave one a gentle tug, it shifted Kellen's foot. This time he shouted with pain. Eric dropped the shoelace and pulled back, but Kellen shook his head and said, "Get it off."

So he untied the shoe. He did it as quickly and gently as possible, but Kellen hissed with pain, and when Eric slid the shoe off, he could see the bone move under the skin and felt a cloud of sickness move through him, leaving him dizzy. He dropped the shoe and it slid down the rock and into the water. Kellen didn't seem to care.

They waited for a moment, Kellen sucking in deep breaths and staring at the treetops. He reached into his pocket and slipped out his cell phone, handed it to Eric.

"See if one of them works?"

Kellen's didn't, and wouldn't—the face was cracked and it was soaked with water, wouldn't even turn on. Eric's still functioned but couldn't find a signal. No surprise down here in the hole, and who knew if it would change once they got to higher ground. The tornado might have taken out a tower or two.

Eric's left arm was shaking now and the pain buried in his head made it hard to focus, his vision starting to swim. He blinked and stared down at the gulf.

"I think it's still rising."

"Coming up fast," Kellen said without even giving it a look. "We're going to need to get me over to the other side."

"No way you're walking on that," Eric said, looking at Kellen's massive frame and wondering if he'd be able to carry him.

"No, but you get me up, and I can hobble."

It took three tries and some intense pain to get him upright. Then Eric dipped under his arm and tried to drag him along, but Kellen was large and heavy and the going was awkward. Every time they took a step, Kellen gave an unwilling gasp. His right foot just dangled below the ankle. They made it around the rim of the gulf, into the tall grass that grew along the flat bottomland near the trail, and then Kellen told Eric to stop.

"Any chance you can make it to the car?" Eric said.

"Maybe. But I doubt there's much left of the car."

Shit, he was probably right. Both of Eric's hands were shaking again. Behind them the water in the gulf gurgled and boiled around one of the fallen trees.

"You need to get to the road," Kellen said. "Going to be police and firefighters out checking on the farms. Tell somebody I'm down here."

He'd lowered himself down into the grass and leaned back on his elbows, grimacing and studying his unresponsive right foot.

Eric saw he was digging into the mud with his fingers. The pain had to be brutal.

"That water comes up much higher, it'll drown you," he said.

"I can get up higher if I need to. But I'm not making it back to the road."

"All right," Eric said. "I'll get help."

He went on up the hill alone.

56

JOSIAH FOUND THE STREETS of town damn near deserted, everyone taking heed of that storm siren and seeking shelter. He blew through a red light, not giving a shit because wasn't anybody out to notice, and then hammered the accelerator when he cleared town, sped past the West Baden hotel without so much as a look. He'd be back for it.

At Anne McKinney's house Campbell's instructions had finally clarified, the reality of this whole fucking mess becoming crystal clear: Josiah didn't need anyone's money. Didn't need their explanations either, didn't need a damn thing from a soul in the whole valley, the whole world.

What he needed was to listen. And now, finally, he was starting to. He heard the goal now, warm as a whisper in the ear. *Take this place down, and watch it burn. They'll know your name when it's done, better believe that. They'll know it, and remember it.*

Eric Shaw's wife was in the bed of his truck, bound with tape and wrapped in a tarp and pushed up next to the dynamite. Way that rain was coming down, the bitch was probably a tad uncomfortable. The wind was coming at him strong enough that it was hard to hold the truck in the proper lane, and he thought it was a damn good thing the roads seemed to be deserted. Fact was, this looked like a hell of a storm. He punched on the radio.

. . . Once again, we have a confirmed tornado touchdown just west of Orleans and there are reports of significant damage. Unconfirmed reports of another touchdown just south of Paoli are coming in. A critical reminder: this is only the leading edge of this storm front, and it's already produced tornadoes in Missouri and southern Illinois. We have more activity on the way in, and the National Weather Service has declared that the tornado warning will remain in effect for at least another hour, if not more. We're being advised that there is a strong possibility of multiple tornadoes associated with this front. Please seek shelter immediately.

He punched the power button and shut it back down. Hell with that shit. Storm would be the last thing anyone spoke of by evening.

The fastest way out to the gulf was to take US 50, but he'd barely gotten on the highway before he heard police sirens. He turned off onto one of the back roads just as a pair of cruisers shot by with lights going, doing at least eighty. Out on some sort of storm-related call, surely, not looking for his truck, but it was better to avoid the risks when you had a kidnapped woman and a stack of dynamite under tarps in the bed.

This detour north was pulling him far from the hotel, but he knew it was necessary, felt that in his bones. Eric Shaw was a part of this, had been from the start and needed to be at the finish. Campbell had placed the man's wife in Josiah's hands just as he had the dynamite, and both would have their role by the day's end. The course was already charted, and now it was merely a matter of listening to the directions as they were issued.

The route change that was forced by the police sighting would have him approaching the gulf from the south now, which would take him right past his own home. He opened the truck up again, curving along through Pipher Hollow. The storm seemed to have died off a bit now, at least here. Out to the northeast the sky still looked fierce, but here things were settling.

He was on his own road and a half mile from his house when he started to see the damage. The first thing that caught his eye was a great gray gouge ripped through the earth in the fields ahead of him, and then he saw downed power lines sparking on the side of the road and a steel farm gate that had been torn loose and bent as easily as if it had been made out of aluminum foil.

He let off the gas and stared around himself as the truck coasted. The row of trees that had grown here was gone, obliterated, the trunks split and the bases pulled from the ground, their mud-covered roots pointing at the sky. He looked past the grove and up toward his home and then he took his foot off the gas completely and put it on the brake.

His house was gone. Any sense that it had been a house was gone, at least. The foundation and portions of two of the walls lingered but the rest was scattered in chunks across his yard and the field beyond. Pieces of his roof littered the yard. His couch was some eighty feet from the foundation, upside down, rain drumming down onto it. The old aerial antenna, no longer functional but never removed, was lodged in the upper branches of a tree in the backyard. The rest of the tree was adorned with pink bits of insulation. Amidst the litter of debris across the yard he saw flashes of bright, stark white. Pieces of the porch railing he'd painted.

He sat there in the middle of the road and stared at it. Couldn't find a thought, really, couldn't do anything but look. This place shouldn't matter — he'd already known he could never return to it — but still, it had been home. It had been his home.

The sirens finally broke him out of it. They were wailing behind him, to the south, coming this way. Somebody coming to see if anyone needed rescuing.

He punched the accelerator and the truck fishtailed on the wet pavement and then found purchase and sped on. He swerved around one downed limb in the road and drove right over the top of another and on toward the gulf. He gave the house one last look in the rearview. It was the only thing out there, the only physical structure in most of a mile in any direction, and it had been destroyed. In the distance, the Amish farm looked solid, everything still standing. Something like that, it seemed almost personal. Seemed like the damn storm had been *hunting* him.

"Well, guess what?" he said aloud. "I wasn't home. And tell you something else? I *am* the storm."

There you go, boy. There you go.

The voice floated out of the air beside him and Josiah looked to the right and saw Campbell Bradford in the passenger seat, just as he had been at the timber camp. Campbell gave a tight-lipped smile and tipped his hat. His suit looked soaked, clinging to his shoulders as if he'd just climbed out of a swimming pool.

That ain't home, he said. *That place ain't even close to home for you, Josiah, never was. You deserved better, boy, deserved a piece of what I'd carved out for you. I was building a kingdom down here, and you're my rightful heir. It was taken right from your hands. Time to take it back. They'll come to know your name, boy. They'll know it.*

"The work will be done," Josiah told him. "You can count on that."

I know it. I'm stronger than ever now, boy, and it's thanks to you. Stronger than I've been in a long time, at least. And that's all I needed—was for you to listen, and let me get my strength back. It's coming now, son. Yes, sir, it is.

"I should have started with the hotel," Josiah said.

No. We'll go back for it, but we have to start with Shaw. You see that, don't you? He's the one who brought me back, then thought he could control me, hold power over me. With water, can you believe it? With water. It's time he sees who's won. Ain't a force in this valley like me, and he'll know it. He'll be the one to tell the others.

Another limb was across the road, this one big enough to do some serious damage, and Josiah saw it out of the corner of his eye at the last possible instant and whipped the wheel sideways. The truck skidded away, branches raking at it, bending the side-view mirror back and pounding dents and scratches into the paint, but it stayed upright. By the time Josiah had it straightened out, Campbell was gone again. He took a deep breath, exhaled, and saw a cloud of cold fog in front of his mouth. That made him smile. Campbell wasn't gone. Hadn't been gone in a long time, in fact, was with Josiah constantly now.

He was suddenly glad that his house had been destroyed and that he'd happened across it. Hell, he hadn't *happened* across it—Campbell had guided him there, and the message he intended to send was clear: there wasn't anything of Josiah Bradford left now. Not the old Josiah, the one these people knew. What remained of him belonged to Campbell now, and that was as it should be. The Josiah that had been known in this valley would vanish completely by the day's end, vanish as swiftly as the cloud that had leveled his house, and with a similar trail left behind.

*   *   *

The R. L. Drake fired up without hesitation. The power in the house was still on, so it didn't need to go to the backup generator, and seconds after Anne found the desk, she had the microphone to her lips. Most of the bands she dealt with were weather-spotter frequencies, but like any quality ham radio operator, she had the local emergency bands programmed as well. These days, some of the communications were encrypted, but there was still access for distress calls. She explained her situation to the dispatcher in as calm a tone as she could manage. Her nerves were rattled and her body felt unsteady but she held it all in check and spoke slowly and clearly. This was what she'd been training for all her life — a real emergency. She'd always known she could keep her poise during one, and while she'd imagined it would be during a tornado and not a kidnapping, her preparation didn't fail her now.

The dispatcher was a woman who sounded at first harried, no doubt from fielding constant storm-related calls, then astonished.

"Ma'am, I need to understand this situation: Are you alone in the house now?"

Anne had specified that at the start. She took a deep breath and willed herself to find patience in the face of panic.

"That is correct."

"But you were held hostage for several hours this morning by a man with a gun—"

"Not just some man. His name is Josiah Bradford. He's a local. Works down at the West Baden hotel, I believe."

"Yes, and your understanding is that he now has *another* woman in his control and that he has left your house with her and the weapon, correct?"

Anne felt a surge of frustration building, wanted to slap her hands down on the desk and shout, *Of course he still has the weapon, now would you please stop asking me to repeat myself and do something about it!* But poise counted in a situation like this, calm counted, and that woman who was with Josiah right now needed Anne's help.

"That is all correct," she said, speaking carefully. "The woman with him is named Claire Shaw. She's from Chicago. Her husband came down here to make a movie and somehow he crossed Josiah. And I would say that time is of the essence. He has a gun, and if he is to be believed, then he is driving a truck full of dynamite. You need to find that truck."

"There's already a bulletin out for that truck. Went up yesterday. A state police detective requested it. I'm going to get in touch with him now."

"All right," Anne said, wondering what Josiah had already done to earn this attention. "He's in the truck now, and so is she. He was taking her somewhere. I don't know where, but it's near his home. I could tell it was someplace near his home."

"Okay," the dispatcher said, "but right now I've got to find someone to come get you out of that basement. Things are out of control... we've got a tornado that hit Orleans, another that went through Paoli not five minutes later, and every one of my units was headed to assist. I'll find one to send back for you."

"No, don't send one of them for me. Please don't. I'm fine. But send one of them to *find that truck*."

"Of course, that's the priority. Be advised there's a bit of chaos right now, though. Got parts of highways closed and all sorts of major storm damage. There's a fire—"

"I know it's chaos out there," Anne said. "But I'm telling you that he could make the storm look gentle before this is done."

*   *   *

The wind was freshening again as Josiah neared the gulf, and here there were so many trees down that the road was nearly impassable. If he'd given the slightest damn about his truck he would have stopped, but at this point the Ranger meant about as much to him as the heap that had once been his house, so he plowed ahead, driving over limbs and fence posts and one snarl of barbed wire wrapped around a stump. All of it deposited in the middle of the road, left behind by a *cloud,* of all damn things. It was hard to believe.

Up ahead the old white chapel was still standing and seemed little worse for wear; the storm must have passed just south of it. He saw the blinking lights of a rescue truck out across the fields, a volunteer fire department outfit, but they had pulled into one of the farm driveways and were paying him no mind. The gravel track into the gulf was empty, and he drove onto it and through the brush and saw two vehicles parked at the end of the lane: Danny's Olds and a black Porsche Cayenne that was sitting upside down. The roof was caved in and glass lay all around it. Pointing skyward were four flat tires. That got Josiah laughing as he stopped the truck and got out to see Danny emerge from the bushes behind the cars, his ruddy, freckled face drained of color, his red hair dripping wet.

"You see it?" he said, walking toward Josiah. "You see it? Oh, *shit,* I never seen anything like it. Damn it all, I never even imagined seeing anything like that."

Josiah nodded at the upended Porsche. "Guess you didn't need to worry 'bout them tires."

Danny stared back at him blankly.

"How'd you miss it?" Josiah asked.

"Drove *away,* is how I missed it. I was waiting down here like you said, and then I heard the noise. I mean to tell you it really *does* sound like a train, just the way you always hear folks say it does. I heard that noise and I saw the sky going black as oil and I said, I got to get away *fast*. So I drove out of here and had hardly hit the road before I saw it. Big old funnel cloud, all white at first, then turning black. And I just hit the gas on this old car like I never have before in my life. Was up at the church when the tornado came in, and I pulled behind the building and set to prayin'. I'll tell you, I was prayin' and cryin' like a little kid, and I think it was that church that saved me because that thing passed by not a hundred yards from me, but I was safe and—"

"Where are *they*?" Josiah said.

"Huh?"

"The ones I'm here for, damn it! Where are they?"

Danny blinked, then wiped at his face, leaving a streak of dirt behind.

"I don't know. They were in the woods. Right there, where it blew through, Josiah. Far as I know, they're somewhere out *there* now." He waved his arm off to the east, in the direction the storm had gone.

"You think they're dead?" Josiah said, and he felt a cold, seething rage nestle into his belly. That storm better not have taken them. He'd come here to settle up, not to collect bodies.

"I have no idea, Josiah. I just want to get out of here. I'm done, all right? I'm—"

"Shut up," Josiah said. "I got a piece of work left to do, and ain't nothing or nobody *done* until that work's been completed. You don't understand the weight of this task, Danny, you don't understand the heft of it at all. Ain't a thing *done* yet."

"Josiah—"

"Stop using that name."

"What?"

"You call me Campbell now. Understand? Call me Campbell."

Danny said, "I think you're crazy."

He was staring Josiah in the face, and when he said it, he meant it.

"I don't know what the hell you're thinking anymore," Danny said. "Don't even seem like yourself, and now you're calling yourself Campbell. . . . It's like you're possessed."

"What I am," Josiah said, "is focused."

He turned away from Danny and walked back to the truck, reached inside the cab and withdrew the shotgun. Then he stood beside the bed and tore the tarps loose and exposed Eric Shaw's wife.

"Josiah! What in . . . oh, *hell*. You are crazy! You've lost your ever-lovin' —"

"I'm going to ask one more time for you to keep silent," Josiah said, and Danny's eyes registered for the first time that the gun in Josiah's hand was pointed at him.

"You going to shoot me? *Me?*"

"Don't intend to. But I came here to finish a task, and ain't nobody going to interrupt me. You least of all."

Danny's jaw slackened. He didn't say a word. The wind was starting to gust again, another round of storms ready to chase the one that had just left this place.

"We're going to find those two," Josiah said, "whether they're out in those woods or up in a damn tree somewhere with their necks broken. We're going to find them."

"Who is she?" Danny asked, staring at the woman in the bed of the truck.

"Shaw's wife. Now tell me where they went."

Danny jabbed a finger into the wind-torn woods. "Down to the gulf. Last time I saw them, they was walking down to the gulf."

"That's fine," Josiah said. "Then we'll take the same walk. You mind helping our friend here out of the truck? I'd like to keep her at my side."

Danny hesitated only a moment, but when he did move, it seemed to be more out of something exchanged in his stare with the woman than in direct obedience to Josiah's instruction. He leaned over the bed wall and tried to gather her up, but he was handling her gently, not getting a thing done.

"Go on and pull her out of there!" Josiah barked. "She ain't that fragile, boy."

Danny ignored him and went to the back of the truck and climbed in the bed to help her to her feet. As he did that, he pushed aside another tarp, glanced down to see what it had covered, and froze with his arms extended to the woman.

"Is that...dynamite?"

"Indeed," Josiah said. "And it would take one squeeze of this trigger to blow the back of that truck into Martin County. Now you want to hurry up?"

Danny got her upright and down out of the truck then, used his pocket knife to cut the tape free from her feet at Josiah's instructions, and then started down the trail. The woman was unsteady with her hands still bound, and he kept an arm on her to help with balance. They'd gotten well into the trees now, the vehicles out of sight, and were crossing over familiar ground, a path on which Josiah knew every root and stone. Trees were downed in every direction, some snapped in half, others torn free at their bases, leaning crazily against one another, but somehow many had stayed upright and largely intact. Even now they were tossing around in that freshening wind. Josiah couldn't help but marvel a little as he watched them. Damn things didn't seem so flexible on a normal day, appeared stiff as the boards they produced, but look at 'em whipping around now. Some would break; some just bend. All depended on the tree and the storm. Some would break and some just bend...

He'd gotten lost in the trees and didn't see what Danny and the woman saw. Didn't understand what was happening until the woman dropped to her knees in the middle of the trail, and when he turned to jerk her upright, he saw Danny was pointing ahead. He looked back down the trail.

Eric Shaw was coming up it.

57

CLAIRE.

Eric saw her before anything else, focused on her so much that for an instant he was unable to see the rest of the frame. The first thing that stood out was the tape: a bright shining silver X across her face. Then she dropped to her knees on the trail and the rest of the pieces clicked into understanding in his brain—Danny Hastings at her side, Josiah Bradford behind them with a gun in his hand. In that first moment, that first blink, they'd been insignificant pieces of scenery around his wife. Now they stepped forward and joined the cast and became significant as hell. Particularly the shotgun.

He'd left Kellen beside the gulf not five minutes earlier and begun the trek back up the hill, thinking that help was a few minutes away. His hands were shaking and his head throbbed but he'd told himself that he needed to think of Kellen, because

Kellen needed help of the kind that could be found—normal, human help, different from that required by Eric. So he'd walked up the storm-ravaged slope, intent on finding rescue for Kellen, and now he was staring at his wife bound and gagged.

For a moment nobody moved or spoke. They all just froze there, looking back at one another, and then Eric started forward at a run, and Josiah Bradford's face split into a grin and he lifted the shotgun and laid the barrel against the crown of Claire's skull.

Eric stopped running.

"What are you doing?" he shouted. "What do you *want?*"

"Only what's owed to me," Josiah said. His voice didn't sound anything like it had two days ago. It seemed to have gained a deeper timbre, gained power. It was the voice of an old-time revival preacher, primed to stir the crowds into a frenzy.

"Take that gun away from—"

"You come on up here. Walk slow, but get closer. I don't want to shout."

No, Eric thought, *I believe we should shout. Because Kellen's back there and he isn't going to hear us unless we're shouting. Don't know what he could do with a broken ankle anyhow, but it's something. I left him to get help. Now I need it.*

He moved forward to join them.

Devastation. That was the word across the shortwave bands— reports coming in from around the area to Anne's basement while she waited for the police. The tornado that had passed overhead while Josiah Bradford was still in her home had touched down just west of Orangeville and moved northeast into Orleans. Houses had been torn apart, cars overturned, utility poles ripped from the ground. At least two fires started in the aftermath. Highway 37 was closed between Orleans and Mitchell, keeping many rescue crews from reaching the scene.

A second tornado had touched down within minutes of the first, this one just to the southeast. It had flattened a group of trailers and then moved back into farmland, taking a cellular phone tower out in its path. Early estimates said that one had stayed on the ground for at least six miles.

She had no view of the sky from down in the cellar, but the spotters to the west were issuing frantic warnings that things were not done yet. The supercell was shifting and realigning and, they warned, possibly preparing to spit out another funnel cloud.

Tornado outbreaks generally spanned a wider area, sometimes putting up as many as forty or fifty or even a hundred tornadoes spread out across a wide, multistate region. To have a cluster outbreak like this, so many tornadoes in one county, was rare but not unprecedented. She remembered studying a similar event that occurred in Houston in the early nineties, when six tornadoes spawned from four separate storms hit one county over the course of about two hours. At one point, three of them were on the ground at the same time. Things like that could happen. You could never predict the behavior of a truly furious storm. All you could hope to do was see the warnings.

That was her role — to see the warnings and hope that people heeded them. She had frequencies for the security outfits with both the French Lick and West Baden hotels, and she contacted them immediately after finishing her initial conversation with the sheriff's department, explained the threat, and suggested they post some guards at the property entrances. She couldn't say whether they believed her, but she'd done what she could. She'd issued the warning.

Fifteen minutes after she'd made initial contact, the Orange County Sheriff's Department dispatcher came back to Anne to report that a detective named Roger Brewer from the Indiana State Police had arrived at Josiah Bradford's home.

And found it missing.

It appeared, the dispatcher said, as if the tornado had in fact touched down almost on top of Josiah's house before beginning its path into Orleans.

"No sign of the truck?" Anne asked.

No sign of the truck. The state police were reaching out to the FBI for assistance — with every available unit out on storm-related calls, the kidnapping called for focused attention that the locals could not provide. But the nearest FBI contact was in Bloomington, which was a forty-five-minute drive in the best of conditions, and these weren't the best of conditions. So there was one detective on the search.

One.

The dispatcher, who was talking to Anne with detached calm, which was of course part of the job but which was also frustrating beyond measure to someone trying to convey a sense of urgency, said that the detective was "making a sweep." Then she told Anne that there were too many other emergency calls going on to prolong this one.

"He was headed toward his property," Anne said. "Some area of woods near his property. Keep looking. And remember that he said his truck was full of—"

"I remember. I've advised our officers. They understand the threat."

No, Anne thought, *they do not. I'm not sure anyone could.*

She couldn't say what she knew to be true: that the storm and Josiah were linked, that something evil had come to town today, and it wasn't leaving soon.

* * *

"What do you want?" Eric Shaw repeated, advancing up the trail toward Josiah. "This doesn't have anything to do with us. Not with her, not with me."

"I think you're wrong on that score," Josiah said. "It has much to do with you."

"How?" Shaw said.

"You give my name to another," Josiah said. "The one who took me from my home, who shed my blood and took me from my home, and you honor him with my name. Don't even see that you brought me *back* home, you dumb son of a bitch. You brought me home, and there's scores to be settled."

The words had left his mouth without a beat of hesitation, and though they were not his own words, he believed them.

"Brought me home and then thought you could control me," he said. "Hold me back with water. A fool's notion, Shaw. There's not a force in this valley stronger than me."

Shaw tilted his head and blinked at Josiah. "He's in you," he said. "Isn't he?"

Josiah didn't answer.

"What do you mean?" Danny said, and Josiah didn't care for the intense interest in his voice.

"Campbell," Shaw said to Josiah. "You sound just like him now."

Above them the sky had darkened to near black, the wind rising to a howl though the rain had ceased altogether. The next wave of storms was here.

"How would you know the sound of his voice?" Danny said.

"Trust me, I know it. I've been listening to him for a few days now. Seeing him and hearing him." He turned back to Josiah. "You don't look like him yet but you carry his voice. He's in you now."

"Always was," Josiah said. "Did you not hear what I said? We're of shared blood, you ignorant son of a bitch. The years don't matter — we're linked, and always have been."

"No," Shaw said, "not like this. He's in your mind, damn it, he's turned you into something —"

Josiah stepped forward and swung the shotgun, caught Shaw in the temple with the barrel and knocked him down into the wet grass. Danny gave a little grunt and stepped forward and Josiah turned and stared at him.

"What do you think you're doing?"

"Nothing. I'm not —"

"You move toward me again, and I'll shoot you just as fast as either of them."

"Damn it, Josiah, he just told you the truth."

"Hasn't been a word of truth left his mouth since he set foot in my valley."

"Bullshit. Campbell's infecting your damn brain just like he says."

Shaw spoke up again, his voice thick with pain. "Let Claire go, at least. Let her go, and whatever problem you've got with me, we'll figure it out. But she's not a part of this."

Josiah stared down at him and watched blood seep out of a wound near his hairline and trickle down the side of his face and drip into the grass. The blood looked black in the shadows, but then the lightning flashed again, and in that instant he saw the bright red of the blood stark against the white of Shaw's face.

"Think for a minute," Shaw said, speaking as if his tongue were hard to move. "Think about what you want, and what you can actually get. You want some money? Okay, I'll get you money. But what else can you hope to get out of this? Why do you have her tied up like that? What does it bring you?"

"It'll bring," Josiah said, "what's been owed."

"What's owed to you?"

"This valley," he said.

"I don't know what that means. And I don't know how hurting my wife can help you get it."

"It's a matter of power," Josiah said. "I would not expect a man of your dull mind to conceive of just what that means. I ran this valley once, held it in the palm of my hand. I'll do it again."

There was blood still dripping off the side of Shaw's head. Josiah must have hit him a good one; his left arm was shaking as if caught by palsy.

"Stop letting him talk for you!" Shaw shouted. "Just *think* for a minute, think about what's real. You've got police after you. If you stay here, you'll be arrested. But I can get you some money and then you can leave —"

"Shut your damned mouth," Josiah said. "If I required a suggestion from you, I'd let you know with my gun."

But Shaw's words were getting to him, crawling in his head and clouding his sense of purpose. What did he want? Why was he here? He turned away from the others, toward the western woods, and let the wind fan hard into his face. He could smell the storm on it, could taste its anger. He wanted to be alone with that wind for just a moment. Just one long blink.

Shaw went for him when he closed his eyes. Josiah hadn't been paying attention to the gun; it hung loose at his side, leaning against his thigh, and Shaw almost got to it. Got a hand on it, in fact, clawed at the stock and almost tore it from Josiah's grip.

Almost.

Josiah snatched it away from him and swept his left fist down like a hammer, caught Shaw square in the forehead. He hung on, though, keeping one arm wrapped around Josiah's waist and throwing punches with the other. Josiah staggered backward and got his free hand on Shaw's belt and heaved. Then he had space to lift the gun as Shaw came back at him a second time. Josiah twisted it so the butt was pointed down and slammed it at Shaw's face, missing and hitting his shoulder. There was a snapping sound and a cry of pain and Shaw fell back into the grass and the mud. Josiah lifted the gun again, hoisting it high this time, and as the woman gave a choked scream against the tape over her mouth, he had a flash of memory, saw himself down in the ditch with that detective again, swinging the cinder block. This time he tempered the blow. Brought the stock of the gun down with wounding force but not killing force. He caught Shaw on the top of the head and he dropped and stayed down. Conscious still, groping around in the dirt as if he intended to rise but eliminated as a threat for the moment. Josiah wanted to hit him again, full strength, but he held back, thinking of the man he'd killed too early last time.

He wouldn't make the same mistake now. The dead couldn't remember you, and Josiah wanted this son of a bitch to remember him. Long may he live and remember. That was Campbell's instruction. Shaw had wanted to tell tales about the family? Wanted to exploit the Bradford name? Let him tell *this* story.

Josiah dropped to one knee beside Shaw, felt through his pockets. No weapon, but there was a phone. Two phones, in fact; one looked already ruined by water. Josiah set both of them on the ground and smashed them with the butt of the shotgun while Shaw lay at his feet and moaned, writhing. Josiah knelt again, took him by an ear, pulled his head back, and looked down into the faltering eyes.

"You ever heard a dynamite blast? Up close, in person?"

Shaw's lips moved but no words came. His eyelids fluttered, then jerked open again when Josiah twisted his ear.

"Picture a full case of it going up, with fifteen gallons of gasoline to help it along. Think you got an idea of what that'll sound like? I hope you do, because you're not going to be there to listen. Won't hear the sound itself, but you'll hear plenty about it. Might start hearing it in your dreams. I'd imagine you will. When they take her bones out of the fire, you won't be able to stop imagining just what it was like. Be imagining for a long time, I expect. Enjoy that."

He slapped Shaw's head back down and straightened up, walked over to the wife, wrapped his hand in her long dark hair, and jerked her to her feet. Danny made another sound of disapproval, and Josiah turned the gun barrel toward him.

"Back up the trail, Danny boy. We're going back up the trail. You walk ahead now. I've got a sense you can no longer be trusted to stand behind me."

"Damn it, Josiah, leave her here. Leave her with him. Ain't no reason to take this thing any farther. We'll get in my car and get you out of this town. Wherever you want to go, man, we can get you there."

"That's where you're confused," Josiah said. "You think I want to go somewhere else. That's not the case. I just got home."

He moved his finger onto the trigger and tilted his chin up the trail, spitting a stream of tobacco juice in its direction.

"Start walking. We got a piece of work left to do."

58

THERE WAS NO WORD of Josiah Bradford or his pickup truck. Anne sat alone in the cold basement that smelled of trapped moisture and dust and scanned the shortwave bands, trying to stay hopeful, trying not to remember the sound his palm had made on that poor woman's face.

Nothing came in to reward her hope.

There were plenty of reports—she couldn't remember a day with this level of activity, in fact—but they were all storm-related. The damage in Orleans was severe. Just to the north, in Mitchell, line winds had brought down trees and blown windows out of buildings, and in the tiny speed bump town of Leipsic, there were reports of a fire that started when a power line came down on a pole barn. The second tornado, in Paoli, had scattered a cluster of trailers, some probably with people inside.

Urgent problems, sure, but what held Anne's attention now were not reports of damage to the north and east, but those of clouds to the south and west. They were accompanied by savage lightning that had been missing in the day's first round—a school nine miles away had been struck—and the area beneath the storm was being raked with nickel-size hail. Two spotters whom Anne knew and trusted called in observations of a beaver's tail, a trailing cloud formation that indicated a supercell with rotation.

Even more alarming, though, were the reports from spotters just outside this new storm. In regions around it, the storms that had been building were dissipating. That might please the novice, but it was anything but a good sign, suggesting that the energy from those outlying storms was being absorbed by the larger front. Feeding it.

The storm was moving swiftly to the northeast. Right back into Anne's valley.

She made contact with the dispatcher again, was informed curtly that Detective Brewer still had no sign of the truck.

"Tell him to make another drive through that area. He's out there."

The dispatcher said she'd ask him to make another pass.

The world would not hold still. Eric blinked and squinted and tried to find steady focus, but it kept shifting, the trees and the earth and the sky undulating around him. Frequently the dark woods were lit with flashes of lightning, and thunder crackled in a way that made the ground seem to tremble, but there was no rain.

He ran his tongue over his lips and tasted blood, tried to sit up and felt a bolt of pain in his collarbone. He reached for the head wound but his shaking hand could not find it, sending his fingers rattling over his face like a blind man searching for recognition.

He was alone.

That meant that Claire was gone.

He gave a grunt and shoved himself onto all fours, then crawled over to a tree and used it to pull himself to his feet. The world tilted again but he held firm to the tree.

Where had they taken her? They'd just left; it could not be far. And he had to follow. Had to follow quickly, because Josiah had a gun and hadn't he said something about—

Dynamite. With fifteen gallons of gasoline to help it along…

He'd heard those words, hadn't he? Was it true? Did Josiah Bradford have dynamite in the back of that truck?

When they take her bones out of the fire…

There was no one there who could help. Kellen was back at the gulf and his car was probably destroyed and Claire was with that man, who was no longer himself. He was infected by Campbell now, Eric was certain of that, had heard it in his voice and seen it in his eyes.

He had to catch up.

He had to catch up *fast*.

Finally Josiah had a purpose, understood it, and knew how to carry it out. He felt like a man who'd long been searching in the dark and finally realized he'd been carrying a matchbook in his pocket the whole time.

His detour to this place, one that had taken him far from the hotel and his ultimate goal, had been puzzling but necessary for reasons he couldn't entirely comprehend. Now, after seeing Shaw, he understood it well—Shaw and Campbell were linked, a part of one another in a way that differed from Josiah and Campbell's bond. Shaw had returned Campbell's spirit to this place, and, somehow, he understood that. Understood the significance.

Campbell needed him to be left to tell the tale; nobody else was capable of giving true credit where credit would be due. Eric Shaw was the exception. In the question of Campbell Bradford's legacy, Eric Shaw was critical.

They moved swiftly up the trail, with Josiah dragging the woman along and keeping the gun pointed forward, toward Danny. The loyalest of friends he'd been for years, and yet Josiah had looked into his eyes and seen the deceit that lurked there and knew well that Danny Hastings was an ally no longer.

That was fine. Josiah was not alone on this day and in this struggle. Campbell rode with him, and the valley knew no fiercer ally. They'd finish this piece of work together, all opposition be damned.

They reached the trailhead and pushed through the fields and back toward his truck. Now that they were out of the trees he could look across the farmland and to the road, and he saw that the flashing emergency lights that had been there when they arrived were gone. Called elsewhere to some other crisis. He reckoned wherever they'd headed, it was the wrong damn direction.

The truck was where he'd left it, covered with dents and scratches but still ready to run. All he needed out of it was one last drive, a handful of miles.

"Here is where we part," he told Danny as they passed the overturned Porsche. "You'll hear the rest of the story soon enough, I expect."

"What do you mean?"

"It's not something I have the time or desire to clarify." He shoved the woman toward the back of his truck, but for the first time she began resisting, twisting against his grasp. Her hands were still bound but her legs were not, and she kicked at his knee. He slapped her hard, wrenched her arm, and slammed her up against the side of the truck. Her sudden show of fight told him that the bed of the truck might not be the place for her. He'd put her in the cab instead, keep her close.

He found the roll of duct tape in the bed of the truck and held her while he wrapped some around her lower legs. Then he dragged her around to the passenger side, paying no mind to Danny, and jerked the door open. She was still struggling, thrashing around so much that she caught his face with the back of her head and he tasted blood in his mouth. He grabbed her by the neck and shoved her forward, slamming his knee into her ass as he did it, and got her inside. He'd just shut the door when Danny said, "No more, Josiah."

Josiah turned back to look at him and saw the knife in his hand.

It was a folding knife, with a blade no more than four inches long, one of those that had a little metal nub so you could flick it open fast with your thumb and fancy yourself a badass. Josiah looked down at it and laughed out loud.

"You going to cut me?"

"Going to do what needs to be done. You can decide what that'll be."

Josiah laughed again and lifted the gun and wrapped his finger around the trigger.

"Knife at a gunfight," he said. "If that doesn't describe your entire pathetic life, I don't know what does, Danny boy."

"Whatever you're fixing to do, you'll do it without her."

"Yeah?"

"Yeah."

"Danny, I squeeze this trigger, I end your life. What don't you understand about that? This bitch hasn't a thing to do with you."

"It ain't right, and I won't stand for it."

"Well, aren't you a noble bastard."

"What her husband told you back there, it was the truth," Danny said. "This ain't you anymore. I don't understand what's going on, but you aren't yourself, Josiah. Not even close."

"What did I tell you about using that name?"

"That's what I mean — it's Campbell's ghost has got in your head, just like he said. You been talking so damn strange, talking about Campbell like he's sitting at your side. The man's dead, Josiah, and I don't know what in the hell has gotten into you, but that man is dead."

"Right there's a mistake that's been made for far too long," Josiah said. "Ain't nothing dead about Campbell."

Danny had shuffled a little closer. There wasn't but five feet separating them now. Josiah was enjoying this little exchange, amused by Danny's attempted show of heroism, but he didn't have time to waste.

"Stand down and step aside," he said. "Me and the missus have to be getting on."

"She's not going with you."

"Danny . . ."

"I'm telling you as a friend, Josiah, best friend you ever had in your life, that you've lost your damn mind."

"That may be," Josiah said, "but I'll tell *you* something: I'm not going to ride into the fire alone. That bitch is coming with me."

"What are you talking about?"

"We're leaving. Go on and get in your car."

Danny paused for a long time, and then he looked at the woman in the truck and pushed his fat pink tongue out of his mouth and wet his lips.

"Anybody going to take this ride with you, it ought to be me."

"You'd take her place?"

Danny nodded.

"And *I'm* the crazy one? She ain't nothing to you, boy."

"And she ain't to you neither."

Josiah felt unsteady again, his mind shifting on him as it had been all day, and that angered him. He didn't have time for it, knew exactly what he had to do and had been on his way to do it until Danny's fat freckled ass slowed him down with this bullshit.

"Get in your car," he said again, emphatically this time.

"All right," Danny said, "but she's getting in with me."

He held Josiah's eyes for a moment, like he was searching for the bluff in them, and then he wet his lips a second time and stepped toward the woman and Josiah squeezed the trigger.

It had been a long time since he'd fired the shotgun, and he'd forgotten the sheer force of it. It bucked in his arms and sent a tremor through his chest and cut Danny Hastings damn near in half.

Eric Shaw's wife let out a low, anguished wail under the tape and pushed herself down to the floor of the truck, squeezing against the dashboard as if she expected him to put another round into the window. Josiah ignored her completely, staring at what he'd done. Danny had been at such close range that the damage was catastrophic. There was blood on the truck and on Josiah's shirt and on his face, hot and wet as tears against his skin.

He wiped at his face with a shirtsleeve and stared down at the corpse.

Best friend you ever had in your life ...

Something trembled inside him, a weakening of the resolve that had filled him on the way up the trail, and he swallowed hard and ground his teeth together as Danny's blood ran through the grass and formed pools at Josiah's feet.

He hadn't wanted to do this. Danny had forced his hand, yes, but he hadn't wanted to shoot. Not at him. Anybody else but not him.

"Damn you," Josiah said and dropped to one knee, staring at Danny's left side, where his torso had almost been freed from his legs. Would have been different if he'd had a handgun; he could have put a bullet into his leg or something and just backed his ass off without killing him. That shotgun had no such option; fired this close, it didn't just kill, it destroyed.

He reached out and touched the grass near his feet, dipped his fingertips into Danny's blood.

Ain't your blood, Campbell's voice whispered to him. *And ain't your concern.*

But it was hard to focus now, hard to listen. The warm, wet touch of his old friend's blood held him like cinder blocks strapped to his feet. He couldn't move away.

He's no kin to you, boy, and you got work left to do.

Campbell's voice, so steady and strong throughout most of this day that it had become Josiah's own at times, suddenly seemed softer. It was hard to hear him, hard to hear anything but the echoing roar of the shotgun.

Josiah had no recollection of having met Danny. They went back that far. Had just walked through their shitty world together from the start, more like family than friends. And the dumb son of a bitch had never stopped walking with him. Not even through this. Shit, he'd come driving up to that timber camp, bringing supplies long after he knew Josiah had killed a man. Had come out here following Eric Shaw at Josiah's command, had waited on him through a damned tornado.

Had offered to take the woman's place in the truck right now. Who in the hell would do that? And why?

Damn it, boy, get your hands out of his blood and step back! You were to listen. That's all. Only thing you're required to do is listen, and now you're not doing it.

He didn't want to listen, though. Campbell would tell him to go, to leave this spot, and it didn't feel right to leave Danny where he'd fallen. No, he couldn't leave him alone...

It was the woman who jarred him loose. He'd taped her wrists together behind her back, but her fingers were free, and somehow she'd managed to reach the door handle. He heard the click of the latch opening, and with it his mind spun away from Danny Hastings and he turned to see her feet go flying through the cab as she fell backward and out of the truck.

He got up quickly and ran around the bed of the truck, found her down there in the dirt. She had nowhere to go, was just thrashing around like a fish on the sand, but he had to give her credit for trying. Josiah reached down and grabbed her by the back of her jeans and got her upright, then dropped the shotgun long enough to use both hands to shove her back inside. He hadn't gotten the door closed yet when he heard an odd, faraway cry.

He slammed the door and snatched the shotgun with both hands, then turned and looked at the woods around him. He heard the cry again, understood the word this time: *don't.* Eric Shaw was on his feet and had reached the trailhead, was just across the field from them. Josiah's finger went to the trigger and for a moment he considered letting it blast in Shaw's direction. He held off, though.

"You watch!" he bellowed. "You watch, and you listen! Isn't a thing you can do to stop this!"

He walked around to the driver's door and jerked it open and climbed inside, setting the shotgun between his legs, muzzle pointed down. The engine roared to life as Shaw continued on his drunken stagger through the field. Josiah threw it into gear

and pulled away. In the rearview mirror, he could see the man
begin to scream.

At the end of the gravel drive he turned left and pushed the
pedal down to the floor, the worn tires howling on wet pavement. He drove south, figuring to return to town the same way
he'd come. It would require passing the wreckage that was left
of his home again, but he was determined to speed past it without a pause or even a sidelong glance.

That was the idea for the first mile at least, until the house
came into view and he saw there was a car pulling out of the
driveway. A police car. Josiah hesitated but didn't touch the brake
pedal. They were looking at the damage, not looking for him.

That idea held until the cruiser pulled all the way out, blocking the road, and hit the lights.

59

ERIC WAS TRYING TO hurry, but his legs were prone to buckling. He fell twice and got back to his feet, reeling, and pushed on. Toward the middle of the field his head began to clear and his legs steadied. There was a terrible burning just above his shoulder and he could feel a wet, pulsing heat along his scalp where bleeding continued — wounds left behind by Josiah's shotgun butt. The pain in his skull was lost between the headache that had been building all morning and the impact of the gun.

He was a hundred yards from Josiah Bradford's truck when the tires spun and it pulled down the gravel drive and toward the road with Claire inside. Eric stopped moving and screamed at them to stop, but the truck flashed through the trees and was gone from sight for a moment. Then it appeared again, marked by a shriek of tires as Josiah made a left turn out onto the road and sped south. Eric stood in the field and screamed until the truck was gone.

The wind blew up in a sudden commanding gust and pushed him sideways, and that got him moving again. The air temperature seemed to have dropped ten degrees, and it was as dark in the field now as it had been in the trees.

Up ahead he could see two vehicles remained—a white sedan and a twisted black mess that had once been Kellen's Porsche. It was upside down now, demolished, but the white car was upright and looked functional. He ran toward it. Made it to within thirty feet before his eyes took in the splash of red across the hood and then dropped to the grass below it. What he saw there took his legs. He stumbled and fell, landing on his hands and knees in the mud.

There was a body in front of the white car. A huddled, blood-soaked mass.

He got up and moved forward, unable to take a breath, the world seeming to go still and silent around him despite the raging wind. There was so much blood. So much...

It was Josiah's partner. Edgar Hastings's grandson. He'd been shot in the left side of his torso, had a massive, ragged hole blown out of him. It looked nothing like a gunshot wound. More like something chopped away with an axe. After he'd gotten close enough for recognition, Eric stumbled away from the body as if it could stand up and hurt him.

Not Claire. That is not Claire. And you only heard one shot.... You saw him put her in the truck, and she was alive. She had to be, because there was only one shot...

There had been only one shot. Right? He felt sure of that, and now he was sure of what that shot had accomplished. But Claire wasn't here, which meant that she was in the truck with Josiah Bradford—a man who'd just murdered his own friend.

Dynamite. With fifteen gallons of gasoline to help it along. When they take her bones out of the fire . . .

"No," he said aloud. "Damn it, no."

He circled around the body and came to the white car, jerked the door open, and looked inside. No key in the ignition. Who had driven it here? Josiah was gone in the truck, so that probably meant the dead man, Danny, had driven this car.

No time to hesitate. He had to move fast, just do it without thinking.

He crossed to the body and knelt beside it, felt bile rise in the back of his throat, squeezed his eyes shut and reached with one of his shaking hands toward the blood-soaked jeans. He felt for the pocket, almost shouting when his fingers touched warm, wet blood, and pushed his hand inside.

The keys were there.

Forty minutes after the first tornado of the day touched down near Orangeville, the third made contact in Martin County, at the point where the Lost River emptied into the east fork of the White River. The funnel cloud tore into the riverbank and then blew northeast, cutting a straight line across the Lost River's snaking course, as if it intended to follow it all the way upstream. Then the storm ran into the hollows of the Hoosier National Forest, two natural wonders colliding, and lost its strength in the uneven wooded terrain. It was as if, one spotter said, the forest had swallowed it.

Anne had been focused on the storm reports, listening to the arrival of this third tornado and quite certain that it would not be the last, that the valley was in the midst of a cluster outbreak now, when the Orange County dispatcher cut in on her.

"Ma'am? Mrs. McKinney? Detective Brewer thinks he has the truck."

"He does?"

"A white Ford Ranger? That sound right? It's a little pickup truck?"

"Yes."

"Well, it came up to Josiah Bradford's house and then pulled a U-turn. The officer is following it now. He's got the lights and siren on but the driver isn't responding."

"That's it," Anne said excitedly. "That's him. Tell him to be careful. There's dynamite in that truck!"

"He's been advised."

"Is there anyone else in the truck?"

"He can't tell."

"She should be with him. She should be inside."

"I understand that. I've advised to exercise caution."

"I don't know if that's a strong enough word," Anne said. "It's going to be hard to stop that truck without..."

Her words trailed off. She didn't want to voice the possibility.

"I understand," the dispatcher said.

Josiah barely pulled the U-turn off. The right-side wheels slid off the pavement and into the grass but the four-wheel drive spun him free and then he was moving again, away from the cop.

Maybe this guy was intending to stop Josiah just to ask what he knew about the house. Maybe he was just going to offer a warning about the storm...

The siren came on then, and such thoughts disappeared. The cop was in pursuit, had gone into it immediately, and that meant he was reacting to the sight of Josiah's truck, and not simply to his behavior.

He was going to have to think fast now, damn it, because his little Ranger was not going to outrun that Crown Vic. If the dumb son of a bitch started shooting at him or tried to force a collision, he'd be in for one hell of a surprise when the truck blew a mile into the sky. Only problem with that, Josiah's load was intended for another target, and he was going to get it there. It was the last task he had, and he could not fail.

That was going to require some time, though, time he couldn't buy as long as this damn cop stayed in pursuit. He dropped his hand to the stock of the shotgun, considering his options. He couldn't fire the shotgun from the moving truck with any accuracy and he wasn't sure that it wouldn't blow the dynamite. Far as he knew, the stuff required a direct electrical charge to safely detonate, but he figured a fire would do the rest. You didn't set dynamite on fire and expect it to quietly burn out. Gunfire might do the job, too, and Josiah wasn't ready to blow this truck up just yet. Had a few miles to go first.

He needed time. That was all he needed — a little bit of time.

He took the truck up to seventy, and now he was aware that the cop was trying to speak to him through the cruiser's loud-speaker. Dumbass didn't even turn his siren off for the attempt, and even if he had, the wind would have washed the words away. It was blowing *fierce* now, the sky gone coal black, sporadic lightning flashes making the world beneath carry an odd green glow.

The cruiser was keeping pace and not attempting to close the gap, which was surprising. Probably the cop was on the radio right now, explaining the situation and asking for advice. How much did he know? Odds were, a description of the truck had been issued after the detective was murdered on this road, but there was a chance — however slim — that the damned old lady had somehow found a way to contact help from her basement. And if that was the case, this guy knew Josiah had a hostage.

There you go, Campbell whispered, and Josiah caught a

glimpse of his face in the mirror again, shadowed but eyes aglow. *He'll stop for her. He'll have to.*

Yes, he would. Protect and serve, that was the motto, that was the promise, and the dumb bastard would have to obey the oath, wouldn't he? He'd have to attempt to protect and serve the dead bitch that Josiah was about to pitch out onto the road.

He lifted the shotgun clear, steering with his left hand, and set it across his lap, the barrel pointed at Claire Shaw's terrified face. He grinned as he leaned across her body and fumbled for the door handle.

"You were going to die sometime today," he said. "A shame it has to be so early."

The Orange County dispatcher had patched Anne through directly to the police officer who'd sighted Josiah Bradford's truck, a state cop named Roger Brewer. He wanted to confirm that it was the right vehicle and understand the situation from her as best he could, he said.

She listened as he described the truck and said, "Yes, yes, that's it," and then began to warn him, as she'd warned the dispatcher, about the dynamite. She hadn't gotten ten words out when he cut in and said, "Shit, something's happening," and there was a half-second pause before he said *"Shit!"* again and then Anne heard the scream of tires searching for traction, followed by the muffled sound of impact and a shattering of metal and glass.

"What happened? What happened?"

"He threw something out onto the road," the officer said. "Dispatch, we're going to need more cars. He just threw . . . I think he threw a body out into the road."

60

THE DEAD MAN'S CAR started on the third try, groaning to
life on the spark of a nearly exhausted battery. Eric, dropping the gearshift into drive, had the sudden, stupid thought: *It's
the Fargo car. White Cutlass Ciera. You saw that movie with Claire
and predicted it would be nominated for a bunch of Oscars...*

He had to back up to get around the body. He made a wide
pass to stay clear of it, and he did not look down. The splash
of blood across the white hood trembled against the engine's
vibrations.

Trees bordered the gravel lane on each side, and only when
he came out to the road did he have a clear look at the sky. The
black clouds seemed to be drifting away from the center in all
directions, isolating a pale circle. The wind that had blown so
violently as he'd run through the field just minutes ago had died
off completely, and ahead of him the fields looked strangely
peaceful.

It can't happen again, he thought, staring up at the separating clouds. *You can't have two of them in the same place.*

He swung out into the road, turned left, in the direction Josiah Bradford's truck had gone, and hit the gas. If another tornado actually did form, it was good that Kellen was still down in the gulf. The gulf had already saved them once.

He had the car up to fifty and was fumbling for the windshield wipers, wanting the crimson smear of drying blood off the glass, when another vehicle appeared down the road. He didn't take his foot off the gas right away, but then the distance closed to the point that he could see it clearly: a white Ford Ranger with dents in the hood and a snarl of fence wire mashed into the front grille and dragging along under the car.

Josiah.

He was coming back.

Stop him, he thought, *you have to stop him.* But the Ranger was flying along, had to be doing seventy at least, and Claire was inside. If Eric swung the car across the road to block the truck and took the impact broadside, they'd probably all be killed. And that was discounting the potential explosion.

Indecision froze him. He slowed the car down to twenty, then ten, hands tight on the wheel, a hundred potential maneuvers floating through his head, all of them dismissed as too risky. The truck was in motion, and the only way to stop an object that wanted to stay in motion was with impact. Simple rules of physics that would be simple rules of disaster today.

And so he sat there helplessly, impotently, as the Ranger roared up and then passed him. Eric was staring inside the cab, trying to catch a glimpse of Claire, but what he saw when the truck shot by him made him give a low shout of fear and slam on the brake pedal, bringing the Oldsmobile to a stop in the center of the road.

Campbell Bradford was driving the truck. Not Josiah, but *Campbell,* hunched over the wheel in his dark brown suit and bowler hat, his mouth twisted into a grin in the quarter second when Eric had met his eyes.

Josiah saw the Oldsmobile pull out onto the road and he was so stunned, so momentarily hopeful, that he almost hit the brakes. *Danny?* But then he got it, understood what must have happened, and tightened his hands on the steering wheel, laid his foot heavier on the gas pedal.

He ain't stopping us, boy, Campbell whispered. *We're going home, and that son of a bitch is not strong enough to stop us. He doesn't have the will for it.*

Indeed, he did not. Josiah kept the speed up and the wheel held dead-on center and clenched his teeth, ready for a collision, but Shaw stayed in his own lane and let the Ranger thunder right by him. Didn't even *try* to do anything, just sat there behind the wheel of Danny's Olds and watched Josiah pass by.

Told you, boy. Told you. He doesn't have the will, and neither does anyone else. You think those police can stop us right now? Not a chance. They ain't strong enough. Ain't nobody in this valley strong enough.

There surely was not. Josiah was flying now, open road ahead, the world yielding to him in the way he'd always known it would.

Dumping the woman in the road had freed him from the first pursuit car, and he'd avoid those that would attempt to join the chase. He'd drive west and take the back roads, a no-brainer as there would be more police near Orleans, and if he drove toward them, he'd make it easier for them. Drive away from them and they'd have to give chase.

He was back on the road to the gulf now, Wesley Chapel a white speck beneath black sky in the distance. Down to the chapel, then bang another left, and keep pushing west at as fast a speed as he could manage. That was all he had to do.

Lightning flashed again, and around him the fields shone with the deep, lush green you could only ever see beneath a storm. He couldn't believe just *how* green everything looked. Above him, something seemed to be opening in the dark clouds. The storm breaking up, maybe. Yes, even the wind had died off. Everything around him was still. That expected furious storm wasn't going to come to life after all.

But something was happening in the sky. He had only a sense of it at first, some swirl of light, and then he blinked and looked up and to the left and saw that something strange was happening in that clear circle that had formed in the center of the clouds. Something was . . . lowering. Yes, a cloud of pure white was dropping down from the center of the dark swirling ring above it.

A thin white rope descended almost all the way to the field ahead, then held. Hesitated. The top end of it whipped around a little and the bottom rose with it, and Josiah was sure the thing was about to retreat when it dropped with sudden strength and a spray of brown soil shot into the air. The windows on the truck were vibrating now, and the trees alongside the road were bending with the force of the wind once again. Only they were bending the wrong way, he realized, they were leaning in toward the cloud instead of away from it.

For a moment he let off the gas. He was beside Wesley Chapel now, where Danny had pulled in and watched a tornado go by, and now Josiah was staring down another one. He'd heard plenty about such storms — they weren't uncommon in southern Indiana — but he'd never seen one himself. The thing looked nothing like the funnel shape you always heard of. No, it was just a rope. A white rope connecting earth to sky, and moving forward. Moving east. Moving toward him.

He raised his eyes to the rearview mirror and saw Danny's car coming on down the road. Shaw had turned around and started in pursuit of him. What in the hell did he think *he* could do?

Still, he was catching up. The tornado sat no more than a half mile away now to the west, the direction Josiah needed to go. It was moving but without great speed. Seemed relaxed, almost. Low-key about the way it was tearing through the land. He watched it come up on one lone tree, saw the treetop bend toward it, and then the cloud was over it and the tree disappeared from sight. An instant later it had cleared the tree, and the trunk remained, but almost all of the branches that had made up the top were gone. The cloud chewed back into the farmland.

It looks like a power washer, Josiah thought, *it looks exactly like a damn power-washer jet. A thin white rope with an invisible and incredible chisel at the end of it, blasting that field away like it was so much dirt on a deck board.*

He looked in the rearview again and saw Danny's car closing in fast.

Can't just sit here, boy. Work left to be done, isn't there? You bold enough to do it? You got the strength, the will?

Sure he did. Sure. Josiah turned left, away from the chapel, and laid into the Ranger's accelerator once again. Ahead of him, the tornado was nearing the road. The base of the white rope had turned brown, and Josiah could see an outer ring of debris circling it. Some awful large objects in that outer ring. All around him the air hummed with a mighty locomotive's roar.

Danny was right, he thought, *damn things really do sound just like a train.*

He could see the spot where the cloud was likely to cross the road, and he knew that if he made it there first, he'd be fine, and Shaw, still trailing behind, would likely be dead. It was a teenage boy's game, nothing more, a bit of that old chicken run. Wasn't nobody else had Josiah's nerves in the game back then, and wasn't nobody else who had them now. He eyed the likely intersection between storm and road and put the full weight of his right leg into the gas pedal, heard the overextended six-cylinder moaning.

You make it through, boy, you are home free. That storm will block everybody trying to come at you from the east, don't you see? The road will be yours. Just got to make it, just got to show the strength and will, keep those hands steady on the wheel and the foot heavy on the gas...

He was right alongside it now, and when he chanced a final glance up at the rearview, he saw Eric Shaw was falling back. Slowing down, afraid to take this run.

"We knew that," he said. "He don't have the strength of will, does he, Campbell? Man doesn't have what we have."

The truck was at eighty-five now and no more than two hundred feet from clear of the storm. The driver's window clouded over with brown dust and then the windshield was covered, too, and Josiah couldn't see a damn thing but that didn't matter, because he knew the other side would be clear. He let out a howl of pure pleasure and bent over the wheel, knowing that he'd made it. Wasn't another man alive would have taken this drive, but he'd not only taken it, he'd made it.

That taste of pure victory was the last thing he knew in the instant before the truck began to slide to the left, and he had time for just one more thought, a final, unspoken question: *Why am I moving this way? This isn't the way I wanted to go...*

This tornado didn't have the funnel shape of that first one, looked like an angry white whip, and Eric could not believe it when he saw the pickup turn left and head directly toward it.

"What are you doing?" Eric said. "What are you doing, you crazy bastard?"

The Ranger was accelerating, speeding into the storm, which was now almost to the road. Eric blew through the stop sign and swung left as well, sped up for a moment, and then saw what would happen and let his foot off the gas pedal, saying, *"Don't let it, no, don't let it..."*

The cloud crossed the field and met the road and enveloped Josiah Bradford's truck. For one instant, there was nothing but the cloud, and Eric had time to form a *they-can-survive-this* hope and then the truck exploded.

The blast was muted by the roar of the storm, but even so, Eric heard it and felt it. The whole car shook and the pavement vibrated beneath its wheels and a burst of orange flame showed itself in the center of the cloud. The wind took the heat and sucked it upward, the flame climbing the center of the white rope into the sky like it was a fuse dangling from the heavens. Then the cloud was past and the flame within it was gone and Eric could see the truck again.

It was upside down on the side of the road, at least forty feet from where it had met the funnel cloud. The roof supports had caved in and it rested flat on the ground, the white paint blistered off to reveal charred metal beneath. Flames crackled across the chassis and licked out of the cab.

Eric couldn't scream. He stared at the burning wreck and wanted to scream but could not. His jaw worked and his breath came almost against the will of his body, but he was silent. He was hardly aware that his car was being dragged until he felt the right wheels slip off the road, and then he realized the storm had been pulling him toward it. Then it was too far away and its grip loosened and left the car sitting half on the road.

He fumbled the driver's door open and got out and ran to the truck. A light rain had started to fall again, a sprinkle that had not the slightest effect on the flames. He got within fifteen feet before the heat drove him back, and he heard himself sobbing now, looking down at the smoldering metal.

No one could have survived it.

He stood there for a long time, with his hands held up to shield his face from the heat. The flame roared and crackled and then burned down, and there seemed to be nothing left of the cab at all. He stepped closer and saw a thin rod of white amidst all the black char, knew it was bone, and fell to his knees and vomited in the grass.

He was down there on his hands and his knees when he heard the voice. Not the scream from Claire that he'd been fearing, but a whisper that now felt familiar.

You brought me home. Been a long time coming. Too many years I was gone. But you brought me home.

He jerked up and stared at the smoldering truck and saw nothing inside, just all that ash and heat and thin black smoke, and then his eyes rose and he saw Campbell Bradford standing just beyond, close enough to the truck that he could touch it but unaffected by the flames.

Think that would kill me? You don't understand the first thing about me, about what I am. I'm strong here, stronger than you can believe, stronger than you can stop. I don't die. Not like your wife.

Eric staggered backward, up to the road. Campbell smiled and ducked his head and then crawled through the burning cab and out onto the other side, following. Eric turned and ran.

There was another car parked beside the Oldsmobile now. A heavyset guy in an Indianapolis Colts baseball cap was climbing down out of a large Chevy truck.

"Buddy, you okay? Shit, did that tornado get it? Man, there

ain't nothing left of it, is there. You see what happened? Was anyone inside?"

Eric stumbled past him and around the open door of Danny Hastings's Oldsmobile and got into the driver's seat. The guy was following him, and over his shoulder, Campbell Bradford walked leisurely down the road.

"Buddy . . . you need to wait for help. I've called the fire department. You can't drive, man, not after something like this."

Eric slammed the door and put the car in reverse and backed up, feeling the jar when the right-side wheels popped back onto the surface of the road. He kept it in reverse as the heavyset guy closed in and Campbell Bradford walked toward them in the middle of the road. The stranger was talking and just a few feet away, but now Eric couldn't hear his voice. He could only hear Campbell's.

She's dead, and I'm still here. Forever. Thought you could control me, contain me, defeat me? She's dead and I'm still here.

Eric backed up all the way to the intersection beside Wesley Chapel. The old white church was still standing, oblivious to the two tornadoes that had snaked through on either side of it today. He cut the wheel then and swung the front of the car around so it was pointing south. He looked in the rearview mirror as he accelerated down the road and saw Campbell just behind, strolling along but somehow keeping pace with the car. Eric dropped his eyes and hit the gas pedal, tore up the road. Ahead he could see police lights flashing, maybe a half mile away. He ignored them and banged a left turn back into the gravel lane, drove all the way to the end, and parked the car beside its dead owner's body. He got out and leaned over and placed the keys in the dead man's hand. This time he did not recoil at the touch or the sight of the wound.

You've left people dead all over today, haven't you? Campbell said. He was no more than five feet behind Eric now. *How many have died today? I can hardly keep the tally. We've got this one, Josiah, your wife...*

There were flashing lights through the trees now, back toward the road, and a police car blew past and continued on toward the wrecked Ford Ranger. Eric watched it go, and the lights set off a blinding pain in his skull, a single burst like all of the headaches of the past days combined into one extravagant stroke of agony. He gasped and dropped to his knees in the wet, bloody grass.

So many dead people, Campbell said. *So many. But guess what? You're still here, and so am I. So am I.*

Eric looked up at him, into the horrible shadowed face beneath the bowler hat, and thought, *He is right. The blood is on me, Claire's is, at least. She came for me, came to help me, to save me, and I left her behind. Went out into the storm in search of that spring and left her behind.*

It was all gone now, everything he'd ever needed and loved was lost because he was too selfish, too stupid, to know what he needed or how to love.

Only Campbell remained with him now.

The muscle tremors in his hands had worked into his forearms, and his left eyelid was fluttering constantly. His skull ached as if someone were piping in additional air pressure; it was hard to walk in a straight line once he got back to his feet and pointed toward the trail, Campbell following him with a strange whispering laugh.

The hell with it—let him follow. All that mattered had been lost; all that was left did not matter.

Eric walked on for the gulf.

61

Eric went left instead of right at the first fork in the trail, ignoring the path that would have taken him down to Kellen and walking instead along the top of the ridge. Soon he left the trail entirely and climbed down into the trees, went out right to the precipice and looked down.

The gulf still swirled. It was higher now than it had been, still climbing those cliff walls. He could hear a churning sound and saw that on the low end it had crested the hill and begun to pour into the dry channel. He could not see Kellen, but that was a good thing. He'd probably climbed farther away, into a safe place.

The truly dark clouds had moved away, passing to the north-east, and the sky now was a winter gray with a light rain falling from it. Eric worked along the rock rim, using trees to keep his balance as he moved toward the far end of the gulf, where the cliff walls were highest.

He circled around to the back, and now he could see Kellen. He wasn't far from where Eric had left him, maybe five feet back. The water wasn't near him yet, though. He was on his back with his hands pressed over his eyes, and he didn't see Eric.

From where Eric stood right now, at the top of the cliff edge above the gulf, there was nothing but trees and farmland to his back and nothing ahead but open air and a damn long drop. He hung on to the trunk of a thin tree that had somehow survived the ravaging that had claimed so many of its bigger, stronger peers, and stared down into the swirling water. Such a bizarre shade...that water belonged somewhere deep in South America, not rising out of an Indiana sinkhole.

You've given up, Campbell said. *You aren't strong enough to go on. Not strong enough to face me, even. I can give you strength. I can purge everything you lost and replace it with the strength you don't have. All you have to do is listen.*

Someone was calling his name, the sound barely audible over Campbell's whispered promises. Eric heard that and realized that Kellen must have seen him, and that was no good because he didn't want to be delayed or distracted. Did not want, certainly, to be stopped. He didn't allow himself to look for Kellen; he focused instead on that whirlpool of blue-green water and the ghostly white limbs that protruded from it at all angles.

Last words. That was what the moment called for, and they should matter—it was the end of the final act, and the last words counted then. It was all you left the audience with. He had none.

I can turn your pain into strength, your loss into power. Don't you want that? All that's required of you is an ability to take instruction.

He heard his name again, louder this time, and he stepped forward so he could see over the edge and down to the rock wall below. When he moved, a loose stone pushed over the edge and fell. It swung back in against the cliff, hit the rock wall, and broke into two pieces and then tumbled into the water. Better remember that, make sure he got a strong enough push to carry him clear.

Last words. Give 'em something, buddy.

"I'm sorry," he said, in a voice so soft no one else could have possibly heard it, and then he stepped to the edge and spread his arms wide, bent once at the knees and closed his eyes and pushed. Pushed *hard,* a good, powerful jump that sent him into the air and over the cliff and then he was falling toward the water below. He twisted as he fell and the world spun around him and he could see Campbell Bradford standing atop the cliff. Beneath the bowler hat, his face looked almost sad.

He heard his name called once more as he fell, and this time, tumbling through the air, he was almost certain it was Claire's voice. How beautiful, he thought, that he could hear her voice one last time. She was waiting for him.

The last thing he felt was the shock of cold.

Anne was close to tears after the dispatcher cut her off from Roger Brewer of the Indiana State Police.

A body in the road. He'd dumped a body in the road.

It wasn't fair, it wasn't right. Anne had been trying to help, trying so hard to play out this role that she had always believed she would have. And they'd been close. They'd been so close…

It was a full five minutes before the dispatcher made contact again to tell Anne that Brewer had recovered the hostage, who was alive but injured, appearing to have suffered a broken arm or collarbone or something. Anne could hardly follow those words. The woman was alive. She was out of that truck, and she was alive. How terrible things might have turned if she were dead. It could have become an absolutely tragic day.

"It seems someone else was killed, though," the dispatcher said. "There's a lot of confusion out there. We're sending more officers to the scene. You did well, Mrs. McKinney. Thank you."

"What about Josiah?"

"Detective Brewer had to stop pursuit when he saw the woman in the road, but there are reports that his truck was destroyed by a tornado just to the north of that spot. That appears to be accurate. Now, Mrs. McKinney, I've got to deal with my officers. I'm sorry."

"It's fine," Anne said. And it was. She was desperate for updates, but the dispatcher was overwhelmed and she knew she had to be silent for a while. Silent and patient. They'd give her the news eventually, and they'd remember to send someone down here to get her out of the basement. There was no rush on such things. She'd done what she could.

She looked at the old ham radio and felt tears crest in her eyes. How she wished Harold could have known the role it had played today. The role *she* had played today.

Her only regret was that she hadn't seen the storms. So long she had waited to see a tornado. She was afraid of tornadoes, yes, but always in awe. Captivated by what they were and what they could do. She'd read so much about them, studied them so carefully, and still she'd never seen one. Now four had blown through the valley in under an hour and all she'd gotten to see of them was that first trailing wall cloud.

That was all right, though. People had been saved today. Josiah Bradford was apparently dead, and that was tragic in its own way because she knew that something had been in the boy's head today that wasn't right. But he'd died alone, without taking any innocents with him, without striking at her beloved hotel as he'd threatened. That hotel was beauty that had outlasted darkness and sorrow, and she'd been determined to do whatever she could to protect it.

A storm spotter, that's what she was. Ever vigilant, determined to spot the warning signs and relay them in enough time to help the people in this valley. Well, she'd certainly done that today. It wasn't the sort of storm she'd envisioned, but she'd gotten the chance to help that she always knew she would. For so many years she'd watched the skies and waited with quiet assurance that she would be needed.

Today she had been.

It felt good.

Around the area, storm reports were still coming in, but it looked as if the tornado that had struck just west of Wesley Chapel would be the last of the cluster outbreak. That put it at four total, not a staggering number for such a storm, but not insignificant either. They'd be clearing up damage for a long time to come. She hadn't heard of any deaths yet besides Josiah's, and that was good. You could put buildings back up. Couldn't restore a life.

She might have dozed a little at the desk. Must have slipped off for just a minute. The sound was what woke her—a hum that seemed to be growing louder, getting closer.

She turned in her chair and looked up at the little windows mounted at the top of the western wall and was shocked to realize that she could see through them. Always before they'd been useless to her except to filter in a tiny bit of sunlight; they were no more than ten inches tall, placed right at ground level, and made of thick block glass. Somehow, from this angle, they offered a perfect look toward the west. She could see the fields rolling away downhill, and at the horizon a band of dark clouds.

The humming increased to a roar, and something white

descended from the dark clouds, and Anne realized with utter astonishment that she was facing a tornado.

First things first—the radio. Do your job, Annabelle. Do your job.

She made a dispatch, curt and to the point—gave her coordinates and said a funnel cloud was on the ground, moving north-northeast. Several of the spotters fired off responses, asking if she was safe, urging her to get as far from the exterior walls as possible. She said thank you and then turned the radio off and rose from her chair.

The cloud seemed to have held almost stationary while she completed the dispatch. Now that she turned back, it was moving again, as if it had been waiting for her.

She got to her feet, thinking that she wanted to walk over to the windows and see if she could get a closer look. The walls of the house were trembling now, and when she walked past the base of the steps, she saw a shaft of light fall across her feet and looked up to see that the door was open. The shaking of the house had evidently knocked away whatever Josiah Bradford had placed as an obstacle up there.

Safest place to be was in the basement, of course, but suddenly that didn't seem to matter. She wanted to *see* this storm. She'd been waiting so long to see one, and it was fitting that on a day like today, when she'd finally been able to play the role she always knew was hers, she would have the opportunity. It felt like a gift, almost, like this one was intended just for her.

She took the steps slowly at first, hand on the railing, but half-way up she realized how firm and strong her stride was. Her legs hadn't felt this way in years. She dropped her hand from the railing.

Up in the living room she turned and looked out the wide picture window. The cloud was closer now, and she could see its movement clearly, the fascinating swirling layers. Everything in the lower portion was pure white, the kind of white that hurt the eyes, like sun on a snow-covered field.

She had a notion that it would be easier to see it from outside. There was an odd sense of celebration to the storm's arrival, and she wanted a toast. Her memory must be slipping; though she didn't remember having had booze in the house in years, there was a bottle of gin on the counter. Tanqueray, her favorite. A glass with ice beside it, with a sliced lime already positioned on its rim.

She poured the gin and tonic into the glass, sure somehow that there was no rush, that the storm would wait for her. She squeezed the lime into the drink and lifted it to her lips, took a few swallows.

Delicious. You could never get too old for a taste like that.

She set the glass down, licked her lips, and walked to the front door. There was not so much as a twinge in her knees or hips, and her back felt strong and supple, ready for heavy lifting. In fact, her *walk* felt supple, felt like the old head-turning walk of her youth. She hadn't forgotten how to move.

She'd left a pair of heels beside the door, beautiful black heels that she hadn't seen in years. What they were doing down here, she didn't know, but given how steady her legs were this afternoon, she'd rather have them on than those silly white tennis shoes.

Off with the tennis shoes and on with the heels, then out the door and onto the porch. Down the steps and into the yard, and then she turned to the left and walked past the house and toward the empty field beyond. All around her the clouds were dark but the funnel remained white. Odd, because it should have been picking up debris by now, lots of it, absorbing the dirt to change into that fierce gray you always saw in the photographs.

It roared just as she'd known it would — the sound of a train.

It wasn't a frightening sound, though. Familiar, really. Took her mind back to other places. Why, it sounded just like the old Monon, the train of her youth.

She walked to the edge of the yard and waited for it, and she couldn't keep the smile off her face now or the tears off her cheeks. Silly, to stand here and cry as she faced it, but the cloud was just so beautiful. There was magic here, and she'd been allowed to see it.

What more could you ask?

62

CAMPBELL STOOD WITH A lantern in his hand and Shadrach Hunter at his side as the rain poured down around them. The boy worked in a shallow ditch below them, pulling aside broken slabs of limestone.

"See there!" Campbell shouted. "There it is, Shadrach. The spring, just as I promised."

The lantern light cast a white glow on the shallow, softly bubbling pool that was exposed as the boy removed the rocks. When Campbell held the lantern directly over the top of it, the pool seemed to absorb the light and hide it.

"Boy, get him a bottle of it."

The boy took a green glass bottle from his coat pocket. He removed the stopper and held it upside down so Shadrach could see that it was empty, and then he knelt and dipped the bottle into the pool. When it was full, he straightened and handed it to Shadrach, who took a drink.

"You tell me," Campbell said.

"Tastes like honey," Shadrach Hunter said. His deep voice sounded uneasy. "Like liquid sugar."

"I know it. This is what the boy's uncle put into that liquor, and there ain't never been any other liquor like it. You know that, Shadrach. You know that."

"Yes," Shadrach said and returned the bottle to the boy.

Campbell grinned, then shoved the boy with his free hand and said, "Cover it."

The boy went back down into the ditch and replaced the stones. When he was done, the water could no longer be seen, and scarcely heard.

"Well, there you go," Campbell said, switching the lantern from one hand to the other. It hissed when rain hit the glass. "You said you wouldn't give me a dime unless you saw the spot, knew that it was real. You seen it now, haven't you? It's real enough."

"It is, yes."

Campbell tilted his head back, his face lost to the shadows. "Well, then. My part of the bargain is complete. Yours is not."

Shadrach shifted, brought a hand out of his coat pocket and wiped it across his face, clearing some of the moisture away.

"Let's bargain while we walk," he said. "I want to get out of this rain."

He started away from the spring without giving Campbell a chance to argue. There was a hill leading away from the spring, and as he walked up it, Campbell and the boy fell in behind him. They walked into the woods.

"What's your plan?" Shadrach said.

"My plan? You know what it is! There's a fortune sitting here, a fortune pooling out of the rocks. That old man never made more than a dozen jugs of whiskey at a time. He was a fool.

Lacked the ambition to see what could be gained from this, the fortune that was waiting. Well, the boy knows how to make the liquor, too."

"So you intend to...expand." Shadrach had his face turned away from Campbell, walking through the woods with a brisk stride.

"Expand?" Campbell stared at Shadrach as if he'd spoken in Greek. "Hell, that's too soft a word. I'm going to make more money than anybody in this valley ever dreamed of. I've got contacts in Chicago—Capone and all the rest of them. The network is there. All we need to do is handle the supply."

"And you want me as an investor."

"That's all you need to be. You'll get your share returned tenfold by the end of the year. Believe that."

"Why me?" They'd crested the hill now and were walking along the spine of a wooded ridge. Campbell was on the left, closest to the brink.

"Hell, boy, everybody else is busted! You ain't figured that out yet? You're the last man left in the valley with dollars to his name."

Shadrach Hunter smiled. "You want to see my dollars?"

"I'd like to utilize them, yes."

Hunter stopped walking. He reached in his jacket and removed a silver money clip. Peeled the bills off and counted them. Fourteen bills—all ones.

"There you go," he said, replacing the money in the clip and offering it to Campbell. "That's my stockpile, Bradford."

Campbell looked at him in disbelief. "What in the hell is the matter with you? I always heard you was cagey smart for a colored. Ruthless. You think I'm making a joke here? There's a fortune to be made!"

"I believe you," Shadrach Hunter said. "But I don't have any money. That's what I got—fourteen dollars."

"Bullshit."

Hunter shrugged and put the money clip back into his pocket. "Ain't no shit but true shit, Bradford."

"Everyone knows you been skimming for years. Just sticking it away somewhere. A damned miser, that's what you are."

"No, that's what the gossiping old fools in this valley *say* I am. Truth is different."

"I don't believe you."

"Don't have to, but refusing to believe ain't going to line your pockets with dollars that I simply do not have."

It was silent for a while. Then Campbell said, "You could have told me that days ago, you son of a bitch."

"Wasn't going to see the spring if I did that, was I? I wanted to know if there was anything to your talk. Now, look here, we can work on this. Find a way to raise a stake. I've tasted that liquor, and I believe what you say—there's gold to be made from it. I just don't have the cash you need. But I'll work with you to see if—"

"Now you know where it is," Campbell said. His voice had dropped in volume and darkened in tone. He'd turned to face Hunter, and his back was to the drop-off of the ridge now, no more than a few steps away. "You played me for a fool, got me to show you where it is."

"Yes, and now that I know it's real, we can try and figure out a way to raise—"

Campbell had to move the lantern again to go for his gun. He'd been holding the lantern in his right hand and he clearly didn't like to shoot with his left, because he switched the lantern before he drew the weapon. That gave Shadrach Hunter enough time to see what was coming, and he actually fired first.

He shot through his coat pocket, and the gun was caught pointing down. The first bullet drilled Campbell square in the knee and dropped him, and the second went through his left side. Campbell finally cleared his gun then and returned fire from the ground, one shot that caught Shadrach Hunter in the forehead.

Hunter was dead by the time he hit the ground. Campbell's mistake was in trying to stand. He lurched up but his wounded right leg collapsed beneath him. He gave a howl of pain and then fell backward, hit the ground, and rolled. The gun came free from his hand and then he slid over the lip of the ridge and there was a long rustling of leaves and a cry of pain.

"Damn it, boy, help me!"

The boy walked over to Shadrach Hunter and stared down at him. Then he leaned down and picked up Campbell's weapon and walked to the crest of the ridge.

"Boy! Get down here and help me!"

The boy wrapped one hand around a thin sapling and leaned out over the edge. Campbell had slid all the way down the slope and into the edge of a wide pool of water, was in water up to his chest. He had one hand wrapped around a hanging root, and now he grunted and tried to heave himself up out of the pool. He couldn't make it. He slid back down into the water and only the hand on the root kept him from going under. His efforts had placed him only deeper in the pool.

"You got one chance to get down here and help me, boy. You waste another second and they'll be picking you up in pieces for weeks to come. You hear me?"

The boy didn't speak. He sat down on the top of the ridge and watched silently. The rain was still pouring down, and the water in the pool was rising and spinning. Campbell's grip on the root loosened as the water tried to pull him away, but he caught hold again and splashed, fighting for his life.

"Get down here, boy. Get your worthless ass down here unless you want to end up like your uncle."

Campbell's voice was fading. His face was stark white. The boy remained silent.

"You don't understand what you're tangling with," Campbell said. "You should by now. You been around me long enough to get a sense. You think I'm just another man? That what you think? I've got power you can't even fathom, boy. This valley's given it to me. You think you'll be safe from me if I drown out here? You're full of shit. There ain't no hiding from me."

The boy dragged the lantern closer to him. He held the pistol in both hands.

Campbell gave a howl of fury and tried once again to pull himself out of the water. This time the root tore, almost pulling free completely, and Campbell was submerged for a moment before he tugged himself high enough to get his face clear.

"You're going to let me drown," he cried. "You're going to let me *die!*"

The boy didn't answer.

"I'll have you in the end," Campbell said in a voice so soft it was hard to hear over the rain. "You will feel my fury, boy, everyone in this whole damn valley will. You think you're safe if I'm dead? Boy, I promise you this—ain't nobody safe from me unless they carry both my name and my blood. You understand that? Only my family will be spared, you little bastard. And you ain't family. I'll come for you. That's a vow. I will come for you and anyone else who doesn't share my blood and my name."

The dangling root tore free. Campbell gave a harsh cry of surprise and pain, and then he slipped backward and was lost to the water. When he surfaced again, he was upside down and motionless. The boy sat and stared at him. After a while, he picked up a few sticks and threw them at the body. There was no response.

He stood and picked his way carefully down the ridge and out to the edge of the pool. Then he set the lantern down, took off his jacket and shoes and rolled his pants up above his knees, removed the green glass bottle from his pocket, and waded into the water with it in his hand.

Campbell continued to float facedown, thumping against the stone that surrounded the pool. The boy reached him and turned him over, exposed his white face. The eyes were still open.

He looked at the dead man's face for a moment, and then he shifted the body and found the wound on Campbell's left side. He pressed the bottle into the wound and watched as blood leaked out of him and joined the spring water that was already inside the bottle. He squeezed out blood until the bottle was full of the mixture, and then he took it away and fastened the stopper.

When the bottle was back in his pocket, the boy grasped Campbell's shoulders and began to tug him through the water. He waded along the southern rock wall, waist deep, moving carefully. Here the lantern light was dim. He stopped moving at a point where water gurgled between rocks, slipping out of the pool and back below ground. He tried to push Campbell into the dark gap, but the dead man's shoulders snagged and held. The boy turned him slowly, rotating him in the water, and slid him in feet-first. He went in more easily this time, up to the waist, and then the boy placed his hands above both shoulders and shoved hard, grunting with effort. The body hung up for a moment, but then the water rose up and slapped against the stone and pushed the corpse out of sight beneath the earth.

He waded back to shore and put on his shoes and jacket. He checked the bottle and placed it gingerly back in his pocket. He then took the lantern and the pistol, climbed the hill again and returned to Shadrach Hunter's body, and knelt and removed the money clip with the fourteen dollars and put it in his pocket.

He rose again, with the lantern in one hand and the pistol in the other, and walked on into the dark woods. A train whistle was shrilling out over the hills. He walked toward the sound.

The lantern's glow turned smaller and continued to fade until it was barely visible in the shadows, and there was nothing but darkness and the sound of rushing water. Then the lantern began to grow larger and brighter, as if the boy had stopped somewhere out in the woods and decided to return. The light grew and grew until the dark woods melted away entirely and there was nothing but that gleaming, flickering light and...

Sky.

Gray sky.

And a voice.

Claire's voice.

EPILOGUE

These are the things he remembers. The lantern coming back through the dark woods, the warm flickering light, the gray sky, Claire's voice.

He is told that he shouldn't be able to remember a thing. That he had been under the water for fifteen minutes before they got him out.

He learns new terms in the hospital: apneic, which means not breathing; cyanotic, which means displaying a bluish discoloration; PEA, or pulseless electrical activity, which means an electrocardiogram test records some heart function although there is no pulse. The heart still lives, in other words, but it is incapable of completing its job.

These are the terms that were applied to him once he was in the ambulance.

Kellen was the first one in the water. He watched Eric leap, saw where he entered, splitting the water directly between two downed trees that could have impaled him. Kellen marked the spot, but with an ankle broken in two places, he couldn't make his way down to the water quickly enough, and the body had disappeared.

One thing Eric definitely did *not* imagine — Claire's voice on his downward plunge. She was coming down the trail with Detective Roger Brewer in tow. She'd forced the detective to go with her to the last place she'd seen him, stretched out there on the trail, and upon finding him missing, began to shout for him. Kellen heard the shouting. Kellen shouted back.

Brewer entered the water while Claire — with a dislocated shoulder and broken collarbone from her landing on the pavement after Josiah Bradford shoved her from his truck — stood on the bank and shouted at every ripple in the water and shadow over it, thinking they all might be Eric.

The way they all tell it now, Eric just floated up from the depths. Surfaced in the middle of the swirling pool, facedown. Like the Lost River had him, and then decided to give him back.

Brewer and Kellen brought him out. The detective began CPR, then turned it over to Claire and went for his radio when he could not get a response. Claire succeeded in getting a few wet, wheezing coughs.

They could not restore spontaneous breathing or a pulse.

In the ambulance, the electrocardiogram registered a brady-cardic — unusually slow — heart rate. Thirty-seven beats per minute. There was still no palpable pulse. The heart's electri-cal system was functioning, but the mechanical pumping sys-tem was not. The paramedics applied a ventilator to assist with breathing and then administered epinephrine. One minute later, Eric's heart rate was up to one hundred beats per minute, and a pulse appeared at the carotid artery.

He was driven to Bloomington Hospital at speeds averaging

ninety miles an hour, and there he was placed on a different ventilator, and steps were taken to warm his core temperature. Claire was with him for the ride and believed that he would be pronounced dead on arrival, that the epinephrine-induced heartbeat was nothing more than a tease.

It was not a tease. Within an hour of his arrival, his heart was functioning normally, and three hours after that, the lungs were deemed capable of unassisted breathing.

They kept him in the hospital for another twenty-four hours. Monitoring, they said, and there were other tasks to be done — putting stitches in his scalp, setting Claire's collarbone, outfitting her with a sling, treating Kellen's shattered ankle.

He does not remember anything of the ambulance ride, or much of his early hours in the hospital. At some point he grows clear-headed again, and soon the police are with him, statements being taken. Claire and Kellen have already offered theirs, and she is in the room with him now. He cannot take his eyes off her. He looks at her and he sees the pickup truck again, the melting, twisted metal and the flash of white bone amid ashes.

I thought you were dead, he tells her.

Likewise, she says.

She believes that Josiah hoped to kill her when he pushed her out of the truck. He had the shotgun in his lap but did not fire it, maybe because he couldn't do that and control the vehicle, maybe because he was afraid of igniting the dynamite in the bed of the truck. Whatever the reason, he settled for shoving her out onto the road, and Brewer crashed into a fence trying to avoid her.

What were you thinking when you jumped into the water? she asks him. How could you let yourself do that?

You were gone, he answers. It does not seem enough for her; it remains more than enough for him. She was gone, and Campbell remained. Now she is here, and Campbell is gone.

He can hardly believe it. He can hardly trust it.

It isn't until late that evening that they hear the news about Anne McKinney. When Detective Brewer shares it in a low, flat voice, Claire weeps and Eric leans his head back and closes his eyes.

Looks like it was fast, and painless, Brewer says. That's something. Old as she was, it was just too much stress. Shouldn't be surprising that she had a heart attack; it's surprising that it happened then, after everything was pretty well resolved.

She saved me, Claire says. Saved us.

Yes, ma'am.

No one even got her out of that basement? She must have been terrified. She must have been so scared.

Brewer doesn't know about that. Says Anne was on the radio with the dispatcher and sounded solid. Then there was a bit of weirdness right before the end.

Weirdness?

She reported a tornado sighting, Brewer explains. That was the last thing she said. Apparently she thought there was one right outside. But of course she was still down in the basement, couldn't see a thing.

So she scared herself to death, Claire says.

Brewer spreads his hands and says that he can't answer that. All he knows is that they said she sounded fine when she made the report. Real composed. Relaxed, even. She was still in the chair in front of the radio when the police got there.

Eric, listening to all this with his eyes closed, is saddened but believes that Claire's worries are unnecessary. Anne was ready for the storm, real or imagined. She wouldn't have been terrified by it. She'd have been ready.

*   *   *

That evening, with Josiah Bradford confirmed dead, Lucas Bradford makes an official statement to the police, explaining the reason he hired Gavin Murray. Seems his father, the recently deceased Campbell Bradford, had written an odd letter just before his passing. In the letter, he took credit for the death of a man of the same name in 1929. He did not murder him, he wrote, not exactly, but he did nothing to help him either. He let the man drown and felt that it was the right thing to do. He was saving not only himself but others. The man, he wrote, was evil.

He identified his fortune as having been built on fourteen dollars removed from a dead man's money clip, all that he had when he hopped a Monon freight train and rode to Chicago. While he felt no guilt over letting Campbell drown, he felt plenty for the widow and orphaned son left behind to suffer both poverty and Campbell's legacy. But he was afraid. For so many years, he was afraid of so many things.

Along with the letter was a revised will — Campbell had designated half of his substantial wealth to be split among any direct descendants of the man he'd let drown. He knew only that there was a son. The rest would have to be tracked down. It was important, he wrote, that he look after the family. That was very important.

Josiah Bradford, the only direct descendant of the Campbell Bradford who had drowned in the Lost River, had been dead for fifteen hours before this was revealed.

The letter made no mention of an odd green glass bottle, or of the reason the old man had for taking Campbell's name as his own.

Eric lets everyone wonder about this. He does not tell them

about Campbell's final threat, that anyone who did not share his blood and his name would feel his wrath.

Claire urges him to tell the doctors about his addiction to the mineral water and the ravaging effects it may have on his body. He tells her this is unnecessary. It is done, he says. It is over.

She asks how he can know this, and it is difficult to answer.

Just trust me, he says. I'm sure.

And he is. Because the water gave him back. His heart had stopped, his breathing had stopped. Those things began anew. He began anew. The old plagues will not return for him.

He returns to Chicago for two weeks before he can convince Claire to go back to the valley with him. He has a purpose there, he explains, and for the first time he understands it. There's a story that needs to be told — so many stories, really — and he can be a part of that. A documentary, though, a historical portrait of this place in a different time. It will not be the sort of thing that makes it to the theaters, but it is an important story, and he believes the film can be successful in a modest way.

She asks him if he will write the script, and he says he will not. That isn't his role. He's an image guy, he explains, he can see things that need to be included in the story but he cannot tell its whole. He wonders if her father would be interested in writing it. His name could help secure some interest. She suspects that he would.

Kellen meets them in the hotel, his foot encased in an Aircast, crutches by his side. He says he has a green glass bottle to return to Eric but left it in Bloomington. He didn't think it should be brought back to this place. Eric agrees.

They eat a celebratory dinner in the ornate dining room of the beautiful old hotel, and Eric explains the documentary and asks Kellen if he would consider being part of it. Kellen is enthusiastic, but it's obvious something else is on his mind. He doesn't address it until Claire has gone to the restroom and left the two of them alone. Then he mentions the spring, the one from the visions, and asks Eric if he believes it is really out there.

Yes, Eric tells him. I know that it is.

Kellen asks if he will search for it.

He will not.

Do you think Campbell is gone? Kellen asks.

Eric thinks for a moment and then offers a quote from Anne McKinney — *You can't be sure what hides behind the wind.*

Claire and Eric stay the night, make love in the same room, and then she sleeps and he lies awake and stares into the dark and waits for voices. There are none. Beneath him, the hotel is peaceful. Outside, a gentle wind begins to blow.

AUTHOR'S NOTE

The idea for this story came wholly from the place itself. The towns of French Lick and West Baden are very real, as is the astounding West Baden Springs Hotel, as is the even more astounding Lost River. I grew up not far north of these places and saw the West Baden hotel when I was a child and it was little more than a ruin. It was a moment and a memory that lingered, and over the years, I continued to learn about the place and its remarkable history. In 2007, when I saw the restoration of the West Baden Springs Hotel near completion, I felt the storyteller's compulsion revving to a high pitch. This book is the result, and because the places and the history are important to me, I've tried to present them accurately whenever possible. Still, this is a work of fiction, and I've taken some liberties — and no doubt made some mistakes.

Two dear friends helped with my research and encouraged the undertaking — Laura Lane and Bob Hammel — and a few people I've never met also deserve credit. Chris Bundy has chronicled the history of the area better than anyone, and his books were wonderful resources. Bob Armstrong, the late Dee Slater, and the members of the Lost River Conservation Association have been dedicated protectors and proponents of an underappreciated natural wonder for many years, and they piqued my interest in the river several years ago while I was working as a newspaper reporter. And to Bill and Gayle Cook, who brought the hotels back from near extinction, I'd like to say a most heartfelt thanks on behalf of the people of Indiana.

ACKNOWLEDGMENTS

It is such a tremendous pleasure to work with the people at Little, Brown. My deepest thanks to Michael Pietsch, editor and publisher without peer, for his efforts and above all else his faith. Thanks also to David Young, Geoff Shandler, Tracy Williams, Nancy Weise, Heather Rizzo, Heather Fain, Vanessa Kehren, Eve Rabinovits, Sabrina Callahan, Pamela Marshall, and the many other key players on the Hachette team.

My agent and friend, David Hale Smith, patiently listened to my wild explanation of an idea for a novella about haunted mineral water and then, with an astounding level of calm, watched it turn into a five-hundred-page manuscript. What can I say, DHS? Oops. An important note of gratitude is due the extraordinary violinist Joshua Bell. This fellow Bloomington native's violin work on the haunting song "Short Trip Home" (written, I must add, by another Indiana University product, renowned bassist and composer Edgar Meyer) pushed me toward an unexpected but rewarding place. It was a melody that needed a story, I thought, and from that grew a large portion of this book.

I fear that I tend to lean too heavily for input and advice on the writers I've long admired, and without fail they somehow tolerate it. It's great to be in a business where amazing work comes from amazing people, and there are none finer than Michael Connelly, Dennis Lehane, Laura Lippman, and George Pelecanos. Thanks to you all, for so many things.

Please turn the page for a preview of
Michael Koryta's *The Cypress House,*
published by Hodder & Stoughton in 2011.

I

THEY'D BEEN ON THE TRAIN for five hours before Arlen Wagner saw the first of the dead men.

To that point it had been a hell of a nice ride. Hot, sure, and progressively more humid as they passed out of Alabama and through southern Georgia and into Florida, but nice enough all the same. There were thirty-four onboard the train who were bound for the camps in the Keys, all of them veterans with the exception of the nineteen-year-old who rode at Arlen's side, a boy from Jersey by name of Paul Brickhill.

They'd all made a bit of conversation at the outset, exchanges of names and casual barbs and jabs thrown around in that way men had when they were getting used to one another, all of them figuring they'd be together for several months to come, and then things quieted down. Some men had slept, a few had started card games, others just sat and watched the countryside roll by, fields going misty with the twilight of a late-summer night and

3

then shapeless and dark as the moon rose like a watchful specter. Arlen, though, Arlen just listened. Wasn't anything else to do, because Paul Brickhill had an outboard motor where his mouth belonged.

As the miles and minutes passed, Brickhill alternated between explaining things to Arlen and asking him questions. Nine times out of ten, he answered his own questions before Arlen could so much as part his lips with a response. Brickhill had been a quiet kid when the two of them first met in Alabama, and back then Arlen took him for shy. What he hadn't counted on was the way the boy took to talk once he felt comfortable with someone. Evidently, he'd grown damn comfortable with Arlen.

As the wheels hammered along the rails of northern Florida, Paul Brickhill was busy telling Arlen all of the reasons this was going to be a hell of a good hitch. Not only was there the bridge waiting to be built, but all that sunshine and blue water and boats that cost more than most homes. Florida was where rich folks went for winter, see, and here Paul and Arlen were doing the same thing, and wasn't that something? They could do some fishing, maybe catch a tarpon. Paul'd seen pictures of tarpon that were near as long as the boats that landed them. And there were famous people in the Keys, celebrities of every sort, and who was to say they wouldn't run into a few and...

Around them the men talked and laughed, some tossing dice or playing cards, others scratching out letters to loved ones back home. Wasn't anyone waiting on a letter from Arlen, so he just settled for a few nips on his flask and tried to find some sleep despite the cloaking warmth and the stink of sweating men. It was too damn hot.

Brickhill was still going, this time expounding on the realization that he'd never seen a true palm tree before and in a few more hours they'd be as good as surrounded by them. Arlen heard one of the men behind them let out a chuckle, amused by the kid and, no doubt, by Arlen having to put up with him.

Damned Good Samaritan is what I am, Arlen thought, allowing a small grin with his eyes still closed. *Always trying to help, and look where it gets me.*

Brickhill finally fell silent as the countryside went fully dark outside the car, as if he'd just now noticed that Arlen was sitting with his eyes closed and had stopped responding to the conversation several minutes earlier. Arlen let out a sigh, grateful for the respite. Paul was a nice enough kid, but Arlen had never been one for a lot of words where a few would do.

The train clattered on, and though night had settled, the heat didn't break. Sweat still trickled along the small of Arlen's back and held his hair to his forehead. He wished he could fall asleep; these hot miles would pass faster then. Maybe another pull on the flask would aid him along.

He opened his eyes then, tugged the lids up sleepily, and saw himself staring at a hand of bone.

He blinked and sat up and stared. Nothing changed. The hand held five playing cards and was attached to a man named Wallace O'Connell, a veteran from Georgia who was far and away the loudest man in this company. He had his back turned, engaged in his game, so Arlen couldn't see his face. Just that hand of bone.

No, Arlen thought, *no, damn it, not another one.*

The sight chilled him but didn't shock him. It was far from the first time.

He's going to die unless I can find a way to stop it, Arlen thought with the sad, sick resignation of a man experienced with such things. *Once we get down to the Keys, old Wallace O'Connell will have a slip and bash his head in on something. Or maybe the poor bastard can't swim, will fall into those waves and sink beneath them and I'll be left with this memory same as I've been left with so many others. I'd warn him if I could, but men don't heed such warnings. They won't let themselves.*

It was then that he looked up, away from Wallace under the flickering lights of the train car, and saw skeletons all around him.

They filled the shadows of the car, some laughing, some grinning, some lost to sleep. All with bone where flesh belonged. Those few who sat directly under a light and out of shadow still wore their skin, but their eyes were gone, replaced by whirls of gray smoke.

For a moment, Arlen Wagner forgot to breathe. Went cold and dizzy and then sucked in a gasp of air and straightened in the seat.

They were going to have a wreck. It was the only thing that made a bit of sense. This train was going to derail and they were all going to die. Every last one of them. Because Arlen had seen this before and knew damn well what it meant and knew that—

Paul Brickhill said, "Arlen?"

Arlen turned to him. The overhead light was full on the boy's face, keeping him in a circle of brightness, the taut, tanned skin of a young man who spent his days under the sun. Arlen looked into his eyes and saw swirling wisps of smoke. The smoke rose in tendrils and fanned out and framed the boy's head while filling Arlen's with terrible memories, ones he'd tried hard to forget.

"Arlen, you all right?" Paul Brickhill asked.

He wanted to scream. Wanted to scream and grab the boy's arm but was afraid it would be cold slick bone under his touch.

We're going to die. We're going to come off these rails at full speed and pile into those swamp woods, with hot metal tearing and shattering all around us . . .